COLD TRUTH

COLD JUSTICE® - MOST WANTED

TONI ANDERSON

COLD TRUTH

Publisher: Toni Anderson. Toni Anderson Inc. C/O Fillmore Riley LLP, 1700-360 Main Street, Winnipeg, MB, Canada. R3C3Z3. Telephone: (204) 808-3112.

Contact email: info@toniandersonauthor.com

Cover design by Regina Wamba of ReginaWamba.com

Digital ISBN-13: 978-1-990721-85-4

Print ISBN-13: 978-1-990721-84-7

For more information on Toni Anderson's books, sign up for her newsletter or check out her website or store.

Love the Cold Justice® series?

Don't miss the gripping audiobooks—expertly narrated by Eric G. Dove—and explore the world of Cold Justice® through exclusive bundles, available on Toni's author store:

https://toniandersonshop.com

ACKNOWLEDGMENTS

I am so in love with this story. In early 2020, when I first wrote that Kurt Montana had left on some Top Secret mission in *Cold Wicked Lies* I had no idea what his story was or how it would end. I'll let you into a little secret. I didn't even know what the story was when I finished *Cold Spite*.

Yep, you read that correctly. I'd set up the framework throughout the Most Wanted books and I knew he hadn't *SPOILER ALERT* died in that air crash, but I didn't know any of the actual story details. I like to think my subconscious was busy plotting in the background the whole time.

Honestly, I wasn't truly convinced Kurt was "hero" material until I began writing his book and crawled inside his head for the first time. I hope you agree that Kurt Montana turned out to be the perfect hero.

I've been wanting to set a book in the amazingly beautiful country of Zimbabwe since I visited in 2015. Needless to say, events and people in this story are completely fictional, but I did use a couple of locales that I was lucky enough to explore, although I changed some of the names. I also borrowed my brother-in-law's cool job for Bjorn Anders profession, but that's the only similarity between them. My brother-in-law may be a former(?) adrenaline junkie, but he's steadfastly honest. Thanks for the tour, Ian! Apologies for the dead body.

I decided to use an area of Shropshire that is near and dear to my heart for where Row grew up—not only to save on research, but also to showcase an incredible place.

I hope you are inspired to visit!

Thanks again to Kathy Altman, who, as always, was the first person to read this and provide feedback. She knows the ugly truth about me and my process. Thanks to Rachel Grant for the great feedback—even as she moved her life half way around the world.

Credit to my fabulous editorial team, Lindsey Faber, Joan Turner at JRT Editing, and proofreader, Pamela Clare (yes, *that* Pamela Clare!). What an amazing group of people who support me.

Appreciation to my assistant, Jill Glass, who helps so much in running the day-to-day business. Thanks also to my wonderful cover designer, Regina Wamba, for her gorgeous artwork. Kudos to Eric G. Dove for being the voice of the Cold Justice® books and for being such a lovely human to work with.

This is my thirtieth published book!!! How is that possible? Throughout them all, I've had one man by my side. Thanks, honey, for being my one constant in a world of chaos.

ABOUT THE AUTHOR

Toni Anderson is a #1 Apple Books, #1 Nook, Amazon Top 10, *New York Times*, and *USA Today* bestselling author whose Romantic Thrillers have captivated millions of readers around the world. Best known for her critically acclaimed *COLD JUSTICE®* series, Toni's work seamlessly weaves together compelling characters, psychological suspense, and unforgettable love stories.

A two-time winner of the Daphne du Maurier Award and finalist in the RITA®, VIVIAN®, and double finalist for the Romantic Novel of the Year Award, Toni's books have been translated into multiple languages and praised for their emotional depth and unflinching realism.

Originally from a small town in England, she now lives in one of the coldest places on earth—Manitoba, Canada—where she writes full time, researches obsessively, and occasionally rescues her dogs from snowdrifts.

Check out Toni Anderson's shop with exclusive merch and offers:
https://toniandersonshop.com
Sign up for Toni Anderson's newsletter:
www.toniandersonauthor.com/newsletter-signup

facebook.com/toniandersonauthor

instagram.com/toni_anderson_author

tiktok.com/@toni_anderson_author

bsky.app/profile/toniandersonauthor.bsky.social

ALSO BY TONI ANDERSON

Cold Heat (Book #7)

"HER" ROMANTIC SUSPENSE SERIES

Her Sanctuary (Book #1)

Her Last Chance (Book #2)

Her Risk to Take (Novella ~ Book #3)

THE BARKLEY SOUND SERIES

Dangerous Waters (Book #1)

Dark Waters (Book #2)

SINGLE TITLES

The Killing Game

Edge of Survival

Storm Warning

Sea of Suspicion

To Librarians.
Guardians of truth. Keepers of knowledge.

COLD TRUTH
Cold Justice® – Most Wanted (Book #6)

Rowena Smith may be a top-shelf librarian, but solid investigative skills won't keep her safe after her newest research project—tracking down her biological father—leads her to a brutally murdered body. The scene offers up one hope for assistance: the card of FBI Supervisory Special Agent Kurt Montana. Alone and terrified in a foreign country, Rowena places the call.

About to board a flight home after a failed mission, Kurt can't ignore the plea in Rowena's voice. She could be the killer or she could be an innocent bystander—either way, he senses she holds information vital to his case. When Kurt's flight takes off without him—only to crash into the African savanna killing everyone onboard—he knows it's no coincidence. Rowena saved his life.

On the run from powerful enemies, he and Rowena pose as a couple—never mind that she's much too young for him. As danger escalates and they inch closer to the secret someone is trying desperately to prevent them from revealing, their fake relationship spirals into something far more perilous. And deeply personal.

The game gets deadlier with each and every step toward the truth. But there's no turning back and they'll need to rely on their skills and their wits—and each other—if they hope to survive.

————

Cold Truth is the sixth book in the Cold Justice® – Most Wanted series, featuring agents from FBI's Hostage Rescue Team.

All books standalone.

Sign up for Toni Anderson's newsletter to receive new release alerts, bonus Cold Justice® stories, and a free ebook copy of The Killing Game:
Toni's Newsletter (https://www.toniandersonauthor.com/newsletter-signup/)

Content Advisory: This book contains common tropes found in the Romantic Thriller/Romantic Suspense genre, including violence, sex, and strong language. If you are sensitive or easily triggered, please take that into consideration and read responsibly. For more details check out my website (https://www.toniandersonauthor.com/books/cold-justice-most-wanted/cold-truth/)

1

JANUARY 11

Monday. Harare, Zimbabwe

Kurt Montana caught the playful smile of a young, pretty, Black woman as she danced nearby. She crooked her finger, beckoning him to join her and her friends on the dance floor. He shook his head ruefully. She looked about the same age as his daughter and made him feel every second of his nearly forty-six years.

Even though it was a Monday night, the place was packed. He'd arrived early and managed to secure a table under the giant outdoor awning. Red bricks formed a wavy booth around his table—the next best thing to having a wall at his back. The man he was expecting, an old friend from his Army days, walked in and Kurt climbed to his feet to greet him.

"Bjorn. How was your trip?"

He'd first met Bjorn Anders in Afghanistan where the man had been working for the NGO he now owned, clearing remnants of war—landmines and munitions discarded after conflicts ended. It was good work, righteous work, but Bjorn didn't do it out of the kindness of his heart. There was always money to be made from war.

"Can't complain, man. Can't complain." The guy was originally from Norway and his accent had a decidedly wonky lilt.

"Take a seat. What are you having? My treat."

They ordered pints of Zambezi beer and stacked burgers accompanied with mounds of fresh french fries. They ate and enjoyed the party atmosphere with the deep throb of African pop intermixed with the iconic sounds of the '80s playing in the background.

The back of Kurt's neck itched as if he was being watched, but he'd had that feeling on and off ever since he'd arrived in Africa.

After the server removed their plates, Kurt eased back in his seat and shook his head when Bjorn offered him a cigar. "Did you discover anything of interest for me?"

"Nah, man." Bjorn shook his head. "Nothing, sorry."

He'd delayed his return to the US specifically for this meet. Having spent nearly two months traveling in some of the most dangerous hot spots on the continent, Kurt was ready to go home. He was tired. Really fucking tired. His bullshit meter was honed to the sharpness of a samurai sword and his patience reduced to a cigarette stub. "Liar."

Bjorn gave him a rueful look and his mouth curved into an easy smile. "Nothing I can confirm from a reliable source."

"At this point, I'll take gossip from your kids' school friends. Shit, I'll take gossip from kids they don't even like."

Ten days ago, one of his men had died trying to save a young woman who was being tortured by a serial killer, and it had gutted him and his men. Kurt should be in Quantico helping his team deal with the grief. He needed something to show for his time here. Going home without advancing the mission would be the ultimate topping on the shit sandwich this op had become.

He should have been there.

Maybe, if he had, Scotty would still be alive. Which was nonsense, but the guilt was real, and he knew every man—and woman—on the team would be feeling the same way.

Instead, he'd been stuck in Africa chasing leads about an

enemy who was proving to be as elusive as the smoke Bjorn drew into his lungs and exhaled in a cloud of toxic vapor. Thankfully, they were far away from any other diners.

"Like I told you at the Falls, it might take a while to hear back from my sources."

"Where are they that they don't have cell service?" Kurt crossed his arms as he leaned back against the rough brick.

"Phone numbers change. People move." Impatience leaked from the other man. "The man I knew who said he knew…*your friend.*" Bjorn glanced around without saying the name, as if afraid someone might be listening in. "He's been dead for a long time. I reached out to a couple of people I thought hung out with him back in the day, but most of them also seem to be dead. I have feelers out with a few other buddies but, oddly enough, being a mercenary is not a job where people get to enjoy old age."

"No shit." Kurt smiled, the skin around his mouth and eyes pulling tight. Bjorn wasn't telling him everything. "Give me the name of this guy who knew my *friend.* I'll have him run through the system."

Bjorn laughed uneasily. "The FBI has fewer resources than my kids have at school when it comes to these sorts of connections. It's not like what we talk about around campfires turns up in some CIA report."

You'd be surprised.

Kurt held Bjorn's gaze. His patience was at an end, and Bjorn was hiding something. "What harm can it do to tell me his name? At least then I can go home with another lead rather than the bust I'm currently sitting with." He softened the demand. "Don't forget, there's a hundred thousand US-dollar reward for any information that leads to an arrest…"

Bjorn's cynical blue gaze sparked at the size of the not-so-subtle carrot Kurt was dangling.

"On the other hand, concealing information from the FBI won't endear you or your NGO to the US government." He was done with pretending to be Mr. Nice Guy. Not about this. "Would hate for any issues to come up in relation to applying for, or renewing, US contracts."

Bjorn's jaw tightened at the threat.

"Just give me the name. An address. What can it hurt? You already said most of the people from back then are dead."

Bjorn scrunched up his face in defeat. "Fine, but it's probably a waste of time. That's why I don't want to tell you. You have to remember, things were different back then, and maybe this fellow was full of bullshit, you know? Most ex-soldiers are."

As they were both ex-soldiers, Kurt kept his mouth shut. Ironically, something he'd learned from his negotiator counterparts.

Bjorn leaned closer. Cleared his throat. "The guy I knew was called Dougie Cavanagh. Scottish guy. Said he knew the person you're looking for from his university days. Talked about doing some kind of business together—your friend wasn't a wannabe despot back then, so it wasn't a big deal or secret. He was just another guy looking to score some money in a place that didn't have too many rules."

"Dougie Cavanagh?" The name wasn't familiar to Kurt. The fact he was Scottish reinforced the possibility this story might be legit.

"Correct. A nice guy, Dougie."

A nice guy who hung around with terrorists.

Kurt's mission was helping to track down the current whereabouts of a shitball who was #1 on the FBI Most Wanted Fugitive list, a High Value Target named Darmawan Hurek.

Hurek had attended the University of St. Andrews at the tender age of eighteen under the name David Hurek. He'd studied political science while socializing with the children of the British upper-crust and wealthy elite. Little was known about Hurek's friends during that time. Email had barely been a thing, social media non-existent with Zuck still too young to be thinking about rating the hotness of his fellow students. Photographs were on film rather than digital. The FBI and NSA had scoured everything they could get their hands on and found nothing. Rental contracts were on paper, with few official records being kept beyond a year or two. The FBI knew what courses Hurek had taken, his classmates, his teachers, and his grades, but little else. It was as if Hurek's history from that time had been scrubbed off the face of the earth.

"Thank you. If it leads anywhere, I'll make sure the authorities know where to send the reward."

Bjorn waved the offer away and glanced around. "It might be more trouble than it's worth. I'm not sure I want anyone knowing I'm in league with the FBI."

"Fair enough." Kurt would see what they could do about keeping the recipient anonymous. The Dougie Cavanagh name was a thread for analysts to pull—or a carefully constructed lie designed to tie up the FBI for the next few months while Hurek continued to evade authorities.

"What happened to Cavanagh? Do you know?"

Bjorn's expression turned into a frown. "He disappeared off the scene. It happened a lot back then. People took off traveling or went home. I assumed he'd get in touch eventually. He'd left some of his belongings at my place. Nothing much. A bag of gear and some books and shit."

"You still have it?"

"Nah." Bjorn licked his lips before he shook his head. "About a year after he disappeared, I heard from someone that he'd drowned in a river somewhere in the Congo. I got rid of everything then."

Kurt had no reason to believe Bjorn would deliberately lie to him, but he wasn't stupid enough to take everything at face value either. Hopefully, this clue would give the task force another angle to pursue, although how it could lead to where Hurek was now was beyond him. He sipped his beer, then caught the eye of a white woman, an attractive brunette, who sat alone at the cocktail bar.

Bjorn looked over his shoulder, but the brunette had turned

away and the dancers from earlier were once again beckoning Kurt to join them on the dance floor.

Did they want to humiliate the old white guy and laugh at what passed for his attempts at dancing?

Probably.

Not that he blamed them.

If his men could see him now.

"Maybe your last night in Africa holds a little more excitement than dinner with an old fart, huh?" Bjorn's smile softened.

"I don't think so."

The brunette at the bar had also been watching him at The Lookout Lodge in Vic Falls when he'd first tracked down Bjorn, who'd been attending an ethical diamond-mining conference on the Zambia side of the river.

Kurt didn't think it was coincidence. Nor did he think it was his rugged good looks that had captured her attention. The fact Bjorn didn't remember that pretty face or mention seeing her at the Falls last week meant either the guy was losing his edge, or they were colluding in some way. Trying to set him up in a honey-trap, perhaps?

Or maybe she worked for Hurek?

"She's a little young for me."

Bjorn scoffed. "She looks legal."

Kurt wasn't sure which of the two women Bjorn was referring to, but both were in their early twenties and had more in common with his kid than with him.

"If I weren't happily married, I'd definitely be chatting her up, and I have a decade on you."

More than. "Yeah, well, you're a dirty old man."

"So my wife tells me, but she'd also cut my balls off if I so much as thought about it." The guy was married to a much younger woman, and they had kids still in elementary school.

Kurt struggled with it. If a guy Bjorn's age tried to date his daughter, he'd probably want to take him out to the woods with a shotgun and a nice shiny shovel. But it was up to Daisy who she dated.

Didn't mean Kurt wouldn't have opinions about the whole thing. Lots of opinions.

Maybe *he* was the old fart.

Loneliness pressed in on him. There was no wife waiting for him back home—she'd given up on him long ago. And while he had his daughter, whom he adored, and his colleagues, he missed having someone to hold at night, to laugh with, to confide in. But he had no desire to dive into the stormy seas of the dating pool. Not at his age.

Some days, Kurt felt twice his years. Especially right now.

The fact he was here, wasting his time on what had turned into a wild goose chase when his team needed him, pissed him off. If the target had been anyone except Darmawan Hurek, whose brutality he'd witnessed on that tiny island in Indonesia last summer, he'd have left with the DEVGRU boys eleven days ago. Instead, he and his right-hand man, Jordan Krychek, had been ordered to stay on so they could hit up a couple more potential sources of information. They'd struck out, and Krychek had left for home yesterday.

The Israelis had tipped off the US that Hurek had apparently been sighted in the DRC in November. By the time he'd arrived with what the public liked to refer to as SEAL Team Six, the terrorist had disappeared into the ether. The fact the guy was on the FBI's Most Wanted list had only brought in more leads that had gone absolutely nowhere.

Being grumpy and frustrated wouldn't endear him to his old pal though. He forced himself to relax, or at least to pretend to. "When is an old fart like you planning to put your feet up and retire?"

"As soon as I can afford it. Unfortunately, Zim doesn't offer much in the way of a pension plan." Bjorn stared thoughtfully into the bottom of his glass.

"A hundred grand could help with that." Kurt wiggled his eyebrows.

A reluctant laugh seemed to catch Bjorn by surprise. "It would."

"You wouldn't go home?"

"Back to Norway?" He shuddered. "Africa seduced me a long time ago, and I've no desire to freeze my balls off every winter."

"You've gone soft," Kurt joked.

"And I'm not too proud to admit it." The guy finished the cigar and stretched his arms wide in a yawn. "I need to head back. The missus wasn't too happy I was going out on my first night back in town."

"You'll have to make it up to her. I appreciate you meeting with me."

Bjorn laughed loudly and clapped him on the back. "As if you gave me much choice."

"Get in touch if you hear anything."

"Sure." Bjorn hesitated. "Watch your back, ya? The man you're looking for... he's very dangerous. No one will want to admit ever having associated with him."

"That's why I'm looking for him. So he can't hurt anyone else."

"You Americans, so full of righteous optimism." Bjorn laughed again and shook his head. "Let's hope you find him. Goodbye, old friend." Bjorn walked away.

Kurt grunted and asked for the bill. He paid, leaving a healthy tip, stood, and tucked his wallet into his pants pocket.

The brunette was nowhere to be seen. Whatever she was up to, he was grateful for the pistol he had unofficially strapped to his ankle. He strolled out of the front door of the restaurant and walked over to where he'd left his rental vehicle in the gravel parking lot.

And there she was, swearing colorfully at an old beater 4X4 with a flat tire. She kicked the deflated black rubber and then, hearing his deliberately loud footsteps, looked over her shoulder. She turned away, shoulders slumped in defeat.

Kurt hesitated by his SUV. There was no one else around, not even the red-shirted security guys who usually patrolled the lot.

He sighed. Was he about to get jumped?

"Need a hand?" he called out.

"No. Thank you."

Her crisp British accent surprised him.

MI6? What was their angle?

She opened the cargo area and started digging around. Kurt climbed into his 4X4 and pulled the Glock 26 out of the ankle holster and laid it on his thigh as he started the engine.

She removed a tire iron and began fighting with the rusted-on wheel nuts.

Was this a setup?

Did she have friends in the shadows who planned to jump him when his back was turned? Was she going to pull a gun on him if he helped her out? Could she lead him to Hurek?

She glanced at him nervously and then back toward the bar where the music blared loudly.

She seemed nervous.

What if she wasn't an operative but instead a sex worker or simply a tourist caught in a predicament that could go from inconvenient to terrifying in the space of a few seconds? What if he'd become cynical to the point of paranoia, losing his humanity along the way?

What if it were Daisy?

Thoughts of his daughter made him take a deep breath. He didn't spend as much time with his kid as he wanted. He'd missed out on her growing up because her mom had moved to Denver after they'd split, and he'd thrown himself into his new career at the FBI. They'd reconnected after she'd gone to college, and he was working his way slowly back into her life.

Daisy was a petite blonde whereas this woman was tall and willowy, but she didn't look that much older than his kid. And if she was an operative working for MI6 or for Hurek, maybe *he* could use *her*.

If she wasn't, then maybe this would be his good deed for the day.

He turned off the engine, got out of the car, slipping his weapon into his waistband at the small of his back and covering it with his shirt.

He scanned the shadows and nearby cars, but he didn't see anyone lurking. The night was still young for the partygoers.

The woman looked up warily as he approached.

"I said, I don't need any help. Thank you." The bite in her tone could have sliced meat.

He stopped about ten feet away as she struggled with the tire iron.

"What happened?"

"I must have run over a nail."

"You have a spare?"

"Of course, I have a spare." The expression on her face wasn't convincing.

Kurt circled to the back of her SUV and glanced inside. A blanket had been shoved to one side. The dirty gray felt base of the cargo area was pulled back to reveal a dubious-looking spare, but at least it appeared to hold air.

"Hey, what are you doing?" She jumped to her feet and took a step toward him.

He eyed the metal bar and slipped his hand closer to his weapon. "Would you like my help, or would you prefer to spend the night stranded in this parking lot?" Although he suspected she might be sleeping in the vehicle, which wasn't exactly safe for a woman alone.

She licked her lips, and Kurt felt a bolt of attraction that took him by surprise. He immediately felt like a sleaze. He was definitely old enough to be her father, which might not bother some guys, but it was a line he wouldn't cross.

"Why would I accept help from a stranger?"

Kurt crossed his arms. "I wasn't aware you were waiting for a friend to arrive to save the day. Forgive me." He took a step back.

Uncertainty painted her features as she examined his face, clearly looking for some assurance she was safe with him. She appeared to come to a decision and held the bar out to him which was foolish as hell.

"The nuts are stuck. I don't think you'll be able to shift them unless you have one of those fancy Formula 1 tools in your boot."

He grabbed hold of the bar, and she took a nervous step back, balancing on the balls of her toes, ready to run. At least she had some sense of self-preservation. He could be a serial killer for all she knew. He kept his awareness wide but hunkered down beside the tire that was almost bald and had a big-ass nail stuck in the wall. No way did she drive over that.

"Who are you?" She feigned casual interest.

Kurt wasn't in the country on official business, although his presence had been okayed by the regional Legat—the legal attaché. Still, he didn't need to advertise his position, especially to a potential threat. The last thing he wanted was a target on his back.

"People call me Joe." That had been his nickname on and off for years.

"*Joe?*" She snorted then looked embarrassed.

He found himself answering her honestly, which was how he generally operated. "Yeah. Joe Montana."

Her brows hiked. "Like the state?"

"Yeah." He smiled. "Like the state. And the quarterback."

"Huh?"

"Nothing." She was both too young and too British to have heard of the famous 49ers' Super Bowl triple MVP. He slotted the head of the tire wrench over the dirt-encrusted, orange-colored wheel nut and prayed that was African dust rather than pure Iron Oxide. His pride was at stake now. He pushed down on the metal bar with all his might, and the damned thing didn't budge. Damn.

The young woman moved beside him, the bare skin of her arm brushing his with a jolt of electricity.

Together their combined weight forced the nut to give, and she fell against him a little but quickly pulled away. He moved on to the next nut and again, it took the both of them to break the rusted seal. Her hair was soft against his shoulder, her scent tropical and floral, like hibiscus and sunshine.

Only a foot separated them now, and he noticed the color of her eyes in the lamp light. They were an unusual shade of green, like moss on the shadowy side of a tree.

"What's your name?"

"Row."

"Row like the boat?"

She laughed. "No, Row as in Rowena. Rowena Smith." She wiped her dirty hands on the back of her jeans and held one out to shake.

Smith? Probably the most common surname in the UK and pretty common in this part of the world for whites too.

He ignored the lick of lust that traveled along his nerves as he took her hand, the frisson of connection he did not want to acknowledge.

She was *way* too young for him. *Way* too young. And even the idea he found her attractive made him feel like a slime ball. He quickly let go.

"What's a Brit doing here all alone?"

"Who says I'm alone?"

Kurt turned to look pointedly around the parking lot.

She didn't respond.

He bent down and loosened the remaining nuts thankfully without her help. "Fetch me the jack, will you?"

She dragged it out and slid it under the jacking point beside the wheel arch. At least she knew *how* to change a tire if she had to. She ratcheted the thing until it began to lift the car.

"Thanks for your help. I can take it from here."

He ignored her and went to the rear, pulled out the spare, and wheeled it around to the side of the car. "You are British though, right?"

"The accent is a bit of a giveaway." She inclined her head.

"What are you doing in Africa, Rowena Smith? Sightseeing?" *Or just following FBI agents around.*

"Row."

He frowned.

"I prefer Row." She pressed her lips together as if annoyed with giving him information. "I have family roots here that I wanted to explore."

Kurt's brows hiked. "Your family used to live here?"

Her brow furrowed with uncertainty. "Yes."

"Were they evicted from one of the farms?"

She shook her head, but didn't elaborate.

He jiggled her damaged tire off the bolts and leaned it against the fender. "If you're here exploring your roots, why are you following me around the country? Looking for a sugar daddy?" He taunted her with something deliberately offensive, hoping for a reaction. "I hate to break it to you, darlin', but I can't afford a girl like you."

"You think I'm a prostitute?" Her voice was pitched so high he thought the windows might shatter.

He suppressed a smile and kept his expression stern. "Pretty thing like you. Turning up in all the places I'm at? Catching my eye at the bar?"

"Are you *out* of your mind?" She rolled her eyes and planted her fists on her waist. "I wasn't following you anywhere."

"I saw you in The Lookout Lodge."

Her gaze narrowed. "So what? It's a free country."

He took a step closer and frowned down at her. They were almost nose-to-nose. Up close she smelled even better. The skin under the soap. He dropped his voice. "What's going on, Rowena? Who are you working for?"

Her eyes widened in alarm, and she took a quick step away. "I was at the Falls, but I don't remember seeing you there."

Liar.

Or maybe that was his ego talking.

He silently considered her. Was a man like him all that memorable to a woman like her? Both restaurants were on the tourist map. But he couldn't afford to believe it was coincidence. Not when he was hunting one of the most dangerous men on the planet.

"I'm definitely not looking for a sugar daddy but thanks for the suggestion should my current career not pan out." Amusement infused her tone, but he refused to be distracted or charmed by the fact she had a sense of humor.

He tilted his head. "If not me, then Bjorn Anders. Why're you interested in him?"

She blinked rapidly. "My activities are none of your beeswax and I don't know anyone called Bjorn Anders." She pushed past him to lift the spare onto the axle. Her arms shook from the effort, but she managed. "Anyway, thanks for your help, *Joe,* but having suggested I'm both a sex worker and a stalker you can definitely go now."

She took the tire iron from his grip and began replacing the nuts.

"Don't over-tighten those, or you'll run into the same issue next time."

"Yes, Daddy." Her sarcasm turned into something else, and they both looked away from one another uncomfortably.

He didn't even remember the last time he'd felt this intrigued before.

Intrigued. That's what the cool kids were calling it nowadays.

He rolled his eyes at himself.

He backed away. If she was a lure for a honeytrap, then the Russians or Chinese or certain corrupt officials within the country had tapped into a weakness he hadn't even known he possessed —although he suspected she'd appeal to most guys.

"You take care of yourself, Miss *Smith.* And get that spare replaced ASAP. You don't want to get caught out in the middle of nowhere without one. Too many predators lurking in the shadows."

He didn't wait for a reply, instead he headed to his vehicle as a small but vocal group of diners left the restaurant and climbed into their car, before quickly driving away. He pulled his head out of his ass and took a photo of Rowena Smith and her SUV and sent it to the task force at SIOC with a request for a background check, then sat and watched her replace the jack, kick the new tire a few times, and maneuver the damaged one back into the cargo space. She sent him a fulminating look before climbing into the driver's seat, well aware he was watching her.

He raised a hand in acknowledgement and grinned when she raised her middle finger back.

The single men in Gold Team would have been lining up to ask her out.

He pulled a face at his thoughts. Right now, the men on his team were likely reeling with no time for romance. And poor Grace… Scotty had been a good man. A very good man. His heart broke anew for the widow who was expecting her third child in a few months.

It had been bad enough to have his wife leave him. Kurt couldn't imagine how he'd have coped if she'd died and made him a single parent.

He followed Rowena's car to the entrance of the restaurant. She indicated right, and he considered following her home to make sure she had somewhere safe to stay. But that risked freaking her out or walking right into the trap he'd so far avoided.

Instead, with an odd sense of wrongness, he let her go and headed left, taking the long way back to his hotel to spend another night alone in his bed—with just the memory of a pretty brunette for company.

2
———————

Bjorn Anders sat outside his gated home and called a number. Waited impatiently for the man to answer. He was balancing on a delicate tightrope with crocodiles beneath him and vultures circling overhead. Either one would tear him apart if they thought he was holding out on them.

He didn't know who the woman who'd been following him worked for. Maybe Montana had paid her to watch his back, but it didn't seem like his style. She looked vaguely familiar. He'd stopped her amateur antics with a large nail he'd spotted in the car park. Now he needed to confront a much larger problem.

"What is it?" Leo Spartan, the Zimbabwean ambassador to the United Nations snapped. "You know I can't be linked to you."

"I met with the FBI agent." Something Spartan would already know from his large network of spies.

There was an interested silence.

Sweat broke out on Bjorn's brow. "I gave him Dougie Cavanagh's name."

The voice hissed dangerously in his ear. "You did what?"

Trying to keep all these powerful people happy was going to be the death of him. "He put pressure on me, insisting he wasn't going to leave the country until he had some new piece of information. You said you wanted him gone."

He heard muffled sounds as the man presumably gave orders to one of his minions.

Spartan came back on the line. "If you told him anything else, I'll—"

"I didn't. I wouldn't." Sweat rolled down Bjorn's temples, and he wiped it away. "But it's not a bad thing, surely? Cavanagh has been dead for years. If Dougie told anyone about his relationship with you, someone would have come forward by now, and it would be public knowledge. Even if someone claimed to know something, there's no proof. Not anymore."

After Dougie's death, Bjorn had been ordered to go through the man's belongings, send everything non-incriminating back to his family in Glasgow, and burn everything else.

Almost everything else.

Bjorn had saved one thing—a single photograph. If Spartan knew about it, he'd already have been dead.

"He's definitely leaving tomorrow? The FBI agent?"

"In the morning."

"Good."

"There's nothing to worry about. Most of the people from back then are gone. The ones who are left would never say anything, *especially* if they get that contract they tendered for last month for the work in Ukraine." He laughed, making it a joke rather than a bribe. His company needed that contract. It would allow him to sell up and retire. He was too old to be chasing around the armpits of the world, clearing up other people's messes. As tempting as the FBI's one hundred thousand dollars was, there was no guarantee it would be enough, nor that he'd live to claim it.

"Hmm." Spartan sounded thoughtful now.

"Kurt Montana will head back to the US, and the FBI analysts will have no more luck discovering what happened to Dougie than they did Hurek. Cavanagh's family are all dead. You have absolutely nothing to worry about."

The silence went on for longer than was comfortable. Spartan had put him on mute and was probably talking to one of his goons.

Finally, "I'll contact someone in that department tonight. Expect Sabelo at your office tomorrow morning with a contract for you to sign."

Bjorn grimaced at the thought of having to be pleasant to Spartan's head of security, but the contract would make it worthwhile. And being able to retire would make his wife very happy.

"If anyone else finds out…" The man's voice got hard.

Spartan was not someone to fuck with. "No one will. I'll send the managers and office staff for coffee. My treat."

"Make sure you do. I don't want any witnesses."

Bjorn grinned and dabbed his forehead with a cotton handkerchief. He didn't want any witnesses either. Backdoor deals weren't uncommon, but they left a sour taste in his mouth. His people risked their lives and did good work.

"Not a problem. Not a problem at all. Thank you, sir. For your business and your trust."

He hung up and climbed outside his vehicle, feeling as if a heavy weight had lifted. He headed inside, greeted his beautiful, patient wife, and hugged his kids. Their life was finally coming together the way he'd promised when she married him, and he hadn't even needed to play the ace hidden up his sleeve.

———

Row drove slowly back to her uncle's house, making sure she wasn't followed before entering the code for the gates and driving inside. Frustration ate at her. She'd learned almost nothing after three weeks of searching for answers. "Joe"—highly doubtful that was his real name—had turned up twice now with Bjorn Anders, and she'd taken his photo in the hope of figuring out his identity.

He was American from the cute accent, and good-looking with it, in that confident, casually macho way some men had.

She'd always had a weakness for a little danger, always watched the bad boys in school with rapt fascination even if she was too reserved to ever act on it.

Not that it mattered.

She rolled her eyes at herself. He thought she was a prostitute, and while she respected workers in the sex trade, she wasn't sure her jeans and black blouse quite fit the bill even if it did have some very cute cutout netting details.

Perhaps "Joe" wasn't the best judge of character.

She was grateful he'd assisted her with the tire because the nuts had been fused solid, and she had not wanted to call her uncle to admit she needed help. Uncle Gamba already disapproved of her traveling alone around the country.

Joe had helped her as much to glean information as to be kind. He'd spotted her watching him talking to Anders, which was sloppy on her part, but it wasn't as if she had a lot of experience with this sort of thing.

Bjorn Anders hadn't seemed to notice her or care about being followed from his home. Tomorrow, she was going to have to confront the guy face-to-face and see if he actually knew anything. It was entirely possible he didn't have the answers she needed or would refuse to tell her if he did. But she had less than a week of vacation left before she had to be back at work.

She was out of time.

She'd discovered Anders was attending the diamond conference from her online research, same way she'd figured out where he lived and worked. She'd tried to gather the courage to talk to him there but had failed miserably.

She headed through the locked back door and into the kitchen and straight into Uncle Gamba who stared at her with disapproval and a pointed look at his watch.

She grimaced. "Sorry. It took longer than I expected. I had a flat tire."

The disapproval vanished. "Are you all right? You managed to change it okay?" His skeptical frown annoyed her, and yet she wouldn't have managed alone.

"I was still at the restaurant. Someone there helped me change it. I can go to the garage and get it replaced tomorrow."

He waved her offer aside. "I'll get Charles to do it." He shook his head as he poured himself some water out of the refrigerator. "I was worried."

"I'm fine."

His dark eyes narrowed. "You know I love you, Row, but you're up to something and that makes me nervous. What's going on?"

Her mouth went dry. She hated deceiving him even by omission, but he wouldn't approve of her quest. Unlike Uncle Gamba, Row was white and had no real roots to this beautiful land. She'd been conceived here, but she didn't fit in, and she didn't fit in back home either.

She needed answers. So did he.

"I wanted to revisit some of the places Aunt Anoona and Uncle Peter said mom stayed."

"Hmm." He turned away and put the kettle on.

Her mother had spent twelve months in Africa prior to Row being born. Originally her mom had been visiting her brother, Peter, who worked as a doctor in remote areas all over Africa. He'd met Anoona, Gamba's little sister, who'd been a nurse, and they'd immediately fallen in love and gotten married. Meanwhile, her mom had gone traveling with some people she'd met while backpacking.

Rowena wasn't sure who her father was, but she suspected it was one of those traveling companions—that's what her Uncle Peter and Aunt Anoona had let slip before they'd clammed up like a couple of, well, *clams*. Thoughts of her aunt and uncle brought on another intense wave of grief. They'd died in a fire late last August, and she'd been struggling to deal with their deaths and the stark reality she had no known blood relatives left alive anywhere in the world.

So she'd decided to try to track down her father.

The main contender was a man named Dougie Cavanagh who'd written letters to her mother that Row had found in a box in her grandmother's attic. Unfortunately, Cavanagh had also passed away, not long before her mother. Row had been unable to track down any of his living relatives—yet—in order to run a DNA comparison to verify. In the letter, she'd found a photograph of a handsome young white guy who had dark brown hair just like hers. He'd been standing in the bush somewhere next to a much younger Bjorn Anders, whom she'd identified using facial analysis software she'd bought off the web.

Hence her trying to get up the nerve to speak to the guy for the past few weeks.

Was Dougie Cavanagh the reason her mother had run home to England without even letting her brother know she was leaving Africa? Had he broken her heart? Had Dougie known Allie Smith was pregnant? The letters suggested not. Her mom had died not long after Rowena was born. Peter and Anoona had immediately returned to England and settled down in Shropshire, where Peter found a job as a GP and Anoona as a nurse in the NHS. They'd raised her as their own, and she'd loved them fiercely. They'd been the most amazing stand-in parents she could have asked for, but she'd never stopped wondering about her biological parents.

Uncle Gamba finished making the pot of tea, then cleared his throat and raised two thick brows. "I don't mean to speak ill of the dead, but some of your mother's choices were a little…reckless by all accounts. It does no good to dwell on the past."

Her uncle and his family were pretty conservative, although he was probably right about the dwelling on the past. Dwelling had done her no good at all.

Hence the action she was trying to take, if only she could get up her nerve.

Gamba was a good man. A kind man who loved her despite

her lack of blood connection and despite her many flaws. And she loved him. She owed him an explanation, but he wouldn't approve of her trying to track down her father this way.

"No one ever really talked about her, and now everyone who knew her is gone…" She'd always thought there'd be more time to badger Anoona and Peter for answers.

"Her death was tragic, especially as she left you behind, a tiny baby." Gamba swallowed thickly. "No one wanted to remind you of your loss. Anoona and Peter tried to do what was best for you."

"And I appreciate that so much." She rubbed her cold arms. "I don't mean to be a burden."

He looked at her sharply and took her by her upper arms. "You have never once been a burden. My sister loved you as her own child, and you know we all feel the same." His eyes grew glassy with unshed tears.

Row blinked to hold back the emotion. "I do know. I guess losing Aunt Anoona and Uncle Peter hit me pretty hard."

"It hit us all hard." Gamba visibly struggled. His wife had also died two years ago. It was a lot to deal with. "But we have to accept God's will."

She nodded but silently disagreed. She didn't have to accept anything.

He let her go. "I have a proposition. I have to go to Jo'burg for the week. I leave first thing tomorrow. After my meetings, I plan to meet Amara and Faith for a few days' vacation and take them shopping. Why don't you come with me?"

She'd love to spend more time with her vivacious cousins, but she still needed answers. Except what happened if Bjorn Anders refused to see her or, worse, didn't know anything? Who knew better than she that life was short and that she should enjoy what was left of her family while she could? "I have plans to meet someone tomorrow. I could fly down after that?"

He looked like he wanted to ask questions about who she was meeting but he held back. "Promise?"

"I promise."

He smiled then turned serious. Squeezed her arm again before handing her a mug of tea. "I worry about you."

She put the mug down and embraced him in a fierce hug. "I'm okay."

She wasn't. Once she found the answers she was looking for, then she would be.

3

JANUARY 12

Tuesday. Harare, Zimbabwe

Row got up early the next morning and waved her uncle off on his trip with the promise to join him and her cousins soon. Perhaps some beach time and shopping were exactly what she needed. She'd gained nothing from following Anders around Zimbabwe. Now was the time to confront him. Then she needed to go back to the job she loved where, as frustrating as it was, she could at least still search for answers.

She found herself sitting in her uncle's old SUV, down the street from Anders' office. A small complex of previously residential buildings surrounded by a high wall and closed gates on the western edge of town. A few minutes after she'd arrived, a big, shiny-black SUV had driven inside the electronic gates, but no one had come or gone since. She hadn't been able to see the driver's face because the glass windows had been darkly tinted.

She memorized the license plates though. That was one of her superpowers.

She gnawed on her bottom lip, trying to figure out the best approach. What if Anders refused to talk to her? Or claimed he didn't know the man she believed to be her father? Did she show him the photo? What if he wasn't at the office today? Should she go to his home again? Actually knock on the door this time?

She didn't want to drive up to the gates because then they might spot her uncle's license plate, and she didn't want him involved. She needed a story to get in the door, but saying she was searching for her as-yet-unidentified father would probably freak Anders out.

She needed to *move* but was frozen to the seat.

Suddenly, the gates opened, and the black SUV sped quickly out of the compound. She ducked, pretending to search through her bag. She wore a green canvas hat pulled low over her unruly brown hair which she'd tied into a loose bun at the nape of her neck. Long sleeves and trousers helped disguise the fact her skin was painfully white. Not that anyone who really looked would be fooled but perhaps she might not stand out quite so much to the casual observer.

When the SUV was out of sight, she sat back up and realized the gates remained open.

Not questioning her good luck, she grabbed her handbag, climbed out of the car, dashed across the street, and strode confidently up the driveway that was lined with mature shrubs and tropical flowers.

Three vehicles were parked off to the left. Excitement hit as she recognized the one that belonged to Anders. A glass door led to a small reception area, and she pushed inside, but no one sat behind the desk.

"Hello?"

A radio played in some distant office, and she poked her head through the doorway and looked both ways down a long corridor covered with framed posters about landmines and the organizations that tried to combat them.

"Hello? Anyone here?"

No answer. Perhaps they were all in a meeting, or wearing headphones?

Gathering her courage, and the memories of acting classes

she'd taken at uni, she walked down the corridor with a half-smile of greeting pasted firmly to her lips. She passed room after empty room. Perhaps all the people who worked here were out on assignment or something.

The main office building was an extended and converted old family home. At the end of the hallway, she saw Anders' name etched onto a fancy nameplate. He was clearly the boss.

Steeling her spine, she knocked firmly on the door and placed her hand on the knob.

No one answered.

They *must* all be in a meeting.

Pursing her lips, she came to a decision. She'd wait in his office. He couldn't avoid her then, could he?

She opened the door and took a step inside. Found herself in a space that looked more like someone's colonial front room with a deep-red tiled floor, large stone fireplace, a couple of hunter-green, leather, wingback chairs. A wide window overlooked a pretty back yard filled with greenery and a stone bird bath.

Her brain refused to register the scene at the other end of the room.

Then her stomach caught up with her brain. She clapped a hand over her mouth as gore rushed up her throat. She forced it back down, grimacing at the bitter taste.

Bjorn Anders was tied to a chair beside a huge mahogany desk and had clearly been savagely beaten.

His head lolled to one side, and blood ran down his neck and drenched the front of his shirt. He looked dead.

Her knees shook as she glanced quickly down the corridor but saw no one.

Was everybody else in the building also dead?

Another terrifying thought struck her. *Is the killer still here?*

She eased the door closed, her heart pounding so loudly she couldn't hear a bloody thing. If the killer was still here, then hopefully they hadn't heard her come in, thanks to the blaring radio.

She gingerly turned the lock. And stood there trembling in shock, not knowing what she should do next.

The lock wasn't much protection, but it might give her time to escape via the back door. She ran across the room and undid the bolts, top and bottom of the door, and turned the large old-fashioned key that sat in the lock. Then she hesitated. What if it was alarmed? Or what if the killer was in the garden? She relocked it and made her way to the edge of the window and stared out cautiously. Multiple birds were feeding on the millet and bread that someone had placed in a basin. She didn't think the birds would be there if a person lurked in the bushes. Her gaze was drawn inexorably back to the grisly figure in the chair.

Bjorn Anders had been viciously beaten and the office ransacked. Pieces of paper littered the floor.

A robbery? Who'd do something like this?

She couldn't not try to help him—even if he didn't know who her father was, she owed it to both of them to try to help him.

She'd had first-aid training.

She stepped carefully over to him, avoiding the mess on the floor, the broken glass of a family photograph that showed his beautiful wife and young kids. She cautiously touched the side of his neck where the pulse should be strongest. His skin was warm, but there was no beat of blood beneath her fingertips. Most of it was spread over his body and pooled on the floor beneath the chair, the scent metallic and cloying.

She jerked her fingers away and took a sharp step back.

He was definitely dead.

Her insides twisted as she fought nausea. She ran for the back door again but hesitated. She glanced at Anders' desk. She wanted to get out of here as fast as possible, but once she was gone, she'd never be able to come back. This would be her *last* chance to find the answers she so desperately needed.

Someone had dumped the contents of the drawers on top of the desk, the items scattered everywhere as if they'd been searching for something. The wooden drawers themselves were tossed against the wall.

She glanced over the items on the desk and saw nothing more exciting than a stapler and paperclips, the usual office clutter. The stuff in the file folders looked like invoices, receipts, contracts. Nothing earth shattering, and she didn't have time to read them all.

Was this a robbery gone horribly wrong? The computer hard drive was missing though a monitor remained.

A flash of gold caught her eye, and she crouched to the floor, sliding aside an envelope. Her fingers closed around the edges of a fancy business card. She frowned at the blue and gold embossed seal.

United States Department of Justice.

Federal Bureau Of Investigation.

Supervisory Special Agent Kurt Montana.

Montana.

Shock filled her. The American from the bar last night.

An FBI agent?

She'd assumed he was some sort of military contractor.

A drop of what was presumably Bjorn Anders' blood marred the textured card, partially obscuring the cell number and reminding her of the carnage beside her.

She turned her head away from Bjorn Anders' mutilated corpse, then frowned. There, on the underside of the dark wood, in the far back corner was an envelope taped to the surface.

Why had Anders hidden it?

She reached inside and scratched at the aged Sellotape until it peeled off and she ripped the envelope away.

She carefully opened it up and pulled out a photograph. A photograph very like the one that had brought her on this quest in the first place, showing a group of men sitting around a fire, including the man she believed to be her father.

Was it what the killers had been looking for? Why? Should she take it with her? She took a quick snap with her phone then hesitated. It was clearly important enough for Bjorn to hide. If she left it here, chances were it would be destroyed or lost. She could take it now and send it to Bjorn's family when she got somewhere safe and figured everything out. With numb fingers she slid it back into the envelope and into a notebook inside her large canvas handbag that doubled as a rucksack.

The FBI agent's card vibrated in her trembling fingers.

Maybe he could help her.

Or maybe he was the killer…

No. She didn't believe that. He'd been intimidating on many levels last night, but he hadn't struck her as a killer.

Not that she was an expert.

She hesitated, heart racing, uncertain as to what to do.

Call the police? Or the FBI?

Or run?

She knew she should call the local police, but why would they believe she didn't have anything to do with Bjorn's murder? And could she trust the authorities after all the tales of corruption she'd heard from her aunt, uncle, and family? She had no desire to spend her life in prison for a crime she didn't commit.

Bjorn's suit jacket hung on the back of the office chair. Deciding she was already in too deep to balk at rifling through his pockets, she pulled a clean tissue from her own pocket and covered her fingers as she pulled out Anders' wallet and his cell phone.

Checking on the garden through the window she opened his phone, relieved he didn't have a passcode. She scrolled quickly through the last few calls he'd made and saw two to Montana's number yesterday.

An FBI agent would know what to do…

He'd probably tell her to stay put and wait for the cops. The lump at the back of her throat grew as her anxiety mounted.

She didn't want to go to jail. She wasn't sure what to do.

———

Kurt sat slouched at a bar in Robert Gabriel Mugabe International Airport, the low murmur of servers and passengers humming in the background. The Legat had been in Nairobi, so Kurt had dropped the weapon he wasn't supposed to have with a contact from the US Embassy—one Martin "call me Marty" Sinclair.

Marty was officially a clerk, but it was obvious to him that Sinclair was a wet-behind-the-ears CIA officer with a too-white smile that didn't quite reach his puppy-bright eyes and an agenda that was way above Kurt's pay grade. Kurt had worked with the type many times before. He was gonna have words with one of his good buddies who now ran The Farm about the caliber of intelligence officers the CIA was putting out these days.

Marty had indicated the embassy was eager for him to get out of the country, which suggested Kurt had maybe rattled some cages with his questions about Hurek.

Who though?

He wished he knew.

Despite everything, he still didn't have any goddamned answers as to the potential whereabouts of Darmawan Hurek.

Someone was helping him. Someone powerful.

Or maybe Hurek was sitting alone in a mud hut in the middle of nowhere, living off the land.

It pissed him off.

All the resources of the US government and its allies, but they couldn't find one guy? At least he had this new lead to pass on. *Dougie Cavanagh.*

However, Kurt's stint on this task force was at an end. His bosses wanted him back at HRT.

He'd spoken to Jordan Krychek briefly before he'd fallen asleep last night. His colleague had been stuck in Frankfurt airport and called for an update on the meeting with Anders, but the connection had been shitty, so they hadn't spoken for long.

He'd see him soon enough.

He downed the last of his coffee, gathered his stuff then headed to his gate. He was looking forward to getting home, despite the failed mission. He wanted to see Daisy, who'd promised to come visit, and to catch up with the guys. Convey his personal condolences to Grace over the loss of her husband. Make sure she had all the support he and the guys could provide.

Someone was going to have to be in that delivery room. Someone was going to have to be prepared to sleep over at Grace's and help out with the newborn every so often to let Grace get some rest and recover from the birth. He knew from experience that the first three months was a sleep-deprivation nightmare comparable to Selection, minus the long runs, heavy loads, and tests of marksmanship.

He narrowed his eyes.

They'd take turns.

They'd set up a schedule that worked for the team and for Grace.

By all accounts, Payne Novak had turned out to be a hell of a team leader, and Kurt knew it was time to step aside for the younger man to permanently take up his position as Gold Team leader. He needed to accept the promotion he'd been avoiding for so long because he preferred getting his hands dirty to overseeing operations. Ackers wanted to retire, but he didn't want to go until Kurt was willing to step into his shoes. Whether the new FBI Director accepted that was another matter entirely.

This op had been a disaster and not how he'd wanted to leave his active-duty roles at HRT. His mind drifted back to the woman with the flat tire last night. He hadn't heard back on his request for more information about Rowena Smith.

If she was a player, she was a good one.

If she was innocent...she was going to get eaten alive.

Why was she following Bjorn? Kurt didn't believe it was a coincidence she'd turned up at the Falls and then at the restaurant last night. Was Bjorn dirty? Or had the inquiries he'd been making on Kurt's behalf stirred up the attention of someone protecting Hurek? Had he put his friend in danger?

On the surface, Bjorn's business dealings had always been

squeaky clean, but you couldn't thrive in an unstable environment without greasing a few wheels. Kurt knew Bjorn had attended the diamond mine conference in order to schmooze with some of the big international firms that sometimes wanted to venture into areas that had landmines left over from various conflicts—new and old.

Kurt was all for getting rid of landmines. It was innocent civilians who lost the most when deploying that type of ground warfare. But sometimes the people footing the bill weren't doing so for humanitarian reasons. Another fucked-up fact of life.

He ambled slowly to the gate with his dusty hand luggage.

He and Krychek had sent their bigger bags and equipment back to the States from DRC with a buddy from DEVGRU who'd promised to drop them off at Quantico. Wanting to travel light, they'd then made their way to Rwanda and flown down to Lusaka, then driven to Vic Falls, and from there to Harare.

There were large blank spots in Hurek's background and whereabouts for several years after he'd graduated from St. Andrews. Kurt believed Hurek had spent some, if not all, of that missing time in Africa. After weeks of subtle inquiries in the DRC, Kurt was convinced Hurek was, or at least at some point had been, involved with the illegal diamond trade.

Blood diamonds.

Despite efforts to clean up the diamond-mining industry, there were still concerns about violence, forced labor, child labor, and environmental issues. Seeing that Russia and China were now the heavy investors throughout the region, those things weren't likely to improve any time soon—not that the West had any moral high ground to stand on with regards to those issues.

Frustration gnawed at him, but there was nothing he could do about global politics. Fuck, he couldn't even track down one Indonesian terrorist with all the might of the US government stacked behind him.

They called for general boarding to commence, and he stood, letting a woman and her baby go ahead of him in the queue. This first flight to Lusaka was packed. From Zambia, he'd fly to Dubai and then overnight to Dulles.

He showed his passport and boarding card to the gate agent and headed out onto the tarmac. It was a beautiful day. The sun was bright, sky a clear crystalline azure. Temperature a perfect 77°F, although it was climbing fast, and the afternoon forecast was for monsoon rains.

'Twas the season.

The weather back home in Quantico was far different so he slowed to absorb a few more solar rays. He wasn't looking forward to being jammed into coach for the next thirty hours.

Unfortunately, the FBI refused to spring for business class even though he'd more than earned it. He'd bet a month's salary Ackers never traveled coach. Another reason to take that promotion.

His cell rang.

Bjorn.

The flight attendant waved him forward, and he thought about ignoring the call. He was tired of being here, tired of being jerked around, and wanted to go home.

But if the guy had something for him, the least he could do was take his call. "Bjorn?"

"It's n-not Bjorn."

Rowena Smith. The girl from the bar last night. He frowned, hesitated, then wheeled around to stand in the shadows of the terminal building. He narrowed his gaze across the shimmer of the airport runway. "What are you doing with Bjorn's cell phone?"

"H-he's dead." It sounded as if her teeth were chattering.

Shock?

"Where are you?"

"Standing in your friend's office looking at his dead body."

What the fuck? Was she telling the truth or was this some elaborate trap designed to get him to stay in Africa? For what purpose?

"I don't believe you."

A notification on his phone indicated a photo coming through. He opened it and winced as he took in the ugly state of his friend. Emotions welled up inside. Bjorn had multiple knife wounds and was tied to a chair so he wouldn't have been able to fight back. Blood soaked his shirt.

"Did you check his pulse?"

"Y-yes. In his neck." The words were shaky and low. "He doesn't have one, but he is still warm."

Sadness rushed through him. Bjorn had been a good man who'd spent his life making the land and people safer. His wife and children now had to mourn a husband and a father.

Who'd killed him? This woman? Why?

Kurt glanced around. The attendant was urging him forward, but there were plenty of other passengers still queuing up to get on.

He waved in acknowledgment and turned away. "Did you kill him?"

"No!"

Did he believe her?

Why should he?

"Why are you there then, especially as you claimed not to even know him yesterday?"

"I *don't* know him. But I needed to ask him some questions about my father."

"Who's your father?"

"I don't know." She sounded as if she were crying.

Dammit.

Sincere or bait?

He couldn't tell.

He shifted his weight. "Why call me?"

"I found your card on his floor. You work for the FBI." That her tone was accusatory was rich. "I figured you'd want to know your friend had been murdered but maybe that's my naivety showing through again. Apologies if I interrupted your morning."

"Why are you using his phone?" But he already knew the answer to that.

"Because that way I thought you'd pick up."

"Who are you working for?"

"*Working for*? I don't understand." The confusion sounded real.

"Come on. You've been following Bjorn for at least ten days that I know about. And now you claim he's dead."

"Claim?" Her voice crackled with emotion. "You think this is some kind of elaborate ruse?"

Kurt didn't trust her one iota, but he was torn. Bjorn certainly looked dead. He stared at the aircraft. "Who's paying you?"

"*Paying me*? For what?" She sounded astounded by the suggestion, her English accent growing stronger with each word. "Forget it. I thought you'd know what I should do, but I'll just call the police—"

"Wait," Kurt warned sharply. If she was innocent, and God help him he couldn't help believing she might be, the local police were the last people she should contact. Not that they were all corrupt, but some of them definitely were. "If you didn't kill him, do you know who did?"

"No. Well, I'm not sure." Her voice dropped even lower. "I was building up my courage to talk to Mr. Anders when I saw a black SUV drive inside the gates. It drove away about thirty minutes later, and they left the front gate wide open. I took the opportunity to walk right in—I never imagined... I didn't see anyone else. I don't know if anyone else is alive in the whole building. I'm too chicken to look and worried the killer could still be here..." That explained why she was speaking in a low, terrified whisper.

That did not sound good. Had Bjorn been killed because of the questions he'd been asking on Kurt's behalf? Was Rowena Smith telling the truth? He had the feeling that even if she was innocent, she was connected in some way to what had happened.

"Did you touch anything?"

A sob tore out. "A few things. I didn't realize it was a crime scene until it was too late."

"Wipe down anything you can easily reach and then get the hell out without anyone seeing you." It didn't sit well with him that he was telling her to interfere with evidence, but until he knew who was involved, he was following his gut. "You have a vehicle?" He'd eased back further into the shadows and, when the flight attendants were distracted, strode quickly around the corner of the building and headed around the terminal.

"I have my uncle's car. The one from last night."

She needed to get out of the country ASAP. He should tell her to go to the British Embassy, but they might throw her to the wolves if they thought she was guilty or if they didn't want to disrupt their fragile relationship with a former colony over one young woman who may or may not be guilty of murder.

She could be stuck there for years.

Whereas the US would be *thrilled* he was about to possibly cause an intentional incident. But only if he was caught. And he had no intention of being caught.

He had a feeling Rowena Smith had information that might prove useful to the FBI. And that information was all he cared about. That, and finding out what had happened to his old friend, Bjorn, and whether or not Darmawan Hurek was involved.

"Meet me at the front entrance of the Epworth Balancing Rocks. Pull up on the side of the road and wait for me there. You know where that is?"

"I can find it."

"Bring Bjorn's cell phone and wallet if you see it. Keep your head down. Don't talk to anyone. I'll be there as fast as I can."

4

R ow carefully wiped down the doorknobs and locks, then
fled Bjorn Anders' office via the back door, scattering the
birds into a frenzy of wings. She ran her sleeve over the front door
handle on the way past, then drove away feeling as if she had a
giant neon sign flashing over her head that screamed "Murderer!"

She followed the directions from her cell, careful to obey the
speed limits and traffic laws so she wasn't pulled over by a
member of the all-too-enthusiastic police force. It took her about
twenty-five minutes to get across the city, and panic made her feel
as if she couldn't catch a proper breath. The entrance to the
Epworth Balancing Rocks appeared up ahead, and she pulled
over onto the side of the road. Cut the engine.

Sweat scored an uneasy path down her spine.

There was no sign of FBI Supervisory Special Agent Kurt
Montana. Maybe he'd called the cops or planned to arrest her
himself. Earn himself some brownie points. She had sent him a
photograph of his dead friend. Why wouldn't he assume she'd
done it? He was already highly suspicious of her motives and a
law enforcement officer to boot.

She gnawed her lip as she rolled down the window then

regretted it as the growing heat and humidity of the day flooded inside.

A few locals were selling arts and crafts on one side of the road and watched her with curiosity.

What was she going to do? The idea of going to prison terrified her but, even if they didn't arrest her for murder, she had interfered and run away from a crime scene without reporting it.

Her mouth went dry as she tried unsuccessfully to swallow. She wouldn't survive prison. She wasn't strong or brave. She liked reading books and eating cupcakes and drinking hot chocolate with lashings of whipped cream.

She squeezed her fingers around the steering wheel as her pulse pounded through her ears. Should she make a run for the border? How long would it take to drive to South Africa? Should she call her uncle and tell him what had happened? He'd know a good lawyer. But then he'd be implicated after the fact, and she wouldn't do that to him.

She stared around her. What was she *doing* here?

No way would an FBI agent help her no matter what he'd claimed, although he was the one who'd told her not to call the police.

Could he be involved in Bjorn Anders' death...?

No. Of course not. That was ridiculous. Unless he turned up in a black SUV, then she'd know she'd been foolishly naive.

She felt sick with indecision. This sort of thing didn't happen to people like her. She put the car in gear, and then spotted the FBI agent jogging up a side road toward her, a work bag slung over his shoulder along with a rucksack. A wave of relief rushed over her. He'd come. Apparently alone. Not in a black SUV with a license plate she recognized. The relief was short-lived, squashed by the unsmiling stare he sent her through the windscreen.

Crap.

She put the car back in neutral. She'd forgotten how intimidating he was in person. Maybe it was a mistake to trust a man like this? Why would he believe her or help her when he worked for the FBI?

He tried the passenger door, but it was locked, and she floundered, searching for the release. Finally, she found it.

He tossed his bags into the back seat and climbed in beside her. His face was tanned, eyes an inky blue that were deeply cynical as he stared intently at her face.

She ran her hands around the steering wheel. "Hello."

"Drive." He didn't smile.

"Where to?"

"You have an airline ticket?"

"It's booked for the end of the week, but I was going to change it and fly down to visit my uncle and cousins in South Africa today or tomorrow." Her eyes filled with tears because she should have left the past alone and traveled with her uncle. Had a little fun for a change. She blinked away the tears. Self-pity was a waste of time and energy. "Now, I don't know what to do or where to go."

His gaze never left hers, but she didn't know what he was looking for.

"I wouldn't fly anywhere if I were you. You might be flagged at the airport. Head out of the city." He pointed southeast so she put the car in gear again and pulled onto the highway.

"Keep to the speed limit, and stop if the police tell you to."

Roadblocks were common in this country.

She swallowed the thickening ball of anxiety wedged at the back of her throat. "Why are you helping me?"

He wiped a light sweat off his forehead. "I don't know. Maybe I'm a sucker for a damsel in distress."

"Ha." Her voice cracked. "Somehow I don't think that's it."

"I'm wounded. I helped change your tire last night, didn't I?" He opened the glove box and started rifling through the paperwork there.

"You did." But he'd done that to confront her. She frowned at him. "What are you looking for?"

"Trying to figure out who the hell you really are."

"I told you who I am."

"Maybe I want proof, considering I'm in a car with a potential murderer who's on the run from the local authorities."

She pressed her lips together. As much as she hated the accusation, she also couldn't blame him for being suspicious. "The car belongs to my uncle. His name and address are on the documents. And you're the one who told me not to call the local cops."

His expression remained impassive as he took a photo of the license and registration documents.

"Please don't get him involved in all this. He has no idea what I was doing."

"If you're his niece he's already involved. Did you call him?"

"No. Just you. From Mr. Anders' phone." Row's eyes stretched wide. "They wouldn't detain my uncle because of me, surely?"

"Depends on who killed Bjorn and why. Give me your phone and his."

Obviously, he didn't trust her, and why should he? He seemed willing to help her though, and she was woman enough to admit she needed help. She fished her mobile out of her pocket. Handed it over along with Anders' and the man's wallet.

"Look at me."

Rowena turned to face him, keeping one eye on the road ahead as he unlocked her cell with facial recognition.

"You can see the last call I made was to Uncle Gamba when he was at the airport early this morning to fly to South Africa to visit his daughters, my cousins. Like I said, I was planning to join them."

He grunted. "Maybe I passed him in the airport."

"You were at the airport?"

"About to board my flight home."

She blinked at him. "And, what, you just *left*?"

"Bjorn looked dead, and you sounded as if you were in trouble. That or you're his killer. At least this way I can keep an eye on you." He stared at her as if trying to read her secrets.

"I'm not a murderer, but I can understand why you might be *apprehensive.*" The idea was so ridiculous she had to force down a laugh. Then she sobered because she was neck-deep in quicksand, and he was the only one who might be able to throw her a line. "I am grateful for your help. Assuming you didn't kill Anders."

He gave her a quizzical look. "Me?"

She rolled her shoulders. "I didn't see the killer. Could be anyone."

"You saw someone exit the premises in a vehicle, and then called me as I was about to board my flight several miles away."

"So you say."

His expression looked respectful rather than scathing. He dug into his pocket and pulled out a boarding pass. "I didn't kill Bjorn, and if I had, I certainly wouldn't have made such a damned mess of it."

She shivered. He sounded as if he knew what he was talking about. "Did you walk from the airport to Epworth Rocks?"

"Ran. It's only 5K and I could use the exercise. Plus, I didn't want a cab driver knowing where I went."

She didn't know what to say to that. She came to a major junction and took a right on R5 heading away from Harare. Her mouth went dry knowing she was on the run from a situation she didn't understand with a strange man.

Montana went back to searching through her calls, texts, and emails but there weren't that many, and they weren't very interesting. She watched him through her peripheral vision.

Finally, he looked up. "You didn't contact anyone at all afterward?"

She shook her head. "Like I said, just you on Anders' mobile."

"Good girl."

She should resent being called a girl at twenty-seven years of age, but in truth it didn't bother her. He checked through Anders' mobile and deleted the image of Bjorn's dead body that she'd sent to his cell. Then he forwarded the same image to someone else and then deleted it from his own phone.

"Why are you deleting it?"

"Because when the authorities realize his cell is missing, they're gonna check his call history with the phone company. Maybe deleting it will slow them down long enough not to consider me a person of interest—considering someone sent me a photo of his dead body from his cell after his death." A frown formed between his heavy brows. "Have to admit I don't know enough about cell phone companies in Africa to know if they store a deleted image on some sort of server or not."

"Why delete it off your own phone?"

"Because if the authorities here stop me and somehow manage to open my phone, the last thing I want them to find is a picture of a friend of mine, tortured to death, and me trying to flee the country with the prime suspect. The FBI should have a copy on their server by now anyway."

"Oh." She shivered and swallowed nervously. In reaching out to Montana she'd involved not just this man, but the entire organization in a murder investigation in which she was a major suspect. The realization was daunting even though she hadn't had anything to do with Anders' death.

They passed a long line of stalls on the side of the road where vendors sold baskets upon baskets of vermillion tomatoes. The vivid red reminded her of the blood dripping down Bjorn Anders' body.

She kept her eyes on the road as her hands gripped the steering wheel tighter. "Why did someone torture him, do you think?"

"Are you sure he was tortured?"

"No, but he was tied up and covered in wounds."

"Some people enjoy others' pain."

She shuddered.

"What do you think they wanted?"

She lifted her hair from her neck and fanned her warm skin. "I have no clue. I didn't know him. I've never even spoken to him."

"So why follow him around Africa? You some sort of private investigator?"

She laughed in astonishment. "I wish. No, I was hoping he could tell me something about my father."

He shifted to face her. "You said you didn't know who your father was."

"Exactly." They were heading past fields of red earth. The heat had started to climb, and the clouds began to boil in the sky above them, building for an afternoon storm. The SUV's A/C was iffy at best.

Row licked her dry lips and felt his gaze follow the move. Probably assessing her body language for lies.

"I *don't* know who my father is. Not for sure. That's what I'm trying to figure out." The tendons in her hands stood proud against the skin as her grip tightened. She couldn't see what harm it would do to tell him the truth now—except make her look pathetic. "I found a photograph of a man who was writing letters to my mom before I was born. It showed him and Bjorn Anders together, so I decided to come to Zimbabwe and ask Anders about the other man and see if he'd ever mentioned my mother. But I couldn't gather my courage enough to approach him. What if he couldn't remember anything? What if he refused to talk to me?"

"Why not ask your mom?"

"She died when I was a baby." Row fought the familiar pain.

"I'm sorry."

She nodded. Nothing to say beyond that really. "My mom's brother, Peter, and his wife, Anoona, raised me back in England in the town where mom and Peter grew up. They met here, in Africa in their early twenties. Anoona is Uncle Gamba's sister. Was."

"Your uncle and aunt know what you're up to?"

She sucked in her lips to suppress the emotions that wanted to swamp her. The last six months had been rough. "They died in a caravan fire while on holiday in North Wales last summer." It still seemed surreal.

"I'm sorry."

She exhaled noisily. "It was difficult to lose them both so suddenly and so violently. They weren't old, and they were both fitter than I am."

"You said your Uncle Gamba flew to South Africa this morning. Any other relatives in the country?"

She shook her head. "Gamba has cousins in the countryside near Bulawayo, but I don't really know any of them. We drove through once, years ago on holiday but I didn't visit any of them this time."

"Good. Hopefully your uncle is smart enough to stay out of the country should Bjorn's death be linked to you."

"Do you really think it might be?"

"Depends on what trace they find or plant. And why he was killed."

Her eyes whipped to his.

"Did you see any security cameras when you went inside?"

Her eyes bugged as she looked at him. Montana grabbed the wheel briefly, but she had it under control.

Relief hit her. "If there was a security camera that will show the real killer!"

Montana's expression grew darker. "Depends on who killed him."

"What do you mean?" Rowena sagged in her seat. "Oh my God. You think they wiped the tapes or turned off the cameras?"

"Or they aren't worried about the police seeing them. Or perhaps they turned them off and back on again after they left, and you'll be seen sneaking onto the property around the time of the murder providing the perfect scapegoat."

Nausea rolled inside her.

She felt his eyes on her face again and realized he genuinely didn't know if he could trust her. The idea anyone would think she could kill another human being was absurd.

She felt a little dizzy.

"So you came to Africa searching for your father. Why not contact him directly? Why the need to go through Bjorn? If you have these letters presumably you have a name and an address to start searching?"

"I have a name, but that's all. He died before I was born."

"Jesus." He rubbed his face.

Yeah, she'd always considered herself a bit of a bad luck talisman. "Dougie Cavanagh."

"What?" he said sharply.

"The man I believe is my biological father was a man called Dougie Cavanagh."

"What makes you think he's your dad?"

"The timing mainly. Mom probably became pregnant when she was in Africa. And why else would she keep his letters?"

5

Dougie Cavanagh.

Kurt had known this young woman was connected to his search for Hurek, but he hadn't known how. He still didn't, but two people had mentioned this previously unknown individual within the last twenty-four hours. One of those people was dead.

"Oh, shit. Up ahead." Rowena's voice was strained. "Police roadblock."

He looked up. Her swearing took him by surprise. She seemed too prim and proper to curse but, if she was to be believed, she'd had quite the day.

Sure enough, three blue uniformed police officers ambled across the tarmac in the increasingly oppressive heat. Dark clouds boiled overhead. A storm was coming.

"Relax. Take a deep breath," Kurt told her. "If they stop us, show them your license but hold on to it. Don't let them take it away. My name is Joe Hanssen. Pretend I'm your boyfriend which is a stretch but do your best. We're heading to Nyanga on vacation. I'm an insurance salesman from Montana, which works if you accidentally slip up on the name. We have a long-distance relationship and have been dating for almost a year but don't see each other much. You were visiting family in Harare—keep to the truth for now, I doubt anyone is looking for you—yet. I joined you after a safari in Zambia with some of my buddies."

"That's all off the top of your head?"

"Not exactly. It's part of a backup plan for worst-case scenarios. My identity is fully backstopped."

"So's mine, *Joe*. So's mine." Her expression was pissed, which beat scared. "Insurance salesman?"

"Proof someone at the FBI hates me."

A laugh burst out of her and had him smiling despite himself. She slowed and began winding the window down as the policeman held up his hand. Then the heavens opened, and rain burst from the sky in a sheet of water. The policeman changed his mind and waved them through as he and his fellow officers scurried to their vehicle at the side of the road.

"Well, that was fortuitous." She pulled a face at him and drove carefully past the barriers.

She was shaking, he realized.

"You cold?" It was in the nineties outside, so he doubted it.

She put on the wipers. Shook her head. Her hair under her green canvas hat was falling out of its haphazard bun and curling against the side of her neck. "Belated reaction to finding a man murdered and the reality hitting home about the very real possibility I'm going to be arrested for the crime—not to mention never finding out the truth about my father."

Her teeth were chattering, and her skin had lost all its color.

He checked the mirror. They were out of visual range of the checkpoint. "Pull over."

She shot him a look of surprise but did as he said, carefully indicating despite the complete absence of any cars behind them.

Rule follower.

He got out, hunching against the downpour that soaked him in seconds as he ran around the hood. Opened the door. "Jump across."

She pushed back the seat and clambered over the console.

He climbed behind the wheel and slicked back his short, wet hair, pulled the shirt from his now soaked skin. At least the rain cooled him down. He put the car in gear and pulled back onto the highway. "Are those the same clothes and shoes you wore at the crime scene?"

Rowena nodded. "Yes."

"You have any other shoes with you?"

"Er, no, just these trainers. Why? Is there a dress code for being on the run?" Despite her attempt at humor, her mossy-green eyes looked anxious.

She should be.

"We need to get rid of anything that might link you to the murder scene and then sanitize this vehicle."

"You mean like blood?" She shuddered and looked at her shoes. "I don't think I stood in any. I don't have anything else with me. I left all my belongings at Uncle Gamba's house. I packed everything up in case I decided to jump on a flight after talking to Anders, but I didn't bring it with me. I never expected…" Her voice trailed off.

"You have your wallet and passport?"

"Yes." She indicated her purse in the back seat. "I always travel with them."

He reached over and grabbed the bag off the back seat and placed it on his lap. "You mind if I go through this?"

"Would it matter if I did?"

Kurt gave her a humorless smile. "Not really."

"You still think I might be involved in something nefarious."

"Nefarious is my *raison d'etre*."

Her brows rose. "You sure you want to do that while driving?"

"Anything sharp inside?"

Her eyes bugged. "Like what? The murder weapon? Or syringes from my heroin addiction?"

"I'm simply asking. I don't want to get stabbed with your knitting needles."

"Tempting, but just so happens I left my knitting needles at home." She crossed her arms and stared pointedly out the side window. "There's nothing I can think of that's going to harm your delicate hands as you invade my privacy, Supervisory Special Agent Montana. Have at it. Enjoy your snooping."

Uh oh. He'd pissed her off. Too bad he couldn't afford to care. He rifled carefully through her stuff keeping one eye on the road. A notebook with a couple of envelopes tucked into the pages, pens. An ereader. Hair bands. Packet of tissues. Tampons. A hairbrush. Lipstick. A British passport in the name of Rowena Smith. A purple wallet.

"Satisfied?"

"If I don't check and you have the murder weapon tucked away somewhere in the vehicle or on your person, I'm gonna look like a prize ass and end my FBI career as a laughingstock for being taken in by a pretty face. Considering I'm putting my career in jeopardy to help you, you could be a little more grateful."

She jerked the bag from his fingers and placed it carefully on the back seat behind her. "You're right. I'm sorry. If someone approached me this way, I'd have already called the cops."

"I am the cops."

She made a sound that might have been a strangled laugh. "I guess you are, though officially you have no authority here or over me. However, you can search the vehicle when we stop. I didn't see a knife in Anders' office, so the killer must have taken it with him." She turned to stare at him. "Why *are* you helping me? Why not just call in the locals and catch your flight home?"

Kurt grunted. Because his instinct was telling him she was innocent? That a killer calling an FBI agent for help would suggest a degree of sophistication and cunning—or plain stupidity—that Rowena Smith did not seem to possess? Or was it that unwanted sliver of attraction making him make poor decisions? Regardless, he believed she had information he needed that might somehow, inadvertently, lead him to Hurek. He wasn't sure how the bosses would view his interference, but if she were locked up in a Zim prison or dead, they'd never find out if his hunch was correct. They had precious little else to go on.

"I'm honestly not sure why I'm here so don't make me regret it."

She looked surprised by his admission. "So what's the plan? I mean I understand the authorities need to question me, but I'd rather be in the UK when they do. Can you help me get home, and then I can talk to the police?"

He wasn't sure coming forward would be a smart move. "What can you tell them if they interview you?"

"I can give them the license plate of the vehicle that rolled in and out prior to the murder."

That was useful information. "Maybe whoever was in the SUV has the same excuse as you do."

She hunched her shoulders and rubbed her hands together. She wore an expensive man's dive watch on her left wrist. "Perhaps, but Anders was still warm when I checked for a pulse. He hadn't been dead long, and they were there for at least half an hour."

A wave of sadness washed over him for his old friend. That he'd died in such a violent manner. They hadn't been close lately, but they'd shared some good times over the years. Some fond memories.

Why had Bjorn been so reluctant to talk to him about this Dougie Cavanagh guy who he obviously knew more about than he'd let on considering Rowena said she had a photograph of them together?

Maybe he'd been afraid whatever he knew might get him killed...

Kurt pulled out his work cell and opened a text message for Krychek who had full security clearance for this mission. "Type in the license plate there and press send. He'll know what to do with the info. Maybe the FBI can figure out who it belongs to. We can see who they're working for before you get involved in the murder investigation. Did you see any faces?"

"Nope. Nothing. Tinted windows and I kept my head down when they drove past. And there was no one else inside the building as far as I could tell."

The black SUV sounded suspiciously like some government entity. The bigger question was whether or not they were sanctioned by the people in charge of the country or someone else with power and money. If they were sanctioned, he and Rowena might be in serious trouble until they could reach safety. They needed to avoid getting caught. He didn't think it would be an issue. No one would miss him for a day as they thought he was on board a flight home.

"We need to pick up a few supplies. What's the next big town?"

She checked the map on his cell. "Marondera isn't far away."

Kurt flicked on the radio to see if the murder had hit the news yet. Instead, it was some piece about a billionaire named Nolan Gilder who was visiting the country and pledging to build a new computer manufacturing factory in the capital.

"Wanker," Rowena muttered.

"You don't like him?"

"Have you heard his views on women in general? He's a misogynistic pig."

Kurt laughed, and she glared at him. He stopped smiling. He liked that she stood up for herself and other women. He happened to agree but also tended to steer clear of making statements about people because he didn't want to end up misquoted on some news outlet. "What? You don't think he's a hero?"

"With his penis-shaped rocket ships designed to rape the nearest planets of natural resources while he lines his pockets? Or his satellite systems cluttering up the sky while he takes control of communications on a global scale? Gilder's the villain science fiction writers have been warning us about for decades."

"You're definitely not a fan." He flicked the station off.

"Most billionaires are selfish egotists with nothing much to recommend them, but Gilder is particularly obnoxious. Uncle Peter and Aunty Anoona met him once, years ago."

He glanced at her then.

"They said he was exactly as you'd imagine that kind of self-absorbed narcissistic personality would be. Uncle Peter said they almost came to blows over some comment he made about Anoona, but Gilder backed down when faced with someone tougher than he was."

"Wanker."

She grinned at his use of the British insult. He was reminded how pretty she was. He looked back at the road.

They were approaching the outskirts of Marondera. "Write a list of your clothing and shoe sizes on my phone."

"I can't come in with you?"

"I don't want anyone seeing you with me. I don't want anyone associating me and what I purchase with you. I'm going to pick up clothes, food, water, a burner phone so we can apply for a visa to get into Mozambique without linking it to our own phones. Maybe some hair dye or a new hat for you. And I'm going to buy some bleach wipes and sanitizing supplies so we can attempt to get rid of any trace evidence linking us to the crime scene."

Her hands formed a twisted bunch of fingers in her lap. "What do you want me to do?"

"Nothing. Sit in the car and keep your head down. Read a book or something."

"Usually my favorite thing."

"Use my cell to direct me to a supermarket and then a shoe store. The FBI encrypts the signal, so it's the best one to use in a pinch, but I'd rather we both fall off the radar until we're on neutral territory if possible."

She did as he asked, and five minutes later, he pulled up outside a fancy-looking Pick-n-Pay. It was still raining heavily, which suited him perfectly. Fewer people going in and out, and hopefully, the rain would remove any traces of blood from his shoes transferred from Rowena's onto the foot pedals of the car.

Her bloodless lips were pressed together in a thin line.

"You gonna be okay?"

Her green eyes were huge and frightened. "I don't know."

"I mean waiting in the car?"

"Oh." She glanced around as flags of color appeared in her cheeks. Nodding briskly, she folded her hands neatly in her lap. "I'll be fine."

"I might be a while."

"I'll be here." She held his gaze. "If I'm not, I'll be at the police station. In handcuffs."

He sighed. He wanted to reassure her everything would be okay but there were no guarantees. "Keep your face averted. Don't catch anyone's gaze. But don't act suspicious either."

She gave him a rapid nod, and he climbed out of the vehicle, leaned back inside. "Any allergies?"

She shook her head and dragged her bag from the back seat into her lap.

He shut the door and headed into the grocery store. He grabbed a cart and mentally calculated the minimum supplies they could get away with. Water was a priority, so he got a flat of still bottled water. Then he picked up a few apples, bananas for the car, sports drinks, energy bars, some packet soups, and a small cheap saucepan in case they ended up having to cook in the open. Some bread rolls. He threw in two big bags of chips because he was starving. He found wipes with bleach in them and tossed in three packs along with a box of tissues and some matches. He grabbed two packs each of ready-made sandwiches and some emergency chocolate bars. They could be over the border in a few hours. Or, if he decided it was too dangerous, they might have to hike cross country through the mountains and figure out a way to contact someone to come pick them up on the other side. His preference would be SEAL Team Six, but it was more likely some local spook who'd shove them in the back of an embassy vehicle and then onto an aircraft in Maputo.

What he did know was that if they couldn't get a visa stamp

from the border guards, then travel in Mozambique would be just as dangerous as traveling across Zimbabwe—especially with someone who might be a suspect for murder.

Not a lot he could do except prepare for the worst. He added another pack of sandwiches. Paid cash and took the loot back to the car, tossing Rowena a sandwich and a Coke and a pack of wipes.

"Wipe off the pedals and the footwells and bottom of your shoes as best you can. I'm going to the shoe shop and electronics store next."

She nodded.

"You have any cash? Or Bjorn?"

She rifled through her wallet and handed him a wad of US dollars. Then she opened Bjorn's wallet and there was a picture of his beautiful young wife and two great-looking kids.

It shook him.

Murder was always shocking.

He inhaled and shoved the feelings aside. She handed him a wad of cash that he'd replace when he was back in the States. He couldn't afford to lose his focus. Not until they were safe.

It was still raining, but he was already drenched so it didn't matter. He was warm and didn't really care.

He got to the shoe store and bought waterproof hiking boots for Rowena along with some good woolen socks for them both. Next door was a clothing store, and he walked inside not really having a clue what Rowena might prefer. He found jeans and T-shirts and a rain jacket and a light fleece.

They were going to look a bit his-and-hers but perhaps that would help sell the girlfriend-boyfriend idea. As long as no one counted the creases at the corners of his eyes, the two of them might get away with it. He added woolen hats too. Where they were going was more elevated than Harare, the nights cooler in the mountains.

He used Rowena's cash for this haul. He would save his alias's credit card for emergencies.

He wished he'd been able to find a tent and a couple of sleeping bags, but perhaps staying at a local lodge or hotel and maintaining their cover as tourists would be wiser for a white couple who so obviously didn't belong.

Or they could sleep in the car.

He went back to the SUV, placed the supplies in the back seat, and met her gaze. Her cheeks were flushed from exertion, and she held a wad of dirty tissues in one hand.

He emptied a plastic bag and held it out to her. "Finished?"

She placed the used wipes inside. "I think so. I scrubbed everything I could think of."

"Pass me your shoes. Put these on."

She took the new boots from him and placed them on the driver's seat. She dragged off her sneakers and passed them over one at a time.

Then she cleaned her hands on another wipe and tossed that into the garbage bag he held.

She bit her lip. "Anything else you want me to do?"

"Just one thing."

"What?"

He frowned heavily at her, keeping a straight face as she nervously waited for him to answer. "Don't eat all the potato chips."

————

Kurt headed across the road to a small outdoor mall that had an electronics store. He tossed the garbage bag in one trash can, placed Rowena's purple sneakers on top of another, and kept walking. Chances were someone would pick them up and take them home because they were nice shoes. That disposed of them a whole lot more effectively than putting them in the trash.

He was soaked down to his underwear which reminded him to go into another clothes store and pick up something for both of them. He checked his cell for her sizes. He thought about calling his bosses, but it would be better if he waited until he had some actionable intel. They weren't expecting him until tomorrow, and no one was waiting for him at home anyway.

He picked up a couple of pairs of boxers for himself because he hadn't done laundry in a week, expecting to be home next time he needed anything clean.

Then he wandered over to the women's section and eyed the array of bras with dismay. What the hell did he know about choosing women's underwear? The woman behind the counter came over and he admitted defeat.

"My, er, girlfriend asked me to pick up some new underwear while she's at the grocery store. She gave me her sizes." He raised his hand at the vast selection. "I don't have a clue what she might like."

"Is she skinny or full figured like me?"

Kurt tried not to stare at the woman's ample figure as she skimmed her hands over her hips. "She has curves." He could feel himself blushing. Fuck. He read the sizes again. "She's a 34C chest and UK 12 pant size. Can you help me out?"

The woman laughed and picked up a piece of lace he realized was supposed to be panties, and he shook his head. "We're doing some hiking. So something comfortable not er… that." He did not need to be imagining Miss Rowena Smith in anything remotely like *that*. He needed to think of her the same way he thought of his daughter.

"Let's pick a selection." She picked out a variety of sensible-looking panties and added a few scraps of material that made heat creep up his neck. Then she headed for the bras.

Kurt spotted a sports bra and grabbed one. "This will do."

The woman eyed him with pity and grabbed a ruby red bra and pantie set. Then she picked up a matching coverup that was practically sheer.

He almost swallowed his tongue.

The shop assistant eyed him over her glasses. "A woman

sends a man shopping for underwear, she isn't asking for practical."

He was pretty sure steam was coming out of his ears. "Fine. Throw it in." The store could probably do with the business. "Put in that flannel pajama set too." He didn't think they'd be together long enough to worry about any of this, but they might have to spend one night pretending to be intimate partners and no way was he dealing with Rowena while she wore sexy red lingerie. He'd sleep in his clothes.

He paid cash again and realized they were going to be low by the end of the day. His alias had a bank account and credit card, but he didn't want to activate Joe Hanssen until they were as far from Harare as possible, and hopefully not even then. All being well, they'd be well-stocked for the next twenty-four to forty-eight hours and in a junk food coma at the American Embassy in Maputo.

He paid the cheerful woman and headed to the electronics store next door. Inside, the smell of component parts and a soldering iron wafted on the air. He stood off to one side as the shopkeeper served a young teen and an older man who was probably his father. Kurt browsed the phones and picked up a cheap pay-as-you-go model. He found two SIM cards that would work across the border and another one he could use on this side if he needed to anonymously call his FBI contacts and tell them what was going on—before he headed off into the great unknown with a woman who might be an ice-cold killer.

And if she was?

He'd get her to an embassy and let them deal with it.

First though, he had to figure out what she knew and how this Dougie Cavanagh fellow was connected to Hurek. Perhaps Cavanagh wasn't really dead. Perhaps Bjorn had reached out to him for information about Hurek like Kurt had asked, and Cavanagh had killed Bjorn—or hired someone else to do it. Maybe Cavanagh was hiding Hurek.

On the TV screen, footage played of Nolan Gilder pressing a

button to set off an impressive pyrotechnic display then shaking hands with the Zimbabwean President. Kurt didn't pay much attention to billionaires in general, but he looked at this one carefully now. The man's hair was short, his jawline was firm. Kurt figured Gilder had to be mid-fifties but looked and acted a lot younger than he was. It was great he was investing in the country, as long as the wealth went to those who needed it.

Kurt headed to the counter as the other customers left. He put his purchases on the desk.

"Will you need phone credit for the Mozambique SIM cards, sir?"

"That'd be great. Thanks. You have any *meticais*?" They didn't take US dollars on the Mozambique side of the border, although they might at a pinch.

"Of course. How much?"

"Fifty US?"

The man nodded, counted out 3000 *meticais,* and Kurt paid.

"You a tourist?"

"That obvious, huh?"

They both laughed.

Then something caught Kurt's eye on the TV screen. News of the crash of a commercial airliner. It made his stomach clench as he should have been on a plane right now.

The shopkeeper followed his gaze. "Oh merciful heavens." He crossed himself. "Those poor people."

Kurt nodded then his whole body froze as he read the number of the flight that was believed to have gone down close to the Zambian border. His mouth went dry as dust.

That was the flight he was supposed to be on.

Without Bjorn's murder and Rowena's phone call, he'd be dead.

He remembered the people he'd seen at the gate. The woman with the baby. The flight attendants who'd urged him onboard. He wanted to throw up. Maybe there were survivors. Perhaps the pilot was able to land it in the bush somewhere. But the ticker tape said they didn't believe there were any survivors, and he felt sick at all those lives lost.

Unease rippled down his spine.

Kurt didn't like the coincidence of Bjorn being killed and then the flight he'd been booked on falling out of the sky—all shortly after they'd spoken about the whereabouts of Darmawan Hurek.

Was it a freak accident? Or had Kurt been the target and the other people on the plane collateral damage?

"Are you okay, sir?" the shopkeeper asked.

Kurt shook his head. "No. Not really. I'm scared of flying and have to take a flight home in a few days. Doesn't exactly make me feel better."

"A stiff whisky beforehand helps me."

Kurt nodded. He'd prefer a parachute.

It was hard to process the deaths of so many innocents. He needed to call HQ and check in with them before they saw the news.

The lights and TV went off abruptly as the power went out in the store.

The shopkeeper cursed under his breath. "The ZESA. The ZESA is out again." He threw up his hands in despair. "Every damned day the ZESA goes out."

The power company, the Zimbabwe Electricity Supply Authority, was notorious for power outages.

"How am I expected to run a business when there is never any power?"

"You have solar or a generator?"

The man nodded. "Yes, but it's no way to live especially in my business."

Kurt wondered how Nolan Gilder's new factory would fare in a country that so often lost power. Perhaps people would adopt even more solar and become self-sufficient. He dropped the shopkeeper another ten-dollar bill to help boost the day's earnings. Then he loaded his purchases into a plastic bag and headed back into the rain.

6

Jordan Krychek ran into the Hostage Rescue Team compound late for the morning briefing.

He was never late.

He'd arrived back in the US after a journey that had been plagued with delays and missed connections. He'd slept like the dead last night, knocked on his ass by the travel and the seven-hour time difference between Virginia and Harare. He was eager to get back to a regular routine with the guys. Running around Africa had been fun for a short time, but when none of the leads had panned out, the last few weeks had been frustrating, especially after Scotty—Dave Monteith—had been killed while performing his duties.

He wanted to hang with the guys. To reconnect.

On arrival, he'd contacted task force leader SSA Reid Armstrong at SIOC at FBI Headquarters where their JTTF was based, checked there were no updates. Armstrong was the former Legal Attaché to Indonesia and intimately acquainted with Hurek. Armstrong had told him to go home.

Instead, he'd gone into the HRT compound and caught HRT Director Daniel Ackers and said "Hi" to some of the guys who were around. After that he'd gone to see Scotty's widow. Grace was still reeling from the loss of the man she loved and had looked visibly aged, probably from grief and the burden of being six-months pregnant.

He knew all about the former and nothing about the latter. He'd ordered takeout pizza for them all and put the kids to bed while Grace rested. Afterwards, he hadn't even had the energy to drive home. He'd passed out on her couch and been woken by five-year-old Katie staring holes through him at seven a.m. that morning.

She'd wanted to know if he'd seen her daddy anywhere, and then she'd started crying when he said he hadn't. To distract them both from the terrible reality her daddy wasn't ever coming home, Jordan had helped her make her mom breakfast, which the little girl had delivered with steely determination.

Now he was late, and he hadn't even been home yet, but it had been worth it to pay his respects to his friend's family.

Jordan wasn't sure where he was being assigned yet. Kurt had told him confidentially about his likely promotion to Director of HRT. As Payne Novak was doing a hell of a job as Gold Team leader, Novak would probably take on that role permanently. With the assaulter and sniper teams at full quota, Jordan was hoping for some sort of assistant role working directly with Kurt, which would be sweet after seven glorious years on Gold Team. In the short term, if the Hurek task force allowed, he hoped to get seconded to the task force hunting the murdering bastard who'd killed Scotty.

His work cell alerted with a Code Red, and his brain instantly switched to high gear. Had Kurt's meeting with Bjorn Anders led to actionable intelligence? Would they send HRT or DEVGRU?

He and Kurt had spoken briefly yesterday but the connection had been so awful Jordan had barely been able to discern what Kurt was saying. He nodded to friends and colleagues as he wove between them and quickly found a seat.

Everyone quieted down when Director Ackers walked into the room and took his place at the front. Jordan had a lot of respect for

Ackers. The man had served on the teams and understood the ropes in a way no outsider ever could.

The director's mouth was grim. Eyes downcast. He raised his hand to get everyone's attention and inhaled a deep, preparatory breath. "I have some bad news and, considering what happened in Houston, I wanted to be the one to break it to you all. You probably know Kurt Montana was due back from a TDY today."

Jordan leaned forward. Had Kurt found Hurek? Was HRT going to be the team to bring him in? Even though he'd only just arrived home, he itched to go bring that bastard to justice.

"Twenty minutes ago, I received word from the State Department that the flight from Harare was involved in a catastrophic incident. I'm afraid State believes everyone on board died. There are no known survivors."

No.

That couldn't be right.

Jordan's head rang with an unreal silence as his heart slammed inside his chest. Then his windpipe closed, and he couldn't swallow.

Ackers held his gaze for a long moment, his brown eyes reddened as if fighting tears. "We're obviously going to be searching for more clarity about the situation, and members of Red Team are being deployed to investigate on the ground." He cleared his throat. "But to my immense sadness, I have every reason to believe Kurt Montana died on that flight. I'm about to go break the news to his family. Operators Novak and Angeletti, I'd like you to accompany me, if you don't mind. Jordan, I need a quick word in my office."

Jordan sat in his chair as everyone else whirled into motion. He felt as if he'd been drained of blood and stuck in a deep freeze.

He felt a hand on his shoulder. He looked up.

Aaron Nash. "You okay?"

Jordan stared at his colleague and friend. He could see the questions burning in Aaron's eyes, feel curiosity that bordered on suspicion. They wanted to know what he and Kurt had been doing in Africa and if that could have had a bearing on Kurt dying in a plane crash.

Dying.

Dead.

Kurt was dead.

Jordan should have been on that flight. He should be dead too.

He'd grabbed a last-minute cancellation because he was fed up with being jerked around by liars and grifters. He'd doubted Bjorn Anders would have anything useful to tell them, and Jordan had been sick of hitting dead end after dead end while Hurek continued to evade them.

Now he wanted to go back. To turn around and get right back on the next plane to find out what the fuck had happened to Kurt.

"Jordan. You okay?" Aaron repeated.

He shook his head. He wasn't okay.

Pressure from a dozen pairs of eyes drilled into him. He needed to go see Ackers. Then talk to the rest of the task force in DC. Make sure they knew about this and see what the hell was going on. He wanted permission to share details of their investigation with other members of Gold Team. He wanted to drown in a bottle of whiskey or fall asleep and never wake up.

This could not be true. Perhaps it was some terrible mistake?

"You're a hell of a lucky guy, Krychek." Birdman leaned back in his chair with his arms crossed, a twisted expression marring his blunt features.

Jordan stood abruptly, his chair screeching across the floor before he headed out of the room to talk to Ackers and then find somewhere quiet to grieve.

He wasn't lucky.

He was cursed.

———

"I hate to say this, but I really need to pee." Row had been crossing her legs for the last ten miles. "If I remember correctly, there used to be a famous tea house along this road." She and her family had visited about a decade ago. "I don't know if it's still open for business, but if it is, could we make a quick pit stop? Otherwise, I'm gonna have to find a bush."

Montana shot her a look and gave a reluctant nod.

She checked his cell to see if the phone service was back yet.

"Still no signal." The power had been off since they'd left Marondera, and the rain hadn't let up. Puddles were forming wide stretches across the roads.

Up ahead, a large, white, bulbous-shaped sign with Halfway House painted on it appeared in the distance.

"Oh, that's the place. You think it's open?"

"Only one way to find out." Montana indicated right and pulled down a side road and into a large gravel car park in front of a thatched, white-painted with fresh green trim, Dutch colonial building with the dates 1891-1991 printed above the door.

The lights were off, but there were a couple of other vehicles in the car park.

Row undid her seatbelt and grabbed her bag. "I'll be quick."

"Wait. I'll come with you. Let's see if they have coffee."

He'd been quiet since he'd gotten back in the car, and she had the feeling he was distracted about something. That, or he was still suspicious of her, which was hardly surprising as he didn't know her.

He dug into the backseat and pulled a rain jacket from one of the bags. He snapped off the tags and handed her the coat, which was a dark purple like the favorite trainers she'd had to give up.

"Thanks." She slipped her arms into the sleeves, which felt cold against her skin. At least the rain had taken the heat out of the day.

He dug into his own rucksack to remove a black Gore-Tex shell which he quickly donned. They both put up their hoods and, after locking the car, dashed through the puddles into the entrance. It was cool inside and dark because of the power outage. But the café was still serving food and drinks, so

Rowena touched Montana's arm and felt his muscles tense in surprise.

She quickly drew away. "I'll be right back."

"Tea or coffee?"

"Tea with plenty of milk please. No sugar."

She used the facilities and washed up. It was cold enough inside the building that gooseflesh formed on her arms. She headed back to the main shop, glad to see there was some fresh fruit and vegetables on sale as well as chocolate bars. Business seemed to be thriving. She spotted Montana sitting outside beneath a covered area at a large picnic table. The other people had left. Rain dripped off the edge of the thatched roof and from the leaves of the tree in the center of the large square courtyard.

He'd bought scones with cream and jam which surprised her. Playing the tourist? Or did he have a sweet tooth? She wished she knew more about the guy. She sat and pulled her cup and plate toward her.

"I'm surprised they have hot water." She sipped the hot tea. Perfect.

"They have a gas burner. Apparently, power outages aren't uncommon especially in the wet season."

"Ah, yes, the constant battle with the dreaded ZESA." She took a mouthful of scone, and felt it melt on her tongue. "This is divine." She covered her mouth as she spoke.

He nodded, running his finger up and down the white bone china mug. "You said you have a photo of Dougie Cavanagh with Bjorn. Do you have it with you?"

She wiped the crumbs off her lips, reached into her purse. Hesitated. "Okay. Before I show you the photo, there's something I didn't tell you earlier."

His dark brows pulled together over serious eyes. "This isn't the time for secrets, Rowena."

"I know, and that's why I'm telling you now. And please call me Row. I hate Rowena. I sound like someone's grandmother."

"I like it."

The admission startled them both.

He looked away and then back again. "What didn't you tell me?"

She dragged an envelope out of her purse. She pushed it across the table. "This contains one of the letters Dougie wrote my mom before I was born. The photograph is inside too."

He carefully opened the letter and smoothed it out. Examined the old photograph of Dougie and Bjorn standing together and smiling.

"The letter mentions him being sorry she left so suddenly and the hope she was okay. The hope she'd write back and he could come visit her in England."

Montana turned the photo over. The date was written there. He frowned again, and she thought it might be his default expression. He still managed to look handsome even when grumpy.

"You said this was written before you were born?"

"About seven months prior. There were three letters in all. That was the first one. I only brought that one with me."

He caught her gaze. "That makes you, what, twenty-seven?"

"Twenty-eight in June." She took another bite of scone.

His eyes traced over her features. "You don't look that old."

She snorted. "Yeah, well, thanks. I feel about seventy-five right now."

"Join the club." He captured an image of the letter and photo with his cell camera and then put it back in the envelope. Slid it back across the table and met her gaze. "What didn't you tell me?"

The blue of his eyes was darker around the edges—like true navy—and cerulean closer to the iris. She'd read somewhere that people with blue eyes didn't actually have any blue pigment, instead they were blue the same way the ocean was blue or the sky, because of the wavelength of light that was reflected back. Those steady eyes watched her now with quiet intelligence. She put the envelope back between the covers of her journal.

She swallowed, nervous now because what she'd done was fundamentally wrong.

"You can trust me, Row." His warm hand closed over hers on the table and squeezed.

His touch sent a shiver skating over her skin that had nothing to do with the cold. He withdrew and watched her patiently.

She pulled his business card from her jeans pocket. Slid it across the table. Presumably she'd have to ditch these clothes sooner or later because of the risk of contamination from the crime scene. "When I was in Anders' office, I spotted your card on the floor amongst all the papers—"

"They tossed his office?"

She sipped her tea. Nodded. "Threw everything out of the drawers and stacked them against the wall. The official seal on your card caught my eye, so I reached down for it and recognized the name Montana from our conversation last night. I was shocked to realize you were with the FBI." She licked her lips. "Anyway. From that angle, crouched on the floor, I spotted an envelope taped to the base of the desktop, right at the back."

Her mouth went dry as she pulled out the second brown envelope with tape still darkening the edges. Maybe this would push the limits of the law too much for him. Theft from a dead man seemed particularly unsavory. She put it on the table. Slid it over the scarred wood. Hugged herself. "I know I shouldn't have taken it, but I was convinced the killer had been searching for something, and I figured it might implicate them. We all know the potential for corruption should the police find it, which they would have, given it was at the scene of a murder."

"You took it?" Those navy eyes sparked with something she couldn't identify.

"I planned to send it to the family. Probably mail it from back home. But I really wanted to look at it myself first. Does that make me a terrible person? Stealing from a dead man?"

"The terrible person is whoever killed him." He shook his head. "I'd have probably done the same thing if I'd been there."

She released a deep breath. "I went to ask Anders if he knew my d— I mean Dougie Cavanagh. That's all. Not to hurt him." She could feel her cheeks heat. She shouldn't assume Cavanagh was her father. It could literally be anyone who'd had sex with her mother back then. Her uncle and aunt had claimed not to know, but she wasn't sure she believed them.

Montana opened the envelope and slipped the photograph into his large palm and stared at it for a few seconds.

She couldn't read his expression.

"When I saw him, Dougie, in that photo, there was no way I couldn't take it with me to try to figure out who the other men were. One guy looks vaguely familiar, but I can't place him. I can do a reverse image search which might turn something up. Dougie died six months after that photo was taken."

Montana turned the photo over. His jaw clenched as he slipped the photo back into the envelope and the envelope into his jacket pocket. "I'll make sure this gets to the authorities."

Oh.

He didn't say which authorities, and his expression had closed down so she didn't feel as if she could ask.

She'd taken a photo of it on her cell, so she'd have to be satisfied with that. She dabbed her finger into the scone crumbs and finished her tea. Montana immediately stood and gathered the dishes onto a tray and carried them inside. She followed him out of the café, and they ran through the rain to the car.

7

The situation had gone from interesting to disastrous in the space of a single moment. Kurt quickly slid behind the wheel of Rowena's uncle's beaten-up old SUV and pulled back onto the highway, keeping an eye out for police roadblocks ahead or any indication they'd been followed from the capital. *Shit, shit, shit.* He scanned the sky. He'd been watchful before. Now he was at DEFCON 2 level of hyperawareness.

It had felt like being jabbed with a cattle prod when he'd looked at the photograph Rowena claimed to have taken from Bjorn's office but figured he'd hid his reaction well enough. He needed a moment to think. To process.

To...

Fuck.

Fuck.

Fuck.

Not only was Dougie Cavanagh looking very cozy around that campfire, so was a young-looking Darmawan Hurek, Nolan Gilder, and Leo Spartan—the fucking UN ambassador for Zimbabwe.

Fuck.

Had Bjorn known all along who Hurek's friends were?

Seemed likely. The photo of Bjorn and Cavanagh looked to be around the same vintage. Was Cavanagh supposed to be some sort of decoy? A deflection?

It might explain why Bjorn was so reticent to talk to him about Hurek in the first place. Perhaps it risked exposing something in Bjorn's own past he wanted to keep hidden. Associating with terrorists was never good for someone working internationally with munitions.

Kurt needed to get both of the photographs to the FBI geeks who could figure out if they were authentic and when and where they were taken.

Could Rowena be working for Hurek, feeding him a line in order to figure out what the FBI knew? But why bother when someone had arranged to take him permanently out of the picture by bringing down a commercial airliner—murdering him along-side hundreds of innocent souls. He flashed back to that babe in arms, and he wanted to vomit.

That plane crash was no accident.

Rowena could be complicit with whoever had killed Bjorn, but he didn't think so. Her tale was so convoluted without turning itself inside out that she was likely telling the truth. If she was involved with the bad guys why show him that photo at all? Why stop him from getting on that flight? No way would the tech billionaire or the UN ambassador want their association, no matter how ancient, with a terrorist at the top of the FBI's Most Wanted list to be made public.

Did they know where Hurek was hiding?

Did Hurek have dirt on them?

The opportunity for Kurt to question them was long gone, if it had ever existed. With this new computer factory, Gilder was effectively holding the keys of the kingdom in this country. He was a national hero. He could probably murder someone on camera, and as long as it wasn't the Zimbabwean president, all would be forgiven.

And Gilder was possibly even more powerful in the US.

Who'd taken that photograph of the four men sitting together? Bjorn?

Given the stakes, chances were someone in the photograph had killed or arranged to kill his old friend.

Why?

To tie up loose ends? To keep a secret that was almost thirty years old? To get this photograph and make sure no one else ever saw it?

In the photograph, they looked like they were in some sort of bush camp. Gilder and Spartan were smiling whereas the other two looked more serious.

Had Bjorn pointed him in Cavanagh's direction as a stalling tactic? Or perhaps some sort of backup plan. Or had the four of them decided that the link to Cavanagh would be a dead end as he'd been deceased—supposedly—for decades. Kurt had a lot more questions than answers and unfortunately, the discovery Gilder might be involved meant the situation had changed drastically and so had his tactics.

"Pop the SIMs out of all three cell phones. I have a paperclip if you need one."

"I have something I can use." Row's mouth tightened as she pulled one out of her voluminous bag. "Why? You think the police can track us?"

He weighed up whether or not to level with her. It was a risk, telling her the truth, but she seemed smart, and the better she understood the stakes the more likely they were to be successful in escaping their current situation.

"I don't think we can trust any electronics right now, not even encrypted ones." Just as well the car was an older model. "Make sure the phones are powered all the way down. If you can pop the batteries, even better."

The fact the ZESA had gone down was a blessing. Without the power outage, whoever blew up that flight and presumably murdered Bjorn would already know Kurt had never boarded that plane. It was possible they already did.

And if they were willing to take down a commercial aircraft to get rid of him, then chances were they'd employ other methods to make sure he didn't leave the country too.

Why? Why kill him?

Because they knew he'd met with Bjorn and were worried about what Bjorn had told him? Or because of Rowena?

The latter didn't make any sense. She felt like a wildcard thrown into the mix at the last moment.

He could no longer assume his communications were encrypted or untraceable. Not when Gilder owned the satellites that bounced the signals around the globe. Nor could Kurt assume any of his messages would arrive at their intended destination. Was that why his connection to Jordan Krychek had been so crappy last night?

Perhaps Bjorn had set him up, knowing Kurt would be effectively incommunicado before being blown out of the sky. He probably hadn't expected to also be eliminated.

Owning the satellites, Gilder could intercept any text or email message that went to an FBI number or employee or have his AI bots analyze everything in real time.

Nope, Kurt had to assume any form of electronic communication was unsafe until he could get to a secure network or SCIF.

He gave Row a minute to double check each phone. The burner wasn't activated yet, so he didn't worry about it.

"Don't suppose your uncle happens to have an old-fashioned map-book around here somewhere?"

"I'm not sure. Let me look." She unclipped her belt and leaned over into the back. "Yes!" She dragged it out of the pocket behind her seat and flopped back down, turned the dog-eared pages. She flipped through until she found the right area and put her finger on the road they were currently traveling on. He was impressed despite himself. Not everyone knew how to read a map these days.

"Who did you tell about your quest to talk to Anders?" He

needed to know who might have spotted this young woman. Whose radar she was on.

"No one." She pushed her hair behind her ear. "I didn't even tell my uncle about him."

"Why now? What triggered you to come here now?"

"It's a long story."

"Do I look like I'm busy?"

She blinked at his tone, and he winced.

"Sorry." Dammit. He softened his voice. "It's important."

Clearly uncomfortable, she chewed her lip and clasped her hands together—a clear tell when she was nervous. "After Peter and Anoona died, I decided to move back into my childhood home—my grandmother's house. She died eight years ago. Peter and Anoona lived there, but I'd moved out after I went to uni and found a little flat to rent when I moved back. My grandmother's house is old—like older than the United States old, and way too big for me on my own, but it's gorgeous, facing the river, with a huge rambling garden." She rubbed her arms. "I'll probably sell it, but…it's a connection to my family that I needed in the aftermath of their deaths."

He knew what it was like to lose people.

"Uncle Peter was the last blood relative I had, which is why finding my father suddenly seemed like a good idea. Trust me"— She cocked her head at him—"I'm currently regretting that decision."

He felt his lips twitch.

"At the start of December, I went up into the attic to pull out the Christmas decorations which was both grief-inducing and comforting. I found an old chest hidden in one corner that I'd never seen before. When I opened it, I realized it was full of my mom's things—schoolbooks, teen diaries, old posters, photographs and even her old SLR camera. Then I found the letters, and I started to do some online snooping about Dougie. I discovered he'd died young, just like my mom, which was a gut check. So I researched the other man in the photo next, Bjorn

Anders, and discovered he was going to be at that diamond conference"—Her long fingers traced the road—"I decided to visit my aunt's family here for Christmas and try to meet with Bjorn and see what he could tell me about my mom and Dougie's relationship. Coming to see Uncle Gamba and my cousins was a lot better than staying home alone among all the ghosts." She hunched her shoulders at the admission. "My uncle has a house up at the Falls. He and my cousins drove back on the twenty-eighth, but I stayed on. I spotted Anders a couple of times, but I never saw him alone, and I didn't have the nerve to approach him with anyone else there, so that was a bust."

"You lied to me."

She raised a haughty brow. "I didn't tell a perfect stranger things that weren't any of his business."

"And after the Falls?"

"I drove back to Harare. Bjorn's workplace was closed all last week. Reopened this morning. I figured it was my last chance to see him before I went home, so I drove over there first thing. We both know how that turned out." She grimaced.

"How did you know he was going to be at the Jam Café last night?"

She looked sheepish now. "I went to his house last night. He came out while I was still building up the courage to knock on the door. I followed him."

"Any chance he spotted you? Could he be the one who stuck a nail in your tire?"

"Why would he do that? I only wanted to ask him a couple of questions?" She rubbed her forehead. "It's possible though. I popped to the loo, and when I came out you were there alone, paying the bill. I headed straight to my vehicle and found the flat tire. I was pretty pissed when you turned up."

He nodded thoughtfully. Had Bjorn been aware of Rowena following him? As a former military man, he'd have been a fool if he wasn't. Bjorn had never struck him as a fool. A man who operated in war zones and dealt with explosives couldn't afford to drop his guard. Had Bjorn told anyone about her? Or did he know who she was and not consider her a threat?

Had Kurt ever really known the other man?

He pushed thoughts of his murdered friend aside.

"It's possible they might not know about you."

"They?" She stared at him, a serious expression hardening those soft green eyes. She knew something was up.

He ignored the question. "My original intention was to head straight to Mutare and cross the border into Mozambique."

It was still a viable option, but *if* someone reported that he hadn't gotten on that flight or if they'd tracked his FBI cell or if they had seen Rowena running away from Anders' office, they could run straight into an armed police roadblock at the border.

That was a lot of potential pitfalls and good reason to be careful.

Much more careful.

"I think we should head north into Nyanga. Stay close to the border or sleep in the car and hike into Mozambique tomorrow before dawn. Once we're there we can activate the burner and call for someone from the embassy to come pick us up." He'd have to figure out who to call to make that happen covertly. Probably Patrick Killion because the spook wouldn't be using a phone that could be tracked by anyone except the NSA and possibly not even by them. Perhaps the FBI's communication was also safe, but he wasn't willing to bet his life on it. Nor Rowena's. "We stay hidden as much as possible to avoid local authorities."

"What happened?"

"What d'you mean?"

"I mean when you came back from your shopping expedition in Marondera you had something on your mind and then"—her voice firmed—"after you looked at that photograph I found in Anders' office, your demeanor completely changed. Has the danger grown somehow? What's going on?"

He hesitated but she'd find out soon enough anyway. "When I

was in the store, I saw a news item about a plane crash in Zimbabwe on the television."

She clapped her hands over her mouth. "My uncle?"

"No." Kurt shook his head. "It was the flight I was supposed to be on this morning."

The blood visibly drained from her face as she stared at him, green eyes vivid against sheet-white skin. "You don't think it was an accident, do you? The crash?"

Kurt gave a slight shake of his head. "Bjorn and I met up last night and he's murdered this morning and the plane I'm supposed to be on falls out of the sky? The odds of that being a coincidence have to be like winning the lottery twice in a row."

She covered her mouth. "Whoever did this is organized and connected and ruthless." Her eyes shimmered. "People died?"

"Everyone on board according to the news report." He cleared his throat as the faces of his fellow passengers flashed through his mind. "If you hadn't called me when you did, I'd be dead right now. I owe you my life."

A single tear ran down her cheek until she swiped it away. "I'm glad you didn't die, but I hate that so many others did."

His throat clogged. *So did he.* "When someone is willing to sacrifice that many innocents to get to one man, it tells me they're worried I know something they can't risk me telling anyone else in the Bureau. The only lead Bjorn gave me was a name. Dougie Cavanagh."

She gasped.

"I recognize a young Nolan Gilder in that photograph and Zimbabwe's UN ambassador. If they are involved in this, then they have far greater reach than I originally anticipated. My guess is whoever killed Bjorn and blew up that plane will do anything to stop the truth from coming out."

Her mouth dropped open. "You think *Nolan Gilder* might be involved?"

He nodded. "There's no proof, but it's a potential factor we can't afford to ignore, considering he controls half the communication satellites in the sky."

"Oh crap—what about the license plates I sent to your colleague on your phone? Will that give away the fact you're alive?"

"I don't know, but I'm worried," he admitted. "Best case scenario, they assume I spotted them at Bjorn's before I went to the airport, and they'll put the timing of the message down to some sort of electronic glitch. Or they simply don't bother to check the data and assume I'm dead along with all the others. And maybe I'm overestimating their abilities or being paranoid. Perhaps they can't track an FBI cell phone."

"But you think they can."

"Plan for the worst. Hope for the best."

"I think I feel sick." She clutched her stomach.

"You need to stop?"

She shook her head. "I just want to get out of here."

He touched her knee, trying to give her some reassurance. He ignored the feeling that felt like closing his hand around a glowing ember. It wasn't anything like touching his daughter.

Rowena's expression was anxious.

Best way to combat worry, in his experience, was to give someone a job to do.

"I want you to find me a route that avoids the major town centers and hopefully any police roadblocks. Nyanga is popular with tourists. We won't look out of place if someone stops us up there."

She was shivering, so he turned up the heater even though he was warm. She looked at the map and then pointed out an upcoming road on the left. "Take this turning, otherwise we're going to end up in Rusape. I've no idea what these roads are like. They'll be dirt for sure. With all this rain, it'll be a mess."

He nodded curtly. The detour was going to slow them down considerably but better than driving headlong into danger.

"Your family and friends are going to think you died once they see the news about the crash." Her voice was soft.

"I know." The fact Daisy and his teammates would believe him dead until he could get to a safe place to contact them sucked. "Nothing I can do about it right now that won't put us at risk." And possibly change their fears into reality.

He didn't say that. Rowena was already struggling to deal with all the things he'd told her.

She shuddered, probably remembering Bjorn's bloody corpse. "Do you have a wife waiting for you back home?"

He shook his head at the question, which heightened his awareness about the fact Rowena was a beautiful woman. Why did she care? "She gave up on me long ago. I have a daughter about your age though. Twenty-three."

She snorted. "I'm not twenty-three."

She made it sound like he'd said Daisy was thirteen. "When you're my age, you may as well be."

She frowned at him. "How old are you exactly?"

"Forty-five."

"Oh boy, you're so ancient." Her laugh was forced, and he knew she was trying to put their predicament out of her mind. "Shall I call you grandpa?"

"Funny."

"You act like you're—"

"Your father? I could be." He shot her a stern look.

"Really? Do you remember having sex with any English women in Southern Africa when you were seventeen or eighteen?"

"I joined the Army a few days after my eighteenth birthday. I didn't come to Africa until I was twenty-two. And sleeping with an English woman is definitely something I'd remember."

Her eyes widened and her mouth opened into a pretty "o."

Jesus, he could feel himself blushing, but thankfully, she was looking at the map again.

"Well, in that case you're definitely not my father, so we don't have to worry about that."

What the hell did that *mean?*

She crossed her arms. "So, Army and FBI. Did you do anything else in between?"

He shook his head. His whole life had been dedicated to service of one kind or another.

"Well, at least you're experienced with this sort of thing."

"I know it's unnerving but try not to worry."

"I'm *not* a child." Her voice was sharp. "I don't need to be humored. I'm a grown woman. An intelligent, grown woman who's very grateful for your help, but please don't patronize me or attempt to placate me with platitudes. I know we're in serious trouble." Her breath hitched. "I might not be a soldier or law enforcement, but I am smart, and I am capable. I have *skills,* and I can help."

Amusement hit him then, but he hid it. Oftentimes grit was as important as skill. "I apologize if I underestimated you. I haven't even asked. What is it that you do?"

She shot him a narrow-eyed look. "You're not allowed to laugh."

"Promise." He crossed his heart over his chest.

"Fine." She raised her chin. "If you must know, I'm a librarian."

She looked ready to defend herself and her profession to the death. He suppressed a grin and inclined his head in acknowledgment. Fuck if he didn't find everything about Rowena Smith, *librarian,* as hot as hell.

8

They drove for hours along endless dirt roads that rattled her bones until her head felt as if it was going to fall off from the constant jarring. Montana barely spoke, just scanned the road ahead for potholes and behind for signs they were being followed.

Row had offered to drive, but Montana had shaken his head and clenched that manly jaw of his. Obviously, he was the strong, silent type, which she preferred to the self-important, let's-talk-about-me versions of the male species.

Finally, they rejoined the A14 and headed north. Being back on the smooth tarmac felt like heaven, and her shoulders and neck instantly relaxed and her jaw unlocked. Until she started to think about police roadblocks and being chased by some of the most powerful men in the country.

The rain had stopped an hour ago, and the sun was beginning to set—early, as always, this close to the equator. Sharp-angled rays streamed dramatically through scattered gray clouds, picking out vibrant spots of green and red in the fertile landscape.

It was truly the most beautiful country.

As the shadows began to lengthen, she shivered, wondering what the night would bring. She was freaked out about everything that had happened today but grateful she had the help of this man, who at least seemed to know what he was doing.

Suddenly, they were driving through pine trees and what looked like granite rocks on craggy moors—the Eastern Highlands. The contrast with the rest of Zimbabwe was dramatic. "Why do I suddenly feel like I'm in Scotland?"

Montana grunted, then swore as the front right wheel hit another pothole, the depth disguised by a puddle of water. The car immediately started pulling to the right.

He slowed and steered over to the side of the road. Sat in silence for five whole seconds before speaking. "Don't suppose you got that tire replaced?"

"No." She hated feeling inept. "I only planned driving to and from Anders' workplace. A few miles at most. My uncle said he'd get one of his staff to take the car into the garage this afternoon."

"Goddammit. I should have picked up a spare along the way. I'm a fucking idiot."

"You're not an idiot. If anyone's an idiot, it's me, and we both know it." Her eyes smarted suddenly for getting them into this predicament. "I should never have tried to follow Anders. I should have left the extent of my poking around to sending my DNA to the family tree research sites and seeing what popped. Then maybe I could have enjoyed my vacation, and we wouldn't be in this mess."

He turned to face her, his dark blue eyes intense on her face. "Only one problem with that. Without your actions today, I'd be dead, and I'm mighty grateful to be not dead."

She exhaled a ragged breath at the reminder. Then nodded. "I'm very glad you aren't dead too, Agent Montana."

"Call me Kurt. Actually, scratch that. Call me Joe, for now. It's a nickname I answer to regularly and easier to not slip up if that's what you're used to using."

She felt inexplicably sad not to get to use his given name. "You really think someone might be trying to kill you?"

"If I'm wrong, everyone back home is gonna think I've lost my freaking mind. But they'll also be happy I'm alive, so there's that." He sighed as they sat looking out at the growing dusk. "Perhaps losing my mind will make it easier to step aside from an active-duty role in HRT, especially, if they don't give me a choice."

"HRT?"

"Hostage Rescue Team."

"That sounds..." *exciting, sexy,* "dangerous."

"The guys train their assess off every day to be masters of what they do, but sure." He shrugged and his eyes looked a little somber. "It can be dangerous sometimes."

"What will you do instead? Play golf? Crochet? I could teach you to knit."

He shifted in his seat, amused by her little joke. "I don't plan to retire just yet. Just step into a more senior admin role which will be a lot less fun."

She looked around at the near darkness, somewhere in Africa, running from God knew what. "Is this your idea of having fun?"

"Maybe." He cocked a brow at her and his very attractive mouth quirked unexpectedly. "I haven't decided yet."

Gosh, the ways she could interpret those words...

"Let me know when you figure it out." She hid her inappropriate thoughts by squinting at the map, although it was hard to see now. "It looks as if there's a resort not far away, and, according to this map, which is who knows how old, there's a garage there too. If we're going to break down this is a good spot."

He shot her a look that questioned her intelligence.

She shrugged. "Beats walking ten miles to the nearest village to beg for help."

He exhaled a long sigh. "Let me look at that."

She handed it over, and he turned on the overhead light and peered down at the page. Well, that helped.

"We need to be up here to find a place to cross the Gairezi safely." He glared down at the paper as if it was personally responsible for their predicament. "Another twenty miles north. Then it'll be a hike to wherever we can get picked up on the other side of the border."

She checked her watch, a Breitling Superocean dive model she'd found in the attic and must have belonged to her Uncle Peter, who'd been a scuba diver back in the day. She'd had it serviced and had been wearing it since the funeral. A constant reminder of the connection they'd shared and of all that she'd lost. What would he say if he could see her now?

He'd tell her to do whatever it took to survive.

"Shall we head to the garage and see if they're still open? We might be able to keep going tonight if they can fix the puncture or if they have a tire that fits."

"Yeah." He sounded reluctant though. "We better take some essentials with us in case this garage isn't there anymore. The hotel should be. Perhaps they have someone who can help us."

She grabbed her purse, which held all her things and the cell phones. She had the feeling he'd have tossed the cells except maybe they contained evidence, especially Bjorn's. And probably hers too, thinking about it. It might help tell the authorities who'd killed the man. Although which authorities, she wasn't sure. She wondered who the FBI was searching for that Dougie Cavanagh's name had come up.

Had Dougie been a criminal?

Her teeth chattered. She didn't like that idea. Not at all. It was possible she'd weaved all sorts of romantic fairytales around the man based on the letters he'd written her mother. Row had no doubt he'd loved Allie Smith. She wanted to believe he'd have loved her too if he'd known about her.

Montana passed her a bag of new clothes and two bottles of water. Her new rain jacket. He grabbed his own rucksack and shoved two water bottles into the side pockets and stuffed energy bars inside. He also rolled up the map book and slid it down the side.

Did he think they might not be coming back? The idea was alien to her.

He turned off the headlights, and suddenly it was pitch black.

"Whoa. I can't see the nose in front of my face."

"I've got a flashlight. Wait a sec while I find it. Here."

He reached for her hand and put something small and heavy into her palm and folded her fingers around it.

"Thank you." She opened the door.

"Careful, it's going to be—"

She went down hard on her ass in the mud.

"Slippy."

She struggled to her feet still clutching the torch. "Slippery," she corrected automatically.

"Yes, ma'am. I'll try to keep in mind the dictionary police are on the job."

She grinned and a quiver slid over her shoulders that had nothing to do with the cool mountain air. She didn't think anyone had ever *ma'am-ed* her before. She kind of liked it.

She closed the door softly, and he did the same. She turned on the torch and pointed the powerful beam in front of her as she carefully made her way around the bonnet and met him at the front of her uncle's old 4x4.

Her footing went again but he caught her and secured a hand around her waist.

"I got you." His breath was warm in her hair. "This okay?"

She nodded as she clutched at his belt. "Yes. Thanks."

Damn, could he hear the hitch in her voice because he was holding her so close? Probably.

His fingers felt hot on her waist. Hot and firm and protective.

She wasn't used to physical contact with men. She'd buried herself in books rather than the opposite sex. She'd been a painfully shy teen, had a boyfriend briefly in college until she'd caught him bragging about having sex with her when they'd barely even kissed. The betrayal had cut so deep she'd avoided any entanglements for long enough that guys had stopped asking her out.

Then she'd gone home to Shropshire, and although she'd

joined a dating app, she hadn't been interested in anyone enough to warrant a third date. Most of her best friends were gay or in long-term relationships, which meant her social circle was not exactly full of available heterosexual men. She'd resigned herself to never finding anyone. To being single.

And was absolutely fine with that.

It was unfortunate that a whisper of attraction had decided to raise its ugly head now. Or perhaps it wasn't so surprising. The guy was helping her flee from shadowy killers and powerful forces. Why wouldn't she be attracted to him? Plus, he was handsome with that classic square-jaw, strong build, and he had the cute accent.

He was also generally unavailable because he lived in America and she lived in England, so, yeah, no wonder she was feeling a little lustful hero worship. It was safe.

He was safe.

They wouldn't be together for long. He'd be going home, and she'd hopefully be heading straight back to Ironbridge and the job she loved, surrounded by books and her co-workers and the capacity for constant learning. Safe from the possibility of suffering from more loss and heartbreak.

Safe.

Alone.

So perhaps she should give herself a little grace. The past twelve hours had been hell. The sort of experience best kept within the pages of her favorite novels, not lived in graphic detail.

"Okay, remember. Joe Hanssen. You're my girlfriend so better act a little ditzy to explain that."

"What do you mean?"

"A woman your age? With a guy like me? You'd need to be a little ditzy."

"What are you *talking* about? You are intelligent, good-looking and"—as she had her hand around his lean waist she could say with confidence—"ripped."

He laughed. "I'm twenty years your senior. Everyone will think I'm your father."

"You are eighteen years *older than I,* and as long as I'm legal age and not being coerced, it's up to me—and you—who we sleep with." Her cheeks flamed in the darkness. She hadn't meant to be quite so blunt, and now the idea had become alive in her mind along with a feeling of ripe anticipation.

Which was stupid. The guy was *helping* her.

"Okay, you can be righteous rather than ditzy. It works better because you look too smart to be ditzy."

She opened her mouth to defend people's appearances and the concept of "ditzy" but then she spotted holiday cabins off to the left and a light on the road ahead and relief filled her. "Looks like the garage is still there. Hey"—she nudged him in excitement—"Joe and Row. Our names rhyme."

He groaned. "Great. Lifetime achievement unlocked." But he laughed the way she'd hoped.

As they got closer, they could hear a generator and smell the exhaust fumes.

"I guess the ZESA is still down."

"Yeah. Row…"

She looked up and caught the stern set to his jaw.

"Do me a favor and stay back in the shadows when we get there. Casually. Pretend to fix your shoes or something. I don't want people seeing your face if we can avoid it."

She nodded. Reminded this was serious business no matter how badly she wanted to pretend otherwise. If someone had spotted her following Anders or caught her on camera at his workplace after his violent murder, the whole country might be looking for her.

All thoughts of whether or not it was reasonable to be attracted to this man fled. Who cared?

They were both in serious trouble. If Kurt Montana was to be believed, someone was actively trying to kill him. And if Nolan

Gilder was involved, the photo she'd taken from Bjorn Anders's office might be a key piece of evidence that proved it. They had to get that evidence into the hands of the proper authorities as soon as possible.

9

Kurt placed the bags he carried near the wide-open garage doors. The temperature had dropped considerably, and he wished he'd pulled on a fleece. Of course, holding onto Rowena had warmed him up more than he wanted to admit, even to himself.

He hoped he didn't embarrass himself. In theory, he believed what people did with their own lives and who they had sexual relationships with was strictly their business.

Yeah.

Sure.

A guy his age in his position of power? A young woman in what had to be frightening circumstances? That would never be morally right no matter how much he might try to justify it.

Not that he had any plans to even think about having sexual relations with Miss Rowena Smith.

Except, now he was thinking about it.

"Hi there." He stuck his head around the door and called out a greeting. Tried to look less like a horny old goat and more like a dumb tourist as two Black guys in greasy overalls swung around to face him. One smiled, and he gave the guy a goofy grin that hopefully made him look harmless rather than certifiable. It was cold inside the workshop, the generator being used to run the lights and machines but not the heater. "My girlfriend and I had a flat a couple hundred yards back there on the road, and the spare is a piece of crap. Any chance you can help us out?"

"Are you staying at the resort?"

"Weren't planning on it. Hoped to head further north tonight."

The guy on the right checked the clock hanging over the office door. Shook his head. "You won't get far. There's a tree down a mile up the road. It's going to be a couple of hours before it's cleared. I can tow your car here and have it ready to go by nine tomorrow morning."

"You can't do it sooner?" Kurt mentally calculated his cash situation.

The man shook his head. "I'll do my best, but I have to get my kids off to school before I come to work in the morning."

Damn.

He drew in a long breath then glanced at the lights across the road. "That's the resort?"

The man nodded. "It's very beautiful. Your girlfriend will love it. You might end up staying for longer."

Not if I can help it.

"My wife works there."

Kurt nodded, resigned to being stuck here overnight unless they wanted to walk. The latter was tempting, but they didn't have night vision equipment, and they needed to cross the river. He'd rather do that in daylight. "Any shops open in town?" He wanted an idea of the layout and population. He jerked his head toward Rowena, who had stayed outside, and lowered his voice. "I wanted to get her a little something as an anniversary gift."

"We have the convenience store and a pottery next to the post office just past the turning to Church Road, but that's closed already. It opens at nine."

Post office? That gave him an idea.

"The hotel has a very fine gift shop. You'll find something she'll like there. Or order her a massage."

"Good idea. 'Preciate it." He could do with a massage too. Or a good close-quarter combat sparring session. Or sex.

Fuck.

Reluctantly, he pulled the car key off the keyring and handed it over. "Do you know if the hotel takes credit cards even when the power is down?"

"Sure they do. They'll process it the old-fashioned way with carbon paper. We can do the same."

That should hopefully give them time to leave the hotel before their names were flagged—*if* they were being followed. Perhaps he was being paranoid after a near miss on the mortality coil. "That's good news. Thank you, sir."

He went back outside and saw Rowena's breath frosting the air as she leaned against the wall. Picked up all the bags in his right hand. Wished he had a weapon tucked away somewhere on his person in case things turned ugly.

"Hard to believe I was sweating earlier today." She sounded pretty upbeat under the circumstances.

"We're a lot higher up than in Harare." He held out his hand because the side of the road was still slick. It wasn't because he liked holding her hand. He wasn't that sort of guy. But to prevent a broken bone? Absolutely. An injury would fuck them up completely.

"So we're spending the night at the swanky resort?"

His mouth went dry at the idea. "We are. They'll fix the tire first thing."

She looked at him, remarkably composed for a woman who'd found a dead body that morning. Perhaps she was still in shock or simply not ready to process everything that had happened yet. He sure hadn't thoroughly processed everything the day had brought, but he was more used to death and danger than most civilians.

Without Rowena's actions today—however unwise or potentially illegal—he'd be dead. That was sobering. But then again, he spent a lot of time training with live ammunition, and brushes with death were one wrong step away. They trained that way for several reasons, but the main one was so adrenaline didn't screw up their physiology with a panic response. To ensure they could think clearly under pressure. He knew it wasn't paranoia driving his actions. It was training, logic, and instinct all working in tandem.

Whoever was in charge of this endeavor had zero scruples, and they weren't afraid to sacrifice innocent bystanders. Someone was prepared to go to great lengths to keep their dirty secrets.

What could be worth killing for? Not just a single impulsive act, but the planned destruction of hundreds of lives.

Land? Diamonds? Fortunes? Reputation?

It wasn't unknown for certain governments to shoot down airliners. It wasn't uncommon for civilians to be massacred. But those criminals rarely cared about what the FBI might conclude about their actions. Or The Hague.

Why was *he* suddenly important? Why now? Why had Bjorn been murdered? Because of the Dougie Cavanagh connection? What influence did a man who'd been dead for decades have on the FBI's current hunt for Darmawan Hurek?

The stakes were obviously high even if he didn't know exactly what those stakes were. One thing was for sure, this wasn't a game, and they needed to play their new roles to perfection.

"I hate to break this to you." He cleared his throat. "But we're going to have to share a bed or at least pretend to."

"Only one bed?" She laughed and he stared at her in surprise.

"Sorry." Her fingers tightened around his as her foot slipped. "It's a romance novel trope."

"A *what*?"

She laughed again, and it looked like she was blushing but hard to say with only the lanterns to light the driveway. "I guess I shouldn't be finding anything amusing about this situation, but I've always dealt with bad times using humor. Maybe it's a British trait."

"Hey, Americans have a sense of humor."

"I know"—she gripped his hand tighter—"like your political system."

"Ouch." He laughed and placed his other fist on his heart. "The patriot in me objects while the pragmatist acknowledges you might have a point. However, at least we don't have a monarchy."

"Ouch, back. Although judging from the number of yanks in London, Americans love the British monarchy—which is irony at its greatest." She grinned and he couldn't help smiling back at her. She leaned closer and lowered her voice. "And don't worry about the bed situation. It's just a place to sleep. I promise you're safe with me."

"Safe from you?"

"From my seductive wiles." Her tone was full of self-mockery.

Maybe she *was* some sort of trained operative, luring him in with her sunny personality and impossibly pretty smile. He'd always been more of a grouch—life was easier that way—but he couldn't deny her appeal.

"I did a little acting at uni. I was terrible, of course, but I think I can handle pretending to be your lover."

Her words struck him like a bolt of lightning out of the sky. She made him feel things he'd never felt before. Want things he wasn't allowed to want.

They reached the front entrance of the hotel and wiped their feet on the enormous welcome mat that stated they'd reached the Salmon Arms Resort. A brass sign above the door said, "Management reserves the right of admission" and below that, "Dress : Smart Casual after 6:30 P.M."

"Uh oh." Rowena glanced up, then down at her muddy jeans. "They might not let us in."

"We'll plead circumstances."

He let go of her hand as they walked up to the counter, and he leaned on the marble reception desk. Thankfully, the TV screen behind the staff was blank. Subdued emergency lighting lit the area enough to see by. Tealights in glass jars had been set up in various locations around the lobby and bar area, but were too weak to penetrate deep pockets of shadow.

"Hoping you have a room for us tonight. We hit some unexpected car trouble."

"Of course, sir. We do have an issue with a lack of electricity right now, but I'm sure it will come back on soon."

Kurt hoped it didn't.

"We still have food available. The heating is gas, and the rooms have emergency lighting in the main room and bathroom. For now, at least."

"Can we get room service?"

"Of course."

The man behind the desk had a smooth round face and a dazzling white smile. He began processing the booking as Kurt pulled out his Joe Hanssen credit card and passport out of the side pocket of his personal bag.

"Why don't you go check out the shop, babe. My treat."

"Okay. Who can resist a chance to souvenir shop?" Rowena pulled a surprised face and then headed over to the candle-lit store.

"It's been a long day," Kurt murmured to the receptionist. "We left most of our gear in the car."

"I'll have someone fetch your belongings—"

Kurt waved the offer away. "Forget it. It's mainly food and clothes. We have what we need for tonight, and the outside temperature is good for our supplies. Can I get a bottle of champagne for the room and whatever nibbles you recommend? We'll order dinner in about thirty if that works with the kitchen?"

"Yes, sir. I'll see to it immediately."

The desk clerk handed him the room key and gave him directions. Kurt headed over to find Rowena ignoring all the beautiful batik paintings and trying on a black ball cap.

"Suits you."

She smiled. "I don't need another hat." She put it back. Her eyes lit up as she picked up a travel cribbage board and playing cards. "But this could be a good way to spend the evening."

Kurt dropped his hands on her shoulders and lowered his voice because the woman behind the desk was listening intently. "I can think of better ways."

Her mouth dropped open, and her eyes flashed to his. Then she must have realized they had an audience because she smiled, went up on tiptoes, and kissed him on the mouth, nearly stopping his heart.

"Perhaps." She grinned as she pulled back. "*If* you beat me at cribbage."

He forced himself out of his state of shock and laughed. Took the board and deck of cards out of her hands. Picked up the ball cap. "I'm a pretty good card player."

"Counting on it." She placed her hand on his chest right over his heart. She lowered her voice to just above a whisper. "We could always play strip poker."

She laughed as she stepped away from him with a flirty grin. He wasn't sure he was going to be able to hold up his part of the playacting bargain without embarrassing himself if she kept this up. Not when he wanted to back her up to the nearest wall and sink deep inside her.

Dammit.

He needed to snap out of it and tease her the way she was teasing him. He knew how to flirt. He wasn't dead. Women came on to him not irregularly. They just generally weren't Rowena's age.

He needed to get over the dirty-old-man syndrome that was dogging him. This was make-believe. He was acting, and actors often dated people of a different generation. Hell, look at Al Pacino and Robert DeNiro.

He cleared his throat, took the items to the desk, and paid the smiling cashier with his alias's credit card. He turned to leave.

"Have a good night." The shopkeeper's tone was full of rich amusement.

He stopped dead for a second, cheeks heating, then drew in a deep breath and continued on. In the foyer, he handed Rowena the card game and hat. He placed his free hand on the small of her back and steered her in the direction of their room.

When they got there, he dumped their assorted collection of bags on the small table inside the door. It was a nice room with cream walls and heavy wooden furniture except for the bright blue easy chairs near the garden doors that opened onto a small patio and presumably the golf course beyond. The emergency lighting was dim, but the staff had placed about twenty candles in jars around the room. It gave the space a decidedly romantic glow.

"I'm going to freshen up." Rowena opened the bathroom door.

"Good idea."

The champagne was already sitting on the credenza in a silver ice bucket.

"I'm going to go order dinner from the bar. Any preference?"

"Anything as long as it's warm."

"Damn. I forgot something I need from the car. I'll be back in twenty minutes."

"I'll grab a quick shower. Open the fizz, please? I need a drink more than my next breath."

He smiled, went over and quickly twisted the cap off the bottle and eased the cork out with a subtle pop as she closed the bathroom door. He poured two glasses and took a long drink from his before stuffing an olive into his mouth.

He scrubbed his face to wake himself up and get his brain in gear. It had been a long day. Quashing his qualms about invading her privacy, he went into Rowena's purse and removed the letter supposedly written by Dougie Cavanagh to Rowena's mother, and the photograph of Cavanagh and Bjorn together. He stuffed Bjorn's cell into his back pocket, then placed both photos into the larger brown envelope and grabbed a pen from the desk. Put the envelope under his shirt.

He pulled on a fleece, picked up his flashlight, and took a

room key with him. He went to the barkeep and put in an order for a pasta dish and another for steak pie and fries. Next, he headed back to the giftshop. He'd noticed they sold postage stamps. "Do you have any jiffy envelopes yay size?" He sketched out the approximate size of the cell phone with his hands.

"Let me fetch one from the front desk."

"Thanks." Perhaps this was the stupidest idea in the history of stupid ideas. But when technology couldn't be trusted, old-school was probably the way to go. If they were caught with these photos in their possession, he suspected they'd be quickly confiscated and never seen again. God only knew what would happen to him and Rowena, but he didn't think it would be good.

He borrowed a piece of headed notepaper. He'd tell Daisy as soon as he got home, but just in case he was detained, he wrote, "Give this to Jordan Krychek immediately."

He hesitated over the address because he didn't want to embroil his daughter in potential danger, but he couldn't assume the post office machines couldn't read or identify FBI addresses or names. Sending anything to Camp Peary where Killion lived wasn't exactly subtle. He didn't have that many options for people who didn't work for one government agency or another. He went with "D. Montana-Sagar." Sagar was Daisy's mom's maiden name that Jennifer had made Daisy use for a couple of years at school, although it had never been legally changed, and Daisy had switched back when she'd gone to college, which had made him smugly happy. He drew a small flower beside the "D." Then he wrote Daisy's address on the envelope and sealed the photos and SIM card inside. When the woman came back with the jiffy envelope, he asked her to guess the postage for the letter. Instead, she looked it up online and sold him the correct postage. Then he asked her for ten times the amount figuring that would cover the stamps needed to send the cell phone, paid and left. He went over to one of the tables and affixed the stamps, then wrote his neighbor's name and address on the jiffy envelope, added c/o K Montana. The guy knew him well enough to hold on to it for him until he got back.

It was a risk to mail anything from this part of the world as post had a habit of disappearing. But he'd at least separated the SIM card. He didn't even know if the phone would hold any clues to the identity of Bjorn's killer or Hurek's whereabouts or Gilder's or Spartan's involvement. He did know he couldn't afford to assume it didn't, and being caught with it would likely embroil him in a criminal case as a suspect for murder that would cause international uproar and steal years of his freedom.

He sealed the phone inside. The battery was already removed. Rowena had seen to that. The lobby was quiet. Muted voices coming from the dining room and the bar. The reception desk was unmanned so he headed back outside into the dark night. He jogged up the road in the direction the mechanic had pointed, using the flashlight to check the uneven surface of the tarmac. A few hundred yards up the road, he spotted a turn off to the right and then a small group of buildings beyond. He ran across the road and found the mailbox.

He stared hard at the two envelopes in his hand. He was leaving it up to fate, but it might be the safest course of action. They had a copy of the photos on their cells. He'd print a copy for Rowena or arrange for the return of the original after examination should it reach its destination. This way, if the two of them were stopped they wouldn't have the originals on them. And, although they had a very good chance of making it out of the country without being detected, he was sure whatever the bad guys were trying to hide was big. Really big. Worth bringing down an aircraft full of people big.

And he needed to do everything he could to ensure this evidence got to the FBI.

The guilt that all those people had died because he was supposed to be on that flight threatened to break through the shield he'd erected against it. Objectively, he knew it wasn't his fault and yet...it devastated.

What secret could possibly be worth that monstrous act?

Perhaps the information somehow implicated Gilder and Spartan in something far more sinister than being acquainted with a guy nearly thirty years ago who'd gone on to become an international terrorist.

Not telling Rowena about his plans for this evidence was a risk. It could shake her trust in him, and he'd need that to get them both safely out of the country. If she didn't know anything, she couldn't tell anyone where these items were, and therefore the bad guys wouldn't think to stop the mail and search for the letters until it was hopefully too late.

It wasn't that he thought Rowena was dirty. Not now. Not at all. But, if they were captured and tortured... He'd gone through SERE training back in the day and a similar program with HRT.

He wasn't dumb enough to think he wouldn't break under extreme duress, but he also knew that if the only thing someone wanted from him was the location of those photographs, then keeping their location a secret was probably the only thing keeping him alive.

The idea of whoever had murdered Bjorn getting hold of Rowena...

Not gonna happen.

The Hostage Rescue Team motto was *Servare Vitas*. To save lives.

That was his priority.

Not Hurek, not the evidence. Rowena's life. And the life of anyone else who might be in danger because of what he'd uncovered.

He opened the slot and slipped the letters inside. Listened to them drop with a hollow feeling in his heart.

Despite not being a particularly religious man, he said a little prayer that he was making the right choice. Then he turned around and jogged back to the hotel.

10

R owena got out of the shower and quickly dried off, feeling a million times better now that she was clean and warm. She figured they should probably dump all her dirty clothes, so she gathered them inside out into a tight ball and put them in the sink. Then she slipped into the thick robe that hung on the back of the door. She patted her hair dry with the towel and untangled it with her fingers.

The lack of a brush would be a problem, but maybe Montana would have a comb in his bag.

She needed her new clothes. Hopefully, he'd remembered something to sleep in, although she could always use a T-shirt.

She peeked through the bathroom door and saw the room was empty. Two glasses of champagne sat on the sideboard. She picked up the full one and took a big swallow, enjoying the bubbles on her tongue and the illusion of normality.

Flashes of Bjorn Anders' dead body formed inside her mind, and she forced them away. Blew out a long, slow breath to try to calm her heartbeat. It was easier not to think about what had happened that morning. Thinking about it brought back all her fears and made acid churn in her stomach along with the champagne.

She lifted the phone handset and put it to her ear to check if it was working, but there was only silence. Perhaps it was a good thing to be cut off. Lack of power must make it harder for the police to track them, assuming they *were* being followed.

Maybe Montana was being paranoid, but after what she'd seen in Bjorn's office, she'd rather be paranoid than blasé and end up like the other man. And though she understood she'd broken the law and should have reported what she'd found, knowing what they now suspected about the plane crash, she didn't regret her decision to run, nor her decision to trust Kurt Montana.

She picked up the bags to see what supplies he'd bought and discovered a plethora of items inside. She pulled out a red silky negligee, and her eyes bugged.

Whoa.

Not what she'd expected.

It was transparent in so many places it was barely worth bothering with.

She realized there were matching knickers and a frilly, half-cup underwire bra for the set.

Who wore a bra to bed? Not someone interested in sleeping—that was for sure.

Was he expecting her to wear that tonight…?

For appearance's sake?

She swallowed hard. She wasn't sure she could do it. She wasn't sure why he'd want her to after all his talk of being old enough to be her father. She definitely found him attractive, but he treated her like she was strictly off limits. Then he bought her underwear designed to set the bed on fire…

It didn't make sense.

She dug deeper, relieved to find there were other things inside the bag, including flannel pajamas and a sports bra and knickers that covered more than her crotch.

It might be awesome to be the sort of woman who was confident enough to strut around in sexy lingerie without a second thought. To have the confidence to seduce a man?

She paused.

What must that feel like?

Did she *want* to seduce a man?

Maybe.

She wasn't sure.

Did the man want to be seduced?

She side-eyed the negligee. Before seeing that, she'd have said definitely no, but no one bought something like that for a cozy night in front of the fire—unless it involved a bearskin rug and some open flames.

She fanned her cheeks.

It was a stupid time to be thinking about that kind of thing under the circumstances, but she was curious to see what all the fuss was about. Before it was too late…

Her mother had died at twenty-two, her aunt and uncle in their early fifties, so maybe she shouldn't dawdle too long. Looking back, she should have just shagged someone in college and gotten it over with.

What exactly was she waiting for? It wasn't a ring or roses. She didn't care about jewelry and had a whole garden of flowers. It was the spark. The connection. The burn of attraction. The zing.

Most of all it was the trust involved. The absolute, unquestionable trust of allowing another person that close—physically and mentally.

Except for watching certain scenes in *Outlander* more than a hundred times, and reading ten thousand romance novels, she was horribly inexperienced. Not because of so-called "morals" or the concept of "saving herself." It was simply not having met the right guy yet.

Was Kurt Montana the right guy?

She'd certainly felt a spark when he'd aided her with her tire last night. She'd felt it again today when he'd helped her get out of Harare. But he didn't seem to feel the same way at all, and as they were on the run from unknown danger, she wasn't ready to expose herself to ridicule by donning the silky nightclothes without at least a little more evidence the guy might be even vaguely interested.

She took another gulp of champagne. Then paced. They had more important things to worry about. It felt surreal, this cloak and dagger stuff. Perhaps they were both being a little crazy, but Kurt Montana had been exceptionally lucky to miss that flight today.

Assuming he was telling the truth about the air crash... But what possible reason would he have to lie?

If he was after what she knew, then she'd already told him everything back at Halfway House when she showed him the photographs. He could have dumped her there or driven her back to Harare and given her over to the local police.

She yawned widely. It was early, but it had been a hell of a day. She suspected they'd eat and then get an early night so they could be ready to go first thing tomorrow morning.

The chances of Kurt Montana doing a one-eighty and suddenly deciding he wanted to give the mattress a workout with her was slim to none, and she was surprised how disappointed that made her feel.

Ignoring the sexual awareness that had suddenly sprouted out of nowhere and made her skin tingle in all sorts of places, she went into the bathroom and donned the red flannel PJs. They fit perfectly and covered everything like she was a Victorian dowager. Disgruntled, she frowned at herself in the mirror and wondered what other people saw. What Kurt Montana saw.

An attractive enough female with unusual green eyes and all her own teeth.

She huffed out a laugh. She sounded like her old pony.

As her hair tended to frizz, she braided it and tied the end and tried not to shiver as the damp rope swung down her back.

She didn't have a toothbrush, but there were some mini mouthwash bottles in the bathroom, so she took a slug and swished it around her mouth before spitting it out.

If she could just determine who her father was, if she had

family, perhaps then she could figure out what she wanted out of life. Be it sexy undies and the courage to offer herself to a handsome American hunk, or the safe solitary fantasies where maybe no one ever got too close and it didn't hurt too badly when people left.

Because people always left.

Impatient with herself, she took her dirty clothes out of the sink and folded them neatly and slid them into a spare plastic bag to dispose of in the morning.

She needed to take it one day at a time. To get home and figure out what on earth had happened. And if she had sex with the handsome American hunk along the way? Excellent.

It really wasn't a big deal.

The door opened abruptly, and she whipped around. She heaved out a sigh when she saw Montana pushing a room service cart inside.

He sent her a warning look even as his eyes swept her body. "Sorry, babe. It took longer than I expected."

Presumably the person who'd delivered the cart was in the hall. Did he need a tip? She didn't have any cash left.

"I missed you." She fluttered her eyelashes at him. "*Babe.*"

He gave her the side-eye as he pushed the cart all the way inside and took a ten dollar bill out of his wallet then went back into the hallway. "Thank you, sir. We'll put the cart out here when we're done."

He closed and locked the door and turned back to face her. His dark eyes swept from her bare feet up to her damp hair. Heat rose in her cheeks at his perusal.

Was he disappointed she'd chosen these pajamas and not the negligee?

Then his expression blanked, and he moved past her to the curtains and pulled them closed against prying eyes.

She should have thought of that.

She sat on the bed, but he didn't look at her.

He went to his rucksack and pulled out a couple of items and a wash bag. "Dig into the food before it gets cold. I'm happy with either dish, but I want to clean up first. Don't answer the door."

With that he headed into the bathroom, and she sat there feeling like a bit of a fool. He didn't care what she wore, for God's sake. This wasn't time or place to try to deal with feelings of attraction, or even with her own issues about still being a virgin. All that mattered was getting out of the country and not ending up the same way as Bjorn Anders.

Then—if she could find someone even half as handsome and gruffly charming as Kurt Montana back in Shropshire—she'd go on a shagging spree.

Her stomach growled.

Annoyed with herself, she topped off champagne for them both and pulled the silver dome cover off one plate. Linguini. The other, a meat pie with a golden crust and a mountain of chips. She stole a chip and then went for the linguini. She sat cross-legged on one of the armchairs and began to eat. The shower turned on, and she twirled her fork in the creamy pasta sauce and popped it into her mouth while she tried not to imagine the pair of them having steamy shower sex.

She took a large gulp of champagne, but it went down the wrong way. She began to choke and cough. Over and over. But whatever was lodged in her throat didn't move. She couldn't breathe.

Panicked, she stood, and carefully, telling herself not to freak out, put her plate back on the tray and tried to draw in oxygen.

Failed.

Crap.

She thumped herself in the sternum and achieved nothing.

She staggered to the bathroom and rammed the base of her fist against the door in a quick tattoo. She desperately tried to inhale but something was blocking her trachea, making her aspirate. Her pulse pounded. She'd never felt more scared in her life. Not even this morning when she'd found Bjorn dead and feared she'd been in the same building as a vicious killer.

"I'll be right out."

Panic gripped tight, and her lungs constricted. *No air. No air.*

She banged again, harder, chest bellowing uselessly as she leaned against the door. She was going to die unless she could get oxygen. Three minutes was all it would take for everything they'd done today not to matter. For her life to cease. For her existence to end.

She did not want to die.

Her vision started to blur.

She shook the doorknob. Discovered it wasn't locked. She stumbled inside and saw Kurt's shocked expression as he stood there naked in the shower.

She grabbed her throat, wheezing, eyes running with tears.

"Oh, shit."

He thankfully seemed to understand what was wrong and stepped out of the shower and spun her around so she faced the sink.

He put one arm across her chest and then started striking her back to try to dislodge the obstruction. He hit her five times with the flat of his hand, but she still couldn't breathe. Oh God. She didn't want to die. Not now. Not yet. She had so many things she still wanted to do. See the pyramids. See polar bears in the wild. Make mad passionate love. Finish that Romantasy trilogy she adored.

He grabbed her from behind, his wet body soaking her pajamas. She felt her blood slowing, energy waning, pulse thumping more slowly in her ears. Her desperate gaze met his in the mirror.

"You're not going to die today, Row." He braced his gripped fists against her diaphragm and jerked her body violently toward him. "I. Won't. Let. You."

It took four thrusts before whatever it was dislodged, and she was finally able to release the pressure in her lungs and suck in life-giving oxygen.

She braced herself on the vanity, coughing violently. Her eyes streamed. Her body felt like every muscle had been beaten. Her chest hurt. Her back hurt. Her throat burned.

But she was alive.

She didn't think she'd ever take it for granted again.

She started to tremble. Caught his concerned gaze again in the steamed-up mirror.

She'd have been gone if he hadn't been there. If he hadn't known what to do.

Just like her mother. Just like her aunt and uncle. Just like Bjorn bloody Anders.

They were even now.

He didn't owe her a damned thing.

If anything, she owed him.

She spun around and threw herself against his chest.

11

Kurt stood naked with his heart pounding as Rowena flung her arms around his neck and started sobbing.

Holy shit.

What the fuck had just happened?

He wrapped his arms around her and held on tight, rocking her gently. Christ. He couldn't decide if this was the worst day of their lives or the luckiest.

He didn't think he'd ever been more frightened no matter what danger he'd faced in the past or how much training he'd done.

She'd scared the shit out of him when she'd burst inside the bathroom, and, sure, for a fraction of a second his dick had entertained the happy delusion she might want to join him in the shower even as his brain had worried the bad guys had found them. Then he'd gotten a look at her distraught features and had known she was in serious trouble.

"I've got you." He rubbed her back, which was now damp from his wet body. He tried to pull away, but she held him tighter, her grip like a boa constrictor.

Resigned to the torture of holding her close and pretending he was unaffected, he reached around behind him and shut off the water. Slid one arm under her knees and lifted her, then carried her into the bedroom.

He glanced around and headed to the armchair because it seemed safer than the bed. Or more proper or some such bullshit.

Jeez.

Since when did he care about *proper*?

What was *proper* about holding a woman connected to his case —who had been through not one, but two, harrowing experiences that day—with him as naked as a jaybird?

On the way to the chair, he put the silver dome cover over her pasta dish to keep it warm. She'd be hungry when this crying jag ended.

She'd had a hell of a day. He sat down and drew her firmly against his chest. Her damp hair tickled his nose, and her tears added to the wetness of his skin.

He resigned himself to being uncomfortable until this was over.

Really uncomfortable.

He could feel the shape of her through those red pajamas, the long lines of her legs, the muscles of her quadriceps, the softness of her ass and breasts pressed against his chest and thighs.

He rocked her gently. Despite the circumstances he enjoyed having her in his arms—like some secret indulgence he would never admit to.

When was the last time he'd held a woman?

Not even during sex for as long as he could remember. Not like this, not like...like they were close. Really close. Holding Rowena like this was more intimate than any sex he'd had in years.

The only people he'd ever held like this were his ex-wife and Daisy when she was a child. He'd missed it, he realized.

Really missed it.

He didn't know where these thoughts were coming from. They were soft thoughts. Tender thoughts. And, emotionally, he was an armored fucking vehicle. They revealed a loneliness inside him he hadn't acknowledged before. An isolation. An *ache…*

Maybe losing his family all those years ago had affected him more than he'd realized. Severed something inside him but at the same time cauterized the wound. Cut him off. Toughened him up. Allowed him to concentrate on being the consummate warrior.

This woman, this situation, was making him confront himself in a way he never had before and didn't want to now.

He should move away. Put some fucking clothes on. But modesty had never been one of his strong suits, and she'd already seen everything there was to see. If she didn't like it, she was welcome to get up and move any time.

But he was hardly pushing her away.

His mother hadn't raised a damned fool.

He smiled reluctantly. Rested his chin on the top of her head. Rowena shivered, and her teeth chattered as if she were freezing. He hugged her tighter, hopefully giving her some of his body heat and the reassurance she needed that she was okay now.

Christ.

What choice did he have?

Pretend like he didn't give a shit?

He gave a shit which probably proved he was an idiot, but no one was debating his intelligence right now. Just his capacity for self-flagellation.

Boo fucking hoo.

This woman had almost choked to death, which was bad enough. On top of that, she'd found a dead man this morning, and if her story was to be believed—and God help him he believed every word—she'd lost every one of her close relatives in a series of freak accidents.

He frowned as he thought about that. Were they all accidents? Could they be connected to his investigation? The FBI had flushed Hurek out of his island stronghold last August, around the same time her aunt and uncle had died in a fire. Coincidence?

Probably. But what if…

Whatever the bad guys were worried about had been bad enough for them to bring down a plane—and fine, he had no proof, but he wasn't in the FBI only because of his tactical skills.

He'd been a damned effective case agent.

From what Rowena had said, Bjorn's murder might be connected to that photograph, likely taken before she'd been born and similar to the one she'd found in her grandmother's attic. Could her uncle's and aunt's deaths be connected to whatever these fuckers were up to? What about Rowena's mother? Could her death be related to what they were trying to bury? Had Rowena's mother been involved in some kind of criminal enterprise?

The length of time since Rowena's mom's death made solving any crime difficult, assuming it was murder—depending on what the statute of limitations was in England.

Certainly, he was way out of his jurisdiction. But if the FBI could help figure it out, he'd make sure they at least tried.

Rowena shifted slightly and snuggled soft and warm against him. Her breathing eased and the sobs quieted.

The room was a little on the chilly side, but he for one wasn't feeling the cold. He could see the two of them reflected in the mirror on the wall opposite. Her in those red flannel PJs. Him buck naked.

His mouth went dry.

He wished his imagination would quit because he could easily see them sitting like this under different circumstances, circumstances that had nothing to do with him comforting her after a near-death experience. In that scenario, he wasn't the only one naked.

His skin heated and he was going to need another shower just as soon as she released him. A cold one.

He soothed her with gentle strokes, ignoring the fact he was growing hard, and hoping she did too. It was autonomic and beyond his control. And maybe that was bullshit. One thing Kurt Montana had never been was a liar.

It was a reaction to *her*.

To this beautiful young woman who pressed every one of his buttons. It was basic biological attraction to the fact she was sitting in his lap and touching him, however innocently.

Maybe she'd fall asleep, and he could pick her up and put her on the bed. And he wouldn't embarrass himself by saying something stupid. Or doing something colossally reckless.

She'd stopped crying now, and her fingers began to tap then trail distractedly over the hair on his chest. She probably didn't realize that her touch was making him hard as stone. Or maybe she did, because all of a sudden, she shifted against him, pressing more firmly against his raging erection and making sweat pop on his forehead.

Her hand stroked up his neck and cupped his jaw. Then she rose up, and he watched her, mesmerized by those mossy green eyes, and by the arousal and desire he saw there.

His gaze dropped to her mouth as she shifted closer, the softness of her lips like petals against his as she kissed him.

Kissed him.

She acted as if she wanted him.

Like she truly wanted him. Despite the fact he was a freaking dinosaur.

She kissed him—driving him in-fucking-sane with want as he sat frozen as day-old roadkill, half afraid he was dreaming.

Hell of a dream.

She dipped her tongue along the seam of his mouth, and he knew it wasn't a dream. Rowena was real, and in his arms, and kissing him like she meant it. As much as he knew he should resist her, he couldn't.

He cupped the back of her head with one hand and dove deep, tasting that sweet mouth and exploring those pretty red lips. Tangled with her tongue, tentatively at first but then boldly. She mimicked his movements, taking it deeper.

She held on to him as if scared he might pull away from her. As if afraid he might come to his senses, which was laughable.

"Touch me," she murmured as she stole his breath. "Touch me like you want me."

Want her? How could she doubt it?

That was all the permission he needed.

He found her breast and cupped the fullness of it as he found the peak of her nipple and teased it through the material of her PJs.

She gasped, and he used that to take the kiss deeper still.

So much for buying her practical nightclothes. He couldn't be more turned on if she were decked out head to toe in fuck-me red lace.

He slid his hands under her top and skimmed over her silky-smooth skin, cupping the breasts that he wanted to see, still holding onto a shred of control. If she were naked, he'd have none. He knew he shouldn't be doing any of this, but fuck if he could help himself.

She sucked in a breath as he pressed her nipple hard enough to make her back arch like a cat. She shifted, and he lifted her so she could straddle him. She swept her hand over the muscles of his shoulders, his chest, his stomach. And then lower until she found his aching cock. She wrapped her fingers around him and moved her hand up and over and back down.

He leaned his head against the back of the chair as he thought his head might explode. As long as it was only his head...

She followed his mouth, never breaking the kiss. Never breaking the connection, her hands on him, driving him crazy. She pulled away long enough to drag the pajama top over her head and toss it onto the bed, and he was toast.

He caught his breath at the sight of her pert breasts, dusky pink nipples, and pretty collarbones. The sweet curve of her stomach and hips made him want to taste her belly button and much, much more. She leaned forward to kiss his neck and run her lips over his rough jaw up to his ear. Pressed her hot core against his desperate cock.

She moved over him, pliant and sinuous. Greedy and definitely willing.

He wanted to be inside her. He wanted inside her more than he needed his next breath.

The fact it was wrong didn't matter. The fact it went against everything he'd ever believed was irrelevant. He wanted her anyway.

Was it because they'd both come so close to death today? That would be a lame excuse because he'd wanted her from the moment he'd first seen her last night. He'd just been too worried about what other people might think to even contemplate the idea.

Ironic because most of the time he couldn't give a flying fuck what people thought of him, but getting older seemed to have made him more rather than less susceptible to being judged. He might not be in his twenties anymore, but what he lacked in youth he more than made up for in stamina and experience.

He lifted her up in his arms and took three steps to the bed, falling onto the soft covers—as close to Heaven as he'd ever experienced. He cradled her head and kissed her long and hard and felt her legs wrap around his hips, drawing his erection against her core.

The only reason he wasn't inside her right now was because of her fucking pajama bottoms. He should have gone with a T-shirt, or nothing at all. Forgotten to buy her clothes of any kind because he'd rather have her naked.

He moved against her gently, angling himself over her clit as he explored that sweet mouth, time and again. Driving her up and up. Relishing the bite of her nails in his skin, digging into his back as her legs twined with his.

Her gasps told him she was close, but rather than let her go over that edge he scooted down the bed to her breasts, sliding his hands under her rib cage and raising her up to his mouth to feast. He sucked her nipple between his lips, scraping his teeth and unshaven jaw gently over the tip until she moaned with want. He drew back and admired the aroused raspberry tip. Then he did the same to the other one, wetting it with his mouth and then blowing over the sensitive skin. Rowena closed her eyes and gripped the pillows.

"I can't take any more."

He glanced up. Hesitated.

Did she mean stop?

He should be stopping, he realized. He shouldn't be touching her at all. He braced his elbows to move away.

She wrapped her thighs tight around his hips and grabbed his short hair firmly, met his gaze with fever-bright eyes. "Please don't stop." She bit her bottom lip which was still glossy from his kisses. "Please."

How could he resist?

"Yes, ma'am."

She melted against the pillows and laughed. "I love it when you call me that. It makes me hot."

Hell. "Yes, *ma'am*." He drew it out and sat back. He put his hand on the waistband of those hated pajama bottoms that he wanted to burn. He drew them slowly over curved hips to reveal pale legs and a neat triangle of dark hair between creamy thighs. She raised both legs in front of him, and he tugged the pants over her ankles and tossed them aside.

And then she was naked before him.

God, she was perfect.

She took his hand and tried to draw him back down to her.

"What's the hurry? I'm admiring the view."

She blushed prettily, then traced a finger over his nipple and tweaked it the way he'd done to her. It didn't have the same effect but seemed to entertain her.

"Where was I?" He cocked his head and slid down her body and kissed a trail down her stomach, pausing to explore her navel, which made her giggle.

"You're ticklish?"

"Very." She narrowed her gaze. "If you exploit that fact, you will be sorry."

He grinned. "Will I? Funny, I don't feel very sorry right now."

Even though he should. Instead, he moved farther south and opened her thighs wide and sank his tongue inside her.

She cried out and grabbed the headboard. "Oh!"

He couldn't agree more. He could feast on her for days and still be starved. He licked and explored this unknown territory like he was memorizing a direct-action plan for an immediate assault.

He held her still when she tried to move her hips. Speared her clit with his tongue until her thighs began to quiver and shake. He slipped a finger into her slick hot core and found the spot that made her cry out with pleasure as her whole body shook from hitting her climax. He'd never seen anything more beautiful.

When she came down from the high, she opened her eyes and ran her fingers through his hair. "I want you inside me."

He crawled up the bed over her, his penis nudging her hot, wet opening. A cold wash of reality penetrated his simple brain. "I don't have a condom."

Usually, he'd carry them for survival reasons, but they were in his other bag this time. The one back in the States.

She held his gaze. "I'm on birth control pills. For my periods but it works just as effectively as actual birth control."

The idea of being inside her was so tempting, clouding good judgment and common sense.

"I don't have any STDs, but I guess you'd only have my word for that." She bit her lip and frowned as if about to say more.

He rested his forehead against hers. "I had a physical three months ago. Bloodwork was normal, and I haven't been with anyone since. But you only have my word for that too."

Holding his gaze, she raised her knees and tilted her pelvis so he was almost there. "I trust you."

He wanted her so desperately he thought his jaw might break from clenching it so tight.

She widened her legs further, and he shuddered with desire.

"I want to feel you inside me." Her words were a whisper. Her green gaze captivating. "I *need* to feel you inside me."

It was every guy's dream to have unprotected sex with a beautiful, willing woman. And if one of his men came to him having gotten a girl pregnant or caught the clap because they'd decided a condom didn't really matter, he'd smack them around until their ears rang. And, dammit, she must have fed him some hallucinogenic drug because he believed every word she said—or maybe he was simply willing to pay the price of being wrong. Any price.

"Please."

He ignored every bit of common sense he'd ever possessed and sank slowly inside this woman, and the sensation was worth every possible worst-case scenario as her tight flesh slowly allowed him entry.

He worked his way inside her, taking his time because the look in her eyes was a little uncertain despite her confident words.

Finally, he was all the way home, her inner muscles squeezing his throbbing cock, and it felt so good he couldn't breathe.

"Is that okay?"

She swallowed. "Not okay. Incredible. Amazing." Her back bowed up off the bed as she stretched against him.

He huffed a laugh. It did feel incredible and amazing. It had been a long time since sex had been this good. Like they were genuinely in tune and connected as opposed to going through the motions simply to get off.

And maybe he was drunk or something because this was just sex, and he'd be a fool to think it was more.

He started to move. Keeping the pace slow until her breathing relaxed and she started touching him again. Scraping her fingernails over his pecs and up to rub the pad of her finger across his bottom lip. They were both putting a lot of trust in one another, her especially. Perhaps that was why it felt different, almost sacred. Or maybe because he was a lucky sonofabitch to be touching Rowena this way and smart enough to know it.

He kissed her again, and she kissed him back. He drove into her a little bit harder, making sure she was okay with what he was doing. She started moving against him, matching his rhythm, matching his force, driving him out of his mind with lust at the fact she wanted this as much as he did.

He pulled her knee up and ground against her, going deeper on each thrust. If there were a way to get closer, he would have.

"Oh, oh. Oh." She cried out, and he wasn't ready for it to end yet. Not yet. But as she rippled around him and squeezed his cock, he was helpless not to follow her over that blinding edge where pleasure burst through him in a wave of pure oblivion.

He lay there breathing into the pillow, scared to open his eyes and see regret on her features.

"You're so pretty." Her words brushed over him like a feather over a raw nerve. Her hand slid over his back to the same effect.

"Is there a mirror on the ceiling?" His voice was gruff.

She laughed. "Has a woman never told you you're insanely attractive?"

He opened his eyes, shot a look up to the ceiling to make sure. "I keep hearing words coming out of your mouth, but they don't make any sense. Are you talking to yourself? Maybe you've lost your mind after all that incredible sex."

"Oh, thanks a lot. Now you're calling me crazy."

Apparently, there was no fool like an old fool. "I'm not calling you crazy, but it would certainly explain a lot."

"I'm not crazy." She pushed at his shoulders even as her eyes sparkled with amusement. "But it was incredible. Thank you."

He touched her face, shocked that not only had she let him make love to her but was now thanking him for the privilege. Maybe it was a British thing, but it seemed wrong.

"No. Thank *you*."

She opened her mouth to say something else, probably to argue from the glint in her eye, but he pressed a finger to her lips. "Let's agree it was phenomenal and exactly what we both needed after a day from hell. Now, you need to eat."

12

Row was hungry—for more sex.

Her heart was still pounding as if she'd been running, and she felt deliciously used and sated, and yet she didn't want it to end. She hadn't expected it to be quite so...volcanic.

So *that* was what all the fuss was about. It was nice to figure it out, to finally be a member of the other club.

She went to shake her head in answer to his question about food when her stomach gurgled like a cement mixer. Kurt reared back with a grin.

"Okay, time to eat. Make sure you chew this time."

"Funny. Ha, ha."

She sat up in bed, leaned on her knees. "I've never choked before. I was so scared. I honestly thought I was going to die. Thank goodness you knew what to do." She admired him as he stood in front of her, "stark bollock naked" as her Uncle Peter would have said. The muscles of Kurt's body were thick and well-defined and made her mouth water.

"Glad I was here to help. It's not a lot of fun—choking. Closest I've come is being waterboarded in the Army."

"Wait. *What?*"

He leaned forward with a grin and tapped her lower jaw shut.

"Believe it or not, we did it on purpose to one another. A lesson in why torture doesn't work."

Was he serious?

"And it fucking sucked."

Oddly, she wouldn't have needed proof to know torture didn't work. She was a wuss. First hint of pain, and she'd tell anyone everything they wanted to know, whether it was true or not, with bells on.

"I've done a lot of combat medic and first-aid training over the years, but that's the first time I ever helped a civilian that way."

Helped? She'd be dead if he hadn't known what to do.

"Saved," she corrected.

He looked uncomfortable with the comment.

"It was your fault anyway."

"How was it my fault?" He cocked a brow as he took his glass of champagne and downed a large swallow.

"I choked after imagining the two of us having shower sex."

He spluttered and coughed, and she froze for a moment, but he held up his hand. "I'm okay. A little surprised, but okay."

His cheeks had gone deep red.

She grinned, grabbed her pajama bottoms and noticed the look he sent them. Disgruntled.

Excellent. She could work with disgruntled. She snatched up her top and headed into the bathroom to clean up.

When she came out, he'd pulled on some trousers, but at least he wasn't wearing a shirt because she liked looking at him.

She picked up her fizz and took a small tentative sip. Then she took her plate off the trolley and sat in the chair opposite him. The food was a little cool but not cold, and she was suddenly ravenous. She was careful to take small bites because she had no desire to repeat her earlier experience even if it had led to something good.

Losing her virginity felt like shedding a heavy weight. She should have probably told him it was her first time, but she'd worried he'd have stopped on a technicality.

The only thing that mattered was they were both consenting adults. And her first time had been magnificent.

She caught him looking at her, but he immediately looked away. "What?"

He shook his head. Then he grinned as he took another bite of pie. A dimple appeared to the right of his mouth, and she wanted to explore it with her tongue. She curled her toes and took another careful mouthful. Chewing and swallowing like a little old lady.

"This was not how I was expecting my day to go," he admitted.

She nodded in acknowledgment. "Same. I thought I'd be heading to South Africa to go shopping with my cousins." She pressed her lips together. "They're going to be worried."

Kurt sobered. "Yeah."

He was obviously thinking about all the people who mattered to him believing he'd died on that plane today.

"Maybe we could risk giving your daughter a call on the burner?" she suggested.

He shook his head. "From what I overheard in the lobby, the cell towers aren't working. Plus, we've been lucky so far. I don't want to blow it." He paused. Sipped more champagne. "The power cut worked in our favor but also theirs." He looked up and those inky eyes met hers. "We haven't been able to call out. I haven't been able to contact my office."

She frowned. "You don't think the power cut is deliberate, do you?"

He shrugged. "My paranoia is busy growing conspiracy theories."

He finished off his pie and most of the chips. She ate about half of the linguini but then felt full. He gathered the dishes and the empty bottle and ice bucket. Put it all on the trolley. He pulled on a T-shirt and fleece before pushing the cart out the door.

He came back inside. "I'm going to take a quick look around before turning in for the night. Make sure there's no sign of trouble. If I see anything, I'll tap on the French doors." He beat out a pattern on the sideboard. "Hear anything else, you run in the opposite direction as fast as possible. And if anyone knocks on the door—"

"Don't answer it. Leave through the French door?"

He grinned. "You're a quick learner."

She smiled. "You have no idea."

He laughed because he didn't know what she was thinking about as he headed out.

She blew out most of the candles and turned off the dim overhead light. Then she headed to the bathroom but paused near the shopping bags.

What if...

She pulled at the corner of the crimson negligee until it came out of the bag and dangled it from her fingertips. She stared at it contemplatively. Kurt seemed content for them to be done and to sleep, which would probably be the most sensible plan.

She'd spent her entire life being sensible.

As soon as they crossed the border and got to an airport or whatever represented safety, they'd go their separate ways. As soon as anyone official joined their party, he'd go back to being a responsible FBI agent, and the lover would disappear. She understood. She really did. He had a reputation to uphold. What they'd done probably went against FBI rules given she was involved, after the fact, with Bjorn Anders' death. She dug deeper and found the bra and panties that matched and went to get changed. If she only got one night with this man, then she was going to make it count.

———

Row had dozed off by the time he came silently back into the room. She lifted her head and blinked.

"Sorry," he whispered. "Didn't mean to wake you."

He headed straight into the bathroom before she could reveal herself in this siren's garb, and she wondered if this was a terrible plan. Just because they'd had sex once didn't mean he'd want to do it again. Was it even possible this soon after? Perhaps that's what he was worried about in terms of being eighteen years older than she was.

Five minutes later, he walked back into the room, and she watched him head straight over to the remaining candles and blow them out, so that the room was pitch black.

So much for the sexy-if-seriously-itchy lingerie. If he couldn't see her then all her efforts would be wasted. Part of her wanted to sneak to the bathroom and change back into the other PJs. The other part was determined to carry this through.

What was the worst that could happen?

Rejection? Humiliation? Embarrassment?

All very possible outcomes and probably the one real advantage of living on different continents.

"Would you, er, mind leaving one light on?"

"Are you scared of the dark? Sorry, I should have asked."

"It's not that..." She smelled the Sulphur of a match being struck then saw him lighting one of the candles on the credenza.

He sat on the end of the bed and began taking his boots off. Then his socks and the fleece and T-shirt. Whoa. Those muscles made her mouth water.

"Kurt?"

"Yeah?"

She sat up and moved toward him. "The thing is...earlier, I was going through the things you bought."

She saw him freeze.

"I found these." She pressed herself against his back, felt his muscles become granite.

She watched his expression, dimly visible in a mirror behind the credenza. His face heavily shadowed as he closed his eyes almost with resignation.

He swallowed audibly. "The woman in the store kind of insisted I buy them. I didn't want to create a fuss by refusing. I didn't expect you to wear them. I wasn't expecting *anything* from you."

"Oh…" That made so much sense. "I thought… God, I'm so stupid."

His gaze found hers in the darkness of the mirror. "What did you think?"

She sucked in her lips and edged back a little, feeling foolish and uncertain. "I thought perhaps this was what you liked."

He gave a strangled groan and wrapped his hand around her wrist dragging her back against his body. He sounded almost in pain. "If you'd asked me an hour ago, I'd have told you lace wasn't my thing." He turned around, swapping his grip to his other hand so she couldn't escape. His gaze ran over the gauzy covering, the pushed-up boobs, and the excuse of panties that didn't even cover her crotch due to a whole void of missing material. "I've since reconsidered and realize you in pretty much anything is absolutely my thing."

She gave him an exaggerated frown. "You don't sound happy about the discovery."

"I'm not."

"Why not?" She tried to pull away, but he didn't let go.

"I still think you're way too young for me, and the fact you've gone through several traumatic events today makes me feel as if I've taken advantage of you."

His expression turned pissed.

She stared down at her lace-clad body. "Does this look like I'm feeling taken advantage of?"

"Maybe?" He shook his head. "I don't know. But I don't want sex to be some sort of payment for keeping you safe."

"Payment? What the hell?" She tried to pull away, but he grabbed her other wrist and didn't let go.

He dragged her to him and banded his arms around her, capturing her, so even though she tried, she couldn't move. He stared down at her, expression fierce but strangely tender. "I don't expect payment in any form because you're grateful for my help today. I will help you without any strings attached. I will do everything I can to get you to safety and nothing is required besides honesty and enough determination to get us there."

Understanding rushed through her as she wriggled to get free. "How many times do I need to say it. I don't want to have sex with you out of *gratitude*, you idiot."

He huffed a laugh, and the anger flooded back.

"I wanted to have sex with you because you're hot and handsome, but I think I've changed my mind."

He didn't let her go the way she'd expected. Instead, his grip tightened, and her pulse leaped in excitement. Her squirming made the lace drag across sensitive flesh and aroused her in ways she'd never experienced before.

His unshaven chin scraped her neck and sent a shiver up and down her spine.

"*Have* you changed your mind?" The words were deep and darkly seductive.

She lifted her chin to give him better access to her throat and shuddered when he bit down on her earlobe. Her breath fluttered out of her parted lips as her blood hummed.

"I'm not sure yet. Keep on trying to persuade me."

He released her and ran his large hands over the sheer material of the negligee and cupped her ass, pulling her against the hard ridge of his erection. There went any concerns he wasn't capable of more than one erection per day. He moved her against him, and the sensation was so good, so heightened she gasped.

One of his hands found her breast, and the feel of his fingers over the rough lace, followed by his lips, made her want to climb him like a tree.

She reached for him, but he grabbed both her wrists and put them behind her back. Held them there.

Well now.

Thwarted, she waited to see what he did next. He gently tugged on the ties of the lace coverup and eased it off to one side.

Excitement raced through her.

Slowly he slid one bra strap off her shoulder and delicately licked the top of her breast. Her breath hitched as the material caught on her nipple. He kissed her softly, close but never quite reaching the place where she most wanted him to touch her. He slid the other strap off with his nose and repeated the exploration with his mouth, breath skimming warmly over her skin, making her edgy because he was only teasing her with what he obviously knew she wanted.

Something he wasn't giving her yet.

She pressed her thighs together to try to contain the feelings, but she was filled with it and didn't know how she was going to stand it.

"Okay, I'm persuaded." She went for humor, but her voice broke.

The smile that curved his mouth was satisfied and totally masculine. He touched the tip of his tongue to the bead of her nipple, and her sex clenched forcefully as she arched her back. He held her up when she might have melted in his arms. He sucked in one nipple and then the other and eased his thighs between hers so her clit came into close contact with his jean-covered erection.

She groaned. "Please, Kurt."

"Joe," he corrected.

"Please, whoever the hell you are. Get inside me now."

He slipped one hand over the barely-there knickers and slid a finger deep inside. She gasped with arousal.

"These have to be the most useless and most awesome panties ever invented. I want to taste you in them."

He let her go and stood to remove his jeans and boxers. She bit her lip as she watched him, changed her mind about where this should go next. Stopped him when he was about to kneel on the bed.

"I want to taste you first." She scooted off the bed, disentangling herself from the bra and lacy negligee. Leaving the panties in place. Pushed him backwards on to the bed.

She pushed between his knees.

"Row," he warned.

She looked up in surprise. "What?"

"I won't last long with your lips around my cock."

"Oh." The crude words made her eyes widen as excitement built inside.

He rubbed his hand against his forehead and blew out a taut breath. "I don't want to disappoint you."

"How would you do that?"

"By coming in your mouth rather than inside you."

The words were shocking and absolutely thrilling to her tender ears.

She took him in her hands and stroked him up and down as he groaned.

"Do your best to control yourself, Joe."

She slid her lips over the tip of his penis and tasted the tanginess of him on her tongue. She traced the length of him, the rigid flesh, the velvety skin. Then she took him into her mouth, figuring out how to breathe as he filled her. Exploring. Teasing. Tasting.

She felt him tense, and he gently drew away. "Okay, we're done." Dragged her up onto the bed with him, moving them both up the mattress.

She grinned. The experience had been more erotic than she'd imagined. The giving of pleasure a turn on in its own way.

He settled her over him, straddling him, his hands bracketing her hips.

This was new. It was all new. She gazed down at where his penis stood proud above his thighs. The look of him made her toes curl with anticipation.

She lowered slowly onto his length. He closed his eyes, and she was grateful he missed her wince. She was a little sore but not too sore.

She knew what she was supposed to do because she might be a virgin but hadn't lived in a cave for the past twenty-seven years. She placed one hand on his chest and rose up again, the glide getting easier with their combined arousal. She slid down and repeated the movement, finding a pace that worked for her. She liked that he could be dominant sometimes but also be passive as she found her way around his body. He didn't know this was her first time doing any of this but seemed content to give and take in the bedroom. That was another big plus for her.

She let her head fall back, looking up at the ceiling, enjoying the feeling of fullness inside her, the friction against her clit.

Then he reared up and took her nipple in his mouth, biting firmly enough to make her buck against him.

"Oh." She grabbed the back of his head and held him to her as he suckled on her breast still buried deep inside her.

He wrapped his thumbs into the side straps of the silly knickers she still wore and began to move them across her swollen flesh.

Oh, God.

The feeling was unlike anything she'd experienced before, and being bombarded from three different directions at once completely overwhelmed her. Sensation pounded into her, until she came in a cascade of stars falling from the sky. As the stars landed, she found herself quickly rolled so that she was underneath him now, and he began to drive into her faster and harder. She wrapped her legs around him and felt his mouth on hers as he went rigid, straining against her, straining, straining, straining. The force of his release triggered another wave of pleasure inside her, and she dug her fingers into his back as she cried out.

For a full ten seconds, they both lay trying to catch their breath. Her blood was on fire and her muscles like melted wax. "I don't think I can move."

"Me neither." But he took more of his weight on his elbows.

He went to withdraw but she wrapped her legs tighter against him. "Not yet."

He rolled them carefully over so she was lying on top of him as he pulled the covers around her shoulders.

She closed her eyes, feeling his heart beat rapidly against her cheek.

"You know the best thing?" he asked.

"The best thing out of that epic sex-capade?" She rested her hand on his chest and snuggled against him, savoring this moment because it would be over soon, and she didn't want to be that desperate, clingy girl trying to hang on for a relationship with a man who was so obviously happier alone.

"Yeah, the best thing." He nuzzled her hair, and she felt the kiss spread all through her body. "I didn't even need to pretend to lose at cribbage."

She pinched the skin at the side of his ribs, and he jumped. "There's always tomorrow."

He chuckled as he squeezed her tight, but she was already drifting off, floating on that pleasure high, and memories that she feared were going to have to last a lifetime.

13

Jordan's limbs were stiff and heavy as lead as he crawled into his Hyundai IONIQ and began the drive home. It wasn't even five o'clock, but the sky was overcast, and the thick, heavy dusk made it seem like nighttime. After the sunshine of Africa these past two months, it was a shock to the system but more fitting to his grim mood. Agitation swirled inside him. Kurt Montana had been one of the best men he'd ever had the privilege of knowing. He'd been honored to call him friend.

Now Montana was gone.

Jordan couldn't believe it.

His eyes filled with tears, and he wiped them angrily away. Tears did no good. First Scotty. Now Kurt. The sickening hollow in his stomach kept growing until it threatened to consume him with grief.

It was a feeling he was well used to.

He wished their last conversation hadn't been plagued by a shitty signal. He wished they could have had a real conversation rather than a crackly, "I'll see you tomorrow."

He'd never see him tomorrow.

Jordan needed to do *something*. Anything to keep his brain occupied. He'd volunteered to assist with the Evil1Geni-us case, but Ackers had ordered him to go home and get some rest instead.

Perhaps tomorrow he could talk Ackers into letting him join Red Team as part of the air crash investigation. He knew the specifics about where they'd stayed, who'd they'd talked to. The routes they'd driven. The individuals they'd dealt with at the embassy. If the crash did turn out not to be an accident, he could jumpstart any investigation on the ground—assuming the local authorities let them.

As much as he wanted to do something, anything, they had to wait to see what the bomb techs found first. Perhaps it had been a mechanical failure. Or a bird strike. Pilot error.

A twist of fate.

"Fuck!" He slammed the steering wheel with his fist.

He exited the Marine base and headed toward his home in the woods out of town. It had taken a long time to get used to living alone and in the countryside after growing up in Chicago and coming from a large family. He pushed the thoughts of family aside before they could gnaw him down to the bones.

He thought of Montana's daughter and the pain she must be enduring. Ackers, Novak, and Angeletti had driven down to Richmond to tell her the terrible news in person. He was selfishly glad he hadn't been ordered to go too.

He'd send her his condolences after the fog cleared from his brain.

Headlights followed as he drove the icy road heading out of town. The temperature had dropped substantially with the threat of snow in the air. He slowed.

The idiot behind him, some yahoo in a big-ass truck, blinded him with his full beams and then revved angrily behind him.

Jordan took control of his own temper and indicated to pull over on the side of the road, but the truck slowed too. He contemplated pulling across the road and blocking it and arresting the sonofabitch for dangerous driving. But there were some sharp corners ahead and a nasty gorge. Jordan didn't want to cause an accident if anyone was coming the other way.

He tipped his rearview mirror to avoid the worst of the blinding glare and was immediately jolted as the truck deliberately rear-ended him.

What the…?

Jordan gripped the steering wheel tighter. He sped up, the truck followed in hot pursuit. This motherfucker was trying to run him off the goddamned road.

Everything left his mind except the road and the truck and the knowledge that if he let the truck pass him on this section of road there was a very good chance it would ram him off the road on the next corner and send him down a steep wooded hillside. The turn after that was a narrow bridge over a jagged gorge.

His car might be electric, but it was fast. Zero to sixty in under five seconds.

He pulled away from the truck but had to slow for the dangerous corner ahead. The truck cut the corners, crossing the white line, oblivious to the fact a vehicle might be coming in the other direction. The truck's nose eased past his rear bumper and nudged his car, causing a skid. Jordan had to speed up to correct.

Sweat formed on his brow despite the winter chill. This fucker was actively trying to kill him.

Jordan pushed the thought aside. He focused and increased his speed, grateful his training included tactical driving and evasion. But the other driver seemed to anticipate his every move, which suggested he also had tactical driving experience.

His fingers tightened on the steering wheel as another ram up the ass flung his car toward the guardrails. He floored it. Ignored the slick road, the deadly gorge. Concentrated on the drive itself. Like some high-speed racing game but with life-and-death consequences. He couldn't let the truck get alongside him, or there was a good chance he'd be through the guardrail and hurtling to a painful death.

Some might say he'd earned it.

Finally, he saw the truck headlights wobble behind him. The truck was forced to slow down or risk losing control.

Jordan raced on, pulling ahead, passing a car going in the opposite direction, jamming his hand on the horn to warn the truck and the innocent occupants of the other car to be alert for possible danger.

He hit the next straight and passed his own driveway, not slowing down. Quarter of a mile farther on, he jammed on the brakes and turned into someone's long driveway and immediately swung the car around to face the opposite direction. The truck also slammed on the brakes but missed the turn. It sat in the dark road with exhaust fumes creating a living, breathing fog that pulsed around it.

Krychek pulled his Springfield Custom Professional 1911-A1 and opened his door, stepping out into the damp, frigid night.

The truck revved angrily as he approached it, his pistol pointed at the driver's seat. The license plate was covered in mud but before he could get close enough to see the occupants, the truck sped away, spitting gravel from the tires.

He lowered his weapon.

What the fuck was that about?

Jordan shook his head and got back in his car, waiting for a few minutes in case they decided to come back. He dialed Reid Armstrong, the former Legat in Jakarta and now in charge of this task force hunting for Hurek.

"Someone tried to run me off the road."

"You in DC? Traffic is always a bitch."

"Near my house."

Armstrong's tone changed when he realized Jordan was serious. "Deliberately?"

"Yup."

"You think it's related to the investigation?"

"I don't know." Jordan tried to unclench his jaw, but it wasn't working. "You think Montana's crash was an accident?"

"That's what authorities are saying at the moment."

"Smells like elephant shit to me."

Armstrong grunted. "I'll send in an Evidence Response Team to you."

"Should be able to collect paint samples and maybe tire impressions." Jordan used his cell to photograph some from the semi-frozen mud at the side of the road. He gave the make and model of the truck.

"Any chance of traffic cams catching anything?"

"No." He ran his fingers through his hair. "Not out here. Unless he followed me from the base."

"Did you cut anyone off?"

"No, I didn't cut anyone off. Is that the road rage equivalent to asking a rape victim what she was wearing?"

"I was just looking for motive. Call the local cops to report it. They might know something if it's some guy with known issues."

"There was nothing simple about what just happened. It was a sustained and dedicated attack using a ten-ton truck. If I weren't a trained operator, you wouldn't be talking to me at all."

There was a long pause. "Any idea why someone might want to kill you?"

"Your guess is as good as mine."

"Maybe you were closer to finding Hurek than you realized…"

"Perhaps." Krychek stared into the stark winter woods feeling like Atlas with the weight of the heavens on his shoulders.

Was it worth the cost?

Compared to losing Kurt Montana, capturing Hurek seemed inconsequential now, and yet, Jordan knew that's what Montana would have wanted. To remove the scumbag from society and put him somewhere he couldn't inflict his brand of violence on anyone else.

"I'm heading to my place now. If what happened was targeted, whoever's behind it could know where I live."

"Want to go to a safe house?"

"No." He pulled back onto the road and drove down the long

winding driveway to his isolated home. "Let these assholes show their faces. I can deal with them."

"Want me to send another agent down to partner with you?"

In his house? "No. Thanks."

"Call me if there's more trouble or signs anyone's been in your place. I'll get the local police to come by, make sure they know there's a serious issue. ERT will be there within the hour."

Jordan hung up as he reached his home. His security lights came on and flooded the area surrounding the rustic cabin. His alarm system app didn't show anyone as having been inside his home since he'd left last November except for the bi-weekly housekeeper he employed, but apps could be messed with and so could people. He got out of the car and examined the damaged rear end, the broken taillights. A hassle to get repaired but minor damage compared to what could have happened.

He grabbed his pack from the passenger seat and put it on his back. Then he opened the trunk, which resisted because of the buckled metal, but he managed to pry it open. He dragged out the bags a buddy from DEVGRU had dropped off at the HRT compound and paused when he saw Kurt's bag there too. His eyes smarted with tears he didn't want to shed.

He grabbed both bags and slammed the buckled trunk shut, locking it with the fob.

He lifted the two heavy bags and headed onto the porch, dropping one bag by the door and pulling his weapon before he entered the familiar space.

He cleared the whole house, top to bottom. Then he went outside and grabbed the other bag and brought it inside. Tomorrow, he'd tell Ackers about the attack, but that could wait. The man had enough to worry about right now.

Fatigue wanted to drop Jordan to his knees, but the flash of blue and red lights told him the cops had arrived. He pulled his creds from his pocket and hung them around his neck to show he was an FBI agent and armed. He glanced carefully through the drapes to make sure they were legit, but the guy was driving the right kind of car and wearing the right uniform.

Jordan kept his hand near his service weapon and went out to talk to the trooper and explain what had happened, leaving out any mention of wanted international terrorists or dead colleagues.

When he slipped into bed an hour later, he kept his alarm system armed and his 1911 on the nightstand within reach.

If anyone came to visit, he'd make sure they felt appropriately welcome.

14

JANUARY 13

Wednesday. Nyanga, Zimbabwe

K urt jerked awake at 4:17 a.m. His brain took a few seconds to catch up with the not unpleasant situation he found himself in. Someone was sleeping on top of him.

Rowena, her skin slick with sweat that glued her to his chest.

Despite that perfect predicament something felt very wrong.

He wished to hell he could see her, but the candle had burned out. He wished they could spend the night lazing in bed, but something had made him wake up, and he never ignored his instincts.

"Row." He stroked her arm and murmured in her ear.

"Um."

She was obviously still asleep, and he wished he could leave her that way.

"Row," he urged.

She moaned and stretched against him. Christ, he hadn't been this horny since he'd been a teen, and he felt vaguely ashamed that it was because of someone who was so goddamned young. But something told him playtime was over.

Everything inside him clamored it was time to go. He eased

away and got up, carefully checking outside without moving the drapes. No one visible in the darkness, but the niggle at the base of his skull told him to get moving. He lit a candle. It wouldn't be enough to be seen from outside but would give him enough light to do what he needed.

He sat at the end of the bed and dressed.

Rowena sat up, groggy. Sank her hand into her hair that had come loose from its braid. "What is it?"

"We need to get going."

"What time is it?"

"Early."

"Can I grab a shower?"

Her words brought back the image of them engaged in shower sex, and he wished with all his heart they were normal people on vacation with only an age difference for him to worry about.

"No. We have to move now."

"Okay."

No argument or pouting. She headed to the bathroom, wearing only the pieces of red string that made up those ridiculous, sexy panties, and he started going through the bags, taking only what they would absolutely need.

He placed clothes for her to wear on the bed. Put another pair of clean underwear and socks in his rucksack. He pulled out some of his clothes, jettisoning anything that wasn't essential. He had plenty of clothes back home.

They'd need to carry water and food.

The red lace number went with the bag of things he planned to ditch before leaving the hotel, which was a damned shame. Red was also the color of blood and a good reminder of the stakes. Rowena came back into the room minus the panties, and he tried not to be affected by her nakedness. A bit like asking a starving man not to look at the buffet table.

Silently, she pulled on the underwear, jeans, T-shirt, and a fleece similar to his. He handed her the black ball cap. He'd packed the woolen hats should they need them later. He stuffed her raincoat inside his pack and pulled it onto his back.

"Ready?" he whispered, uncertain as to why he was suddenly so on edge.

She grabbed her big purse and nodded. Her eyes looked anxious. Mouth drawn tight.

He didn't mean to worry her, but if he was right, they were in deep shit. They needed to keep moving. If he was wrong, he'd look like a nervous jackass, and he was fine with that.

He gathered all the bags they were leaving behind and went to the door. He checked the peephole, and all was clear. Everything seemed quiet and appeared normal. It didn't matter. He went instead to the French doors, eased through the drapes, and unlocked the doors, opening one quietly because noise traveled at night.

He wished he had a firearm. He felt naked without one.

He stepped outside and paused for a moment, absorbing the quality of the night. Frogs sang their chorus. He couldn't hear anything unusual.

Rowena joined him, and he gently eased the door closed.

This was not the time to make foolish mistakes.

He touched her lips with his finger so she knew to be quiet. She nodded, and he took her hand as they began making their way around the front of the resort and up to the main road.

He headed back to the garage and spotted their vehicle outside the doors, new tire already fitted.

He saved his anger—the mechanic had either unexpectedly found time to fix it last night or had wanted to boost the number of guests staying at the resort because his wife's livelihood depended on it.

Kurt ignored the frustration that they could have already been in Mozambique by now. No point wasting energy. They'd needed the rest anyway. And if they hadn't stopped here, he may never have gotten to make love with Rowena.

But that wasn't worth the risk of her being detained.

He dropped the bags of things they didn't need any more into a dumpster at the side of the garage.

He found the car unlocked, key in the ignition. He put the rucksack on the back seat. Pulled out a little so Rowena had enough space to climb in.

He rolled down the window and thought he heard a car engine in the distance. She twisted in the seat. She heard it too. He drove off slowly up the road, past the entrance to the resort and then off the main road into something that looked like a fish hatchery.

He turned off the lights and ducked down as headlights from two vehicles swept into the driveway of the hotel behind them.

Two big, black SUVs.

Shit.

He started the engine again, and they set off, leaving the headlights off for as long as he could. But the sun hadn't risen, and he couldn't risk crashing or hitting another giant pothole in the pitch black.

What he wouldn't do for a pair of NVGs and his trusty SIG Sauer.

"Those vehicles look like the one I saw at Anders' place yesterday morning." Rowena's voice was soft in the darkness.

He nodded, unsurprised.

"They might not be looking for us." She sounded as if she were trying to convince herself.

"In which case, no one will care that we left already."

"But you think they are after us, don't you?" Her voice was sharper now, all traces of sleepiness gone.

He gave her a curt nod.

"How did you know?"

He shook his head. "I didn't."

"I would have still been sleeping. What woke you?"

He wasn't about to suggest he had a sixth sense about these

things, but it wasn't wise to ignore instincts that had been honed over decades.

"I put myself in their shoes. Assuming they're after me and not you, assuming they were monitoring my cell, it would niggle at them—where did that last ping come from? They'd see I'm headed east—or at least my cell signal was. Then, perhaps at first, they think it's a glitch, and then someone checks some of the surveillance cameras around the airport, as they are bound to do after a plane crash, and sees someone who looks very much like me hopping over a security fence.

"Hello, ready-made terrorist suspect when and if the authorities declare it a bomb rather than an accident."

"Or they picked up my uncle's vehicle outside the murder scene and used street cameras to follow me through the city and determined which road I left on."

He nodded, but he didn't think the cops would be as motivated to solve Bjorn's murder as whoever was capable of bringing down a plane full of people just to stop him getting back to the States.

"From there they start working gas stations, hotels, and rest stops."

"Halfway House," she murmured. "That was my fault. Sorry."

"No. Not your fault. I didn't realize at that point how high this thing might go. What the implications were." He glanced through the night sky and wondered how many of Gilder's satellites were watching them right now.

Would the FBI believe he was dead? Why not? Unless he could contact the authorities, they'd never know he'd survived the crash. Hopefully, once the letters arrived the truth would come out for sure, but that could be months away.

He ached for his fellow FBI agents and most especially for his daughter. They'd all been through too much already.

The FBI would send a team to help investigate the crash, but how much access would they really have, and how much of the crash scene would be staged to look like whatever the bad guys wanted it to look like? This assumed the government, or at least *someone* powerful within the government, was complicit in the crash. But Leo Spartan was the ambassador to the UN with plenty of friends in high places.

What did those four men—Nolan Gilder, Leo Spartan, Darmawan Hurek, and Dougie Cavanagh—have in common? What secrets were they trying to hide?

Had Cavanagh been murdered to keep him quiet?

Had Rowena's mother?

What had Bjorn known, and why hadn't he told him? Why give him Cavanagh's name unless Kurt had managed to rattle him?

Thinking back on that press conference about the new factory, which would be a lifeline for many struggling Zimbabweans, chances were the government would protect the billionaire before they'd protect their relationship with the US.

It was the perfect bribe from one of the richest people on the planet.

However, it was one thing for government officials to look the other way and ignore the fact someone had tried to murder a serving FBI agent. It was quite another to actively help kill an FBI agent. That could be considered an act of war, and the US was not someone you fucked around without finding out payback was a bitch.

"Hang on." He pressed his foot to the accelerator as fast as he dared under these conditions. He was risking another flat, but the people behind them had muscular SUVs that would eat up these roads, and they were probably armed.

"Get the map book out of my pack and find a road that gets us as close to the Gairezi River as possible. We need to get off this highway ASAP."

Rowena fumbled for the map book and had to turn on the light to see.

He called out markers until she found where they were on the page. They passed a business center. A primary school.

"Here. Take this right."

"Hold on."

She grabbed the handle above her head as he took the turn and immediately hit a dirt road. He slowed down. He had to.

They rumbled past farmland and a small number of houses, some modern, some traditional circular thatched homes. Dust churned up behind them, a definite marker if anyone was following behind. Rowena peered at the map about an inch away from her nose, straining through the darkness for landmarks.

"The road curves to the right up ahead. Yes. Here." Her finger traced the map the way they'd traced his skin last night, and he had to jerk the wheel back into position as he lost his concentration for a fraction of a second.

Focus, dumbass.

"There's a left turning up ahead, but if you miss it the first time, there's another turning just beyond it, like a fork." She looked at his face. "It's more of a farm track than road by the looks of it."

Didn't matter. "How close are we to the river?"

"Less than a kilometer away, and this track gets us within a hundred meters."

He nodded and concentrated on the road ahead. Suddenly, headlights cut through the darkness behind them and Rowena glanced over her shoulder with big fearful eyes.

Shit. Fuck.

He hated being right.

"When we get to wherever this track ends and we can't drive any further, we jump out and run as fast as we can to the river. I'll take the backpack. Don't wait. You run and then swim as hard as you can. I'll catch up. The other side is Mozambique, and when we get there, we need to hide ourselves in the trees. If we get separated for any reason, head northeast and ask someone to drive you to the US Embassy in Maputo. Ask them to hide you, and tell them you'll pay them a thousand US dollars if they do so. The embassy can pay them for you. Give the ambassador my name—only the ambassador—and tell him everything that's happened." He grinned manically. "You can leave out the sex if you want, but bottom line, tell him everything, and tell him Kurt Montana said to take care of you. I'll pay him back."

"I can pay him back, but we won't be separated."

"Row."

"I'm not leaving you."

"You might have to."

She closed her mouth.

"Promise me."

"No."

"Row."

"No!"

"*Rowena*," he warned. "I might need to peel off to create a diversion. I can't be worried about you walking straight back to them if I do that. I'll meet you at the embassy if not before."

She didn't answer.

Headlights were getting closer.

Fuck fuck fuck.

"Rowena...*please*." He wasn't used to begging. He was used to people obeying orders.

"Fine." She tugged a few pages out of the map book and rolled them up. Stuffed them into her giant purse.

He gunned it. Driving along a dirt road, then a walking path, busting through a gate on the track that led down to the edge of the Gairezi itself.

"Go right." She pointed. "The river is wider and probably slower there."

It was the wet season. Kurt didn't let his worry show, but he was scared the water might be too fast for her to swim across safely.

"Are there crocs?" Fear rang out in her voice.

"No crocs." It was insanely dangerous to even think about

swimming with crocs or hippos. He'd take his chances with humans—but this time it was fifty-fifty as to which might be worse.

He turned off the headlights as they rumbled across a muddy field. A faint tinge of pink skimmed the top of the mountainside on the Mozambique side of the border. The sun was starting to rise in the east.

They could do this. *If* the guys behind them didn't have guns. *If* the river wasn't too high. *If* they got lucky.

He had no doubt whoever was chasing them were ruthless killers. He needed to get the information he had to the Joint Terrorism Task Force that had been put together to find Hurek. But right now, protecting Rowena was his number-one priority.

He reached a line of trees and stopped the car. Rowena leaped out and ran toward the river like he'd told her. He grabbed the backpack and a bag of food and water. Closed the top securely as he raced after her to the edge of the Gairezi.

The headlights had almost caught up with them.

Rowena waited for him at the edge, and he ran in, dragging her with him as he aimed upstream.

"Can you swim?" A little late to ask.

"Yes, but not particularly well."

They were in a wide meander, and he wanted to give her as much chance as possible to cross before it narrowed again to a series of rapids. He heard voices shouting above the noise of the water. Chasing them. He took her arm and urged her into the cold water. Deeper and deeper. She held her bag up trying to keep it dry. The water hit his thighs, his balls. The current tugged at his clothes, his limbs.

He heard her gasp.

Unstable rocks beneath his feet made him stumble. "Go. Strike out hard for the other bank. You need to get out of the main flow, then you'll be fine. Put everything into it and then hide in the trees. *I'll find you.*"

"Okay."

"You've got this, Rowena. You've fucking got this. I'm right behind you."

The sound of gunshots rang through the night, and a sharp pain bit into his shoulder.

Sonofabitch.

———

Rowena cried out in fear at the sound of a gun being fired. She flung herself into the deeper water. The current took her, her limbs heavy from her waterlogged clothing. Panic swept through her. Her bag was soaked, and she thought of the photograph inside, ruined. Thank goodness her uncle's old watch was waterproof.

"Push hard, Row."

Kurt was behind her, and his words launched her muscles out of paralysis. She struck out and kicked forcefully, dragged along by the current but also making gradual progress. Her clothes and boots and bag felt like they were made of grasping fingers, but she kept swimming forward, inch by inch. The river wasn't that wide compared to the Severn beside her home, but it was the rainy season and full and strong and full of large rocks that could easily crack a bone.

Her bag caught on a boulder and almost pulled her under. She swallowed a mouthful of water and spluttered, reminding her of how it had felt to almost choke to death last night. Drowning would feel the same. She struggled with the strap and had to duck under water and wrench it over her head and let it go. Her notebooks. The photo. Her mobile phone. Her contraception pills. Her *passport*. Treasures, memories, junk. Gone. Swept away by the mighty Gairezi.

She blinked to clear her vision and plowed on. She couldn't see that well, but she knew where she was supposed to be headed.

She banged into a boulder and inhaled sharply. Fought on. She'd never taken the power of water for granted. She'd witnessed too many floods in her hometown not to respect the unstoppable force of nature. She used her technically terrible front crawl and dug deep to find the strength to drag herself toward the other side.

Kurt gave her a sideways shove, helping her escape the grip of one particular vigorous stream. She was suddenly out of the main torrent and being pulled less aggressively.

The thought hit her. If she could cross this river, what would stop these men from following them?

"Swim, dammit, swim."

When her foot hit the bottom, she staggered upright. The noise of more gunshots speared her with terror and made her crouch.

"Go. Quick. Get into the trees."

"What if they follow us?"

"They will." His voice deepened to a low growl. "Get into the trees, run, and hide. Don't come out until I tell you. Otherwise, don't come out at all. Do what I told you to do earlier."

She went down hard on one knee and a bullet whizzed through the air close enough she could feel the air move. The spit in her mouth dried up. She jerked upright and started to run, feet slippery in the gravel and silt. She zigzagged her way up the short beach on the other side. Headed into the deep shadows of the forest, Kurt behind her, shielding her with his own body she realized.

Tears formed, but she blinked them away. The idea of anything happening to this man was unbearable. She concentrated on doing what he'd asked so he didn't have to worry about her as well as the bastards who chased them.

She reached back and squeezed his hand and then streaked ahead. She hoped that wouldn't be the last time she saw him alive. The idea made something swell inside her like a balloon against her sternum. It was too much to contemplate. Too much to comprehend.

She forced it out of her mind.

He was a professional. So was she, although she wasn't sure

how being a librarian was going to be helpful at this point. But she wouldn't let him down. They'd get out of this alive.

It was still on the dark side of dawn, and she was on the leeward side of a mountain beneath a thick canopy of trees. She led with her arms, but her eyes gradually adjusted, and she was able to make out a faint game trail ahead. She followed it, trying to be quiet, knowing she would leave tracks because of the mud, but it couldn't be helped. The land started to rise, the incline increasing. She slipped repeatedly and could hear men shouting at one another as they forded the river. Coming after them. Hunting them.

Her heart pounded, and her chest heaved with exertion and fear. She forced herself to draw her breath in slower, deeper.

To hide, she'd need to be silent.

To be silent, she needed to stop bellowing like a winded horse.

She scanned her surroundings and spotted an even narrower path off to the left. It was less muddy there. She ran along it a short distance and then backtracked walking backwards in her own footsteps. At the main trail she made a leap onto a grassy mound beside a large tree. She hugged that tree and swung herself around to the other side of the trunk. The smell of ferns and bracken rose through the air. Gingerly, she tried to stay out of the dirt and step on small tufts of grass. She picked her way carefully through the forest, her breath deepening even as her fear mounted.

Where was Kurt? What did he plan to do?

She headed up the slope again, another fifty feet and then turned back to the left, paralleling the original direction she'd taken.

The noises indicated the men were across the river now. Getting closer. She spotted a fallen log which would make a good hiding place and almost headed there.

She paused.

It was surely the first place they'd look...

Her gaze traveled up into the trees above her head. Another

gunshot sounded so loud it made her blood freeze. If she wanted to survive, she needed to hide. And she really wanted to survive. She wished Kurt was here with her. The thought of him out there, fighting these guys alone was terrifying. She swallowed the knot that strangled her throat. Then she began to climb.

15

K urt stowed his backpack and supplies in what he hoped was a safe spot, doubled back to the river, and observed three men crossing.

At least one person stayed in the SUV and moved one of the chase vehicles so the headlights angled across the river, helping the hunters see and presumably attempting to pick him and Rowena out of the forest.

He scanned his eyes over the area without moving anything else.

No sign of Rowena.

He looked back at his would-be assailants whose faces he could see vaguely but didn't recognize. One Black guy. Two white guys. One of the white dudes was yelling orders, coordinating the crossing. Running the show.

He moved like a motherfucking merc.

Kurt faded back into the shadows and headed up the slope again, out of the range of those powerful headlights.

No sign of Rowena, which was a good thing. If he couldn't see or hear her then neither could they. He hoped she'd found somewhere to lay low. He doubted the people chasing them would kill her straight away, and fear for her heightened his resolve.

He wasn't about to let anyone harm her.

He moved silently through the forest, so deep in the zone he could hear the rustle of individual leaves on the trees and the huffing breath of each of the three men as they clambered out of the rushing water. Those barked instructions.

South African accent speaking English rather than Afrikaans. They were fanning out, which suited him just fine.

He cut across the forest and crouched within the protective embrace of three giant ferns. He waited. Let his senses flow out into the forest. Ignored the discomfort of soaked clothes, the throb in his shoulder. Found the gray zone, the killing zone. Finally, he heard footsteps approaching, seemingly unconcerned about being seen or making noise. The guy was armed and thought that meant he had the upper hand.

This man thought he was the predator.

And Kurt was the prey.

Kurt had news for him.

Dawn was beginning to break, but they were in the murky stage of darkness, where shadow and substance merged into ghosts.

He listened to the guy pass by. Waited for him to move a few steps ahead before Kurt rose silently up out of the foliage. In one motion, he wrapped his hand around the man's mouth and slipped the guy's own hunting knife from its sheath. Then he slit the guy's throat before he could make a sound or get off a shot.

Kurt eased him gently to the ground, rolled him onto his back and looked at the man's face. Blond. Five eight. Stocky build. Blue eyes red-rimmed as if he had a cold or a drinking problem—or had just had his throat slashed. Nose that had been broken too many times to ever be straight. Probably mid-thirties.

What a waste.

Kurt took the handgun. A 1911 and some spare ammo. He rifled through the guy's pockets and came up with nothing.

Definitely a merc of some kind. Private security?

If so, what was he doing in Zim, aside from chasing Kurt and Rowena through the Eastern Highlands?

He wiped the blade on the dead man's khaki shirt.

Then he melted into the shadows and followed the barked commands of the asshole who'd once been in the center of this little posse.

Kurt used trees to provide cover, extended his awareness behind him in case the other bastard decided to cross the river and join his friends.

Kurt followed the second man up the trail. Moved behind a large tree as the guy did a slow 360, shining his powerful flashlight through the forest.

Listened as he gave an excited shout as he picked up Rowena's trail. The guy jogged along and then paused, cut left. Kurt followed. Moved fast and silent through the mist-soaked forest until he was right behind the big fuck. He didn't hesitate. He caught the man around his lantern jaw and slid his stolen blade through the man's common carotid.

He held that strong jaw shut as the man sagged to his knees, blood spurting warmly from the slash, coating them both in blood like they were starring in a horror movie. Slowly, the man's heart stopped pumping, and he keeled over, dead.

One to go.

For now.

He rolled the body off the path. Dug into the wet pockets of his shirt and pants.

Nothing.

Presumably they had some ID in the vehicles. Otherwise, they wouldn't be able to get around the country without the police stopping them.

The crack of a branch had him diving behind a tree trunk a split second before a bullet scored the earth where he'd been kneeling.

The last guy started yelling, calling out for his buddies to help.

Kurt popped around the other side of the tree and used his left hand to send a bullet center mass.

The man clasped his chest and dropped with a startled grunt and an almost comical look of surprise. He hadn't expected Kurt to be armed or to fight back. He began crawling through the undergrowth as Kurt walked toward him, keeping the gun aimed. The man in the dirt didn't go for his weapon. Just kept trying to drag himself to safety.

Kurt kicked the discarded weapon aside then pressed a foot onto the man's back to stop his progress. He frisked him for any other weapons. Took another knife from his waistband. "Who are you working for?"

The smile flashed white in the dawn. "Someone who wants you dead."

"Give me a name. You may as well. It's not like you're going to make it out of here alive."

Fear entered the man's yellowed eyes. Jaundice? Hepatitis?

"Please. I have a wife. A child."

"It's not me you need to persuade." Kurt crouched. "I'm not going to kill you, but you think your pals are going to help you back across that river or carry you to the nearest town to a hospital?" Kurt shook his head. "We both know they'll likely put a bullet in your head and blame it on me."

Those burnt umber eyes acknowledged the truth of Kurt's words.

"Who're they after? Me or the girl?"

The injured man rolled onto his side and held both hands to his gut in an attempt to stem the bleeding. He gave a baritone chuckle. "What girl?"

Kurt nodded and straightened. That's what he'd figured. The man shifted warily away from him, but Kurt wouldn't kill someone who wasn't an immediate threat. He started to walk away. He needed his pack, and he needed to find Rowena. Get the hell out of the area before they brought in reinforcements.

"Hey, Mr. FBI."

Kurt swung around.

"You can't outrun these people. They're everywhere. In government, security forces, police. Not only here but all over the world. You saw what they did to that aircraft..."

Kurt clenched his teeth. "Maybe if you give me a name, I can start making them pay for what they did."

The man choked out a laugh. "They're more powerful than you can imagine."

"I think I heard that line in a movie once." He wanted them rooted out. Exposed and left to wither and die, preferably in a prison cell. "The bad guys always claim to be all-powerful. It's a bullshit mind-control tactic that makes the weak succumb without a fight." He flicked the point of the knife at him. "Make a sound in the next fifteen minutes, and I will come back and slit your throat like I did your friends'."

"They weren't no friends of mine."

"Then you should have chosen better work colleagues."

The injured man shook his head. "You think a man like me has a good way to make a living in this country?"

Kurt didn't point out that they were no longer in Zimbabwe but in Mozambique. The situation here was just as difficult.

"There has to be a better way than chasing two innocents and getting gut shot for your troubles."

Shaking his head at the sheer amount of human suffering and waste, he left the injured man, went and rescued his pack from the patch of ferns where he'd hidden it. Then jogged back up the path to where the second man had picked up Rowena's trail. As he walked to the place she'd turned right, he noticed mud on the trunk of a tree and paused, circled, picked up her tracks heading northeast. Clever girl. He jogged, caring more about speed than stealth right now.

"Row?" He called out quietly when he lost her spoor.

"Joe?"

The reply came from overhead, and he looked up and saw her straddling the limb of a large tree about twenty feet up.

"I think you may as well call me Kurt now." Cat was well and truly out of the bag. "Can you get down from there?"

She shot him a wry grin. "One way or another."

The fact she still had her sense of humor in this situation rocked something inside him. He was well acquainted with grit and determination. They put their HRT candidates through the wringer looking for those same qualities. Rowena had them in spades.

She clamped her long legs around the trunk and shimmied down to the ground. He caught her the last few feet and helped her to stand. Took her hand with his left and pressed it to his lips. "Thank God you're okay."

"What happened?" Her green eyes went wide with concern as they took in his appearance. "You're hurt."

"It's not my blood." He wiped his face with his sleeve, then checked his shoulder. "Except for a graze on my arm." The bullet had ripped the skin, but it was a minor flesh wound. Though some antibiotics would have been useful right about now. "Come on. We need to put some distance between them and us." He squeezed her fingers.

They headed farther up the mountain but kept below the tree line, out of sight of the man he'd shot—in case the guy made a miraculous recovery and decided to try to fulfill the mission regardless of his injuries.

"Is it safe now?" she whispered as she glanced around.

As if he'd have taken her out of her hiding place unless he was certain she'd be okay. For now, at least. But they had to get moving.

"They sent three men after us. I took care of them. Others stayed with the vehicles. I don't know how many but at least one." Enough to report their location to others. Enough to concentrate the search.

"*Took care of them*?" Her brow furrowed.

"Killed two. Injured the third, but I doubt his colleagues will get him medical attention."

Her eyes widened. He braced himself for disgust but instead got sympathy.

"I'm sorry you had to do that." She pressed her lips together, clearly fighting emotion. "What do they want, do you know?"

"Me."

"You? You're sure?" She sagged with relief.

He nodded. "Me. I apologize for dragging you into something this dangerous."

"I flung myself into it when I walked into Bjorn Anders' office and found him murdered."

He squeezed her hand again then forced himself to let go. He needed to keep his hands free for his weapons. "I'm glad you stopped me getting on that flight, but I'm not happy about the fact you're stuck with me now. I don't think they've linked you to Anders' death, so don't mention it if they or anyone else asks, understood? You never saw the guy."

"What guy?"

"Exactly."

She grinned at him, looking so damned beautiful…

"You'd be a lot better off without me."

"You are the only person keeping me alive right now."

He turned away. She needed to get the hell away from him. But they were in the middle of Africa with bad guys on their trail. And, if the bad guys had identified her, she'd be in as much danger now as he was.

Dammit.

He moved quickly, wanting to get away from the area before reinforcements arrived.

"I lost my bag in the river. Along with the photograph of Bjorn and Dougie Cavanagh."

Guilt hit him hard. He knew he should tell her it wasn't lost, that he'd mailed it, but he also knew it made more sense not to. The only real secrets were the ones only one person knew. "Do you have copies?"

She blew out a huffed sigh. "No. But maybe I have similar back home. Of Dougie at least."

He frowned. "What does that mean?"

"I found some negatives with my mom's things in Granny's attic, including an undeveloped roll in her camera. Seems as if she took lots of photos during her time in Africa."

He stopped. Her mother might have been the photographer of that group of four. She might have more photographs pertinent to their investigation.

"I asked a friend who teaches art and photography at a local secondary school to develop all the old negatives. I don't know what happened to the actual photos, but I couldn't find them. I'm paying for the chemical supplies and photographic paper. John enjoys that kind of thing."

"John."

She shot him a glance. "Yes, John. He's been a friend of mine since elementary school."

"Sure he has." He couldn't deny the whip of jealousy that curled through him. "I'd like to get copies of those negatives and photos if possible. We'll pay for any supplies."

She frowned again. "Why?"

"I'm not sure. A feeling I have. It might be nothing but…"

Her nostrils flared as she inhaled. "If my mom was taking photos in Africa around the same time as those other pictures were taken, they might hold clues."

"It's not like we have a lot of insight into what the hell is going on right now, let alone all those years ago."

Was this why Rowena's mom was dead?

Her breathing grew hoarse from exertion, but he didn't slow down. Not yet.

"Kurt." Her tone was pensive. "Who exactly are you looking for in Zimbabwe?"

He shot her an innocent look. "What d'you mean?"

Her eyes narrowed in irritation. "Don't treat me like a fool. I get that you have a job to do and secrets to keep, but do *not* treat me like an idiot."

He rolled his shoulders and felt like a dick. "It's mission sensitive."

"I'm not asking for Top Secret information. Just anything you can tell me as to why you were talking to Bjorn Anders in Vic Falls and Harare. You want my help with my mother's photos, which I'm willing to give without reservation." She swallowed. "I just, would like to know anything I'm allowed."

He inhaled, the cold air catching in his lungs. "Officially, I'm not allowed to say a single word about what is a Joint Task Force operation." He scratched his ear. His arm was sore now, and he was worried about the risk of infection. The river water and dirt weren't exactly sterile.

But this situation was more important. What the hell. He trusted her.

Not because they'd had sex. Right now, they needed one another. "I'm going to tell you anyway."

Her pupils dilated in surprise.

"I'm searching for a terrorist who was last reportedly seen in the DRC. I tapped Bjorn as an old friend who's been in Africa for the past thirty years and who always had his ear to the ground. I think Bjorn knew a lot more than he admitted." How were Bjorn's wife and kids coping after the murder, he wondered. "The FBI is searching for a fuckwad named Darmawan Hurek. Number one on the FBI's Most Wanted Fugitive list."

She slipped, and he caught her, held her upright.

"You think my mom might have known a *terrorist*?"

"He wasn't a terrorist back then. He was a guy dicking around Africa after he finished college, presumably searching for his way in life. Unfortunately, his way turned out to be hurting others to get what he wanted. He went to St. Andrews."

"Like Dougie Cavanagh." Her eyes widened. "You think Dougie and Hurek were friends at uni?"

She sounded so disappointed he almost smiled. Instead, he gave her a curt nod. "That photo you found in Bjorn's office showed Cavanagh, Hurek, Gilder, and a man who looks awfully like a young Leo Spartan, the current Zimbabwean ambassador to the UN."

Her complexion went sheet white. "Gilder went to St. Andrews too."

"Did he now?" Interesting. He narrowed his gaze at her. "You seem to know a lot about him."

"I like to research people I vehemently don't like in case I'm doing them a disservice."

That made him smile.

"He spent four years studying computer science but only came away with a general degree, which doesn't exactly scream genius." Her tone was derisive. "No one knows where all his money came from, but his parents died when he was about the age I am now. He's an only child and inherited close to ten million pounds. I felt sorry for him when I found that out—not about the inheritance, but the fact he doesn't have any relatives left."

Kurt wished he could take away some of the obvious pain she felt at being alone in the world.

"Then I found several photos of him online posing with big game animals he'd shot and killed, and that destroyed *any* sympathy I might have felt." Her disgust was obvious. "Those photos were subsequently scrubbed from the internet probably when he started getting involved in politics, but"—she tapped her nose—"librarians like to keep records of things."

He fucking loved librarians.

"He apparently began investing in the startup tech sector. Gained a reputation for being some kind of wonder-bro with a nose for the next big thing without ever inventing anything himself."

She pulled back on his grip hard enough to stop them both as she caught her breath for a few seconds. "He developed blood cancer when he was thirty, which also made me feel a bit sorry for him, again until I read his opinion about women in the tech sector." She raised one brow. "He fully recovered—that type always do—but the rumor is he can no longer father children. I don't think they were that into freezing sperm back then or they messed up something?" She snorted derisively. "What am I saying? He probably has gallons of the stuff in his minus eighty freezers in some underground bunker in Idaho."

"There's a thought." Kurt tugged her onwards. He wanted off this steep slope and into the forest on the other side.

"Apparently, he's obsessed with slowing down the biological aging process and has turned into a bit of a health nut."

Cancer could do that to a person, he supposed.

Kurt and his fellow Hostage Rescue Team operators could be considered fitness freaks, but none of them expected to live forever.

"Did Bjorn tell you anything useful about Hurek?" she asked.

"I pushed him hard at the Jam Café, mentioned the hundred-thousand-dollar reward and how the US government could be both grateful and displeased when it came to awarding contracts." He'd pressured him, and now Bjorn was dead. "Eventually, he gave me Dougie's name. He wouldn't confirm that Dougie and Hurek were friends but claimed to have heard rumors they'd known each other back in the day."

"Why give you any name if Bjorn was also involved with Hurek? He must know it risked exposing himself?"

Kurt shook his head. "Not really. Either Bjorn knew it was a dead end or, if he was also involved, maybe he told Spartan or Gilder I was poking around asking questions about Hurek and his cohort in Africa back in the day. Maybe he foolishly decided to use that photograph to blackmail them. Or maybe the fact I was in the country asking questions was enough for the bad guys—whoever they may be—to get rid of any potential loose ends including me and Bjorn."

"Why hide the photo?" She shivered.

"I don't know, but I do know we need to get you out of those wet clothes."

She banded her arm across her body as her teeth chattered. It was almost fully light now. "I'm fine. I don't have anything to change into anyway."

He tapped his bag.

She frowned. "You have clothes for me in there?"

He nodded.

"Won't they be soaked?"

He shook his head. "Waterproof backpack. They might be a bit damp if it leaked, but overall, they should be dryer than what you're wearing."

"Thank you." Her shoulders started to shake. "You think my mother was somehow involved in all this, don't you?" Those soft green eyes met his. "You think her death might not have been an accident."

"How'd she die?"

"She went for a night out with some of her old school friends. I was home with my grandmother apparently—a couple of months old. Mum stumbled into the street and was run down. They never found the driver."

Suspicious. "Could have been an accident."

"Could have been murder." Row's expression turned faraway.

They crested the ridge using a game trail and keeping low to the ground even though they were surrounded by thick bushes. Over the rise, he stopped in a small clearing.

"Let's change here. Nothing we can do about your boots, but I have dry wool socks. Do you want some privacy?"

She snorted and started stripping off her gear. "You've already seen more of me than any other human outside my GP."

He frowned. Did that mean she was shy? Or not? As she tugged the wet fleece and T-shirt from her body and wrung it out, he figured that was a no.

He dug for her clothes while she sat gingerly on a log and eased off her boots, then peeled off her damp jeans and panties. She sat there shivering and naked, and he shook himself out of his distraction and located her dry clothes. Handed them across and tried to keep his gaze above her mouth.

She tugged on the sports bra and shimmied into panties that were plain black but just as awesome as that red lace from last night—apparently, his gaze had wandered. Then she pulled on the pair of pants he'd picked up yesterday and a wool undershirt. He didn't have a spare fleece for her, but he had one of his own, so he handed it over.

"Thank you." The socks came last, and she grimaced as she slipped her feet back into the wet boots.

"The wool should dry as the boots do."

She shook out her hair and redid the braid, rapid style. Frowned up at him. "You aren't getting changed?"

He shook his head. "I want to find a place to wash up first."

He indicated the blood smeared on his shirt.

She nodded. Her expression grew serious. "You're sure you weren't seriously hurt?"

He stuffed her wet things into a plastic bag he'd taken from the hotel that morning, using his injured arm to prove a point. Tucked the gun into his waistband and the knife in the side of the pack. "A scratch. Hopefully we can find some antibiotics or alcohol today."

"Well, I could certainly use a drink."

He laughed. "For that too."

She climbed to her feet, and he offered her a bottle of water which she drank from and handed back.

"I thought we'd be safe once we crossed the border," she admitted quietly.

His eyes held hers. "So did I."

She twisted her lips. "I lost my passport in the river."

He'd figured she probably had. Thankfully, neither of them were flying out of Africa on a commercial airliner.

He set off through the forest.

"What's the plan?" She hurried after him.

"We head to Beira. It's a bit of a shithole for various reasons and therefore dangerous. It was hammered by a hurricane. As the city is a stronghold for the official opposition, the government didn't give it any money for repairs afterwards."

"Seriously? Is that how democracy is supposed to work?"

Kurt shrugged. "It's not uncommon. Why worry about making the people who will never vote for you happy?"

"I can never figure out why people get into politics if it's not to help society in general, but I suppose that shows my naivety." She shrugged.

"Right now, we have other things to worry about." Too many things.

"Why Beira?"

"It's closer than Maputo by several hundred miles and has a major port. If I can contact my people, they can hopefully arrange a boat. We just have to get there."

"We're in deep shit, aren't we?"

"Seriously deep shit," he admitted.

"If they are after you and not me, what will they do with me if they catch us?"

Kurt glanced at her sideways, unwilling to paint the picture with ugly words.

She didn't need him to. "They'll rape then kill me." She swallowed. "Well, at least my first sexual experience was wonderful and positive. I'll hang on to that if things get bad."

He frowned, caught her arm. "What?"

She averted her head. "Let's keep going."

He held on to her as she tried to move past him. "Row?"

He stared into those changeable eyes that looked slightly embarrassed now.

"You seriously couldn't tell?"

"Tell what?" Shock sank into his bones. "No."

He let her go, and she strode on ahead of him. He shook himself out of his stupor and the unexpected but all-consuming guilt.

"You should have told me."

"Why?" she countered. "You'd probably have stopped."

"Damned right I would have stopped." Not a lot surprised him, but this cut him off at the knees. He'd known she was way too young and inexperienced for him, but he'd never imagined... "Your first time is supposed to be special."

"It *was* special." She turned and those brows sank into a fierce frown. "I don't know what it meant to you, but it was special to me. Better than fumbling around with some jerk in my college dorm. A jerk who told his friends he'd already had sex with me even when it wasn't true."

Kurt narrowed his gaze and clenched his jaw. "Give me his name, and I'll make sure he never walks again."

She shot a feral grin over her shoulder as she walked away.

He kicked his own ass and caught up with her. Swung her around. Put a hand on each of her upper arms to keep her in one place and stared down into those suddenly wary eyes. "It was special to me too, very special. But I'm hardly—"

She threw her arms up in dismay, breaking his hold. "If you're going to go on about how *old* you are and how your horrible, wrinkled body shouldn't be touching my young, nubile virgin one, I might scream." She hissed it instead. Keeping the volume low because they were still on the run from violent men who wanted them dead.

He laughed at her words and her pissy response. "My body isn't wrinkly."

"I *know*!"

"It enjoyed the hell out of touching your young nubile one." He refused to think about the virgin part.

She laughed. "I know that too."

Had he hurt her? He tried to remember any telltale signs or indications but couldn't recall anything that wasn't pleasure. The sex had been good. He frowned. For him anyway. And she'd definitely orgasmed more than once and had taken the lead both times.

Because she wanted to lose her virginity?

He chewed on his lip. It was her business who she let touch her. But he felt as if it was something he should have known before they'd messed around. Except when was the last time it had even crossed his mind to ask?

"How could you possibly still be a virgin?"

She tilted her head. Tone frosty. "What do you mean?"

"I mean the guys in England must be fucking blind not to be knocking on your door and begging to date you and then treating you like a fucking princess."

"I *know*, right?" She grinned and touched his face, rising up on tiptoes to kiss him unexpectedly. It was so carefree it took him completely out of the moment, out of their situation.

He kissed her back, deeply, before he reminded himself where he was and what they were running from.

Maybe he was being an idiot and needed to chill. Not take things so damned seriously. It wasn't as if this thing between them was going to lead anywhere. They'd been thrown together by fate, and if they escaped unscathed, they'd be torn apart by reality. As much as he liked her, the idea of a long-distance relationship didn't appeal.

He was too old for that shit.

But he did really like her, this virgin-turned-siren who'd turned his world on its head, not to mention saving his life. For now, he wanted to enjoy whatever they could salvage out of their time together.

It was no one else's business anyway.

He scanned the forest around them as they walked on. Antelope tracks in the dirt and plenty of different bird species flitting around the trees. He needed to keep up his awareness so they didn't walk headlong into another group of mercenaries coming from the other direction. Bush was growing thicker, and he figured the most obvious direction they'd take would be northeast to the major road then south to Maputo.

He'd bet money there would be some sort of settlement or farm if they cut straight east. Perhaps someone would have a car they could borrow. Or steal. Or they could simply walk out, as long as they didn't meet any hostiles along the way.

Mozambique was dangerous in places, but he was pretty sure this area was relatively safe and stable, and he was armed now. It was a hell of a long walk to Beira. They could be on the road for days—but it might be better than getting stopped by the cops.

"Hey, Row."

"Yes, Kurt?"

His name sounded good on her lips. He turned to meet her amused gaze. "After we get out of this alive..."

She cocked her head to one side. Cute as a fucking button.

"I'd like to take you to bed again and make you scream. In a good way."

Those eyes widened and lashes blinked as her lips tried unsuccessfully to suppress a smile. "Well now."

"That's all you have to say?"

"Deal." She grinned.

16

"What the hell happened to your car? Did you leave half of it at home?" Ryan Sullivan gazed derisively at the electric SMART car Jordan had unfolded himself out of.

"Shrank in the wash." Jordan had dropped his own vehicle with the dealer to get a quote on fixing the damage.

Cowboy narrowed his gaze at him. "You okay?"

Emotion blindsided Jordan. Christ. "Not really. You?"

"Not really," Cowboy admitted. "Did you find what you were looking for in Africa?"

Jordan glanced sharply at his teammate. He wasn't even allowed to say they'd been in Africa, let alone who they'd been looking for. No point lying though. He gave the slightest shake of his head.

Ryan's mouth twisted. "Figured."

An attractive woman with long dark hair arrived, got out of her vehicle, and strode into the compound.

Jordan frowned. "Who's that?"

Ryan's eyes gleamed with amusement. "Ah, you haven't met the FNGs. Behold, the first woman to get through Selection and NOTS, Operator Meghan Donnelly."

Jordan knew a woman had passed but hadn't seen her in person. "She any good?"

"Nope." Ryan Sullivan shook his head and watched the woman head into the building. "She's fucking brilliant."

Jordan nodded. She'd have to be. "Montana requested her for Gold Team." His friend's name hit his tongue with a heavy rasp.

"Yep." Cowboy's voice got rougher too. Another long pause that Cowboy filled. The guy didn't do silence unless it was mandatory. "I think he'd have gotten a kick out of her. I do, although, I don't think she likes me very much."

"Do *not* hit on her."

Cowboy grinned. "I don't date co-workers." He drew a cross on his heart.

The mood turned sour again as they headed inside the building for the morning briefing. "I'll see you in there. I want a quick word with Ackers first."

Cowboy shot him a glance that said he knew Jordan was keeping information from him and he didn't like it. Jordan didn't have a choice.

He'd woken at 3:43 a.m. and spent the early hours searching the news in Zimbabwe. He'd read hundreds of media and social media reports about the accident—zero eyewitnesses, no survivors.

The authorities were still in the recovery stage of the investigation, finding and identifying human remains—a situation complicated by the large number of predators and scavengers in the park where the aircraft had come down.

Even the thought made him want to puke.

Then he'd done a search on Bjorn Anders and discovered something that had startled the hell out of him.

Inside, he split off from Ryan and headed to the admin area of HRT.

Maddie Goodwin was Ackers' personal assistant and the unofficial mother of all HRT personnel. The recent deaths had hit her hard.

"Can I see him?"

Her usually smiling eyes were bloodshot. She picked up the phone and stuck the receiver to her ear. "Jordan would like a word." Her eyes raised to his. "Go right in."

Jordan headed into the corner office and shut the door behind him.

"There's no news. Red Team isn't even on the ground yet." Ackers brushed a weary hand over his mustache.

"Someone tried to run me off the road last night."

Ackers' eyes widened. "You think you were targeted?"

Jordan gave him a tight nod.

"Hurek?" He leaned back in his seat. "Doesn't make any sense."

"No, it doesn't, but I also discovered the guy Kurt stayed on to talk to was murdered in Harare yesterday."

Ackers leaned forward and started typing on his computer. "I'll be damned." He looked up. "Any idea what's going on?"

Jordan shook his head. "Unless Kurt discovered something after I left, and they think I know it too."

"Do you?"

Jordan shook his head. "We spoke briefly when I was in the Frankfurt airport. The connection was terrible. I could barely make out anything he was saying—but perhaps they don't know that."

"You told the task force?"

Jordan nodded.

"I want you moved into a safe—"

"I'm not going anywhere." Jordan straightened.

Ackers gave him an expressionless stare that had gotten him his way a thousand times, but Jordan wasn't backing down.

"Firstly, I've just gotten home, and the last thing I want to do is camp out in some hotel."

Ackers went to speak over him, but Jordan plowed on.

"Secondly, why don't we use it? Set up electronic surveillance all around my property and on my vehicle. The fact I live in a sparsely populated area works in our favor. Rather than running, let's invite whoever is doing this in and see what the hell they have to tell us when we catch them."

Ackers propped his elbows on his desk. "What if they put a bullet in you before we can grab them?"

"They could do that any time I leave the base, boss. I'll be careful. I'll vary up my routine. Local cops can escort me home—I don't want to worry the guys."

Ackers dragged a frustrated hand through his thick gray hair. "We're stretched thin with this serial killer hunt and now this plane crash investigation."

Jordan knew it. The serial killer who operated on the dark web, auctioned off exactly how his victims suffered for the highest bidders to watch while they jerked off. He'd not only murdered innocent victims but deliberately set a bomb that had killed Scotty and injured many more. "Those things both take priority. Let's talk to HQ. If they set up enough cameras around my place, then I'll have all the warning I need to protect myself. I have a space that can double as an impromptu safe room if I need it, and we could have the local police at the other end of the alarm for a rapid response. I'll be as safe as I can be, and I have plenty of firepower at home."

Grief swelled again, and Jordan forced it away. "Kurt *must* have been onto something before he died. We need to track down everywhere he went and everyone he spoke to after I left."

Ackers narrowed his gaze thoughtfully. "Did Armstrong agree with how you want to handle this?"

Jordan nodded. "It makes sense to try to draw these scumbags out. If Hurek has people doing his dirty work on American soil and they're willing to go after an HRT operator...no one is safe. We need to catch them."

Ackers raised a bushy brow in acknowledgment.

Jordan cleared his throat. "How did his daughter take the news?"

Ackers looked down at his desk. "Exactly the way you'd expect."

A burning sensation started behind his breastbone. God.

Ackers checked his watch and rose to his feet. "You can't talk about any of this with anyone else on HRT."

Jordan bristled. "I know that." They'd been over it yesterday despite Jordan's objections.

"But I'm not sure you realize how hard it's going to be."

Misery welled up inside him. "I have a pretty good idea."

Ackers nodded. "I'll call TacOps after the briefing, arrange for that surveillance myself. Assuming Armstrong doesn't want you in DC, I want you to spend your time trying to piece together Kurt's last twenty-four hours. You can use the office next door." He inclined his head. "But it might not be a bad idea to head up to SIOC on a regular basis to see what they're up to. In case they aren't sharing everything."

Jordan nodded. "Understood."

Ackers rested his hand on Jordan's shoulder as he walked past him toward the door. "Glad you made it back okay, son, but watch your back. I don't want to lose you too."

———

Rowena followed Kurt, trying not to worry about the very real danger they faced. Suddenly, a kudu raised its head then pranced away, the stripes on its back like dripping white paint running down its side. *Crap.* She put her hand on her heart. She wasn't sure who'd been the more startled.

They were skirting a large mountain on the right of them, and her thighs ached from the exercise even though she was used to walking up and down steep hills back home in the Ironbridge Gorge. They'd seen a large sable antelope earlier, its magnificent deep brown coat gleaming in the sunlight, hooked horns like twin scimitars on its head.

She hoped her uncle and cousins weren't too concerned about her. Hopefully, they'd just think she'd gone off investigating something—assuming Kurt was correct about the police not linking her to Bjorn's murder. She'd prefer Uncle Gamba to think she was irresponsible rather than in danger—or that she was a killer.

She checked the time on the ever-reliable Breitling. Nearly three p.m. They'd been walking for hours, and she was starting to get hungry but refused to be the first one to crack. Birds sang overhead. Frogs chorused nonstop. Insects buzzed but not as many as near the Falls. Malaria was less of a risk here because of the elevation but could be more of a problem the lower they went and closer to the Mozambique coast.

"Do you have any malaria pills with you?"

"I have about a week's supply of Malarone in my pack. We'll each take one tomorrow depending on how far we travel today. Good reminder." He wiped his hand over his brow, a light sweat creating a sheen.

At least she wasn't the only one feeling the burn.

Earlier, they'd found a small stream, and Kurt had washed up then changed clothes. He'd placed the bloody shirt and trousers under a rock in the stream and left them there.

In case they brought a K9 unit, he'd said.

She hadn't liked the idea of littering, but the thought they might be tracked using dogs freaked her out. She'd been on high alert ever since.

"How many miles do you think we need to cover before we can be sure they aren't tracking us?"

He shot her a measuring look. "If Gilder's involved probably about four thousand."

Tears smarted against her eyelids. That seemed like an insurmountable distance over which to evade capture and way too much power in the hands of one man.

"Once we're debriefed under oath, he can't do an awful lot to stop the information we have getting to the right people. Whether it means anything is something else entirely. And whether or not we can prove it…"

Because the photo linking Anders to Cavanagh was gone, and the one she'd found in Anders' office proved nothing except she'd been at the murder scene. It might indicate a friendship, or it might be a one-off meeting that none of them even remembered.

Seemed unlikely considering the fact she and Kurt were being chased, and Bjorn had hidden the thing and was now dead. It suggested the men had done something together that wasn't legal. Or maybe they were still aiding their friend, the terrorist who'd kidnapped innocent Westerners and ransomed them off for cash. She'd read one hostage had been repeatedly gang raped and knew it was a definite possibility should she be captured. It was a tactic as old as hominids to dominate and suppress women, keeping them firmly in their place.

Cockroaches.

Row pushed the possibility out of her mind. It was a fear women always carried with them and something she fervently hoped she never experienced.

"I want to see about getting you into protective custody until Gilder's arrested."

Protective custody? For how long? In the US? Or back in the UK? She didn't like the sound of that. Not at all.

She didn't want to die either.

"Assuming Gilder's involved." She picked at the dry skin of her thumb cuticle. "I'm selfishly hoping he's not because the other two, Spartan and Hurek, as scary as they may be, don't have the global reach of the billionaire."

"I'm hoping the same."

She looked up at the sky through a gap in the branches and realized they'd been keeping beneath the shade of trees and weaving through thick scrub all day. Avoiding being spotted by satellites wherever possible.

Kurt definitely believed Gilder might be involved.

She shivered again. How did you outrun someone who had a network of satellites and who controlled communication networks around the world?

One step and one second at a time.

"Water?" Kurt stopped and pulled out their last remaining full bottle. Held it out to her.

She took a sip and passed it back.

"You need more than that."

"What happens when we run out," she argued.

"We'll be able to refill as soon as it rains."

She stared at the crystalline blue sky. "Not looking like that's going to happen anytime soon."

He looked around. Pointed. "There's a stream ahead. Drink. You have to stay hydrated."

She took a long swallow. The refreshing liquid cooled her throat. She passed it back to him, and he followed suit.

"Do you still have the burner phone?"

He nodded. Wiped his mouth. "Yeah. Once we're back in civilization I'll fire it up and call for assistance. Then we lie low until someone comes up with an exfil plan."

She felt like she was in a movie and this wasn't her life anymore. At least she got to be in it with a handsome leading man who was capable, considerate, and sexy as hell.

He pointed to a line of trees in the distance. "Let's go that way to fill up the bottles."

The canopy was getting thinner and thinner.

They headed down to a clear, bubbling stream, and he filled the bottles while she relieved herself downstream.

As she rejoined him the sound of a dog barking in the distance had them both going motionless. He tilted his head to listen. "Probably a farm dog. Doesn't sound like a bloodhound."

She released a tense breath when the barking stopped. What did a bloodhound sound like? She hoped she never found out.

They followed the stream for a time, stripping off their

footwear and rolling up their trousers. Wading or stepping from rock to rock, careful not to slip. The last thing they needed was a twisted ankle. They were able to do that for almost a mile before the stream turned into a fast-flowing river. They drank again and topped up the bottles, headed east.

She rubbed her neck, wished she could wash her hair because her scalp felt dry and itchy after her swim in the muddy river.

The fact that she was worried about her hair rather than her life told her she was an idiot. She rolled her eyes at herself. "Tell me about your daughter."

He looked at her then, the way someone assessed a threat, which startled the shit out of her.

Then he grimaced. "Sorry. I tend not to talk about her much. Not even with the people I work with. I guess I see it as protecting her, but maybe it's just habit. Like I said yesterday"—it felt like a decade ago now—"she's twenty-three. Graduated valedictorian from her degree at Virginia Tech last summer. Started her post-graduate program in the Fall. Smart as a whip."

"You sound proud." She wrapped her arms around herself, unaccountably cold despite the beautiful day.

"I am proud, but I can't take the credit." He clenched his jaw. "I wasn't there much for her as a child. Her mother left me after I joined the FBI. Said she'd thought I'd do something where I was home more after leaving the Army. Decided she hated the FBI without really giving it a chance." His expression twisted. "And that's not fair to Jenn either. I was an adrenaline junkie." He laughed softly and looked around. "Probably still am. I loved my wife, and I adored my child, but I was also happy to let Jenn do all the heavy lifting when it came to parenting while I went off and played soldier—at the expense of her career aspirations."

"Sounds like you have regrets."

"I do. Lots. Jenn's an amazing woman, but I would suck at most 9-to-5 jobs, so the marriage was probably always going to fail. Just a shame Daisy was caught in the middle."

"Do you still love her? Jenn that is? I mean, *obviously* you love your daughter."

He stared at her for a long moment, those dark eyes examining her face and seeing things she hadn't meant to reveal. She didn't know why it mattered if he was in love with someone else. It was no business of hers just because they'd had sex.

He shook his head. "I did love her. For a very long time, I did even though I didn't admit it to myself." A soft smile touched his lips. "I don't love her anymore."

A knot formed in her throat, and she couldn't speak. Thankfully he didn't seem to notice.

"With Daisy being in Virginia rather than Colorado, I was able to see her much more regularly the last few years. When she was little, Jenn wasn't great at following the visitation rules, and as my job was so demanding, I always felt like she had final say given she was doing most of the work. I should have pushed harder though sometimes. I guess I was terrified it was Daisy who didn't want to see me, rather than Jenn laying down the law, which she is exceptionally good at." He checked his watch and pressed his lips together into a grim line. "Daisy was supposed to come to Quantico and visit me this weekend after I got back. I hate to think what she's going through. And my team..." He cleared his throat. "We already lost one man this year. On New Year's Day. A bomb."

"Oh my God, I saw that on the news. It was horrible. I'm so sorry." A serial killer had set a trap for the FBI and blown up members of the Hostage Rescue Team. Her mouth went dry at the realization of how dangerous his job was.

"We were lucky we didn't lose more. I was in Africa, obviously." He sent her a sideways look in reference to seeing her at the Falls over New Year. "I spoke with my commander and to the widow of the man who died. I wasn't allowed to contact anyone else, which pissed me off but also made sense. We are trying to keep this investigation on the down low. But I know the team was hit hard, and I wasn't there for them. Now they probably believe I'm dead too..." His jaw clenched as he looked away.

It sucked that all those people would suffer until the truth came out, but at least Kurt hadn't been on that plane. More than two hundred other souls had been.

All those families devastated.

She knew what that felt like and wished she could change what had happened. But wishes were useless. They had to figure out how to get to safety.

Kurt took another deep drink and offered her the bottle. She took a quick sip. Kurt rubbed his head, and she noticed twin red patches rode his cheekbones. She reached out and touched his forehead. "You're burning up."

"I'm fine." His eyes were a little glassy.

He wasn't fine.

"Stop." She tugged the pack from his back and started peeling his shirt up.

"I'm not sure this is the time, darlin', but I'm game if you are."

"Funny." She helped him shrug off the right sleeve and bunched the material up onto his shoulder so she could examine his wound.

The gash was ragged, and blood had crusted into a thick black scab. The edges were red and inflamed, and there was yellow pus gathering at one edge.

"We need to get this cleaned out."

He took a look at the wound. Pulled a face. "I'm pissed with myself that I don't have a better first-aid kit with us."

"You have any painkillers?"

He shook his head. "My colleague left the day before I did. He had everything in his luggage. I had malaria pills left over from last time in the backpack and told him I was good."

She'd seen him with another man at the restaurant at the Falls. A tall guy with a Michael Fassbender vibe. "You have any money left? Perhaps we can buy some topical antibiotics."

He wiped the sweat from his brow though the day wasn't that

hot. "I have about a hundred US and about fifty dollars' worth of *meticais*."

Not a lot, but the cost of living here was a lot lower than back home.

"I also have credit cards, but that false identity is burned now they found us at the hotel. We can use one as a last resort but only if we are prepared to move."

She slid the pack onto her back.

"I can carry that." He tried to take it, but she shied away from him.

"I can take my turn. You need to conserve your energy until we can find you some treatment."

He rolled his eyes, but the fact he didn't fight her told her he was in worse shape than she'd realized. He pulled his shirt back on, carefully rolling it over the wound.

"Come on." She tried to keep her tone upbeat, but his hand was hot in hers.

They walked for another hour until the sun began to descend in the sky.

Kurt stumbled, and she gripped his arm and helped him stay upright.

He clutched his forehead. "Fuck. I'm sorry, Row."

Emotions clogged her throat. Fear chief amongst them. "None of this is your fault. Don't you dare be sorry."

"I'm supposed to be the professional. I'm supposed to be looking after you."

"Unless you can magically wish away germs, none of this is your fault. And you were shot protecting me."

"Felled by microbes." He caught her waistband. Held her for a moment in a hug that was pure comfort.

She squeezed him back, worry seeping into the edges of her mind. If she couldn't get him to safety or at least find some sort of medical treatment soon, he was going to be in serious trouble. She couldn't carry him.

She wasn't strong enough.

She'd have to go for help.

They stumbled onwards, him using her to help steady himself, signaling exactly how poorly he was feeling. They both spotted the buildings at the same time and froze at the edge of the tree line.

He moved them back into the shadows. Crouched. She copied him.

He stared at the place for ten minutes without speaking. Eventually he said, "Looks like some sort of citrus farm."

They'd seen one man get into a truck and drive off.

"It's not harvest season right now, and they all look done for the day."

"We could search for a first-aid kit."

Lines cut between his brows. "They might have security on the buildings, or they might employ guard dogs."

"We need help."

He nodded. Conceded. "Let's wait for dusk, and I'll head across the field. See if I can access soap and hot water or a vehicle. I'll signal you when it's safe."

"Nope. Not on your Nelly."

He laughed quietly. "What?"

"It's an expression."

"I figured. What's it mean?"

"It means we're both going. Together. I'm not sitting here like some delicate flower while you keel over halfway across that field."

He smiled, but it didn't reach his eyes. His cheeks were flushed, but the skin around his eyes was pale and drawn. "If the danger is there, then they'll take me and forget about you."

"You don't know that for sure."

"You're right. I don't. But I can sure as hell hope." He looked away and then back. "If we both walk across that field, I do know we are both needlessly exposed and the people who are after me can pick us off one at a time."

"*If* they're there." Her breath shuddered on an exhale. "Look, I know you want to protect me, but the bottom line is we're both in trouble here. We need one another. Now you have an infection, it's even more important we stick together." She gripped his shirt. "And I'd rather be with you facing that danger than here safe alone. Whatever happens. I'd rather be with you."

17

E motion punched him in the throat. Damn if she didn't make him feel like an ass for trying to do the right thing. He sank back against the trunk of a large tree, hidden from the sheds and barns but where he could watch the farm and the forest around them.

"Take off the pack. We'll rest until dark."

She did so, and he tugged her down until she sat between his spread knees.

She leaned against him and slowly began to relax. They'd been on the go for twelve hours straight, feeding off adrenaline with little in the way of food.

So much for planning. He'd relaxed his guard and almost gotten them both killed.

He had protein bars in his pack, but he was rationing them.

She hadn't complained or whined, not even once, and he couldn't help comparing her to his team who were among the best of the best.

She'd held up pretty damned well.

He rested his fevered face against her hair. Held her in his arms even though the one throbbed like a bitch and felt as if the muscle there had turned to hot lead.

How could something so small set his system into overdrive? He understood the biology and knew thousands of men had been killed from infection following wounds gained in battle. He couldn't afford not to take an injury seriously, but dammit, he hated being the weak link. Thank God he'd had all his vaccinations.

Rowena's hair smelled like the river and like someone who'd finished a good sweaty hike. He preferred it a thousand times over any French perfume. He wanted to nuzzle the delicate skin beneath her ear, but he also knew he shouldn't. Whatever their current circumstances, Rowena Smith was way too young for him.

He knew where this hangup came from. His father had dumped his mother for a trophy wife when he was a teenager, and he'd despised the man from then on. His mom would turn in her grave at the idea of Kurt dating a much younger woman.

Or would she?

Perhaps he needed to stop imagining her judgmental reaction. It wasn't his fault his father was an asshole. Nor Rowena's. Neither of them were cheaters.

He pushed the thoughts aside. He barely had the strength to keep his eyes open, let alone anything else. No point torturing himself. He needed to conserve his strength.

He needed to save them both.

Slowly, Rowena's breathing settled into a steady rhythm, and he knew the instant she fell asleep.

The shadows were lengthening, and the fever made it feel as if his head were glowing like a neon bulb. His mouth was parched, but he didn't want to risk waking Rowena by pulling out a water bottle. Not yet. He kept his awareness wide—for pursuers or people simply walking through the woods.

Frogs croaked incessantly, and a couple of klipspringers pranced past like baby goats. He was grateful this wasn't a stronghold for big predators because he couldn't fight off a kitten, let alone a lion right now—but leopards would be around. *Shit.* He edged the pack closer so he could reach the knife if needed. He eased the handgun out of his waistband and put it on the ground beside him. He didn't want to shoot anything and bring unwanted attention to them, but he didn't want to be supper either.

They needed to get out of the mountains and head to the city. But if they were stopped and asked for papers along the way…

He couldn't risk it.

Didn't have a choice.

Stuck between the proverbial rock and a hard place.

The burner phone was tempting, especially while fighting this fever, but he knew Gilder was involved, and he knew the billionaire would be using all his resources to track him down for his own illicit reasons. If it was Gilder and Leo Spartan who were after him, they'd already proven they'd stop at nothing to prevent Kurt from getting home and revealing what he knew about their association with Hurek.

What if it went deeper than a friendship from thirty years ago?

What other secrets were they desperate to conceal? Aside from the bombing of a civilian aircraft, which was a pretty giant fucking secret anyone would kill to keep.

Rowena's hair tickled his nose, and he smoothed it down and then smiled at how relaxed she appeared in sleep.

If someone had told him two days ago that he'd be here cuddled up with Rowena Smith, a sexy, twenty-seven-year-old British national, or that they'd have become intimate last night he'd have thought they were out of their minds.

The situation had come out of left field, completely unexpected—both being on the run and having sex. The fact he was her first was something he needed to get over. What was virginity anyway, except the choices Rowena made about when and with whom she had sex?

Wasn't he all about choice?

Damned right, he was.

He was grateful, not at being the first, but at being chosen at all.

He was a damned lucky guy.

His mind wandered to Bjorn and then to his team members back at Quantico. Had they caught the guy who'd killed Scotty and all those other people? Were Gold Team on a different op now? Were they safe?

Was his daughter crying over his death?

Remorse ate at him as dusk folded into darkness, but there was nothing he could do to change things. Not yet. Especially not when he felt as weak as a newborn.

He drifted off into a light doze. After an hour or so, Rowena jolted awake in his arms.

He squeezed her gently. "Shush. I've got you."

She relaxed instantly, which made him feel like a fucking superhero when in reality he was a liability. She snuggled in for another moment and then rolled her shoulders and crawled onto all fours to turn to face him, slowly blinking awake.

"Pass me some water, would you?"

She gave him a bottle and took another for herself. "I'm going to assume we can refill these from a tap over there."

He glanced at the farmstead, wishing his head wasn't pounding like the inside of a drum at a Springsteen concert. There were lights on in some of the buildings but nothing that looked like a house or as if people were working. Not from this angle, anyway. Who knew what lay beyond the massive shed.

He finished the water and pulled a fleece from his pack, easing into it as he began shivering. Chills. He slipped the gun into his waistband and the knife into the side pocket of the pack. Pushed himself up off the ground. Clawed for stability as the world rushed around inside his head.

Rowena grabbed his good arm. "Are you okay?"

He leaned his head back against the rough bark and stared up through the leaves and branches at the night sky. "I've been better."

She followed his gaze. "Can he see us? Even in the dark?"

Kurt knew who she meant. Gilder. He was a scary adversary—a real James Bond villain.

"Some satellites can see in the dark." Many could, but he didn't want to worry her more than she already was. "Depends if he happens to have one positioned directly above us at this exact moment in time." He stared upwards for a full minute. He didn't see anything with the naked eye, which was something at least.

"Well, we can't stay here forever."

Patience clearly wasn't her strong suit, but it could be taught—if she wanted to sign up for HRT and try out to be a sniper.

He rolled his eyes at himself.

"Let's head to the buildings. We'll look for somewhere with a small office area. See if we can find a first-aid kit or a stove or microwave where we can boil water and clean the shit out of this arm."

Rowena put her arm around his waist but that pressed the handgun into his spine. He shifted and pulled it out, placed it in his fleece pocket even though it wasn't ideal. She wrapped her arm around him again.

It felt amazing.

He wanted to ask her questions. About her life, her job, her friends. Now wasn't the right time. His head was thick and fuzzy, and he had to concentrate on where he placed his feet so he didn't stumble over the uneven surface.

They walked in silence across the field, and he was grateful for Rowena's help which was beyond humbling for a man who'd overcome so many obstacles and passed so many tests in his career. To be brought low from such a minor wound was embarrassing. Not his fault, but it pissed him off.

At the edge of the main barn, he used the wall to prop himself upright as she scooted forward and peeked around the corner into the large space.

"I can't see anything. It's too dark."

He pulled out his flashlight and handed it to her. She shone it around the interior.

"Empty," she whispered.

Kurt eased around the corner looking for a telltale red or green box as Rowena tracked the beam across the walls, but there was nothing inside except a large tractor.

"Check inside the machine." He nodded toward the vehicle, and Rowena dashed across the concrete floor, climbing up the steps and opening the driver's door.

She disappeared inside but re-emerged a few moments later with a triumphant grin on her face, waving a small green box.

She climbed down and closed the door with a quiet bang that made him wince.

"Sorry," she whispered before scurrying back to his side. "Let's see if we can find a small kitchen area so we can get you cleaned up."

Kurt nodded and fought off another wave of dizziness.

She caught his good arm and pulled him along. He hadn't felt this out of it since he'd been best man for one of his old Army buddies about a decade ago. He hadn't been drunk since.

They walked around the corner, and there was a shipping container obviously being used as an office. Rowena tried the door, but it was locked.

"Let's go this way." He pointed. "I suspect they employ seasonal workers who'll need to be fed, so there has to be a kitchen somewhere."

They struck out in the next two buildings but found what they were looking for in the third. It was open on three sides and looked like a canteen with a sink and refrigerator over at one end and two long trestle tables running down the middle.

Rowena dashed away with the flashlight and filled the tea kettle with water. She checked the cupboard. "Oh, my God. They have Tetley!" Her eyes shone as if she'd found a great treasure. "Do you think they'll mind if I steal a teabag?"

"Hopefully, they never find out." He smiled reluctantly and slumped heavily onto a bench. "Flick the light switch, would you?" He doubted the bulb over the sink area would be any more noticeable than the erratically moving beam from the flashlight. It looked like a Jedi battle was going on in here, but he was too exhausted to take command of even something as simple as a flashlight.

She found the switch and slipped the flashlight into her back pocket.

He opened up the first-aid kit, relieved to find Band-Aids and a tube of antibiotic ointment. He shrugged out of his fleece and shirt, grateful for the cool breeze.

Rowena placed a tall glass of water in front of him, and he downed it in two seconds flat. She got him another one and filled the bottles for the next stage of their journey. He downed that glass as well, and Rowena filled it again. He hoped to hell neither of them caught anything from the water they'd been drinking, but they didn't have time to stop and boil every drop.

"Did you find any acetaminophen in the kit?"

He shook his head. She frowned and then checked under the sink, squeaking with delight when she came up with a second, much bigger, medical kit.

She placed it on the table in front of him and undid the clips. The bottle of painkillers looked as amazing as any uncut diamond. His hands shook as he fought with the lid.

After a few moments, Rowena took the bottle from him and twisted the cap down and off. She handed him two red tablets, and he swallowed them with relief and another swig of water.

He slipped the bottle into his pocket.

Next, he examined the furrow on his arm, which was festering nicely.

He poked the swollen, hot skin. Winced as yellow pus oozed out of the edges. *Ugh.*

"Stop touching it with dirty fingers." Rowena sounded like she was scolding a naughty child.

She was worried about him.

He couldn't blame her. Her white knight had turned into an

anchor around her neck, dragging her down and holding her under.

She scrubbed her hands with soap and water. The kettle boiled, and she took a pack of gauze from the first-aid kit and soaked it with boiling water. Then she beckoned him to the sink.

He stood wearily, legs a little wobbly. He needed to shake off this funk. Hopefully, the drugs would help calm the fever, and he'd be able to think more clearly.

He winced as she pressed the cloth to his arm, holding back a hiss as she cleaned out the wound. *Fuck.*

The redness was all around the two-inch long gash.

Her eyes turned serious. Expression pinched.

He tucked an escaped strand of hair behind her ear. "Don't worry. It'll be okay."

Her mouth curved, unconvinced. "I was thinking how easily the bullet could have hit you or me somewhere fatal. They didn't seem to care about keeping us alive."

She pressed her lips together as if holding back tears, and he raised her chin and kissed her. She sank into him and returned the kiss, made him feel like the luckiest man in the world. Apparently, he'd have to be dead not to respond to this woman. She pulled back, swallowed her very obvious fears about what had happened and what might still happen, and instead washed the rest of his arm with a hot soaked cloth.

He gritted his teeth.

"Sorry. It has to be done."

"Yes, ma'am."

Her eyes flashed at him, and he suppressed a grin.

Once she was convinced the wound was as clean as possible under the circumstances, she let him sit, then she dried it off with another piece of sterile gauze before slathering on ointment. Then she placed a large Band-Aid over the wound.

He knew it might not completely solve the infection issue, but it was a damned good start.

He carefully pulled on his shirt and slipped the gun back in the waistband of his pants, packed up the smaller first-aid kit, augmenting it with some supplies from the larger one, which they put back under the sink. Overheated now and a little bit woozy, he stuffed the fleece in the straps of the backpack and shouldered it. It was his turn to carry the load.

He tossed the litter in the garbage as Row quickly finished her cup of tea and washed the mug and placed it back in the cabinet.

Satisfied the room was almost exactly as they'd found it except for the garbage and missing supplies, they turned off the lights.

"What next?" she asked.

He heard the noise of a footfall on dirt a split second before a flashlight blinded his eyes.

Fuck.

He'd let his guard down. Forgotten they were nose-deep in shit.

He stepped in front of Rowena as he raised his arm to cover his face.

"Who's there? What the hell are you doing on my property? Stealing?"

The voice was female and angry. He could make out the vague outline of a shotgun propped on the arm holding the light.

"I'm so sorry. We didn't mean to trespass." Rowena stepped out from behind him even as he shot her a glare. Did she think this was a game?

Fear and anger rushed through him. She was going to get herself killed, and he didn't think he could live with that.

"My boyfriend and I were hiking in the hills when Joe took a fall into the river, showing off even though he'd never admit it."

Kurt scowled, in character as idiot Joe, but also for real.

"I fell in trying to help him, and we lost some of our supplies, including the map and compass. I tried to run on and catch them, but the river was flowing too fast."

"Rainy season. Of course it's too fast." The woman sounded less angry though, caught up in Rowena's story.

"Joe was stabbed by a branch, although he didn't think to

mention it until hours later." Rowena rolled her eyes dramatically. He didn't think she was faking her nerves as her voice shook. "W-we got lost and couldn't figure out how to get back to the place where we'd left the hire car. I think we crossed the border, although Joe thinks we didn't."

Rowena was either brilliant or going to get them both killed.

"Could you tell us where we are, please?"

"As in, what country?" From the tone of the snort the woman obviously considered them both idiots.

"Yes."

He slouched against the table and tried to look more like an insurance salesman than a Hostage Rescue Team leader. He didn't want to draw his weapon and shoot an innocent woman. Wasn't a hundred percent convinced he could hit the barn door let alone a moving target right now.

"You're in Mozambique. That where you started?"

He shaded his eyes again as he looked at Rowena. "See, I told you we hadn't crossed the border." Because being right was the most important thing for Joe rather than keeping the sweet woman who was so clearly out of his league happy.

"Well, thank goodness for that." Rowena hugged her arms around her waist. "I lost my bag in the river, and it had my passport, mobile, and wallet inside. I'm going to have to go to the embassy and get an emergency one issued to fly home."

"Could you put the gun down and maybe get that light out of my face?" he muttered impatiently.

"Joe." Rowena admonished sharply, and he almost laughed. "If we were in the US, the landowner would probably have already shot us."

He pulled a face. Definitely a possibility.

"But you're English, right?" The woman seemed to be softening to their story. Why else would two bedraggled people be wandering around in the middle of the country? Being on the run from mercenaries hired by one of the richest men in the world was too far-fetched for words.

"Not me," he grumbled.

"Yes, I can tell." The woman lowered the flashlight beam away from their faces, flicked on the light using her elbow on a switch on the wall near where she stood. She was white. Mid-fifties—closer to his age than Rowena's. Jeans patched at the knee and a loose cotton shirt tied in a knot at the bottom.

"Joe's from the US. I'm English. From Shropshire. Do you know it?"

"No. My great-grandparents were from Yorkshire. Settled here years ago and built one of the biggest citrus farms in the country."

"Have you been back to visit at all?" Rowena was happy to have a polite conversation while someone pointed a presumably loaded shotgun at her.

"I've been twice." The woman gave a mock shudder. "I didn't like the cold."

"You mind lowering that gun?" Kurt was used to live weapons pointed in his direction but someone doing it to Rowena pissed him off.

The woman hesitated.

Rowena sent him a look. "I hope you don't mind. I stole a teabag and had a cup of tea while we cleaned up Joe's wound. Joe has some money left to pay you with, right, babe?"

"That's fine about the tea." The owner waved the offer away, but her eyes sharpened on his face. "You have ID?"

Kurt inclined his head, slowly dragged his wallet out of a side pocket of his bag. He extracted the driver's license belonging to his alias. Held it out.

Come to papa.

He left his handgun where it was, covered by his shirt. He didn't want to shoot an innocent civilian who had every right to defend herself and her property, but neither did he want to be detained or shot again himself. If he could get close to that shotgun, he could disarm her and tie her up—raging fever or no raging fever.

Rowena snatched the license out of his fingers and walked over to the woman, holding the card at arm's length.

He closed his mouth. Gritted his teeth.

The woman peered at the ID then nodded.

"I can understand why you'd be concerned finding us here like this." Rowena sounded genuinely empathetic as she delivered his card back to him with a "behave" look. "I'd be terrified. If you point us in the right direction, we'll get out of your hair and be on our way."

"Where are you staying?"

"Beira," Kurt interjected. "I forget the name of the hotel, but it's modern. By the beach. We sent our luggage ahead from the place where we were staying and are supposed to fly to Madagascar tomorrow night. Rental car is in the bush somewhere north, but the company will have a tracker on it. I'm not too worried. I paid extra for insurance. Now we have to go to Maputo and sort out passports which will change our plans." Kurt tightened his lips. "Is there a bus or a taxi service we could call?"

"You don't have any papers at all?" she asked Rowena.

Rowena shook her head, bit her lip nervously. "Not on me."

The woman exhaled audibly. "The police will likely stop the buses coming from the direction of the border and same with a taxi. Without papers, you'll end up sitting in a cell until they can verify your identity."

Kurt swore. "I'm not leaving her alone in some police station in Mozambique."

"I don't like the idea of the police getting their hands on a sweet, young woman either." The woman gave him a look that judged him to be someone else who might be taking advantage of the sweet, young woman. "I'm heading there in the morning with one of the trucks to pick up fertilizer. Beira that is. They hardly ever stop me, and there is a compartment in the back of the cab under the bench seat that one person *could* conceivably hide in. My late husband used to smuggle various things off the black market."

What kind of things? Didn't matter. "Are you offering to give us a ride to Beira tomorrow?" Kurt held his breath.

"If you like, but it'll probably be as uncomfortable as hell especially for whoever has to sit in the back."

"Seriously?" He didn't believe in this sort of good luck. "How much do you want?"

The woman's lip curled. "I'm not asking for money or anything else for that matter."

Her disgusted expression suggested she thought he was worried about having to perform sexual favors which, in his current condition was laughable.

It was a kind offer, but he didn't trust her. He didn't trust anyone.

18

"Oh my goodness. That is so kind of you! You're a lifesaver." Rowena couldn't believe their good fortune and could barely control her happiness. "But we don't want to put you out… Sorry, I don't know what I should call you."

"Marianne. Marianne Van Hoogen."

"Marianne. Hi, I'm Ro—short for Rogan." She wasn't used to lying, but she figured a little deception wouldn't be a bad thing under the circumstances. "And this is my boyfriend, Joe." She winced because she was pretty sure there was someone famous called Joe Rogan. "Joe's not normally quite so grumpy, but he's got a nasty infection, and it's been quite the day. Both our mobiles stopped working, not that it matters about mine as it's at the bottom of the river, but Joe wanted to call for help and couldn't." She ran her hand down his good arm. "Then he started with this fever, and I honestly thought I'd be carrying him all the way to the city… It hasn't been a good day."

"Phones are down all over. Some sort of cyberattack, apparently. Can't wait to see how the government handles that," Marianne scoffed. "Come into the house. I have some antibiotics I use for the pigs." The woman shot Kurt a look. "Probably won't do you any harm."

Row suppressed a snort. "Obviously, *you* made a good impression," she murmured.

He grunted.

"I have stew on the stove if you want some," Marianne offered.

Row's stomach audibly growled at the mention of food. "Yes, please."

Kurt indicated she lead the way, and she joined Marianne as they walked to the house. She kept half an eye on Kurt over her shoulder as he rolled his shoulders and moved his head from side to side. He still had the handgun. She hoped they didn't need it.

The woman cracked open the double barrel, and Row breathed a little easier.

"Keep the shotgun to deter break-ins and to scare away the odd predator who wanders too close. I have a dog, pigs, chickens, and goats."

"You live here all alone?" Row couldn't imagine running a farm in the middle of Africa alone.

"I have a farm manager who has his own house other side of the orchard."

"No Mr. Van Hoogen around the place? Or Mrs.?" Kurt asked from behind them.

Row shot him a surprised look. "You don't have to answer that. Joe's nosey."

Marianne gave him a wry look. "I'm used to men. Trust me. This one doesn't bother me."

Funny, he bothered the hell out of her. They arrived at the back door and went inside to find a springer spaniel barking and wagging its tail so hard Row was surprised he didn't fall over.

"That the guard dog?"

Marianne popped the cartridges and placed the gun on a rack beside the door. She answered Kurt's wry comment in a monotone. "Spencer. He used to have a sister called Hepburn, but a leopard got her." She shot Kurt a narrow look. "That leopard is now a rug on my living room floor."

"You shot it?" Row tried to keep the shock out of her voice.

Marianne looked at her sharply. "I did what needed to be done. That old cat needed to be put down before he decided to take one of the kids from the village." Her brows lowered. "A single shot through the head—he never felt a thing. His skull is on my desk. To remind me of all the predators in the world."

Kurt nodded slowly at what sounded like a warning.

Row watched the two of them measure each other up.

Great. The last thing she wanted was to upset this woman when she'd offered them a ride to the city, saving them days of walking and potential peril. But Kurt had good reasons not to take things at face value. His job probably required a degree of mistrust.

It wasn't how Rowena operated but she'd try to be circumspect.

The smell of fragrant cooking filled the air. Row pressed a hand to her belly. She didn't remember the last time she'd been this hungry even though she'd stuffed her face last night. But they'd walked all day, dawn to dusk, on nothing more than a protein bar each. They hadn't expected a warm meal tonight.

"That smells delicious."

Marianne smiled. "I like to cook. Makes a change to have someone to feed."

The dog jumped up on its owner, and she bent to give it a scratch on his liver-spotted head. "Come on. I'll find those antibiotics and serve us all up a bowl with some bread I baked earlier."

They followed her into an old-fashioned kitchen with a large dining table in the center. A dark red Aga oven sat in one corner, pumping out heat. A pot on the stove top.

Kurt put the rucksack on the nearest chair, and she could see he was burning up. His coloring worried her. As did the sheen of sweat clinging to his brow.

"Can I trouble you for some water?"

"Help yourself." Marianne waved a distracted hand over her

shoulder as she rifled through a drawer filled with everything from screwdrivers to birthday candles.

Row found a glass and ran the tap until it was cold.

Marianne pulled on a pair of reading specs and peered closer at the orange pill bottle in her hand. "Here we go. My late husband, Newt, was a veterinarian and he regularly fed me animal drugs. Never did me any harm."

She tossed them to Kurt.

Kurt caught the bottle and asked cautiously. "And what exactly did he die of?"

Row's mouth dropped open, but Marianne took it as a joke.

"Melanoma." She pressed her lips together in a watery smile. "Took him fast, which is how he'd wanted to go. Now I'm the last one of my family and no kids to leave it all to. End of an era."

Rowena knew exactly how that felt. "Perhaps you should sell up and spend your retirement living it up somewhere."

Marianne snorted. "Maybe I will."

She pulled out mismatched bowls for the stew.

"Cutlery is in the drawer." The woman pointed to the drawer next to the sink.

Rowena grabbed spoons as Kurt read the pill instructions. Then he popped off the lid with a determined clench of his jaw before he swallowed two tablets along with another glass of water.

"That landline work?" He pointed at the old-fashioned phone hooked onto the wall that Row had failed to notice.

Marianne shook her head. "Not last time I checked it."

"You mind if I try?" He angled his head toward the receiver.

"Knock yourself out."

He put the earpiece to his ear then, after a second, hung up with a grunt. Obviously still dead.

They sat down to eat informally at the kitchen table.

"You grow fruit?" Rowena took a piece of fresh bread from the loaf Marianne had carved.

"Yeah. Oranges mainly but some limes too. And guava."

"Do you ever get lonely out here on your own?"

Marianne's smile grew rueful. "Probably wouldn't be feeding two strangers who turned up on my doorstep if I didn't. What do you do in Shropshire?"

Row smiled. "I'm a librarian."

Marianne chortled. "And your boyfriend?"

The label "boyfriend" did not sit easily on this man's shoulders. He was too rugged. Too experienced.

Kurt forced a smile. His eyes were glassy and cheeks flushed. "Insurance salesman or antichrist. Take your pick."

Marianne's brow rose, unimpressed. "Well, at least you have a sense of humor about it."

"I keep telling him to come over from the dark side, but he says he has a good pension he doesn't want to jeopardize."

He shot her a look from under his brows that told her the pension quip had hit its mark. Despite his hang-up about their age difference, he wasn't even close to retirement.

"We have a long-distance relationship which is difficult because we only see each other a few times a year." She would hate living so far away if she were truly in love. "This vacation was supposed to be our big romantic adventure to last us for another six months."

"Sorry, babe." Kurt reached out and squeezed her hand.

Her heart tumbled over in her chest. The fiction was taking root in her mind as a form of reality, in terms of emotions if not the details. She needed to remind herself they weren't really a couple.

"We went to the Falls together and saw the Big Five, then the private house that belongs to a friend of Joe's boss was very fancy."

Marianne eyed her, and Row wondered if her lies had become too elaborate. She spooned up some fragrant gravy and potatoes.

Kurt mopped his brow with a napkin. Pushed his empty bowl away and leaned back looking miserable.

Her throat swelled. She didn't think he was a man who was

used to being incapacitated in any way. "Is it possible for Joe to get a cold bath or shower?"

Marianne eyed him more critically then. "Of course. Bathroom's through that door on the right. If you run him a bath, I'll make up a bed for the two of you."

"Oh, give me the bedding. I can make it up."

Marianne shook her head. "From the looks of him one of us needs to make sure he doesn't drown in the bath, and I think he'd rather that was you than me."

Row glanced at the man in question who had closed his eyes, a reluctant smile on his face. "You're probably right."

He muttered. "I can handle a bath and getting into bed without help."

"And if it were I who was sick?" Row demanded.

He blew out a frustrated breath. "Fine."

She finished her stew, chewing the last morsel of beef. "At least let me wash the dishes as soon as I have Joe tucked up. Hopefully, the paracetamol and antibiotics will kick in soon."

Marianne nodded. "I'll make us a hot drink while your man gets some rest. We'll set off early tomorrow. He'll be as good as new in a few days, but make sure he finishes the whole course of antibiotics."

Your man.

Rowena liked the sound of that even though it wasn't true. It was nice to pretend for a while though. Pretend she wasn't alone in the world. Pretend FBI agent Kurt Montana was her long-distance boyfriend, not a relative stranger helping her escape from unexpected danger while enjoying a few mutual benefits along the way.

She walked around the table and touched his good arm, noticed his skin was hot and dry. Even so, he remembered to pick up the rucksack as he rolled slowly to his feet.

"Thank you, Marianne, for your hospitality. We're very grateful." Then he followed her through the old-fashioned house.

The bathroom had an old, iron, claw-foot tub with the enamel worn away in places from a constantly dripping tap. She put in the plug and ran the water so the bath was tepid rather than frigid.

"Come on, soldier, strip."

Kurt placed the pack on the floor and reached back to pull the handgun out of his waistband. Placing it under a towel on a stack beside the bath, within easy reach. Then he began to peel his shirt over his head, and she forced herself not to ogle those heavily muscled pecs and solid abs.

The window was cracked open an inch despite the colder weather, and she shivered. A spider clung to one wall, and she forced herself not to think about the number of arachnids likely in the house. She'd had to deal with them in her uncle's homes, not to mention a scorpion on her way to the bathroom one night in Vic Falls.

The locals didn't seem to care, but she hated anything with eight legs.

He wobbled as he began to undo his trousers.

She grabbed his elbow. "Sit on the edge of the tub and hold onto my shoulders. I'll help."

He did as she suggested. His expression bemused as he watched her. "Slightly different from last night, huh?"

She smiled up at him as she removed his boots and socks. "I'll try to control my baser urges until you're feeling better."

"There go my fantasies."

"I don't think you'd survive."

"Be a hell of a way to go though, wouldn't it?"

She laughed and then reached around and tested the water. Turned off the tap. Pulled a face. "It's cold."

"Thank God."

"Rather you than me."

He kicked off his trousers and underwear, then slid slowly into the water, his body visibly jerking in reaction to the icy temperature.

"Fantastic." He kept his injured arm on the edge of the bath. "I have to admit I feel like shit."

"Funny, because you look *really* good."

He squinted over his arm. "Pervert."

"Guilty." She found a washcloth and dipped it into the cold water. Wrung it out and placed it on his brow as he leaned back and closed his eyes.

He gave a low growl that was almost a purr. "That feels good."

"Better than sex?"

His eyelids cracked open. "What do you think?"

A blush heated her own cheeks. "I would be shocked if it could feel that good, but it's been a while since anyone placed a cold washcloth on my forehead, so maybe I'm missing something."

He laughed then groaned as if his head hurt. Closed his eyes. "You're funny. I like that. A lot."

His words filled her with some unidentifiable emotion. She liked it too. Making him laugh. The man was far too serious, but he dealt with terrorists and life-and-death situations on a not infrequent basis. She dealt with small research projects, community literacy support, overdue fines, making sure the books were in the right order, and the occasional plumbing issue.

She could afford a little levity.

Not that her job wasn't important. Librarians were the wardens of knowledge and truth. The checkers of facts. The gatekeepers to a million tiny universes. Libraries were still important in the modern era of ereaders and the internet. They could be sanctuaries and safe places for people who needed that. Tardises for mind expansion and entertainment for those who couldn't afford to buy books or DVDs.

She dipped the now warm cloth back in the cold water, repeated the process until his body temp cooled, and his color faded back to normal. She tried not to check out his impressive body, but it was difficult under the circumstances. Everything was right *there.*

He'd closed his eyes, absorbing the coolness of the water.

The well-defined muscles spoke to a life of physicality and action—not someone who sat behind a desk all day selling insurance. Marianne would know that in an instant if she got a look at him naked. His knees were bent to fit in the bath. Thick, strong thighs relaxed and spread. Not a man to be bashful, and Rowena was not a prude. She was curious.

The tiny crow's feet edging the corners of his eyes were definitely not unattractive. Tiredness from their long day and his raging infection were evident in the deep creases bracketing his mouth. His lips were wide and firm, perfectly symmetrical. That elusive dimple making a brief appearance. On his chest, two moles sat just above his right nipple, forming the perfect triangle, and made her fingers itch to touch. A sprinkling of dark hair formed a center line that traveled south from his navel providing more tempting territory. There was a scar on his thigh, a small white puckered circle, that looked suspiciously like a bullet hole. Another scar ran down his shin.

Despite the scars, he was a very well put together man.

Very well put together indeed.

Her mouth went dry.

She searched for a distraction. God knew they had plenty to choose from. "What do you think of Marianne?"

"Don't trust her," he grumbled. "Be careful what you say to her."

"Why don't you trust her?"

He opened one eye. "Probably because she got the drop on me."

"Beat you at your own game, you mean."

He laughed quietly. "I guess. I just don't see why a woman on her own would invite two strangers into her home when we could be cold-blooded killers out to rob and murder her. It's foolish, and she doesn't strike me as a fool."

"She seemed nice."

"Exactly."

"You're a cynic."

"I thought you'd figured that out the night we met."

"When you accused me of being a sex worker, you mean?"

He winced.

"And you kept asking who I worked for as if you thought I was some kind of spy."

He grimaced. "I was right about you following one of us. I figured you could be a honeytrap—one that tempted me to dive headlong into it regardless and worry about the consequences later."

She held his deep blue gaze, glad she wasn't the only one who had been attracted. "I was shocked you thought I could be anything other than what I am. I live a boring little life in a quiet little town."

"You're a smart, beautiful woman."

The throwaway compliment took her by surprise.

He ran a thumb across her bottom lip. "I bet you wish you were back home now surrounded by your books."

She looked away to hide the emotions that threatened. She loved her books, but they couldn't hold her hand or hug her when she was lonely. They couldn't give her everything she wanted. "I wish we weren't in danger. I wish people hadn't died. But there are several things I wouldn't swap for anything, except maybe you not getting shot."

Their gazes locked, and she could tell he thought she was talking about the sex, but it was more than that. More than she wanted to admit.

"Why me?" he asked. "Why last night?"

She folded the damp washcloth and put it on the edge of the bath. "Because I was once again reminded life is short, and I didn't want to die without having experienced sex. I hadn't been waiting for someone special *per se*—just someone I liked and trusted enough to be intimate with." She watched him from under her lashes. "And someone who looked like he knew what he was doing in the bedroom and who I found incredibly attractive."

"No wonder it took you so long. I was lucky to be at the right place at the right time."

You *were the right place and the right time.*

She didn't say it out loud. It was too heavy for a casual relationship, and she owed him too much to put pressure on him like that.

He caught her hand. Dragged her toward him. "Kiss me."

She laughed. "You're ill."

"I'm fine."

"I can't take advantage of you!"

"I saw you checking me out... I know you're curious."

She almost pulled away, mortified, but he held tight to her hand.

"Look at what you do to me. Even now."

He slowly wrapped her fingers around him, and she was shocked to find him rock hard. Her lips opened in surprise even as he cupped the back of her head to pull her in for a kiss.

She squeezed her fingers tighter, and he braced his feet against the end of the bath.

"I want you." His words came between kisses.

"I want you too." She kissed him deeper and touched him. As turned on and willing as she might be, having full-on sex right now wouldn't be right. But she could give him something. She copied how he showed her to touch him, stroked the long, hot length of him, up and down, tip to root, faster, keeping the rhythm. Kissing his mouth, his jaw, feeling tension build there as he strained to hold back.

"Row. Wait. Wait. I'm gonna—"

"I want you to." She gripped him more firmly and kept stroking him, faster now, his own fingers joining hers, changing the tempo, the pressure.

"Are you sure?"

"Yes."

His jaw clenched. Eyes hot on hers. He opened his mouth with a silent cry, head thrown back as his release ripped through him.

She watched as he pulsed hotly over his stomach and their joined hands.

He collapsed down into the water, panting, eyes wide with shock, a little pale now. "Holy fuck, you're going to kill me." He swallowed thickly. "I wanted to…"

"Next time." She hoped there would be a next time. "When I can be *sure* I'm not taking advantage of you."

"I was trying to take advantage of you. I did take advantage of you." He corrected as he washed himself off.

"No, you didn't. I enjoyed it. Another first." She smiled as he stared at her, not letting her escape his scrutiny.

He touched her cheek. "You can take advantage of me anytime. Any time at all. And anything you have an interest in exploring…let me know. As long as I don't have to wear high heels and pantyhose, I'm game."

She met those eyes, the color of the deep ocean, and a quiver of pleasure slipped through her. She'd like that too. A lot.

Suddenly, she noticed the hairs on his arms had formed goose bumps and he'd begun to shiver.

"I'll hold you to that." She grabbed a large towel and held it out for him. "And you can make me scream with pleasure any time at all—except when you're suffering from a nasty fever."

"Yes, ma'am. It's going to be my absolute pleasure."

She turned away and hid a secret smile. Despite everything that had happened over the past two days, she felt sexy and powerful. She liked it. Loved it, actually. Hated the thought that they'd be going their separate ways soon.

Still, the sooner they got out of this mess the sooner she could begin her campaign to see him again. Perhaps he'd let her visit him in the States. Assuming they got out of this mess alive.

19

JANUARY 14

Thursday. Mozambique.

For the second night in a row, Kurt woke a few minutes after four, with the dull throb of a headache pounding gently at the base of his skull. Feeling better overall if still a little weak. He'd slept like the dead.

Rowena getting him off in the tub seemed like a fever dream. An incredible, *let's do that again sometime but with me inside you,* fever dream. She was curled up beside him now, not touching, but facing him, as if she'd fallen asleep watching over him. Worrying about him. He wished he had the strength to do more than kiss her on the forehead before he got out of bed. He rose, dressed, and placed the pistol into the waistband of his pants. He loathed that carry, but without a holster, he had no better option. In the kitchen, he checked the landline to see if it was working yet.

It wasn't.

Gilder? Or a coincidence combined with his growing paranoia? Nah, he'd always been grounded in reality rather than fantasy. He had to assume Gilder was hunting him. If so, how long could the billionaire disrupt a nation's communication services before the population rebelled? How long would his government co-conspirators let him?

Kurt found the makings for coffee and put on the pot, staring out into the darkness, wondering if and how many mercs were on their trail. A yawning Marianne walked into the kitchen along with Spencer, who ran to the back door and scratched to go outside as the percolator came to a boil.

She opened the door and let the dog out to do whatever he needed to do and run back inside again. She slid the bolt home after he did so.

It was a little humbling to know she trusted them enough to let them sleep in her house overnight. He hoped she hadn't played them in some way and betrayed them to the authorities. She'd seemed to have taken a shine to Rowena. There was a lot of that going around.

"You look better." Her voice was gruff with the gravel of morning.

"I feel a lot better. Thank you." He'd taken another dose of antibiotics and could already feel the difference as the medicine helped combat the infection. "Oink."

She laughed in surprise.

"Sorry I was an ass last night." He rolled his arm. It didn't feel nearly as heavy or as sore as it had yesterday.

"Don't worry about it. I'm used to men being asses."

He grimaced. "I'm sorry for that too."

She inclined her head. "Not my husband, but a lot of people I used to respect who now struggle to deal with me as the person in charge rather than Newt. It's been eye-opening to say the least because"—her eyes flashed with wry amusement—"I was always the one in charge."

Kurt passed her a coffee. "You know you don't have to come with us to Beira. I could pay someone to deliver the truck and the fertilizer back here." He shrugged. "I can afford to make it worth someone's while. I hate to think of you making the return journey alone."

She watched him carefully. "I've been driving that road for nearly forty years and was going anyway. This way I have company one way. You don't need to worry about me."

"Well, thanks. Appreciate it."

She looked out the window into the darkness. "Henry can manage on his own this time of year. Hell, maybe I'll spend the night at some fancy hotel, see if I can pick up a boy toy."

His mouth-tightened at the obvious jibe about the age difference between him and Rowena.

The edge of her mouth curved up. "He was a lot older than me. Newt. My late husband."

Kurt cast her a sideways look.

"I can see it bothers you, though she doesn't seem to care. But I know it doesn't always matter what the woman thinks." She rolled her eyes and blew the top of her coffee. "Newt struggled with it our entire married life—he was thirty-nine and I was eighteen, but I knew what I wanted. He was a close family friend, and his first wife died young, which was a damned shame. He was miserable for about a year, and my parents invited him to stay here, which worked for them as they received free vet care. We started to spend more time together and"—she popped her shoulders in a carefree shrug—"events took their natural course one night when my parents were away and I persuaded him to go skinny dipping in the pond with me."

Kurt wasn't often at a loss for words, but right now he was struck mute.

She joggled his sore arm. "My advice, not that you asked. Don't be ashamed of the age difference if you're still happy to shag her blind in secret. Otherwise, she might wonder at some point if you're actually ashamed of her and the only reason you're together is for the hot sex. And what man would refuse hot sex?"

Kurt coughed, and she slapped him on the back.

"Newt made that mistake and had to come groveling with a big-ass diamond ring to get me back." She extended her right hand where her diamond engagement ring sparkled like the sun. "He had to prove to me the age difference didn't matter and that he considered me his equal, not a child, even though he was two decades older. Once you reach adulthood, sonny, age is just a number."

He huffed a laugh and took a drink of his coffee. "*Sonny*?"

"Just trying to make you feel better." Her lips quirked.

"I'll bear that in mind, grandma."

She smirked.

Not that he and Rowena were an item. He wasn't sure what they were, but right now, it felt a lot like partners, and he was okay with that. He needed to get them both out of this situation alive. If they found a way to see one another again in the future, he'd flaunt her every chance he got. Probably.

His hangups were a problem for future Kurt. His current issue was figuring a way to get them out of the country without Gilder knowing.

"I'll take Sleeping Beauty her coffee and then go check out the truck." Figure out how to make it safe and comfortable for someone hiding in the back.

"I'll throw together a quick breakfast, keep us going. Along with some supplies for the journey."

"Appreciate it."

They set off just as the African sun started to rise. Kurt had lined the bottom of the rear bench seat, which was basically a metal box with a padded lid that was bolted to the chassis, with cushions from the garden chairs and wool throws from the couch. He'd found two pieces of wood that could be used to prop the seat open and allowed Row to sit upright but out of sight. Marianne had draped a blanket over the back of the two front seats, and he'd placed the backpack with the gun in it on the floor in the back where Row could grab it should they be stopped on the road. Marianne had loaded a crate of water into the back, and he'd refilled all his and Rowena's bottles before they'd left.

Marianne handed him an old sunhat to wear with her farm logo on the front along with some wonky sunglasses. He put them on, wondering if she knew he was trying to avoid being recognized by people and any surveillance cameras that happened to be around.

It was hard to tell what she really thought was going on or why she would help them. Maybe she was simply a romantic and thought they were star-crossed lovers. Or maybe Gilder or Leo Spartan had offered a reward for their capture, and she was driving them right into the hands of their enemy.

He figured they were going to find out.

They passed banana, rice, tea, and tobacco plantations. Saw evidence of the mining frenzy that was consuming whole chunks of Africa in the search for precious gems, metals and now rare earth metals.

They'd almost reached Chimoio when Marianne's cell phone burst to life with a series of dings.

"Looks like the cell towers are back in action."

He nodded. He needed to contact someone to get a US Navy ship offshore. Should he call his boss directly? He feared a man with Gilder's resources would be smart enough to tap the phones of Kurt's FBI workmates, and his nearest and dearest. If not to hear the conversation, then to ping the location of the caller. He didn't want to do something rash when he could smell freedom. Even Gilder wouldn't attack the US Navy. Or British Royal Navy for that matter…

The CIA should have contacts within the country.

Killion's number had changed when his friend had retired from his Intelligence Officer role to manage The Farm, and Kurt didn't recall the new one without starting up his work cell which he had no intention of doing. He did remember the number for the intelligence officer from the embassy in Harare though. Marty Sinclair.

"I need to pee." Rowena's voice was high and slightly desperate.

They were about halfway through the journey.

"I'll pull off onto a quiet road and we'll find some bushes. There's a place not far away I've used before."

As soon as the women clambered out of the truck, Kurt pulled the burner out of his pack and inserted the battery and SIM card. It took thirty seconds to activate the phone cards, then he punched in Marty's number.

The guy picked up on the first ring. "Sinclair."

"It's Kurt Montana."

"Where the hell—

"Listen carefully. I don't have much time. What Navy vessels are in the vicinity of Madagascar and how soon can they reach Beira?"

"That's where you are? I thought you were dead."

"Naval vessels."

"I'd have to check."

"Do it. Tell the FBI I'm alive and need exfil with a twenty-seven-year-old female British national. I'll be there in a couple of hours, and it would be nice if there was someone friendly to meet us."

"Who's the female?"

"Classified. I'll make a full report to my bosses when I get onboard. All normal communication channels need to be assumed to be compromised. Use the SCIF to contact FBI HQ. You can't talk about this in person or on unsecured channels to anyone, not even the ambassador. Fuck, not even the president. I'm going to hang up now. I'll call back in a couple of hours, and I want a boat or a chopper waiting. Got it?"

He hung up before Marty could reply. Popped the SIM and battery and placed them in his shirt pocket, cell in his pants.

He picked up Marianne's phone, reading the texts he could see on the Lock Screen. No obvious signs she'd contacted authorities and told them about him or Rowena.

He put the cell down as he heard laughter getting close. The women climbed back into the truck.

Marianne opened the glovebox, and Kurt spotted an old revolver inside. She rifled around and pulled out a bottle of hand sanitizer. She squirted some onto her own hands and handed it back to Rowena.

"She can probably sit up now. Chances of a roadblock goes down dramatically from here on out."

"I'd rather not risk it. The idea of Row ending up in a jail cell is pretty scary for the sake of another couple hours of being careful. Once we're at the hotel, I'll make a few calls."

"I'm fine back here," Rowena said brightly. "Probably going to snooze for a while anyway."

"Want me to drive?" he offered.

Marianne grinned and tilted her head coquettishly. "You're not insured. Hey, did you call the car hire place? Let them know you survived?"

"My cell's out of juice."

"Use mine."

"You don't mind?"

"Hardly." Marianne pulled back onto the main road. "Code's 1232. Original, I know."

"Thanks. You mind if I check a couple of other things while I'm at it?"

She shook her head. "Knock yourself out."

He pulled up the news first, saw reports on the crash and the fact an investigation was happening as soon as they'd finished recovering the dead. Reporters claimed bodies had been scavenged by animals—convenient if you wanted to lose the remains of someone who never actually boarded the aircraft. He scrolled down, and the fact an off-duty FBI agent had been onboard along with his name was mentioned. Then a long list of photos of the dead including his official FBI mug shot.

His heart ached anew for Daisy and his FBI family, and for all the people who'd needlessly died a horrific death because of someone's twisted need to keep secrets.

Authorities believed it was "mechanical failure" but were

investigating. He wondered if the killers would get away with that.

He searched for news about Bjorn's murder and found a short reference to a vicious attack in Harare. Nothing to suggest they had a lead on a suspect. The air crash had probably diverted resources away from the homicide investigation.

No mention of Rowena.

He deleted his search history.

Then he made a fake call to a car rental place apologizing and begging forgiveness for not returning the car. Next, he checked out the Beira hotels and picked a new modern build on the beach-front. They could hang out and have a meal if nothing else while Marty made arrangements.

This was going to work.

They were going to get out of here and back home. He forced his jaw to relax. And perhaps he could figure out a way to keep seeing Rowena. He was due some vacation time. He wondered how Rowena would feel about that idea. Maybe he should ask her and find out.

Just as soon as they made it out the other side of this mess.

20

Row yawned widely and shifted position. The box was disconcertingly like a metal coffin and the idea of being shut in completely freaked her out—not that she'd admit it. She kept up a series of stretches to stop herself from stiffening up. The cushions helped.

Kurt seemed a hundred times better than he had last night. The fever had gone, and his wound was healing nicely. Marianne handed out egg salad rolls, and they were some of the best things Row had ever tasted. She seemed to be obsessed with food right now. Food and sex. Fighting for survival seemed to have triggered hunger on several levels.

She and Marianne had spent a little time talking last night about their lives in general, and Marianne's struggles since her husband had died.

Row had felt like the worst kind of liar not telling the other woman the truth about the situation she and Kurt found themselves in, but their lives were at stake. And possibly something more. She'd figure out a way to make it up to her later. It was also possible that knowing too much would put a target on Marianne's back, and Row didn't want to be responsible for anyone else getting killed.

Her nerves were fraught, but at the same time, the long drive made her drowsy. She took another sip of water but didn't want to drink too much in case she needed another trip to the non-existent bathroom. Seven hours in the truck with the constant motion wasn't helping.

The side and rear windows were tinted so she could safely look out from her low perch. They were passing through areas that were becoming more and more built up as they neared their destination, the city of Beira, and hopefully an escape from this nightmare.

"Would you mind helping load the fertilizer onto the truck before I drop you at the hotel? Then I can get back on the road faster."

"You're still planning to drive back tonight?" Kurt turned in his seat.

His voice was deep and lovely. Row shivered as it flowed over her.

Marianne shrugged. "I'm used to the drive, and I can stop for dinner in Chimoio on the way home. Row can get out and help too if she wants. I doubt people down at the ports are going to ask about her passport. Not unless she tries to get on a boat." She snorted.

Ha.

"I wouldn't mind having a couple extra pairs of hands down there. And eyes. A lot of thieves and rough characters about. They don't usually bother me, but in the past, I'd have Newt or Henry or my dad with me."

Row watched Marianne lick her lips as a flicker of unease crossed her features.

"Not a problem," Kurt assured her.

He'd never leave someone in danger. Row knew that about him now.

"Of course we'll help," she added.

Without Marianne, she wasn't sure where they'd be, but Kurt would be in bad shape. She'd noticed he'd been popping the antibiotics at a faster rate than the label suggested, but he was doing okay, so she wasn't about to mention it. They had other things to worry about.

Anticipation competed with worry as they drove into the city. If it hadn't been for the men chasing them with guns yesterday morning and the grim memory of Bjorn's tortured body, she'd think they were on some sort of Amazing Race adventure. But people were dead, and they could have been too. It was sobering how a near-death experience could alter your perspective on life and make you reconsider what was really important.

The need to discover who her father was would always be a tug, but perhaps the search through open DNA channels would provide all the closure she needed. She didn't even need a direct hit. Any hint of a family tree, and she'd have a good idea of whether or not Dougie Cavanagh was related.

They pulled up in front of a large warehouse beside a wide-open space filled with various ginormous piles of grit, gravel, and presumably fertilizer. Marianne got out and marched off to the big, wide-open warehouse door. Kurt leaned over the seat, dark brows pulled low as he peered over cheap sunshades that sat lopsided on his nose. The hat looked equally ridiculous, but he somehow managed to make her stomach quiver with something that was definitely not laughter. "You want to help? It's going to be dirty."

"You think it's safe?"

One side of his mouth twitched. "I think we need to act natural. From what I saw on the news, your name and face weren't mentioned publicly. I'm listed as dead from the air crash, but we know whoever is after us also knows that's not true. Otherwise, they wouldn't have sent the mercs. They might know about you now too." He reached out and touched her hand. Squeezed gently then let go. "I'm going to use the 'loo' and call my contact on the burner. See if he arranged transport to the ship yet."

She felt her heartbeat flutter. They were so close to safety. It was nearly over. It was nearly done. As soon as they were rescued everything was going to change. They wouldn't have to pretend to be together anymore.

He wouldn't need to protect her.

She caught his hand. "When this is all over, I'd like to see you again."

A smile lit his eyes as he looked at her over those wonky glasses, but his mouth stayed stern. "That was supposed to be my line."

She bit her lip. "Sorry. I get the feeling that if I hadn't pushed that night, we'd never have..."

He looked away. "Not because I didn't want you, Row. Just because of all the other stuff."

"The age difference."

He looked at her. Removed the glasses. "I've never allowed myself to even think about hooking up with a woman twenty years my junior."

"Eighteen."

"What?"

She allowed herself a little quirk of a smile as she knelt up so they were eye level. "The age difference is only eighteen years."

"A generation." He drew a thumb over her bottom lip. "Not a bridge I ever thought I'd cross, but we did, and maybe the numbers are less important than I always believed. You might have figured out by now I'm a little stuck in my ways."

She hiked her brows. *A little?*

"So perhaps I could come visit you in your 'boring little town' sometime? When I've sorted everything out with my daughter and work."

She felt her eyes bug wide. "Oh, I'd love that. You'd love Shropshire. It's the UK's best kept secret for history and beauty."

He laughed softly. "You sound like a tour guide."

"I love it." She had the horrible feeling she loved something else too, but him agreeing to them maybe seeing each other again made her pull back on any wild declarations. She couldn't be the only one pushing for them. It had to be both of them, or else it simply wouldn't be worth it.

She was quite capable of living alone and dealing with loneliness—she thrived on it even. She hadn't been single all this time because she had no other choices. What she wanted was a man who made giving up all the perks of being a single woman worth the downside of sharing a life together. Of making compromises. Someone worthy of the pain of missing them when they were gone.

Someone who loved her the same way she might be starting to love them.

He leaned over and kissed her, igniting flames that built into passion despite everything. It was still dangerous, but as she grabbed onto him and pulled him to her, none of that seemed to matter. He made a low groan that made the kiss all the hotter.

They broke apart as the need for oxygen overcame them.

The heat in his gaze made her fingers tighten on his shirt. She wanted to drag him into the cramped back seat right here and now. She swallowed because he looked like he might let her.

Marianne tapped on the window, and they both jumped apart.

"Shit. Head in the game, Joe. Head in the fucking game." Kurt picked up the knapsack and got out of the truck, speaking with Marianne for a brief second before heading into the building.

Row climbed over the front seat and got out the driver's door.

"What do you need?" She was blushing and hyperaware of the gazes of the men working in the area. Boys no older than ten ran around playing football barefoot, in dirty, ragged clothes, in the large dusty clearing between mountains of potash.

Marianne raised a brow. "Joe seems better."

Row smiled at her, coyly. "Seems to be getting his strength back."

"Uh huh." She handed Row a shovel. "Fill that wheelbarrow with the white stuff over there. You want a bandana for the dust? I've got more sunglasses around here somewhere too."

"Yes, please." Row nodded and rolled her shoulders. She was

used to lugging heavy stacks of books and digging the heavy clay soil from home so hopefully this would be easy.

She tied the green bandana over her nose and mouth like a bandit out of a Spaghetti Western and slid the too big glasses up her nose. She rolled up her sleeves and felt pretty badass as she pushed the barrow to the pile and began scooping shovelfuls of cream-colored fertilizer into the barrow where it landed with a dry whoosh against the metal. Pale dust floated off on the breeze to mix with the industrial smells of coal, petroleum, and sulphur. Row grimaced at the thought of the chemicals that surrounded her and what those growing children were exposed to daily.

She filled the barrow, then tested the weight and pushed it back to the truck where Marianne had set up a sturdy ramp. Thankfully, Kurt arrived back at that moment and ran the barrow up into the bed of the truck and dumped it. She grabbed a second empty barrow and began the process of filling it again.

It took a while. Almost an hour before they were done, and the bed of the truck was full. Kurt carefully secured a blue tarp over the mound, so it didn't all blow away on the drive back. Or wash away in the oncoming monsoon.

Sweat dripped down her back as she eyed the ominous clouds forming overhead.

"How would you have ever coped alone?" She accepted a fresh bottle of water from the other woman to wash away the grit in her throat.

"I'd have probably paid some of the boys that hang around to help load." Marianne nodded toward the children now kicking a ball against a battered brick wall. "Many of them are orphans from the last hurricane."

Pity swelled in Rowena's chest.

"Don't worry. I'll give them some *meticais* before I leave. Although they should be in school. At least they'll eat tonight."

Row wished she could help them, but it wasn't her place, especially when she couldn't even save herself. She knew there were far too many people who found themselves in difficult situations

—but it was hard, really hard, to imagine being an orphan with no home or food security in a place like this. She'd been lucky, she realized. Sure, she had issues, but it had never been life or death, not until she'd begun this foolhardy quest. She'd always had a home and food on the table and love in her life.

Kurt tossed the shovels in the back of the truck and returned the barrows to where they'd found them.

"I'm glad we could repay your hospitality and kindness in a small way." Kurt removed his own bandana and wiped his forehead and neck. He grabbed the water and took a swig. Row watched the line of his neck ripple as he swallowed before he splashed the rest over his face.

She shook herself out of her current obsession. The thought of losing him was starting to eat at her nerves, and she didn't like it. They'd only known each other a few days, and she wasn't the kind of woman to rely on a man.

"Thank you." Row hugged the other woman even though she didn't seem like the hugging type. Marianne surprised her by giving her a tight squeeze.

"Come visit again sometime, okay?"

"I would love to." Assuming she was ever allowed back into Africa. "And you come see me in Shropshire. I'll send my address to your website."

Kurt stepped forward with his own hug. "Thank you for your help."

"You're not bad for someone who sucks the life and soul out of people for a living." She patted his cheek. "Don't forget what I told you."

"I won't forget." He kissed her cheek. "I'm sorry you lost your husband."

"But I had him." Her voice broke. "I had him for all those years. I wouldn't swap that for anything in the whole world."

Marianne headed inside to pay the man for the fertilizer. She obviously did business here regularly.

"What did she tell you?"

A thoughtful smile curved his lips. "Things I needed to hear."

The sound of squealing tires had Row lifting her gaze in concern. Kurt reached into the backpack and pulled out the pistol. "Get in the truck. Quickly!"

She ran around to the other side, but the rat-a-tat of automatic gunfire and the spit of bullets in the ground near her feet made her freeze with her hand on the door handle.

The bullets stopped as soon as she stopped moving.

Oh my God.

Oh my God.

Her heart raced so fast she thought she might faint.

She didn't want to get shot. Didn't want to die.

A small army of men bristling with weapons leaned out of every window of a white SUV. Her mouth turned to ash. Kurt and one measly pistol had no chance against such overwhelming firepower. He seemed to realize the odds were not in their favor and stepped forward, raised his hand with the gun dangling uselessly from his fingertips.

"I'm not going to let them hurt you, Row. Whatever happens, whatever I say to them from now on, know you're my priority." He spoke quietly and urgently.

The men tumbled out of the car and pointed their weapons at him.

"Try to avoid gaining their attention. It's me they want."

Were they going to shoot him even as he surrendered?

Her heart banged in her chest.

The thought of losing this man...

"Joe?" Her voice wobbled even as she was proud of herself for not using his real name.

One tall lanky man ran toward Kurt in a loping gait, yelling at him in Portuguese.

"Stay absolutely still. Hopefully, they'll leave you here. Go to the British or US Embassy and tell them what happened. Don't trust *anyone* else."

The man yelled some more and hit him with the butt of his

weapon—straight into the arm that had been injured yesterday. Kurt staggered in pain.

"No!"

Kurt shot her a concerned look as the man started to frog march him to the car at gunpoint.

Marianne stepped outside the building, but a man pulled her back into the shadows. Row didn't want the other woman to get involved. She couldn't just let them take Kurt.

"You can't do this!" She ran toward the SUV, unable to bear the thought of them hurting him and her doing nothing to stop them. If they took him now, she doubted she'd ever see him again. "Leave him alone!"

Another man ran over and grabbed her arm, fingers biting viciously into her skin.

"Leave her the fuck alone." Kurt began to struggle then. "She has nothing to do with any of this. I don't even know her. She's some skirt I picked up along the way."

But the man with the bloodshot eyes either didn't believe him or didn't care. He dragged her across the rutted ground and threw her into the back of the vehicle beside Kurt.

The look in Kurt's eyes was pure fury.

"I couldn't just let them take you," she whispered.

His eyes shimmered, and he blinked away something that looked suspiciously like tears. "Whatever happens don't fight them. I'll get you out of this. I promise, but it might get hairy for a while. Don't give up. Promise me you won't give up."

She nodded slowly, terror sinking into her lungs. He thought they might rape her. Her pulse tripped and stumbled. She took a couple of deep breaths. Nodded, wishing she hadn't tried to stop them, knowing she couldn't have done anything else and lived with herself.

Her hands shook as the men bound her wrists together with old rope. One of them punched Kurt again while she sat slack-mouthed in shock, unable to help him. Another pulled two black canvas bags out of somewhere and forced one over each of their heads.

The darkness was suffocating, the camphor smell cloying to the point of nausea. She started to hyperventilate.

"It's okay, Row. It's okay. Try not to panic."

Try not to panic?

Tears formed even as she held back sobs. Everything they'd done. Every step they'd taken while running away from Harare was all for nothing. They could have saved themselves the trouble and gone straight to the Zimbabwean police.

She cried harder as Kurt's bound hands found hers.

They'd been captured by these bandits with no one to save them. But why? By whom? And maybe more importantly, what did these gun-wielding maniacs intend to do with them now?

21

R owena's tears were like stabs to the heart. Thankfully, she'd managed to stop crying before they were dragged noisily out of the vehicle and hauled into this dank room that smelled of sweat and desperation. Not that Kurt begrudged her some heart-felt tears, but every noise she made, every movement, drew these men's attention to her. And *that* he fucking hated.

The rain had burst through the clouds on the drive here. Only about ten minutes from the warehouse, so still in Beira.

They kept him and Rowena tied up on cots on opposite sides of a small office-like room in a heavily shadowed adobe building. Three men were in the room with them.

Two men sat playing cards at a small table to one side.

The man Kurt figured for the leader sat behind a big, old mahogany desk, going through Kurt's backpack and examining everything carefully before putting the contents neatly back inside. Except for the knife, which he kept. He sent him a long look as he slipped the blade into his desk drawer. He was short with sharp eyes and close-cropped hair. His skin was deep brown and glistened with sweat.

He spoke Portuguese so was probably local.

These guys seemed like a street gang, rather than mercs.

Perhaps he could persuade them with reward money from the US government. What would he be worth, Kurt wondered?

Not even a Business Class airline seat on an average day, but this was different. This was an assault on the whole organization, and he intended to make sure someone paid.

So would the FBI.

The other gang members had dispersed around the building. Perhaps as guards. Perhaps sleeping. They seemed to be waiting for something to happen. Maybe a phone call? Or for darkness to fall?

They'd removed their black hoods, which meant he could at least keep an eye on Rowena, but Kurt wasn't sure it was a good thing they could both identify their captors' faces. He would do everything to imprint them on his memory and bring these motherfuckers to justice.

He caught Rowena's muted green eyes. Tried to convey the depth of his remorse that she'd been taken with him, the depths of his feelings for her. Didn't matter he'd told her not to get involved. She'd been trying to protect him. He understood her motivation. Respected it. Even as he hated the fact she was now being held captive with him.

He wasn't sure what he could do if these men attempted to hurt her, but he'd die trying to protect her.

And then she'd probably be dead too, or living in sexual slavery.

No.

Surviving was the most important thing even if it meant short term pain. Getting her out. And then making sure every motherfucking one of these bastards paid with blood and tears.

"If it's money you want, give me a phone. I can get you money in a few hours. No questions asked."

The leader's glance flickered suggesting he spoke English, but he didn't respond.

Kurt had counted eight men so far. Seen six AKs, multiple Glocks glued to skinny hips or lying around like the one on the desk in front of him, more tempting than a naked woman to an incel. At least he knew what to do with a gun—and a woman—once he got his hands on one.

He looked at Rowena, and their gazes meshed. A quiet connection that bolstered him. She was stronger than she knew, and he respected the hell out of her.

Loud laughter came from the two playing cards as one scooped up his winnings. Every one of their abductors also carried a large hunting knife.

The room was crumbling old yellow brick on three sides and exposed wattle and daub on the fourth side, with a large double door open onto some kind of courtyard that had a broken stone fountain at the center. Old, colonial Portuguese architecture. Beautiful, grimy, decaying. Ruined by time and neglect. Mother Nature reclaiming her due.

Two vehicles were parked inside the courtyard.

The dirty window behind him was large and ornate, glass missing from half the panes. Water spat at him through the broken shutters. The rain was still pouring down.

One of the men playing cards kept sending Rowena hungry glances as she sat with her nose pressed to her knees. Her eyes were either on the floor or on Kurt.

The man's glances were sly.

Predatory.

The leader seemed to know what his men were thinking when they looked at Rowena but, so far, he hadn't allowed them to do more than touch her with their eyes.

Which made Kurt want to snap bones.

Mosquitoes buzzed, and Kurt wished he and Row had both taken a malaria tablet that day. Stupid but he'd been distracted by more obvious dangers. The antibiotics Marianne had given him were still in his back pocket, although they'd found the burner and SIM card in his shirt pocket and placed it in his backpack.

Smart in some ways.

Sloppy in others.

Sloppy not to search him properly. Sloppy to tie his hands in front on him and not bind his ankles. Sloppy to leave handguns scattered carelessly on the desk. If he'd been alone, he might have gone for one. If they attacked Rowena, he still might. Two steps would take him to the desk. Glocks had no safety to worry about, and he could probably finish off the kidnappers in this room before they could get off a shot. But Rowena was directly behind the leader and in the line of fire. Somehow Kurt didn't think that was an accident.

The man was cleverer than he first appeared, and Kurt had to wonder if this setup was a test.

Why?

To see if he attacked, or to see if he was a kitten.

He was happy to pretend to be a kitten. For now.

Was it the classic kidnap-for-ransom scenario where they would be moved regularly until someone negotiated their release? That could take months or years. If it was, he planned to do what Quentin Savage had done with Haley Cramer and claim Rowena was his wife in the hopes it would protect her.

Presumably they wanted Kurt alive as he was the one they'd targeted.

The fact Rowena was in danger made him crazy, but the fact she'd tried to save him also moved him deeply. It was the sort of thing he would have done for his daughter, for his team. The sort of thing he'd have done for her...

If it wasn't a classic K&R, was it Gilder, Spartan, and Hurek tying up those loose ends?

If so, why not shoot him on the spot? Why take him and Rowena captive? Were they searching for the photographs? Did they even know about them?

Had Marty fucking Sinclair betrayed him? Sinclair had said there was a US Navy frigate three hours out from port when he'd spoken to him from the warehouse bathroom. Had Gilder somehow picked up that call from the burner? Traced it. Was this all Kurt's fault?

Or had one of those kids running around the warehouse been shown a photo and told to be on the lookout for him? Easy enough to spread the word to gangs like this along the coast while offering a large reward. The gangs would put the word on the street.

Or had some drone or satellite picked him up somewhere, somehow, and notified Gilder or Spartan who'd then mobilized this little gang of hired thugs?

Or, worse, had Marianne delivered them into the arms on the enemy?

Somehow the idea of that betrayal seemed even worse than some dirty CIA officer.

Kurt could offer these abductors more money or threaten them with FBI reprisal, but he'd wait to see what they wanted first. Never make the opening offer. He knew enough about negotiation to know that.

He hoped this was a run-of-the-mill kidnapping because as soon as they demanded money from Daisy, the whole FBI would be alerted to the possibility he was still very much alive. And at least they could stop mourning him and concentrate on finding him.

Delta Force or DEVGRU or HRT could track him down and take these motherfuckers out in a firefight. The only worry was Rowena getting caught in the crossfire.

The most dangerous time for any hostage was during a rescue.

But if this was a simple K&R, the mercs who'd been chasing him and Rowena through the Eastern Highlands would likely hear about the kidnapping via the criminal network long before any rescue attempt and have zero qualms about making sure these men never told anyone who they'd caught in their net.

Which meant he and Rowena had to escape sooner rather than later. Preferably tonight. If there was a frigate off the coast, he could find a way to contact the ship and get him and Rowena onboard. If there wasn't a ship, he'd steal a boat and get into international waters before calling for US assistance.

The guy at the desk turned on a lamp that cast a warm yellow glow over the weapons. The sun had disappeared. Sounds outside suggested there were people in the street, dodging the rain and living normal lives. His Portuguese was a little rusty, but from the tone of the conversations, these men belonged in the community.

Running away wasn't going to be a breeze.

The rotary phone on the desk rang, an old-fashioned strident noise. The leader snatched up the receiver, listened carefully, then slammed it back down in the cradle.

Those eyes glittered as they stared at him.

"*Vamos!*"

Let's go.

The other two men dropped their cards and picked up the AKs and dragged Kurt to his feet. He stared at Rowena and braced for a fight. No way was he leaving without her.

"*Os dois.*"

Both of them.

He relaxed a little. They shoved him toward the vehicle, the butt of the AK digging into his kidney in a way that made him want to return the favor—with a blade. He refused to say a word. Refused to give them an opening to use as an excuse to hurt Rowena.

They forced him back into the SUV, but one of the men tried to drag Rowena into the back seat with him and his friend.

Kurt stiffened.

The leader cuffed his subordinate and pulled Rowena out of the car and shoved her beside Kurt in the cargo area.

She was shaking as she pressed herself to his side. He wanted to wrap his arms around her and tell her it was going to be all right, but he wouldn't lie. The best bet was for him to work on the rope binding him and then grab a gun and shoot their captors while they were en route to their next destination. Except, chances were high one of them would get a shot off, and one bullet could be enough to end Rowena's life for good.

He ground his teeth, pissed as the black hood was placed over his head again.

When the trunk slammed shut, he grabbed Rowena's hands in his and squeezed. She squeezed him back. She hadn't given up hope yet.

He worked on loosening her ropes, the knots were tight, but he felt the first one begin to give. The stink of the canvas hood overrode most scents, except he swore he could smell baked seaweed and dead fish. Were they at the harbor? Could this be Marty fucking Sinclair's idea of a rescue, rather than an abduction?

A tendril of hope began to curl inside him.

When the vehicle stopped, it was quiet outside, and no one spoke. The door opened, and someone dragged him out by his injured arm and led him onto what felt like an unsteady gangplank.

"Struggle, and you'll end up in the water." The voice was low and threatening, speaking English.

It *was* a gangplank, and they were getting on a boat. "What about the girl?"

What if they forced him onboard and kept Rowena for themselves?

"Your girlfriend is coming. For now. Although, she won't be yours for much longer. I'm hoping I get a turn before we leave because she is *fine*." The dark chuckle told him this wasn't a rescue.

Kurt shoved the guy hard, ripped the hood from his head in time to see the bastard go flying through the air and land with a splash between the hull of a large wooden vessel and the harbor wall.

He turned and the leader stood behind him, a gun to Rowena's head.

Shit.

The man glanced sideways as his man spluttered in the water. He shouted something down to him then raised his chin at Kurt.

"Keep moving, Mr. FBI. Otherwise, I'll shoot this one right here, and no one will even notice, let alone care."

Rowena visibly shook.

Kurt pressed his lips together and nodded. Turned and walked onto a large green boat that looked a lot like a fishing trawler.

Onboard, he was once again shoved along, but Rowena was by his side now, the hood removed, and despite the danger, he felt reassured. Maybe this was a rescue designed to look like these guys were bad guys rather than working with the American government.

And who'd have thought he'd have become a raving fucking optimist?

They were forced onto the floor of a small room beside the main cabin where the captain stood behind the wheel, legs spread wide, not even glancing at his human cargo.

Perhaps he was being forced into this. Perhaps he didn't want Kurt to see his face. Kurt studied the man's reflection in the glass and vowed to remember each and every person involved in this nightmare.

There was a shouted exchange between his abductors and the crew, but the armed men quickly left, and Kurt heard them laughing.

Presumably they'd been paid.

Would Gilder let them live? Kurt doubted it. They'd seen Kurt alive when he was supposed to be dead.

If Marianne had betrayed them, she'd be in danger too. He really hoped she had the sense to disappear for a while. He'd liked her.

The boat set off, the stench of diesel fumes so strong his stomach clenched.

"Are you okay?"

Rowena met his gaze and shook her head. She looked as if she might throw up. "Could be worse though, right?"

He smiled at her attempt to look on the bright side of such a shitty situation. "Maybe they're taking us out to that Naval frigate."

Her eyes widened in hope. "You really think so?"

He grimaced. He couldn't lie. "Probably not, but the CIA have done crazier things rescuing people."

"If this is a rescue, I'd hate to experience a rendition." Her bottom lip trembled. "I'm sorry."

"What for?"

"If I hadn't been with you, something tells me you'd have already escaped these guys."

His mouth tugged into a reluctant half-smile, the warmth of her seeping into him from where they were pressed together. "I might have tried, and I might already be dead." He lowered his voice further. "I hate that you're in danger."

They sat quietly for a few moments, the noise from the engine effective white noise against their conversation.

"Try to loosen the knot in my ropes, will you?"

She reached over and started playing with the knots as he wriggled his wrists, trying to build give into the binding.

Twenty minutes later, he figured it wouldn't take much more to slip them now.

But a man carrying a pistol stepped into view, and there was a shout and scramble of activity. People started running around as a large red tanker loomed out of the darkness.

———

Rowena didn't know how her life had gone from boring librarian to being winched by armed men up the side of a massive container ship on an open platform in the undulating swell of the Mozambique Channel.

The breeze was cold, but that wasn't why she was shivering. She had the feeling her life was about to change for the worse, and there was nothing she could do to stop it. She was an idiot for interfering.

Kurt's expression was tough and grim. None of the lover. All of the operator who looked ready to shove their companions into the water below them.

The wind buffeted, and she grabbed onto the back of his trousers to steady herself. She wanted to be sick, but refused to give these people the satisfaction of seeing her succumb so completely to fear.

She was in this now. In it for good. And she and Kurt would get out of it together too.

The platform jolted, and she yelped, but Kurt stood steady, holding her up and supporting her.

The men with them laughed.

"Ignore them, Row."

She swallowed the knot that formed in her throat. "I plan to, Joe."

As they reached the top, arms reached out to drag her aboard, touching her ass and breasts. She lashed out at one man, and he struck her, making her vision spin.

Kurt headbutted the offender and then kicked him in the balls, so he lay crying on the deck.

The sounds of rifles being lifted had Kurt placing himself in front of her, but there was nowhere to hide. She stepped to his side and raised her chin.

The rifle barrels parted, and a man appeared. He jerked his head, indicating they follow him toward the main part of the ship.

"I'm scared," she admitted quietly.

"So am I."

You'd never know it though from the fierce expression on his face. Row tried to quell the shaking of her legs as they were led inside the hulking tin can. She had the horrible feeling she'd never come out, or if she did, she'd be irrevocably changed.

22

Jordan had spent the better part of the day driving up and down to the J. Edgar Hoover Building, fighting rush hour traffic on the beltway, and feeling a whole new appreciation for commuters who didn't commit road rage. He strode into his new temporary office, dumped his bag on the desk. Shrugged out of his jacket. He spotted Ackers about to head home and strode out to intercept him.

"Any news?" Ackers kept his voice low.

"Yes." He moved closer. "Apparently, Montana sent a photograph of a woman called Rowena Smith to SIOC and asked for a background check on her Monday night." He paused when he heard footsteps. Shane Livingstone, one of the Gold team assaulters, came into view. He wore a cast on the arm he'd broken during a nasty op at a courthouse last month—a break that had probably saved his life. Jordan nodded to Shane and would have called out a greeting, but Ackers drew him back into his office. Shut the door.

"Who is she?"

"British national in Zimbabwe visiting family. No criminal history. No known criminal associates. She's a librarian from

Shropshire—attended Oxford. I recognized her though. She was in Vic Falls at the same time we were."

Ackers' brow puckered. "Where did Kurt spot her on Monday?"

"A popular restaurant in Harare."

"Was she following him?"

Jordan pulled a face. "Maybe. Or maybe he was being rightfully cautious when he saw the same face in two locations. I would have run her too."

She was pretty. Hard not to notice a woman like that.

Ackers frowned. "He didn't mention her to you when you spoke?"

Jordan shook his head. "It was a terrible line. If he did mention her, I didn't hear it."

Ackers heavy wrinkles bunched. "Did he take his personal cell? Did the task force check that?"

Jordan rubbed the stiffness from the back of his neck. "It crapped out in DRC after a particularly heavy rainfall. He said he'd replace it when he got home." The fact Kurt was never coming home hit him again. Hard.

"Dig into this woman. See what you can discover. If she checks out, then try to talk to her. See if she has an explanation for being where she was or if she remembers seeing Kurt."

"Yes, boss."

"Anything else?"

Jordan pulled a face. "Electricity went down almost countrywide not long after the crash, and the cell towers were out of commission for more than twenty-four hours. Not unusual, but the length of time meant lack of communications significantly impeded the response to the crash and the recovery operation." His voice roughened. "They still haven't identified Kurt's body among all the others."

"It could take some time, especially if we have to rely on DNA." Ackers sighed heavily. "What a shit way to die."

Agreed.

"Any news on the Bjorn Anders murder?" asked Jordan.

"Nothing the team at SIOC can glean through official channels."

Ackers stroked his mustache. "Some days it sucks having to play by the rules."

Jordan was willing to throw the handbook in the trash. He just didn't know where to start or what he was looking for, if anything. First and foremost, they needed to know if the crash was an accident or deliberate. If it was deliberate, who was behind it? Until that had been determined there was little he, or the US, could do, rules or no rules.

A yawn caught Jordan by surprise. "Sorry, boss."

Jetlag had kicked in again, and he was exhausted to the bone.

"Time to get home. You call the locals for an escort yet? I cleared it with VSP." He searched his desk and handed him a piece of paper with a Virginia State Police phone number. "Local switchboard will have someone in the general area and available when you need them."

"I'd hoped to put in another hour before going home—"

"Leave it." Ackers patted his arm. "Call the number and get the hell out of here. As much as it sucks, Kurt Montana is still going to be gone tomorrow. He wouldn't want you to work yourself to death tying up a few loose ends."

Jordan bristled. "I'm not working myself to death, boss."

Ackers looked at him. "Armstrong have any progress on the Hurek investigation?"

"No. HQ are talking about upping the reward to $250,000."

"Hell, I might go freelance for that. Maybe it'll help." Ackers opened his door and indicated Jordan go ahead of him. He turned and locked the door. "Get on home now. That's an order."

Jordan nodded and grabbed his jacket off the back of the office chair he hadn't even sat in yet. He left the laptop where it was on the desk and locked the door. Called the number for the VSP on the way to his EV and found the trooper waiting for him at the main junction. He headed home half hoping the sonofabitch from last night would try something again.

Unfortunately, not.

The trooper tailing him a few hundred yards behind radioed as they neared his property. "You want me to come in and help you check the place?"

The trooper's voice held a tone he hadn't expected. Sexy. Sultry.

"I'm good. Thanks for the backup." No one had gone inside according to his security monitor. TacOps were sending techs down tomorrow morning to install a better system of motion sensors and high-spec cameras around the property.

"Anytime, sugar."

Jordan reached his driveway, and the cruiser followed behind. The officer slid down her window, a pretty blonde with a confident smile and a flirty gaze. Then she turned the patrol vehicle in the wide arc and slowly rolled away.

He went inside, a chill rushing over him. Was the heating off? He turned on the lights and couldn't resist drawing his weapon as he went downstairs to check the furnace. The pilot light had gone out, so he relit it and went back upstairs. Headed into the bedroom ready to collapse on the bed in pure exhaustion. Hesitated.

He'd placed his and Montana's big black kit bags against one wall in his bedroom beneath the window. He was positive he'd put his on the top because he might need things out of his, but he didn't need anything out of Kurt's. Now Kurt's bag was on top.

Krychek slid his hand back onto his 1911 and called the trooper back. "Hey, can you take a quick swing by? I think there's been an intruder."

"10-4."

He went to call Ackers. Paused. If he told Ackers he thought someone had been in his house, his boss would insist he go into some kind of protective custody, which would be both a pain in his ass and a burden on precious resources.

The surveillance being installed tomorrow would be monitored by the techs at TacOps, and he'd get those same techs to check his current security system to see if someone had tampered with it. And if he pretended he hadn't noticed, maybe they'd feel emboldened enough to come back, and they'd catch them in the act with the additional surveillance measures.

And what if he'd mixed the bags up in his exhaustion? They looked almost identical, and the last thing he wanted was for Ackers to think he was losing his mind. He scrubbed his face with his free hand.

He did a thorough sweep of the inside of his home, going over every inch, including taking the cover off the furnace and checking in case someone had put explosives inside. Nothing. There was a firm knock on the door, and he went upstairs and checked the camera. The trooper was back.

He opened the door. "Hey. Sorry. False alarm. I cleared the place. Apologies for wasting your time."

The light in her eyes changed, and a different kind of smile touched her cherry red lips. "Oh, well now. Perhaps I should take a quick look as I'm here?"

She came inside, hips swaying in her trim blue-gray uniform as she glanced around with interest. "As I don't have much time, how about I start in the bedroom?" She looked over her shoulder expectantly as she walked away.

Jordan stood there in shock. Did she think he'd called her for a booty call? She knew he was FBI. Maybe she had a thing for G-men or wanted sex with a stranger who wasn't likely to be a threat to her or her career. He flipped the lock out of habit and stood there indecisively for a few seconds. He headed slowly into the bedroom, wondered if he was hallucinating.

She'd tossed her hat onto the dresser and unbuttoned her neat jacket.

"Trooper—"

"Mires. Ellen Mires." Her fingers had already undone enough buttons on the plain gray shirt to reveal the top edge of a lacy black bra.

"Ellen." He cleared his throat. "I, er, think there's been a misunderstanding."

"No misunderstanding." She removed her weapon and placed it beside her hat, then walked toward him and slid a hand around his neck to bring him closer. "But, like I said, I don't have much time." She bit his lip hard enough to hurt, and he pulled back in surprise. That stab of pain was the first thing to penetrate his dark fog since Kurt had died.

She pressed against him, and he found himself reacting physically to her. This woman, this stranger. Not because he wanted *her* necessarily, but because the lure of sex was better than the numbness and grief currently engulfing him.

And she wasn't pretending this was something it wasn't.

She tugged his T-shirt out of his pants and dragged it over his head. He put his weapon in the bedside drawer. Pushed her jacket off her shoulders. Undid the buttons of her shirt and cupped a full breast. She gripped him back. Worked him. Stripped them both. Rolled a condom on him and then rode him like a rodeo queen.

Afterwards she kissed him lightly on the mouth and quickly put her uniform back on. "Mind if I use your bathroom?"

He stared at the ceiling. Stunned. Bemused. "Knock yourself out."

He forced himself to get off the bed. To ditch the condom he wouldn't have thought of if she hadn't.

Shit.

He walked her to the door. The fact he was naked didn't seem to bother her.

She slipped him her card. "If you need another escort tomorrow, call me up. I'll make sure I'm *available* to you."

She batted her eyelashes at him, and he gulped. He stood staring blankly into space after she left.

He locked the door and reset the alarm. Turned off the lights and leaned against the wall.

Had he dreamed that whole thing? He wasn't sure. Was Ackers right about him working too hard? No. Never. But he was so tired he swayed in place. He headed to the bathroom for a quick shower then fell into bed. Ellen Mires' business card and the scent of sex hanging in the air were the only things that suggested she'd ever really been there.

23

Kurt kept looking for an opportunity to escape, but there were too many men, too many eyes on them, and too many damned guns. If he'd been alone, he might have thrown himself over the side and taken his chances at sea. That fantasy lasted until they were thrust into a large lounge where the man he'd spent months searching for stood preening like a peacock.

Shit and fuck balls.

Not a rescue with a grinning Patrick Killion at the end of it after all. Not that he'd held out much hope.

Two men started to drag Rowena in another direction. She screamed.

"The hell you do. Leave her alone!" Kurt fought against the men who held him, shouldering one man in the jaw so hard he dropped to the floor like a felled tree. Then twisting another man's arm so he fell to the ground. But three others grabbed him, binding him with rope around his torso. Still, he didn't stop fighting to get to Rowena.

The terrorist he'd spent months searching for whipped out his expandable baton and struck him on the side of the head.

Blinding pain fried Kurt's brain, and when the agony eased everything was blurry and Rowena was still gone.

He felt as if he'd died and gone to Hell.

Hurek paced. "We don't need the girl. She's more useful as entertainment for my men. They grow restless and we've been at sea a long time."

Kurt spat out blood as he was hauled to his knees. "Entertainment? Like the 'gang rape of Darby O'Roarke over an extended period' entertainment? Highly enjoyable if you're a rabid animal. Just one of the reasons you're top of the Most Wanted list, motherfucker. You touch her, you hurt her in any way, I'll kill everyone onboard this boat with my bare hands, including you." He held Hurek's gaze, made sure he understood Kurt meant every word.

Hurek tilted his head. "Women should know their place. She's not your wife, she's just a whore."

Rage filled Kurt. Rage and a bone-searing fear at what was already happening to a woman who'd somehow burrowed into his heart. No one deserved what Hurek's men would do. He'd feel the same rage for anyone, but Rowena was different. Rowena was his.

Hurek tapped that steel baton against his palm. "She's of no consequence. You can even have her back when they're finished with her. Take your turn."

Kurt straightened as fury fused his bones together. "Her name is Rowena Smith. And she has consequence."

"Smith?" Those dark eyes fixed on his for a moment. Shrugged. "Smith is a common surname. Common, like the girl."

There was nothing common about Rowena.

Did Hurek remember Allie Smith? Was that what had caused the spark?

"Forget about her. I don't care about her. I care about you and what we can do for one another."

Hurek wanted a deal?

Kurt pulled his reactive ass off the floor and shook off his brain. "If you think I will do a damned thing except snap your neck unless you bring Rowena Smith back right this minute, unharmed, you're an idiot." He narrowed his gaze. "And I don't think you're an idiot."

"You will deal with me whether the girl entertains the crew or not." Hurek waved his hand regally.

"No." Kurt allowed all the anger, all the rage to show in his eyes. "I won't."

"You'd sacrifice your own life, Supervisory Special Agent Montana?"

"If my life is the price, I'll gladly pay it. You damned well bring her back here, and she stays with me. She's mine." He figured the other man could understood the need to possess and claim something whether it belonged to him or not. "You obviously want something from me. Give me the girl, and I'll help you get it." His gut churned at the thought of offering to deal with this dirtbag, but he didn't care. He'd never allow Hurek to go free. But right now, saving Rowena was his first priority. Save the girl. Then make the bad guys pay. "It has to be now before they touch her."

"Ah, you don't want damaged goods. That I understand." Hurek jerked his chin at one of his men. "Bring her back. Shoot anyone who complains and throw them overboard. We'll stop at the next port and pick up a couple of prostitutes for them to play with."

Bile filled Kurt's mouth at the way this man considered women to be nothing more than vessels for a man's pleasure. All Kurt wanted was to save Rowena, and he'd cast aside all his training, caved like a new recruit. But this was going to be a long game now, and he was good at the long game.

Patience. He'd been a sniper once upon a time, and he knew all about patience.

"What makes you think I want anything from you?" Hurek was curious.

"You would have shot me on the spot otherwise."

Hurek's eyes widened and didn't deny the accusation.

"Why haven't you killed me?"

"There's still time." A slow smile spread over the man's pale brown skin. "Maybe you have information I want."

Kurt had no doubt. He wouldn't betray the FBI or his country, but he could pretend for a while to give himself and Rowena the opportunity to escape.

He heard a scuffle in the hallway before the man pushed Rowena back inside the lounge. Kurt breathed a sigh of relief.

Tears stained her cheeks and her lip was bleeding. The button of her pants was undone. Anger hardened inside him. "Are you all right?"

Her wild eyes met his. She raised her chin. Wiped her mouth with her bound hands. "Yes."

Hurek sneered as he took a couple of steps toward her. He stopped. "Who are you?"

Sensation prickled over Kurt's scalp. "I thought you said it didn't matter who she was."

Hurek strode over to her and grabbed her wrist. "Where did you get this?"

Rowena struggled and was rewarded with a strike of the baton against her side.

"Ow!"

"Leave her the fuck alone!"

The men guarding him held his arms tight behind his back and another braced his hand against Kurt's chest to stop him rushing forward.

Rowena staggered against the wall as Hurek undid the dive watch she wore around her wrist. He held it up to the light.

"Where did you get this?" he asked almost in wonder.

"My uncle."

"What is your uncle called?" He pulled back his arm as if to strike her again, and she cowered.

"It's a fucking watch, what does it matter?" Kurt bellowed.

Hurek's eyes shot to him. "Your uncle's name?"

"Peter Smith."

Hurek lowered his arm and asked in a soft voice. "And who is your mother?"

Rowena visibly swallowed. "Allison. Allison Smith."

"Allie." Hurek's eyes widened and took on a mad gleam. "Poor Allie Smith. I haven't thought about her in years..." He placed the baton under her chin and lifted. "Now I see it. You look like her."

"You knew my mother?"

The curl of Hurek's lips turned ugly. "Everyone knew Allie Smith. I didn't know she had a child. How old are you? Don't lie. I can find out soon enough anyway."

"T-twenty-seven."

Something moved in Hurek's eyes.

"And your father?"

When she hesitated, Hurek yelled. "Who is your father, girl?"

Rowena flinched in fear.

It took all four men to hold on to Kurt as he tried to get to her. To shield her from the sonofabitch.

"I-I don't know."

Hurek pulled a fresh handkerchief out of his pocket and dabbed the side of Rowena's mouth with it, mopping up the blood.

Kurt didn't think it was because he was kindhearted. The terrorist was collecting a sample. For what? DNA?

"Put them in the room we prepared. Make sure our guests are well cared for—for now." He paused at the door and addressed his men. "If anyone touches her, tell them I'll peel their penises with my penknife then toss them overboard."

Kurt stared at Rowena, and she stared back. What the fuck had just happened?

———

Rowena was pushed along until she reached some steep metal

stairs that led into the bowels of the boat. "I can't go down those with my hands tied."

She'd break her neck. Desperate, she looked back at Kurt. Perhaps if they were both freed from their bonds there was still the chance of escape.

The guard impatiently untied her wrists and signaled her ahead, considerably gentler than he had been before Hurek had threatened him. She didn't want to think about any of that. She didn't want to be grateful to a disgusting human being who was keeping her safe from the men he'd already tried to throw her to. Nor did she want to think about how he'd known her mother. She gripped the handrail, the swell of the ocean making the uneven trip down these twelve stairs feel like she was drunk. At the bottom, C deck, the guard brought her to stand well back and placed a pistol to her head as the men above released Kurt from his bindings and indicated he go down the stairs ahead of them.

Hard metal jabbed her forehead, and she nearly peed her pants.

There was nothing good about this experience.

Kurt looked at her briefly, but he wasn't telegraphing any secret escape messages. He looked ridiculously calm, as if he were walking to a weekly meeting.

At the bottom of the stairs, they went to bind him again, but he held up his hands docilely. "You don't need to tie me up. I'll come quietly."

The men looked at one another in confusion, but the man who held her seemed to understand English and shouted something to his compatriots. They stood back from Kurt. Her captor pulled her backwards about halfway down the corridor, opened a door and pushed her inside. She caught herself before she fell to her knees, absurdly grateful there was a porthole to look out of. Kurt stepped in after her and the door was immediately slammed shut behind them. A key turned in the lock, the sound like a death knell.

She met Kurt's worried gaze. "We're not in Kansas anymore, Toto."

"No shit." He held his arms wide, and she threw herself against him. She wasn't sure how he felt about her right now. She'd messed everything up, and it was probably her fault they were stuck on this boat. He hugged her to him, and she buried her nose to his chest. He smelled like sweat and the dusty fertilizer they'd shoveled for Marianne, but he also smelled like the man she'd come to know and love.

What a terrible time to fall in love.

Was it circumstantial? Or fate? Or her old bad luck raising its ugly head? The thought of Kurt dying hurt too much to even think about. There was only so much loss she could take.

"Why are they doing this? What do they want from you?"

"I don't know but I have the feeling we'll find out soon enough." Kurt gave her a firm squeeze then let go, turning to examine every inch of the room. There was a small bathroom off to the right. He checked that too. "Looks like we got the fancy digs. I was expecting a blindfold and a bucket to piss in."

"What are you doing? Can I help?"

"Give me a minute."

He went over every light fixture, crevice, and bolt in minute detail. Finally, he stood in the middle of the room and ran both hands through his hair until it was sticking up on end. "Doesn't seem to be bugged, although he obviously wasn't expecting two of us."

Row sagged. She hadn't even thought about the possibility of bugs.

"I'm sorry I got you into this mess, Row."

"What?" She grabbed his hand. "It's not your fault. If anyone is to blame it's me."

He didn't look convinced.

"I know I'm the weak link. How's the arm?"

He twisted it to check it out. "Fuckers made it bleed again, but it seems clean." He dug into his back pocket and pulled out the orange pill bottle. "Still have these."

"That's a relief." She crossed her arms over her chest as a shiver raced over her skin. "I hope Marianne is okay."

"Yeah, so do I." Kurt nodded. "Unless she's the one who betrayed us, in which case I hope she burns in hell."

Her eyes flashed. "You think someone betrayed us? It wasn't simply bad luck?"

"It might have been bad luck, but I doubt it."

She wasn't about to tell him she considered herself a bit of a curse. She didn't want him to hate her. "It wasn't Marianne. She liked us."

Kurt grunted. "She liked you."

Row smiled. "You grew on her."

He scratched his head. "Thing is, if it wasn't Marianne then it was my contact at the US Embassy. And that means he lied about everything and there's no rescue ship nearby and no one in the US government knows I'm still alive, let alone that you're with me."

The cold truth of that statement curled over her shoulders like a metal yoke. They could be held hostage for months or years or shot tomorrow and thrown into the ocean, and no one would ever know. The thought was unbearable.

"That vile man called my mother a slut."

"I wouldn't take his views on your mother personally. He doesn't strike me as a man with a very positive opinion of women in general. He got very excited about your dive watch though."

She looked at her naked wrist. "I found it in the attic. I assumed it was Uncle Peter's. He used to dive a lot."

"Hurek recognized it."

"Yes. He did." She didn't know what that meant. "He knew my mom was dead. The way he said 'poor Allie.'" She could tell from his eyes that he'd noticed it too. Even though her mother supposedly meant nothing to this man he knew she was dead even though she'd lived far away.

Her mouth went dry.

"Look, it's late. We've had a shit few days. I've no idea what's going to happen next, but what I'd like to do is get cleaned up while I have the chance before I crawl into bed for some rest so I can think more clearly. I don't want to dirty the sheets."

She glanced at the single narrow bunk. "Only one bed." She choked up and looked away. Pretended her eyes hadn't filled with tears by staring determinedly out of the porthole that contained nothing but blackness.

Kurt came up behind her and turned her in his arms, placed her head against his shoulder as she lost it. He pushed out a chair with his foot and dragged her onto his lap and rocked her like a child. For the second time in forty-eight hours, she found herself bawling all over him. For someone who rarely cried, it was humbling.

Finally, the tears subsided, and she sniffed loudly, needing to blow her nose but not wanting to move from the illusion of safety in his arms.

Kurt angled away so he could catch her gaze. "We'll get through this, Row. It's not going to be easy. It's not going to be fun. But we are going to have each other's backs and make a plan, and we are going to get through this. Understand?"

Her breath shuddered out as she nodded.

"Okay, you grab the first shower."

"I have a better idea." She took his hand as she led him to the small bathroom.

"I'm not sure it's a good idea…"

"Not sex. I don't want to be alone, and we can at least close the door."

"We can do that."

The small bathroom was well stocked with towels, soap, shampoo.

"Pretty cushy digs for a kidnap victim," she commented.

Kurt looked around with narrowed eyes. "It really is. And knowing what I do about how he used to keep his hostages, it makes me wonder what the hell he wants from me and how long he plans to keep me—and now you."

"Your last big adventure is turning into a bit of a nightmare." She stripped off the long-sleeved shirt and bra and the trousers, which had been new and were now filthy with dirt and sweat. Unfortunately, she'd have to put them back on after the shower. They were all she had.

A smile lit his eyes as his gaze ran down her naked body. "It's had its compensations."

She laughed as he'd meant her to and ducked her head under the warm spray. She undid the braids and massaged her fingers into her scalp. She half hoped he'd climb in with her, but instead he picked up her dirty clothes and started scrubbing them clean in the sink. A lump the size of Everest lodged at the back of her throat.

"It's a risk, but I figure they'll leave us alone at least for the next twenty-four hours while Hurek gets out of the area. We have water and supplies. They can toss in food if they want to via the slot in the bottom of the door like a prison cell." He shrugged, but she could tell he was not happy about any of this. "These should be dry enough to wear by morning. I'm hoping that by the time we stop at the next port, we can figure out some way to escape." He rinsed and wrung out her clothes as she washed the shampoo out of her hair.

He stripped, and she ran worried eyes over his gunshot wound.

Neither of them were in the mood to fool around. Not when it felt this dangerous, this unpredictable.

Clean, she stepped into the towel he held wide for her and went up on tiptoe to kiss him. Savored that miracle then moved away, wrapping the towel tightly around herself as he stepped into the shower. She picked up his dirty clothes and returned the favor.

"I can do that."

"I know you can. So can I." She paused, startled by the reflection in the small, steamed-up mirror. She looked exactly the same as she always did after a shower, and somehow, she hadn't expected to. Not after what they'd endured. What she'd been through. "I need to contribute my fair share."

"You already do, Row. You do." He paused, considering her carefully. She didn't know what he saw. "You're beautiful—did I tell you that yet?"

She shot him a surprised look. "Once. So are you."

"No, I mean it." He seemed somber. Serious.

She meant it too, but perhaps she should learn to take a compliment. "Thank you."

She scrubbed his clothes vigorously with some hand soap and rinsed them off. Wrung them out as much as she was able and left them in the sink.

There was only a single toothbrush and some Colgate toothpaste, but she was willing to share under the circumstances. Hurek hadn't been expecting her, and she was the biggest fool to have followed Kurt into this nightmare. If she'd stayed behind, she could have contacted the embassy. Alerted the authorities Kurt was still alive, and they could have rescued him.

She handed him a towel. "I'm sorry I didn't do what you told me to do back at the warehouse. If I had, we wouldn't both be in this mess. I could have found a way to raise the alarm about you being alive and kidnapped."

He dried off and wrapped the towel around his waist, then his arms around her. "Maybe they wouldn't have let you escape or contact anyone. And without you here, I'd have already told Hurek to go fuck himself. Without you being here, he'd be busy ripping out my fingernails, one at a time. Then he'd beat me to a pulp because I wouldn't do whatever it is he wanted me to, and that would continue every day until I was dead or caved—and I wouldn't cave."

She started shaking at the thought. She wouldn't have wanted that. Not at all. Not ever.

He dragged his fingers through her hair and tried to work through the tangles.

She winced. "It'll take hours to do anything with it."

He picked up a narrow-toothed comb that sat on the sink. "I've got nothing better to do. You?"

Tears pricked again, but she forced them back. Shook her head.

He squeezed more water out of his wet clothes in the sink, hung them up around the cabin, and propped himself in the corner of the bed, wearing nothing but the towel. Spread his legs wide and indicated she sit in front of him.

He parted her hair on one side and worked through each section a little bit at a time. "Tell me something about yourself, Ms. Smith."

"Like what?"

"Your best friend at school. Your favorite food. Pets. Embarrassing secrets…"

He was trying to help her relax, and it was working. She needed to figure out how to build resilience within herself. To enjoy the moment because it could really be her last—or she could be handed over to a bunch of savages who considered her body nothing more than an object to use. She'd bet they'd never consider it rape. It wouldn't cross their minds.

Or they wouldn't care.

It was still a very real possibility, but she couldn't let the fear destroy her. Women endured. They'd endured for millennia. She'd make the most of this time with Kurt and not think about the ugly possibilities around every corner. Enjoy the present until she couldn't.

"My best friend at school was a girl called Deb, who was constantly getting me into trouble. She moved to Lincoln after we left school."

"Nebraska?"

"Lincolnshire. North East England. I suspect ours came first."

"Show off."

She told him tales about her hometown and the old house

she'd grown up in and inherited from her grandmother. About the memories and the history. He listened patiently as he painstakingly combed through her hair and even plaited one side.

"You're really good at this."

"My kid has long, blonde curly hair that gets snags if you blow on it. You bet your ass I'm good at this. The last thing I needed was my ex complaining I couldn't even brush Daisy's hair."

His voice broke, and she grabbed his hands and pulled them around her and hugged him to her as he hugged her back. It was the first sign of weakness he'd shown since this began.

"We're going to get through this, Kurt. You're going to see your daughter again."

His fingers gripped hers. "Yes, we are. Together. We're gonna get through this together."

He finished braiding her hair, and she got up and turned off the light. They lay down together, him spooning her, the thin blanket spread over them. They were on the edge of an abyss with no idea when someone would give them that final shove. She intended to hold on for as long as she possibly could.

24

The next morning Jordan awoke and yawned so hard his jaw cracked. There was a knock on the front door, and he thought about Trooper Mires.

Had *that* really happened?

Part of him hated himself for having mindless sex last night, but more for knowing he'd do it again in a heartbeat.

Would he call her tonight for an escort home?

Why not? Mindless sex beat thinking about his ghosts.

The knock came again, louder this time, impatient. It was still dark out. He grabbed a black bathrobe from the back of his bedroom door and walked to answer it. He checked his security feed and saw a man he recognized as Unit Chief Jon Regan himself, head of TacOps, standing with a tool kit in hand and a pissed-off expression on his face.

Jordan unlocked the door, and the other man pushed inside, closely followed by a geeky-looking girl in black glasses that peeked out from thick black bangs.

"They sent the big guns, huh?"

Regan tossed his bag on Jordan's kitchen table. "I've got one team with HRT, another in Brooklyn, and one in Texas—doing things I can't even think about outside a Sensitive Compartmented Information Facility. Figured I'd deal with this myself as it was close to home and on friendly territory. This is Crisco—not her real name. She's in training."

"I need—"

"It was Crisco, San Fran, or something vaguely lard related, but apparently that's not allowed anymore." Regan smirked, clearly trying to get a rise out of someone.

"I threatened to shoot him if he went with anything even remotely body-shaming." Crisco stuck her hands in her back pockets. "So we settled on Crisco."

"Fair."

"You got any coffee?" Regan asked.

"Yes."

"Black. No sugar. Crisco likes cream and two sugars, even though I keep telling her all her teeth are gonna fall out."

Jordan glanced at the clock. 6:03 a.m. He filled the coffee pot and rubbed his eyes. "Sorry. I'm fighting jet lag."

Regan nodded. "I'm sorry about Montana. He was a pain in the ass and a damned good friend of mine." The man's mouth pinched. "He was in Africa?"

"I'm not allowed to say."

Regan laughed and clapped him on the back. "You don't have to."

Regan was a legend in the FBI. Same as Montana and Lincoln Frazer. The cases they'd worked, ops they'd run were taught at the academy. Montana would be glad Regan was here.

"Look, you probably know someone tried to run me off the road on Tuesday night, which is why I initially asked for additional surveillance, but"—he lowered his voice until it was barely a whisper and leaned closer—"can you check if anyone fiddled with my alarm system yesterday and maybe got inside without me knowing?"

Regan was paying attention now, and it was unsettling to be his entire focus. He pulled a gadget out of his pocket and turned it on. "We can speak freely now. This blocks all transmissions from devices within a ten-meter radius. Bugs can still pick up your voice outside that zone though, so keep the volume down, especially if you're outside. Tell me why you think someone got inside?"

"I thought I'd left Kurt's bag under mine in the bedroom, but when I came home, they were the other way around." He sounded like a paranoid idiot.

Regan strode into the bedroom and took a look at the bags. His gaze also hit on the used condom in the waste basket. Although he didn't say anything, his mouth took on a knowing smirk.

Christ.

"You check inside the bags?"

"No. I planned to drop Kurt's at his place, but I didn't figure there was any rush. I need to go through it for HRT equipment first."

Regan nodded. "Let's do it now. Just in case there are any hidden surprises."

He looked carefully at the bag then placed it on the unmade bed.

Jordan shoved aside the flashes of having his brains screwed out. He wasn't a stranger to anonymous sex but never here. Never in his home.

"You know what was supposed to be in here?" Regan asked.

"I was there when he packed it, but I wasn't staring over his shoulder or anything. Friend from DEVGRU brought it back and dropped it at the HRT compound for me to pick up."

Regan ran a wand over it—checking for bugs or explosives? But if it were the latter, they'd have gone off last night. Shit.

"Hmm." The man unzipped it slowly, inserting another machine into a tiny gap. "No explosive residue."

"Skippy." Crisco's happy tone seemed to bounce off the other man's abrasive exterior.

Regan started pulling the neatly packed items out of the bag and going over everything individually. Crisco wielded a wand-like black light and inspected every item a second time— for electronic rather than biological residue.

The wand changed color when it ran over an adapter, and Crisco shot him a look.

Jordan wasn't stupid. That meant there was a bug inside it. Someone had been inside his home—unless the bug had been planted before that. At DEVGRU or even back in Africa?

Regan removed several handguns and a bottle of G96 gun oil. "Where can I put these? I don't wanna get grease all over the bedcovers."

Jordan grabbed a towel and laid it out on the other side of the bed.

Ammo followed. Lots of ammo. Regan swore. "You guys are a walking armory."

Just because they'd been away from the compound didn't mean they'd stopped training. It hadn't stopped death from finding Montana though.

"Okay. Nothing here. We'll take care of that for you." He pointed at the adapter.

Regan put everything back in the bag and placed it back on the floor.

Regan repeated the procedure on Jordan's own kit bag and found another bug, this one tucked into the inside piping of the bag itself. A wave of unease moved over him in a cold shiver. One of his ghosts giving him a friendly warning? Or something more sinister?

Regan repacked the bag, and this time left the bug in place. Jordan wanted to smash it under a hammer.

"Let me take a good look around. You go outside and help Crisco with the ladder."

Jordan realized he was still in his robe and pulled on some underwear, black tactical pants, and a black T-shirt. Before he could leave, Regan ran the wand over every inch of him and then over his socks and black tactical boots. He gave him a satisfied nod. Drew a finger across his lips.

Jordan got it. They were leaving the bugs in place for now. Who the hell would bug him or Kurt? Why?

Obviously, someone somewhere worried they'd been on to something.

What though?

"That coffee would be great about now. Thanks."

Jordan poured coffee for each of them and then went outside to help the shorter agent haul a large ladder down from the top of a panel van with a painting company logo on the side.

She slung a bag over her shoulders and grabbed one end. They tromped through the wooded area around his lot. "We'll start here. Create a complete perimeter with cameras and motion sensors."

"The deer—"

"We know we're gonna spot wildlife in the woods, Operator Krychek." She rolled her eyes.

Ouch. "Call me Jordan."

She smiled at him. "We already have a Jordy at The Center, so I'm gonna go with Krychek instead. It's cooler. Very X-files."

He was getting whiplash from the conversation, but he wanted to know about the bugs. "Back there…"

"I have the first bug in a box in the van that shields the persons being spied on but still allows the signal to transmit. Once we get it to the lab, we can try to trace the signal back to its origin. To have a hope of doing that we have to leave the other bugs in play for the time being."

"So they just assume the FBI is incompetent?"

Crisco smiled coolly. "They get to think they're safe. Right up until the moment they aren't."

He helped her set everything up and was impressed by the coverage the cameras gave in all directions. "Can someone come in and cut the power?"

"Battery operated."

"What about block the signal?"

"Sure. We'll have an alarm set up that goes straight to us, the local cops, your boss, and the nearest resident agency if that happens."

"What about blocking that alarm?"

"Any interruption or change in the signal results in an alarm being sent regardless. If they block that..." She cocked her head as she considered. "Pretty sure that would mean we'd lose all our feeds, in which case, the alarm would be raised."

"How would you bypass this system?" They trudged back slowly to the house, carrying the heavy ladder. The mist was rising through the trees in the early dawn.

"We do brainstorm this kind of thing, you know. One of the reasons we have multiple cameras in each position is so that no one can approach the camera from a blind spot." Her eyes lit up. "If it was me, I'd use a drone with a paint sprayer. Do it at night and block out all the lenses. But I'm pretty sure that would trigger an alarm, as we have infrared cameras at night. Bottom line is we will know immediately if and when anyone tampers with or sets foot on your property, and that will alert local cops and feds and alert you on your phone, hopefully giving you time to protect yourself. It won't stop an army, but..."

Jordan grunted. "I don't know why anyone is wasting their time bugging me. I don't know anything."

"Someone thinks you do. Be careful what you say inside until Regan gives you the all-clear."

Had whoever bugged him heard him having sex last night with Ellen Mires? Should he warn the Trooper? Was she in danger? Did it matter if he had sex? It wasn't illegal. It hadn't been intimate. In fact, it would have been more intimate if they'd had a romantic dinner or played chess.

He and Crisco arrived back at the house. Secured the ladder back on top of the van.

Regan was smoking a cigarette on the wraparound porch. "Didn't find anything to worry about." He held up his hand with four fingers—obviously he'd turned off his signal blocker.

Shit. "Well, that's good news. Thanks for coming out. Apologies for it being a waste of time."

"No problem." Regan crushed his cigarette and strode over to Jordan, indicating he follow him out into the woods where the birds had started to sing.

He turned his signal blocker back on. "No cameras, just audio. Act normal. Pretend like you don't know you're being bugged. Put the radio on or the TV or something until you go to work. Any belongings at work that have been out of your sight for any length of time?"

Jordan shook his head. "My car is still in the garage. I'm driving that vehicle over there temporarily."

Regan's eyes narrowed. "You think they were trying to scare you the other night or kill you?"

"Kill me."

He looked over his shoulders and nodded for Crisco to examine the vehicle.

"These bugs are not something I've seen before. I don't know if this is state sponsored or some private enterprise. I do know they're pretty sophisticated, so now I'm curious."

"Can you track it back to source?"

"My guys can do anything, given enough time. Give me your cells."

Jordan balked. "The work cell has classified—"

"I'm not interested in reading your messages unless it's with the person you got it on with last night."

"How did you know—"

"You think I couldn't smell sex when I walked in the room? Either that or you jacked off into a condom, which is weird, but whatever. Each to their own. Girlfriend?"

Jordan dug into his pocket and handed over his two cell phones.

Regan put a replacement in his hand. "It's the same work number but monitored and tracked. Who was the woman? I'm assuming it was a woman, which is my bad."

"Virginia State Trooper who gave me an escort home last night. I called her when I saw the bags had been tampered with in case there was someone still in the house. She, er, took it for a booty call."

"Well, now, if I'd known that came with the service, I'd've gotten someone to run me off the road too, but with my luck I'd get Hank Previtt, and I have no desire for him to bounce on my balls. What's her name?"

"Ellen Mires."

"You know her before last night?"

"No, sir."

"You're just that fucking hot, huh?"

Jordan felt his cheeks singe.

"Relax. I'm not your mother. I'm not judging you except with pure envy. I'll get your cell phones back to you this afternoon. I am going to do a background check on this Trooper Mires. And let me know if any other women suddenly find you irresistibly attractive, okay?"

The thought the trooper could be involved depressed the hell out of Jordan. "And what should I do if she's my escort again tonight?"

"Enjoy the fucking ride, you lucky sonofabitch. And don't tell her about the listening devices or any other damned thing. Don't let her out of your sight either. Not for a second. No sleepovers. Last thing I want is to have to come back every morning because you're screwing the enemy."

Jordan shook his head. "All of a sudden I'm not interested in any more hookups."

Regan narrowed his shrewd blue eyes. "You want to figure out who is doing this and why, don't you?"

Jordan jerked his chin up and down. Of course.

"So if she's involved, she's involved. If she's not, she's not. Either way, try not to tip her off." Regan placed the signal jammer in his palm. "Use that if you want to talk about something sensitive. They shouldn't be able to penetrate it."

Jordan stared at the jammer with a sinking feeling.

"Remember what Sun Tzu used to say in *The Art of War*. 'Keep your friends close: your enemies closer.'"

"I'm not sure this is what he had in mind."

Regan laughed. "Then you obviously don't know much about women."

———

Kurt woke up with Row in his arms and darkness around and inside him.

He'd failed her. For all his training, his supposed smarts, and his upbeat talk they were both wrapped up like a couple of dying flies waiting for the spider to come and suck them dry.

She twisted in his arms and twined her legs with his. At some point in the night their towels had come undone, and both of them were naked. Despite the situation, he found himself growing hard. He had no intention of taking advantage of her or reminding her about the threat of torture and gang rape being dangled over their heads like Damocles' sword.

He felt her tense against him. "It's okay. I've got you."

She relaxed again and seemed to go back to sleep.

It was a damned lie. He couldn't save her if they came for her again. He'd die trying, but the reality was likely a severe beating for him, and they'd still do whatever the hell they wanted to her.

He couldn't protect her, and the knowledge was humbling.

What did Hurek want from him? Classified information? Secrets? Intel? Before he'd have said they could do anything to him, and he wouldn't tell them a damned thing. But he'd gone and given the bastard a weapon to use against him. A goddamned nuclear bomb to blow up everything good and noble he'd ever done.

They could have used Daisy too. He was grateful they hadn't taken Daisy—as far as he knew—but Rowena meant so much to him already. So much. They'd found his kryptonite, and now he had to figure out how to limit the damage. To deflect and delay. Lie if he could get away with it. Hope they could get out of this mess or signal for help somehow. In the meantime, he'd play the willing, cooperative captive.

Survive.

He'd never cause real harm to his colleagues or his nation, but he might have to sacrifice a few principles in the dance between keeping Rowena alive and protecting everything else he held dear.

Perhaps he could lay a trap...

He thought about the photos in those envelopes sitting in the mail. Bjorn Anders' cell phone. How long would they take to arrive at their destination? Would the people on the receiving end know what they meant? The implications? Would they prove Anders had been in league with Spartan, Gilder, and Hurek?

He wasn't sure.

Fuck. He didn't know if they'd ever reach the people he'd sent them to or convey what he needed them to understand.

Rowena stirred again. This time she stretched languidly and ran her thigh over his, stroking his raging erection. He wanted her, but fear for her threatened to drown him.

"I can't. It feels wrong."

She inched up so her lips were close to his ear. "This might be the one choice I get regarding my body. I'd very much like to choose you for as long as you'll have me."

Jesus. What she had to be going through all because he'd decided to "save" her.

The reality was she'd saved him, not the other way around. And now he'd doomed her with his confidence and self-belief.

His hands spanned her waist as she rose up over him, keeping in their little cocoon beneath the blanket. "If it was up to me, I'd choose you forever."

She opened her mouth in a small gasp of surprise.

It was true.

Somehow, the two of them meshed in a way he'd never meshed with anyone before. Not one single person on the whole planet. He'd come close with some of his buddies, but it wasn't the same—and it wasn't only because of the physical aspect of his and Rowena's relationship.

She inspired him with how she thought and how she behaved under pressure. She'd held up better than most agents he knew. Almost as well as a trained operator.

She moved over him, kissing his neck, touching his chest, dissolving his resistance like water eroded a wall of sand. It wasn't desire but an inner rebellion.

Fuck Hurek. Fuck them all.

His hands shook as he positioned himself against her, and he moaned as she slid over him, enclosing him inside her. Taking him in. Filling him up in a way he'd never experienced before.

The fact that he knew she wasn't experienced when it came to sex made him want to be gentle, especially in the face of what might come next, to treat her like the most precious thing, because she was.

He could faintly make out the details of her face in the darkness. That too-wide mouth. The straight nose. The faint glimmer of pretty eyes. He rose up, cupped the back of her head and brought her down for a kiss that was both sacred and sweet. He explored her mouth while his hands traced her breasts, her back, her legs. She rocked over him gently, and he found her nipple with his mouth, sucking softly at first and then with more pressure. He felt her reaction, figured out the sweet spot between too hard and not enough. Heard her whimper. Felt her clench and tremble around him and then shudder in wild abandon.

But he wasn't done. She was right. Maybe this was their last time together, and he intended to give her everything he was able to give. He slithered down the bed and sank his mouth into her folds, loving the taste of her as his tongue sank inside learning every intimate detail. She whimpered again as he sucked on her clit. He knew he was doing something right when her thighs began to shake, her fingers gripping his hair painfully tight.

"I want you inside me now." Her voice was a whisper on the night air.

He'd never deny her anything if he had a choice, but he wanted to give her experiences. Good experiences. He moved behind her where she'd braced herself against the cabin wall.

He nudged her thighs wider apart and drew her back against him, so she got to decide how much of him she wanted to take while he teased and played with her breasts and explored the elegant line of her spine.

She pushed against him, clearly enjoying being in control. The woman was responsive as hell and made him feel like a goddamned god. Although both of them tried to keep quiet, she made these little sounds that told him she was close.

She slid up and down one last time, driving him to the edge, and he knew he wouldn't last much longer. He found her clit, pinched the sensitive bud, felt her shudder and clench around him as his release hit him. When they both stilled, he rested his forehead against her back.

"I think I'm in love with you, Ms. Rowena Smith," he admitted, feeling as scared of that as of anything else.

But he wanted her to know. In case things got bad. He wanted her to know someone in this cruel, uncertain world loved her. Didn't matter if she said it back. He wasn't expecting it.

She nodded, rocking, head down. He was worried she might start to cry again. Instead, she twisted and pulled him down under the covers and wrapped his arm around her waist, so he held her tight.

"I love you too, Kurt Montana. I think I've loved you since you came over to fix my tire and accused me of wanting a sugar daddy."

The idea she might love him blew his mind. He'd forgotten he'd said that to her in Harare. "I guess you've got one now, huh?"

He felt her laugh. "You are the least sugar daddy material I've ever encountered, but I've got exactly who I want, even if circumstances are less than ideal."

He huffed a smile against her hair. "Less than ideal" was a bit of an understatement.

"I always thought finding out who my father was would finally make all the pieces of me click together. I was wrong. It was you and this horrible situation." She swallowed. "I know who I am now. I know I'm strong. I know I'll survive or die trying."

Emotions crashed over him like the roiling surf. Jesus, he didn't want to lose her. Not now they'd found one another. "Come with me to Virginia when this is all over. It's pretty. Might not be Shropshire but we have a history."

"A short colonial history," she said slyly.

He scraped his jaw over her shoulder. "It seems wrong for the colonizer to show off about the size of their own history."

He sensed rather than saw her grin.

"Ouch. You have a point. I'll be on the first flight out to educate myself. I'll grant sexual favors every time you show me something older than my grandmother's home that isn't natural rock."

"How old is your grandmother's house?"

"There's an engraving from 1770 on one of the lintels. I suspect there are parts that are older, but we'll take that as the benchmark."

"So anything pre-Declaration of Independence will be a win?"

"Hmm. It shaves a few years off, but I'll throw you a bone."

"Trust me, I'm the one who's going to be throwing you a few bones." She laughed like he'd hoped. "I think we're gonna spend some time in Jamestown for starters then move on to Williamsburg."

She twisted to face him with surprise lighting her face. "Are you a closet history buff, Supervisory Special Agent Montana?"

"Like any good tactician, I know my military history, Ms. Smith."

Her eyes shone, and he knew he'd scored a point in his favor.

"I should have known." She reached out and cupped his stubbled cheek.

"You're about to get a whole hell of an education on American history. And lots of sex."

She laughed a little breathlessly. "I can't wait."

The laughter in her eyes died a little as their current situation crowded in around them.

"Get some sleep. It's early yet."

She nodded and yawned loudly. Gradually, she drifted off while Kurt lay awake in the darkness, running every possible escape scenario through his mind. Every one of them would depend on luck as much as skill. And luck could go either way and turn a relatively stable situation into a shit show.

How long did DNA results take to come in? He had no doubt that's what Hurek planned to do with the sample of Rowena's blood he'd collected yesterday. Did he suspect one of the four friends of being her father? If so, what would that mean for Rowena?

He suspected that it much depended on which of them it was, if any.

Dougie was supposedly dead, and Kurt doubted the Scot held much sway over Hurek's current motivation. Kurt couldn't see the father being Hurek or Spartan because Rowena's complexion was milky white. Except, he knew that was bullshit. Phenotype depended on more complicated genetics than what the parents looked like. If either man had a white parent or grandparent, it might not show in the color of their skin, but it could be reflected in their daughter's.

Kurt figured he had three weeks max to figure out a way out of this mess before the dynamic shifted and pitched them all into the fire. But in the meantime, keeping the status quo, drawing things out, hoping those envelopes arrived back in the States would be the safest possible scenario for both him and Rowena.

He hated it, but patience was a virtue for a reason.

It could be tactical.

He hoped it wasn't a misjudgment that got them both killed, or worse.

25

JANUARY 15

Friday. Quantico

J ordan had gotten to work too late for the briefing, only to find most of the guys had left for Charlotte following a break in the EvilGeni-us case.

Frustration at being kept on the sidelines ate at him. He knew why Ackers was doing it. Officially, Jordan was still part of the task force chasing Hurek and could be called away at any point. But he suspected Ackers was also trying to keep him separated from the team, so he didn't blurt out something Top Secret. He resented the hell out of it, but he also knew it was possible. These men were his brothers, and it wouldn't take much for them to crack him like an egg and cause everything to spill out. Especially as he couldn't see the harm in them knowing the truth about what he and Kurt had been doing in Africa.

But it could cost him his career, and it would be unprofessional, and most importantly of all, Kurt Montana would not have approved.

He went out in search of coffee and bumped into the beautiful and mysterious Dinah Cohen who was on secondment from the Israelis.

"How was Africa?"

He frowned at her as he stirred his coffee. He could pretend the Israelis hadn't given them the lead that Hurek was in the DRC, or he could be direct. "Your intel was out of date."

She poured herself a mug. "Wasn't our intel."

"Whose then?"

"Above my pay grade, I'm afraid."

"Someone fed you a line. Might be nice to know who." He raised his chin and looked down on her. "Why are you here? Are you spying on us? So help me God, if you had anything to do with Kurt's death—"

Her mouth dropped open. "What possible reason would we have to kill a member of the FBI?"

"What possible reason would you have to abet a terrorist like Hurek?"

"None," she spat. "We want him to face justice as much as you do."

"Why? He didn't kidnap any Israelis I'm aware of."

Her lips twisted. "He did not." Her mouth firmed. "But he's had dealings with people who want Israel wiped off the map. Your great-grandfather was Jewish, you should understand…"

"You've run background checks that deep on me?" Jordan stared at her in surprise. "You've done that on everyone working here?"

She backed up a step. "We always run checks on people. It's automatic. We want to know the potential red flags before people start waving them."

"What did you find out about the people working here?" He tried to keep the threatening edge under control, but she heard it.

"Nothing of interest except that you're well-trained and loyal to one another. That's a trait we admire, Operator Krychek, not exploit."

He wasn't sure he believed her, but it struck him then that perhaps he could use her and her connections to the Mossad. Rather than treating her like the enemy he should feed her some of the information that was proving impossible for the analysts at SIOC to figure out. Regan's words from earlier came back to him. Keep your friends close…

"What do you know about a man called Bjorn Anders?"

She pursed her lips. "We know he had connections with some people we consider corrupt and that some of the contracts his firm were awarded were not the lowest or best bid."

"Who murdered him?"

She hesitated. "We don't know that. We do know someone was following him."

Jordan frowned as something clicked into place. "A Brit? Rowena Smith?"

She looked surprised. "Yes, but we can't find any connection, and now she's disappeared."

"You've looked for her?"

She nodded. "Not full scale, but we've had our feelers out. She's supposed to catch a flight home tomorrow from Harare. If she's on it, we'll let you know."

"I'd appreciate that. Thank you." He headed outside into the cold dank day. Called Regan on his new cell. "Hey, can you come over and check mine and Ackers' offices? Maybe the whole compound? Make it a routine training exercise or something? Most of the guys are in Charlotte on a mission anyway."

"I'm aware. What are you worried about? Specifically?"

"It's probably nothing."

"Uh oh—that's when I really start to worry. You haven't had a visit from Matt Lazlo's girlfriend lately, have you?"

Jordan had no idea what the guy was talking about. "We have an Israeli operative over here on an exchange."

"Ah, Ms. Cohen."

"You know her?"

"We're aware of her."

They were bugging her.

"Look, it seems stupid to do all that work at my house if my workplace is also compromised…"

"I'm not disagreeing, but I doubt the Israelis would do anything to jeopardize their relationship with the US."

"I agree. I just don't trust anyone very much right now."

"We could do a sweep as a standard check. Probably a good idea considering what we found at your place. Ackers agree to this?"

"I haven't spoken to him about it yet. He's up in DC for a meeting. The thought just occurred to me after a conversation I had with Dinah."

"Don't bother telling him. He'll say no."

"Why?"

"Because he thinks I'd bug his office."

"Would you?"

"I don't do what I do for fun, Operator Krychek. I am given orders, and I follow them." The tone was hard.

"You didn't answer the question."

"Hell, yes, I'd bug his office *if* I thought he'd ever do anything interesting enough to warrant it. But he won't, so no."

Jon Regan was giving him a headache. "So are you coming?"

"We're driving onto the base right now. I have your phones for you. Both were clean."

"That's good news, at least."

"Preliminary check on your personal storm trooper raised no obvious red flags, although I'd keep an eye peeled for an ice pick during the throes."

Jordan was relieved. The knowledge he'd been reckless enough to let a stranger into his house when he knew there was danger circling all around ate at him. Was he actively trying to invite trouble? To punish himself?

"And the bugs, did you track them?"

Regan growled. "Fuckers were on to us before we cleared three levels, but the fact they had more than three layers tells us something. I'll pick up the other electronics tonight because we want to dissect them. If you aren't planning on playing cops and robbers with fluffy handcuffs, I can be your escort home. See if we pick anything up in an unmarked."

Jordan spotted the painters' van heading his way and hung up. What the hell was going on? Who was powerful enough to bug, not to mention try to kill, a member of the FBI? And why? The obvious answer was to shut him up because he knew something, but what? He was drawing a blank.

They needed to figure it out. And soon.

———

Friday, January 22.

Kurt had officially been dead for nine days. Every day the lie continued, it amplified the pain his family and colleagues must be suffering. He scratched off a mark low on the cabin wall beside the bed, hidden from immediate view should someone come in and inspect the cell.

No one had bothered yet. He assumed they were too scared he might overpower them.

He and Rowena had been left relatively undisturbed with the exception of meals being thrust noisily through the slot three times a day. He ate more here than he did normally.

They saved any imperishable items in case Hurek changed his mind about how he treated them and decided to starve them instead. They'd stored apples, packs of crackers, and cans of soda in a recessed space in the closet. They'd formed a bit of a routine since they'd left the last port somewhere in mainland Africa or Madagascar. Their hopes of escape there had been thwarted. They'd only been in port for a couple of hours, just long enough, presumably, to drop off a blood sample to be sent for DNA analysis and to pick up supplies. He hoped to hell that didn't include unwilling women. It had been broad daylight, and their porthole faced the harbor, hampering any hope of breaking out without detection.

So they'd sailed away without a glimmer of escape.

He'd spent time dismantling the porthole without it being detectable. He could remove the casing easily enough and figured he'd probably be able to pry the window fitting out if he had a crowbar. The chair legs might work. They were tubular steel, and there was a place on the base of the chair where the steel was pinched and might be thin enough to ease into the gap between the glass and the metal for leveraging. But he needed a screwdriver to detach the legs from the base of the chair, and so far, every knife they'd been given had been wooden and useless for that purpose.

Ever since they'd left port, he'd been trying to file down the metal handle of a spoon into something he could use as a screwdriver or a shiv, or both. But it was slow going because he was using the metal edge of the bed frame as a rasp.

One thing he did know was everything had to be in place for them to bolt if and when they had the opportunity to escape. But it didn't make much sense to escape when they were so far out to sea they couldn't see land.

The seas were rough, and poor Rowena lay in bed looking green.

He gave up on the spoon and slipped it inside the hollow leg of the chair in case their guards decided to search their cell. "Okay. Ready for some PT?"

Sweat shone on her brow, but she struggled upright.

"I'll try as long as we start with yoga. Anything more strenuous might lead me to vomit all over you."

"Fun. Let's work on our downward dog." He raised his brows suggestively but only to tease.

"Perv." She swatted him gently and lowered herself carefully to the scratchy brown carpet.

He scrubbed at the beard on his face, which he hated but Rowena seemed to enjoy. Maybe it was the thread of silver in the black that he really disliked, the visual evidence in the mirror that he was older than this beautiful woman.

Though he'd searched the cabin repeatedly for bugs or peepholes, neither of them could shake the worry they might be spied on. They made love in the darkness—*coitus interruptus,* the only contraceptive method available to them. At night, when they felt safest, they abandoned their fears and indulged in each other, and it was glorious. But not today. Today the ocean was too turbulent for Row to do anything except fight the need to throw up.

They set up on the floor and started stretching, if you could call it that. He wasn't exactly known for his flexibility. It helped that they sat legs spread and feet touching. Talk about sappy. It was both a physical and emotional connection, and the only reason he was holding it together.

Once Hurek got serious about whatever the hell he wanted from them, the first thing he'd probably do was split them up. The threat to the other would be enough to control them. It was something Kurt was going to have to deal with in the moment. No point pretending he could predict what a sociopathic dictator might do, but he'd worked through various scenarios in his head.

Hopefully, they'd be long gone by then.

He flexed his foot against hers, and she laughed. She was very ticklish in all sorts of interesting places.

"I think we may be sailing around the Cape of Good Hope."

"That is not something I ever imagined I'd do."

"As soon as we reach the Atlantic side and get out of the zone where the two oceans mix the seas should settle down."

She crossed her fingers. Bent toward him offering her lips if only he could match her flexibility. Amazing what a little incentive could do for you.

"Not that we might not experience bad weather." He couldn't lie to her.

"I know." She wiped her sweaty brow. "But thanks for giving me a little hope. I never knew seasickness would be quite so vomworthy."

He'd never been afflicted, but he'd known plenty who were.

Sailing in this direction was preferable than heading toward the Suez Canal or the Indian Ocean. At least there was a vague hope they'd head West and be more able to escape.

Was Hurek plotting some kind of terrorist attack on US soil? Kurt wouldn't put it past the man, although he didn't think Hurek wanted to be a Bin Laden-esque figure. He had no real ideology, save looking after his own skin. So what was his endgame?

Why had he kidnapped Kurt rather than feeding him a lead bullet back in Beira?

They switched so one leg was bent over the other, and he leaned forward feeling his hamstring loosen a little. Rowena was quiet, and he didn't disturb her concentration, not when he was pretty sure it was the only thing keeping her from puking.

The thought that maybe it was morning sickness rather than seasickness had crossed his mind, but he figured it was too early for that to be the case.

It gave him pause. What would it be like to raise a kid from scratch again? Would Rowena want to keep it? Would they be out of this mess by then? No way would he want Rowena to deliver here in this room with no medical support.

He didn't want to put the additional worry about pregnancy into her head. He wouldn't mind another kid, but what sort of asshole risked making his girlfriend pregnant under these sorts of circumstances when the possible consequences for the woman and baby included death from complications?

They needed to stop taking risks.

The metal hull groaned audibly as the ship tipped into a deep yawing motion and then rocked violently back up the other side of the wave.

Rowena dashed to the bathroom.

Damn, he felt for her.

Maybe they had some seasickness tablets onboard.

Who did this ship belong to? Did Hurek own it? Had he always owned it? If so, how had they missed that? The FBI had been scouring the world for any sign of this sonofabitch since last summer with zero success. If he owned this vessel, they should have known about it.

Footsteps sounded in the corridor, and he tensed as the footsteps paused. The slit in the bottom of the door, about four-inches tall by twenty-inches wide flapped as something was shoved through.

Clothes.

"The captain expects you to join him for dinner, Mr. FBI. Any attempt to escape or hurt anyone onboard will end with you being beaten and the woman punished appropriately."

Appropriately? What the fuck did that mean?

Rowena leaned on the doorjamb.

He held her green eyes. "Both of us?"

"Just you."

Shit.

He opened his mouth to argue, but Rowena shook her head. She was even more green now than before.

"Tell the captain I'd be delighted. One thing. You got any seasickness tablets? I'm sick as a dog and don't want to puke all over the captain's table."

"I'll see what I can do."

26

Jordan had watched open-mouthed that morning as one of their team had been arrested and frog-marched out of a briefing, accused of vehicular manslaughter. There was no way Grady Steel was guilty, but the furor had yet to die down, and Grady hadn't returned to the compound.

Kurt had been dead for nine days with still no sign of his body. DNA was being run on all the remains found by the Zimbabwean authorities, but it was a slow process. They'd rejected offers of help from the US.

At least no one had tried to kill him lately, although he was still getting an escort to and from work. The escort home had involved a strip search and sex on two subsequent occasions — which Ellen had instigated, but he'd been more than happy to oblige. There had been no repeat of the bugs found in his home, and TacOps hadn't found any at HRT either.

Did that let Dinah Cohen off the hook? He didn't quite trust the agent even though she'd told him that Rowena Smith had not caught her scheduled flight home, which FBI analysts had confirmed.

He'd started to run his own deep and thorough background check on Rowena Smith and was finding some interesting details.

He uncovered a phone number for the relative she'd supposedly been visiting in Harare and decided to call it.

"Hello?"

"Can I speak to Mr. Gamba Moyo, please?"

"Speaking."

"My name is Jordan Krychek. I'm with the FBI."

"The FBI? Oh, Holy Jesus, is this about my niece?"

Krychek wasn't sure Gamba was legally Rowena's uncle, but the concern in his voice was genuine.

"I've been trying to locate Rowena Smith to ask her a couple of questions. Do you have any idea where your niece is at this moment?"

"No, I thought that was why you were calling. With information, not questions." He sounded angry now.

"She's missing?"

"Yes!"

"I'm afraid I don't have any information at this time. I have some questions about what she was doing in Africa."

"She was on some fool's errand. Told me she was revisiting the haunts her mother had visited when she was here nearly thirty years ago, but I know what she was really doing."

"What was she really doing?"

"Searching for her father."

"Who was her father?"

"That's the problem. Her mother didn't know. Allie went gallivanting around the country and then suddenly without a word caught a plane home to England. Didn't even tell her brother until she was back in the UK. Next thing I hear, she's pregnant, and her brother is mighty pissed. She wasn't dating anyone he knew about. The baby was born, and they seemed to make up, and then Allie died in a terrible accident. Peter and my beautiful baby sister rushed over there to take care of Row and Peter's mother. They decided to stay."

Jordan knew the aunt and uncle had died in a fire last year. "Did your niece mention how she was going to find her father?"

"No, but maybe she found a clue in her mother's belongings. She brought me some letters I'd sent to Anoona back when we all still wrote letters. Said she'd found them in the attic. I'm worried about her. The day she was supposed to join me in South Africa, she simply disappeared, and my car turned up near the border of Mozambique. I had to pay a tow truck a lot of money to fetch it back here. There was no sign of her inside, but she had replaced the spare tire."

The Mozambique border? Had she made a run for it? Why? "Could you tell me exactly where the car was found?"

"About ten miles north of the Salmon Arms Resort. If you don't know where she is, why are you calling and asking questions? What does the FBI want with my niece?"

"I'm making some inquiries about a friend of mine who died in the air crash, and I believe they may have crossed paths—Kurt Montana?"

"I'm sorry but I never heard of him."

"And she wasn't planning to leave the country?"

"Yes, she was planning to change her flight and come down to South Africa with me and her cousins." Gamba sounded impatient. "Her bags were all packed and ready to go on her bed, but she simply disappeared. I haven't heard anything since."

"Is that unlike her?"

"Son, it is so unlike her. She loves her family. She wouldn't leave us without word unless she didn't have any choice." The man choked up.

"I'm sorry. If I come across anything during my investigation, I will make sure to call you and let you know."

"I appreciate that. May God grant mercy, and we find her safe."

"Yes, sir." Jordan hung up. The uncle sounded worried, and Rowena didn't sound like some undercover agent or *femme fatale*. But maybe the uncle wouldn't know if she was.

He should have asked what date the car was found but he didn't want to call back. Not right now. He checked the time and decided instead to call the local library she'd listed as her supposed workplace.

"Good afternoon. Madeley Community Library."

"Hello, can I speak to the manager?"

"I'm the head librarian. How may I help you?"

"My name is Jordan Krychek. I'm with the FBI."

"Oh my."

The voice sounded as if its owner was old. Very old. He cleared his throat. "I'm trying to get hold of a woman named Rowena Smith. I believe she might work there."

"Rowena?" There was a second voice in the background asking who it was. "He's looking for Row. She was supposed to come back to work on Monday at nine sharp. She usually comes in earlier and sets up. I confess, at first, myself and the other librarian were a little annoyed she didn't turn up on time as we'd both worked over the holidays so she could go on her little trip. Alasdair was supposed to take a vacation the next day, but as the day went on with no word, we both grew more worried. It wasn't like her at all. Not at all. We went by her house after work, but she wasn't back. Alasdair canceled his vacation."

He heard the Scottish accent—Alasdair presumably—telling her it didn't matter.

"Then I started thinking maybe she was on that flight that crashed? I tried her cell but no reply. Filed a police report, but no one seems to be taking our worries seriously. Say she probably met someone and took another week on a beach somewhere. Row would never leave us in the lurch this way. Never. I'm terrified something bad has happened to her."

"So no contact since before Christmas?"

"She sent us photos after that, didn't she, Alasdair? We share a group chat. But nothing since the eleventh of January, even though we both texted her multiple times."

"Do you have access to Ms. Smith's home?"

"Of course. Alasdair waters the plants when she's away and collects the post."

"Have you been inside since she was supposed to be home?"

"Yes. Of course. Just to check on things, you understand. We had a cold spell this week, and we wanted to make sure the pipes hadn't frozen. Everything's fine there. I knew her granny, and she'd love to see her sweet grandbaby living in her old home. Has something happened to Row? You must tell us."

"I'm afraid I don't have any news." Jordan didn't have any reassurances to give the woman, neither did he have any data about what had happened to Rowena Smith. The fact she disappeared around the time of the crash wasn't something he could afford to ignore. Not when Kurt had requested a background check on her the night before he died.

She was connected. He just didn't know how. "Thanks for the information. This is my cell number. Would you mind letting me know if she contacts you?"

"Of course, young man. And promise me that if you hear anything, anything at all, you'll let me know."

"I'll let you know what I can." He hung up. There was a knock on his door.

Dinah Cohen slipped inside without waiting for a response. "Can I come in?"

"Sure. What do you have?"

"Our analysts found some anomalies." She was turning into a very useful source of information.

"What kind of anomalies?"

"Montana's cell phone signal. As far as we can tell, Kurt Montana didn't contact anyone after Monday night when he spoke with you. However, our analysts found evidence that his phone may have pinged off a cell tower a few hours after the flight went down."

"Cell could have carried on working after the crash."

She shook her head. "Signal was picked up way outside the crash zone. Did he take his personal cell too? We didn't find any sign of that."

"No. His personal cell died on the trip. He said he'd replace it when he got back." He'd never had the chance.

A headache began to dig into the back of Jordan's skull. "How do your analysts explain this signal?"

"Ghosts."

He shivered.

She shrugged. "Or someone might have stolen the phone."

The idea someone had stolen a cell phone after a tragedy made anger surge inside. "Did your people track the signal?"

"It disappeared after a few hours on the Mutare Road."

Jordan rubbed the back of his neck. The thought of Montana sending some kind of message from beyond the grave freaked him out. He believed in ghosts. He had his own. Hope had bloomed inside him for a few precious seconds but was dying again. "Can you push them to dig deeper until they figure out who has his phone now?"

"I'll ask them."

After she left, he pulled out the map of Zimbabwe they'd used on the trip and attached it to the wall. He put yellow and purple pins in Harare, and Victoria Falls. He added yellow at the plane crash site and googled the location of the Salmon Arms Resort— gotten to by driving along the Mutare Road. He marked off ten miles north.

He stared at the map. That was the shortest distance from the road to the border with Mozambique, only a mile from the main road. He placed a purple pin there.

Had Rowena Smith somehow gotten hold of Kurt's cell phone? Was she simply a thief, or something much more threatening? "What were you doing, Miss Smith? Who were you running from—or to?"

27

That evening Kurt, wearing a flamboyant Hawaiian shirt that stretched uncomfortably tight across his chest and white pants straight out of Miami Vice, watched guard #1 slip the door key into his pocket after he locked their prison cell door behind him.

Rowena was feeling better, and the rough seas had calmed down considerably. Unbelievably, their captors had provided a small bottle of Gravol, and Rowena had been able to take a tentative spoonful and keep it down.

He followed guard #1, while guard #2, carrying an AK, walked too close behind them.

His fingers itched to reach back and grab the gun from guard #2, use it to shoot guard #1 before grabbing the second man's knife strapped to the side of his waist and sliding it into his kidney. But although it might get him and Rowena out of the cabin, it wouldn't get them off the ship.

Ships like this usually had life rafts. He wondered if he and Rowena could get on one and launch without the rest of the crew knowing. Possibly. But probably not when he was expected for dinner.

What he really needed was that key. Or to pick the lock. But the door was also bolted on the outside which complicated things.

He was led up to the stateroom where they'd originally been brought and saw a long table set for a banquet with two places set at opposite ends.

To prevent Kurt from grabbing Hurek and using him to bargain their way up to the bridge where he could call for help? Probably.

He had a sudden thought. Hurek probably had a helicopter on the ship. It might take a little time to make it flyable, ten minutes at a pinch, but if they were close enough to land or a friendly naval vessel then perhaps that was their way out. He just had to find it, then figure out where the hell in the ocean they were, or else they might not have the fuel to reach safety.

Kurt was ordered to sit at the far end of the table, and Hurek arrived wearing a white suit with gold piping and brocade on the shoulders like some military dictator or ornate table lamp. It took everything in Kurt not to laugh. The man was petty enough to take any perceived slight out on Rowena, and Kurt wouldn't risk her. Not even for the satisfaction of mocking this asshole.

The man with the AK held Hurek's chair out for him and then stood back against the far wall with his weapon drawn and pointed in Kurt's direction. Kurt doubted he'd be able to clear the mountain of food to get to Hurek before even the most incompetent bodyguard could shoot him. Good chance Hurek might catch a bullet too, but Kurt would still be dead. And then God help Rowena.

"I trust you find your accommodations adequate?"

Kurt nodded. "Better than I was expecting."

"Well, you promised to work with me if you got the girl. I gave her to you—for now. I trust you are making good use of her in the meantime."

The threat of taking her away as if Rowena was some kind of chattel hung in the air.

Rather than react to the obvious bait, Kurt moved the conversation where he wanted it to go. "I don't understand what you want from me."

"Please." Hurek waved his hands as if they were in some fancy restaurant. "We will talk as we eat."

A waiter draped a large bib over Hurek's white and gold suit and tried to do the same to him. Kurt shook his head. He wasn't a baby.

Kurt eyed the lobster and prime rib and wondered if he'd fallen asleep days ago and was still dreaming. To say everything that had happened lately was surreal was an understatement.

Kurt helped himself to steak and salad and hoped Rowena was okay. The danger they could take her while he was dining with this motherfucker was high on his radar.

"You're probably wondering by now why I offered you my protection."

Protection?

Kurt cocked his head. He wasn't the only one living in fantasyland.

He couldn't react to the lies. He needed information. "The people chasing us in the mountains tried to shoot us. Are you telling me they didn't work for you?"

"I can assure you they were not working for me. I heard about your plight and decided to rescue you from those brigands, even though the FBI has been less than fair with me." Anger lit the back of the man's eyes, and Kurt knew he was on a rollercoaster with an unstable psycho. An unstable psycho who held the welfare of the woman he loved in his hands.

"Do you know who was shooting at us then? Who they work for? The FBI would be very interested in that information."

Hurek waved a lobster claw in his direction. "No idea, but Americans have made many enemies in that part of the world."

Hurek knew. He wasn't ready to show his hand.

"Did you know I'd been sent to Africa specifically to track you down, Mr. Hurek? I guess I have you to thank for successfully completing my mission."

A sly smile formed on the man's glistening lips. "I heard something about it. From various sources."

"You seem to have a lot of friends."

Hurek shrugged and looked uncomfortable for a moment. "Rich men always have friends. Whether they are trustworthy is another thing entirely."

So the brotherhood was cracking. "I understand you went to university in Scotland. That was a long way from home for a young man from Indonesia."

The man's smile looked sincere. "That was probably the happiest time of my life. It's the sort of experience you can never repeat, no matter how you try. I hope—" He cut himself off and frowned again.

"You a fan of haggis? I still can't bring myself to try it." It felt weird to make small talk with a guy he wanted to arrest but who instead held him captive. But he was a professional. He'd do whatever it took.

Hurek smiled. "Dougie cooked it for us, and I liked it well enough, but I couldn't stand the turnips that he insisted went with it."

"Dougie Cavanagh. He was a friend of yours?"

Hurek's mouth thinned. "He was. He was a good man until a woman ruined him."

"Allie Smith?" Kurt held his breath.

Hurek's brown eyes flashed. "She was a little bitch, always taking photos and poking her nose into everything we did. Everything changed after Dougie met her and brought her to our camp." His expression turned petulant.

"But she went back to England alone. Did she dump him?" He deliberately didn't mention the letters or photographs.

"She left." Hurek shrugged again, looking amused.

Kurt could tell he desperately wanted to share the full story but couldn't because Kurt was law enforcement. That gave him some hope that Hurek might plan to release him.

"She stole another friend's very expensive watch when she did so. A gift from his parents who died not long afterwards. He'll be glad for its return."

Gilder? Or one of the others whose background he didn't know yet? He didn't want to reveal his hand too soon. "What exactly do you want from me?"

"A little information about people in your acquaintance."

"Something tells me your friends could easily get this information for you at the press of a button."

Hurek's eyes shot to him and away. Yeah, Kurt knew who his friends were.

"I'm not at liberty to ask them at this moment."

Ah. There was definitely a rift. "Who do you want to know about?"

"Quentin Savage and Haley Cramer and a little bitch called Darby O'Roarke."

Kurt held himself very still. "You can't honestly believe I would help you hurt those people again."

"You forget I can take your girlfriend away from you at any time and make her the ship's whore."

"You can make her a rape victim, but you can't make her a whore." Rage rose up inside him. No way would he sacrifice those people. Not even for Rowena. "What's your plan exactly?"

"The Cramer woman has an island. I threaten the O'Roarke girl, and she gives me the island—a fair exchange for the one she took from me."

This guy had a lot of anger toward women. Haley hadn't done squat to him. Neither had poor Darby.

"And you presumably hold onto Darby O'Roarke as insurance."

"O'Roarke and Ms. Smith."

Kurt's jaw clamped shut. "That's a terrible plan."

Hurek flashed him a narrow look. "You'll tire of her before then."

He would never tire of her. "I work for the FBI. We don't sacrifice innocents to people we view as criminals. Why do you really want to hold onto Rowena Smith?"

Hurek looked flustered, then angry. "Women have their uses."

"Haley Cramer's island isn't much bigger than this ship and a hell of a lot easier for your enemies to track you down on."

"I can't live my life on a ship! My s—" Hurek's breathing grew labored as he cut himself off.

What had the other man been about to say? It had sounded a hell of a lot like "son."

Did Hurek have a child he cared about? On this ship or squirreled away somewhere?

"I want to be off that damned list. I want the Interpol red notice canceled. I want immunity."

Never gonna happen. He stared at the man stonily.

"I rescued you from certain death." He wagged his greasy finger at him.

"And now you are holding myself and Ms. Smith captive."

"They'd be grateful for your safe return whatever your condition. You can force them to grant me leniency."

"The American government does not negotiate with terrorists."

"That's bullshit, and you know it. Semantics. They negotiate. They just use third parties so they can lie about it like they lie about everything else—"

"They might be willing to do a deal." No point letting Hurek build himself up into a rage. "What could you offer them?"

"You."

"Besides me." Kurt cut into his steak, wondering if he could sneak the knife into his pocket. Pity the shirt had short sleeves.

"You aren't enough?" Hurek gave an ugly laugh. "From the outpouring of grief I've witnessed over your death, I'd think your return from the grave would be enough to make me quite the hero."

Thanks for the reminder.

"I'm not saying this 'rescue' counts for nothing. But it strikes me that a man like yourself would know who brought that airplane down and why. A smart man might have certain insurance policies in place to protect himself if others of his acquaintance turned on him. And if he did have evidence of someone bringing down a commercial airliner in order to target an FBI agent, well, the US has certainly been known to grant immunity to lesser charges if it means we get a conviction on the major offenses."

Kurt's stomach threatened to revolt at the fact that he was trying to sell the idea of an immunity deal to this bastard. But it was perhaps a way of telling the world he was still alive, and of saving Rowena. And perhaps, even though he hated the idea and hoped to find a way around it, he was beginning to think Gilder was the bigger threat and far more dangerous than this tin-pot dictator.

Hurek tried to look affronted, but intrigue gleamed in his eyes. "I don't betray my friends."

"Are they as loyal to you?" Kurt let the question hang in the cold air. These men didn't have a clue about true loyalty. What they had was a weak cover-your-ass imitation, not a fight-to-the-death determination.

Hurek thrust his plate away with the remnants of the lobster shell strewn everywhere. "You'd broker this deal for me? Immunity for information?"

"You'd have to let Ms. Smith go first."

A sly kind of amusement glinted in Hurek's brown eyes. "She must be better in bed than her mother was."

Kurt froze at the direct reference to Hurek having had sex with Allie Smith. "You and she were intimate?"

Hurek sneered. "She spread her legs often enough. Except for Dougie. Dougie believed they were in love and mooned over her like a little bitch. We decided to prove to him she was just a little slut looking for a payout."

Hurek looked away. Red tinged his cheeks.

So he didn't truly believe his own lies. Not even now.

Kurt wanted to leap over the table regardless of the automatic weapon pointed in his direction and punch this guy in the face until his features were unrecognizable. Instead, he picked up his glass of wine and took a small sip. Asked casually. "How did you do that?"

"It wasn't me. Nolan and Leo"—He'd stopped pretending Kurt didn't know who he was friends with—"got it into their heads that if Dougie realized she'd slept with one of us then he'd stop pining over her and boot her out."

His scalp prickled. "One of you seduced her?"

Hurek looked at him scornfully. "Who needs seduction when a girl likes her wine?"

Kurt's gaze flashed to his glass.

Hurek waved his concerns away. "I have no need to drug you, my friend. We are on the same side it seems."

The meal Kurt had eaten wanted to crawl up his throat.

"Nolan slipped her something while Dougie was…busy elsewhere. By the time he got back to camp, she was in Nolan's tent and quite obviously…entertaining all three of us."

Gang rape was something this man had been participating in for decades, and he'd persuaded himself women were somehow complicit and to blame. It seemed on brand for an animal like Hurek.

"Dougie immediately went off in a sulk for a few days, but we knew he'd get over it. Allie disappeared. We didn't know where she'd gone at first. I thought she'd wandered into the jungle in a drunken stupor and been eaten, but it turns out she cleared out before we even woke up—we'd all been pretty wasted." He laughed as if excusing their behavior. "Turns out she ran back to England with her tail between her legs, taking Nolan's precious watch with her and, interestingly enough, a baby in her belly."

"Rowena could be your daughter." What would the knowledge do to her? She'd been searching for her father but in all likelihood had not been expecting anything like this.

"She's the right age, but the girl doesn't look anything like me." Hurek lifted his wine and took a long swallow. "Who knows how many men Allie Smith fucked back then."

Even though Kurt wanted to kill the man with his bare hands, he knew Hurek spoke this way as a defense mechanism. Cast the victim as the villain, and you didn't have to spend emotional energy dealing with your crimes and failings.

Had Hurek been born this way or become twisted over time?

"If you are so disinterested, why test her DNA?"

That gaze narrowed in surprise. "Because knowledge is power, my friend. Knowledge is power. I'll think about your kind offer."

"You know the terms."

Hurek's eyes widened as if only now realizing Kurt was serious about only helping him if he released Rowena.

"If there's anything you need in the meantime to make your stay more comfortable, don't hesitate to let my men know. Take him back to his room." Hurek clicked his fingers at the guards.

Kurt had a feeling Hurek hadn't meant to reveal quite so much, but that was Kurt's charming personality for you. He figured the man planned to play the Department of Justice off against Rowena's biological father should it turn out to be one of his friends.

"Thanks for dinner." Because this was war, and war required strategy, not kicking sand in someone's face. He'd do whatever he must to get Rowena out of here safely, including being polite and palming the butter knife he'd hidden beneath his napkin. He'd also happily stab the guy in the heart and hold him while he bled out. He just needed the right opportunity. "Appreciate the hospitality."

———

Rowena's stomach had settled, and the seasickness had eased off. She felt a lot better now the ocean had calmed down, but she wasn't hungry. Just as well. They hadn't bothered bringing her any dinner. Which told her where she stood in the pecking order. Lower than the chickens.

Kurt had been quiet since he got back to the cabin. He'd immediately taken a shower and came out of the bathroom looking tired and drawn. He'd stripped off his new clothes and pulled on his freshly washed boxers which were still a bit damp. The wound on his arm had completely healed, the pale scar the only visible legacy of being struck by a bullet.

"Are you all right?"

He curved his lips but couldn't meet her gaze.

"What? What is it?"

He turned away from her. His shoulders sagged.

"Kurt," she said sharply. He was worrying her.

He sat on the bed, head bent as he took her hand and folded it in his. "I have some information that might be distressing for you. Part of me wants to keep it to myself."

"Tell me. Please."

He closed his eyes.

"Hurek told me that Dougie was sweet on your mother to the point his friends decided to stage an intervention to drive them apart. According to Hurek, Gilder slipped something in her drink and the three of them raped her in Gilder's tent, made sure Dougie found them all together."

Her skin turned to ice as she held that inky blue gaze.

"Dougie apparently thought it was consensual, at least at first. Stormed off in a huff. The rapists all passed out, and it seems your mom woke up before them and was able to get the hell out of there. She took Gilder's watch, which was why Hurek noticed it. Apparently, it pissed Gilder off that she took it."

She started to sway, Kurt pulled her down beside him, slid his arm around her and held her tight.

Her bones felt brittle and old. "Are you trying to tell me that one of those animals might be my biological father?"

He pulled her into his chest and rested his chin on the top of her head. "She might have already been pregnant at that point, but I think it's a possibility you need to prepare yourself for."

She started to tremble. All this time she'd been chasing a romantic notion of a doomed love affair, and instead she was nothing more than the product of misogyny and sexual violence.

"It doesn't affect who you are, Rowena. It doesn't affect the fact that I love you and want you the hell out of here."

This awful knowledge rang around her skull like someone banging a gong. She felt dizzy and disoriented. "Tell me the rest. Tell me everything that happened."

By the time he was done, she was lying against him, covers drawn as the dark flowed over them, protecting them from the harshness of their confined quarters. She refused to cry.

"I think Peter and Anoona knew."

"Why do you say that?"

"Because whenever I brought up the subject, they'd change it. They never encouraged me in seeking out my father. Ever. I know Peter was close to his sister. I wonder if she told him about what happened."

"Tell me how they died again?"

Her fingers clenched into a fist on his chest. "They had a static caravan on a campsite in North Wales. Portmadog—I think you call it like a trailer. My grandparents used to take my mom and Peter there as kids, and Peter and Anoona took me in turn. It's a great spot. Huge beaches and nice scenery." She could see the blue sky and golden sand. Hear the rumble of the waves. "It's only a couple of hours from home. They'd go up there whenever they had a long weekend. Mainly to escape the chance of being called into work. I haven't gone with them since I finished university, although I did go up on my own or with friends occasionally.

"They went for a week in August. They'd been up in June before the schools broke up for summer, but Anoona loved the heat if she could get it and didn't mind the crowds. So they went up again in late August, start of September. According to the local fire department, the gas burner on the stove malfunctioned, and the van caught fire. They didn't get out."

She held back tears because she'd cried a million times over their loss. "Fire department said it was an accident."

"Timing is pretty damned suspect."

"Why?"

"Hurek's lair was discovered in August last year after he kidnapped a couple of American citizens including a colleague of mine named Quentin Savage." Kurt huffed a laugh. "The two of us go at it sometimes, but it doesn't mean we aren't friends. He's a negotiator, and we work together a lot.

"We were able to track them down after they escaped and sailed to another island. They managed to signal for help, and a rescue mission picked them up. By the time we got to Hurek's island, someone else had massacred Hurek's followers, but Hurek had managed to escape on a boat he'd stolen, presumably with a few of his trusted henchmen."

She remembered the story. The implications hit her. "So Hurek was thrust back on the world stage with maximum media coverage last August."

"Maybe your Uncle Peter recognized him and got in touch with authorities. Or perhaps he contacted Gilder and threatened him…"

"You mean like to blackmail him? No way. Uncle Peter would never have done that. Wait. I do remember a weird comment he made on social media not long before he died." She frowned. "Something about oligarchs and chickens coming home to roost." She sat up. "Do you think Gilder had them killed?"

He tipped up her chin. "I think the fact you have lost so many relatives to untimely deaths might bear further investigation. I think it's also why Hurek took a sample of your blood the day we arrived."

She sat up, startled by the idea. She leaned against the wall, knees to chin. The thought of any of these awful people being her biological father made her sick. "Hurek doesn't have the results yet, right?"

"I don't think so. It usually takes a few weeks from what I understand." He sat up too. "I told him I'd help him broker an immunity deal with the FBI"—Rowena felt her mouth drop open —"if he releases you."

"But if he thinks I'm one of his friends' daughters, he'll hold onto me for them." Like property or a bargaining chip.

"I don't think they're friends right now. I got the impression Hurek was hiding out from his old buddies, which is probably why I was taken rather than shot on sight. Maybe Gilder and Spartan want to get rid of Hurek the same way they got rid of Dougie Cavanagh. He's a threat to their current positions of power."

"Did Hurek admit that they'd killed Dougie?"

Kurt shook his head. "But it makes sense. Perhaps Dougie figured out what they'd done to the woman he loved and started threatening whatever business they were in together. My guess is diamonds or gold mining in a conflict zone. But, yeah, if those DNA results say you're Gilder's or Spartan's kid, then I suspect Hurek will try to cut a deal with his old friend—a private island somewhere and a new face—rather than risk dealing with the US government."

"Why hasn't Gilder or Spartan killed Hurek already?" She shivered. Her preconceptions had been turned upside down these last few weeks.

"If I was in any of their positions, I'd have damning information squirreled away that became public in the event of my death."

"Dead man's switch."

"Yeah." He looked surprised. "They already killed one of the group—what is to stop them killing another?"

Rowena's teeth chattered. Kurt pulled her down on top of him and covered them both with the blanket again.

Her mouth tasted bitter like iron. "What's the plan?"

"Keep playing the docile dummies until we have a chance of getting out of here alive."

"Would the FBI cut a deal with him?"

"As much as I hate to admit it, the Department of Justice might. If he could deliver clear evidence Nolan Gilder is a corrupt criminal, that is. Gilder has defense contracts, not to mention his fingers in every global communications pie with his satellite empire and space projects. DoD would want to know they were dealing with a criminal and potential enemy of the United States."

The thought a man like Nolan Gilder might share her DNA was abhorrent.

"Leo Spartan also needs to be exposed. He's in a position of power for a country that deserves better. Would they prosecute him?"

"We might not have the proof they'd need unless we can tie him to the plane crash and Anders' murder." Kurt squeezed her gently. "But that's up to the Zimbabweans. Gilder is a US citizen now, and he answers to our laws."

Rowena huddled against Kurt and tried to draw some comfort. Thoughts about what her mother must have endured and what kind of a person her unknown father was kept her awake long into the night.

28

JANUARY 26

Tuesday. Shropshire, England

Jordan shifted down a gear as he drove through narrow, windy streets more suitable for horse and carts than modern vehicles.

After his conversation with the librarians and Smith's uncle on Friday, he'd spoken to both Daniel Ackers and Reid Armstrong, and they'd agreed it might be worth digging deeper into Rowena Smith's disappearance, especially with those faint echoes of Kurt's cell signal along the road to Mutare. On Monday evening, he'd boarded a plane to Heathrow and then driven the rental car for four hours to Shropshire.

At least he was arriving before the library closed, which was four p.m. on Tuesdays.

This trip was strictly under the radar. His bosses had decided it wasn't necessary to alert the legal attaché in London, so he'd bypassed that step and hoped it didn't bite him in the ass if the Legat discovered he was in-country. He was hoping to use his dubious charm to talk his way into looking around Smith's home. If, as her uncle suspected, she'd found something that had sent her on some urgent quest, perhaps he'd be able to find it, and it might tell them why she'd been on Kurt's radar—and why she'd disappeared.

A full two weeks after the crash, after *extensive* and *unrelenting* pressure from the US government, investigators from the US's National Transportation Safety Board were finally being allowed access to the hangar full of pieces of the aircraft and personal effects of the victims. Unofficially, a bomb tech from the FBI was also part of the team to verify it was an accident and not terrorism, but the team had been told they weren't to analyze or photograph anything without the express permission from the Zimbabwean officials in charge of the investigation.

Plane crashes in foreign countries could be difficult to examine, but the aircraft hadn't come down in a conflict zone. Why was the Zimbabwean government being so territorial? Was the airline to blame? The manufacturer? Or was it something more sinister like a bomb, and if so, had Kurt Montana been targeted specifically?

The idea drew a low-level rage inside him that wouldn't quit. Until he knew the answers, he couldn't rest.

Finally near his destination, he drove past the impressive red-brick building with its arched upper windows and felt as if he'd dropped into some Georgian novel. He parked around the back and walked inside to The Anstice and made his way to the small library.

The tiny woman behind the desk might also have been from the late eighteenth century.

He cleared his throat.

"How may I help?" The woman smiled tremulously with neon orange lips.

"Ma'am." He leaned against the counter and kept his voice low. "We spoke on the phone on Friday." He slid his business card across the counter, and she gazed at it through her thick bifocals. "Jordan Krychek. I wanted to follow up—"

"Have you found her?" She grabbed his hand with deceptively strong fingers.

Jordan shook his head and opened his mouth to speak when she cut him off again.

"Is it about the fire?" Her voice shook.

Jordan narrowed his gaze. "Fire?"

"Careful, Betty." A man joined them. Dark hair shaved close to his skull. Broad features. "We haven't verified his identity." He reached out for Jordan's card and then went to the computer and pulled up the FBI's government website.

They spoke in hushed voices, as if they were in church.

Jordan pulled his creds and slid them across the counter. "You won't find me in the database, I'm afraid. The FBI is big on keeping our identities out of the public eye as a safeguard from all the lunatics and criminals. Plus, I'm not here officially." He decided to level with them. He opened his cell and found a photo of him and Kurt standing with Victoria Falls in the background. He held his cell out. "Look up the passengers for the flight that crashed in Zim. An FBI agent named Kurt Montana is listed among the dead. He was a good friend of mine."

Betty's brimming eyes went from Alasdair to him as Alasdair entered the search. When Kurt's official FBI mugshot appeared on screen, looking like a handsome motherfucker, she reached out with her soft wrinkly fingers and firmly squeezed his hand.

He found it difficult to swallow.

"What does that have to do with Rowena?" Her voice was a rough whisper now.

He swiped his photos avoiding any that could be deemed classified, such as images of the bugs from his home and any of his HRT buddies—not that they felt like buddies right now. The rift between them grew with each passing day. He found the grainy image of Rowena Smith that Kurt had taken outside the Jam Café on January 11.

They both looked with concern at his phone and then at one another. "Montana asked HQ to run a background check on Rowena Smith the night before the crash. It was the last time we heard from him."

"You're not suggesting—"

"I'm not suggesting anything. I'm simply looking for answers." He didn't have time for Alasdair's overprotective outrage. "Would Rowena be the kind of person to"—Christ, there was no diplomatic way to put this—"take someone's cell phone?"

"Steal, you mean?" Alasdair's nostrils flared. "Never."

Maybe Kurt and Rowena had shared a night of passion, and he'd accidentally left his cell behind. "What if she found it and knew it was important. What would she do?"

"Drop it at the nearest police station or do her best to find the person it belonged to and mail it to them."

Hmm. That was worth thinking about. "Tell me about the fire."

A woman with two young children came and checked out a stack of books that Betty scanned through with some kind words for the youngsters.

When the woman left, she waved him through into the admin office of the library.

"Rowena's house burned down on Saturday night. More than two centuries old, and now it's gone."

Alasdair crossed his arms and nodded pointedly. "Less than twenty-four hours after we spoke to you."

Jordan stared at the man as his brain whirled. He was thinking not about the conversation he'd had with Betty, but the one he'd had with Rowena's uncle when the man mentioned the possibility Rowena had found something in her grandmother's attic that had started her on her quest to find her father.

Could someone be somehow intercepting his phone calls? They were supposed to be encrypted, but the timing seemed like too much of a coincidence. Regan had assured him his cells were clean but what if someone, somehow, had found a way to unravel the code. Or perhaps they'd tapped the uncle's phone... that would be a hell of a lot simpler.

"Was everything destroyed at the house?"

Betty's bright lipstick flattened into a thin seam of tangerine.

"The brickwork is intact, but the fire and water destroyed everything inside. Can't blame the firefighters. They're only doing their jobs, but all her grandmother's things. All *her* things." Tears filled the woman's watery eyes and drew a line down her papery cheek. "Gone."

"Did they say how it started?"

"Garry, chief firefighter, suspects arson." Alasdair spoke. "Figures some kids got inside as they knew she was away. Put a little gasoline on the curtains and 'whoosh.' No witnesses though."

"Poor Rowena. If she does come home, she's got nothing left except her car. I don't even know what to tell the insurers. Until she comes back, she can't make a claim."

"Not 'if,'" Alasdair corrected with a pat on the woman's shoulder. "When. Our Row is made of stern stuff, and she's smart and resilient. I'll talk to my friend who works in insurance. He'll tell me the best things to do so she can deal with it more easily when she gets home. I know she took videos of all of the rooms and uploaded it to her cloud like you're supposed to before she went away."

Jordan's ears pricked up at that, but he decided to talk to Ackers and Armstrong about whether or not they should apply for warrants to access her cloud and see what else was in there.

"Did she ever discuss her father with you?"

The two of them exchanged a glance. "Well, she mentioned something about looking for him. She also mentioned putting her DNA on one of those family tree sites."

Jordan stared. Could this be related to who her father was? Had she found him? Was he some puritanical bigwig who couldn't afford for his sins to catch up with him and was willing to pay any price to keep a secret? Was it Bjorn Anders? Was Rowena Smith dead just like Kurt?

"Any idea which database?" They gave him a name, which he wrote down. "May I see her car?"

"Sure. I've been driving it most days since she's been gone to keep it running—she told me to, and it meant I could pop down quickly to the Bower Yard to check her house." He looked crest-fallen. "Not that that will be an issue now. Saved me the walk up the bridge bank. Car's outside." The man was babbling now. "Can you manage alone for five minutes, Betty?"

Jordan's hopes faded as he followed Alasdair to a gleaming powder-blue Mercedes hatchback. The inside was equally immaculate.

"I was hoping to collect a DNA sample. See if I could use it to run against..."

Alasdair went pale. "Against the DNA of any unidentified bodies you mean."

Jordan pulled a face. "Sorry. It's a tool in the box. Like finger-prints. Doesn't mean she's dead." But perhaps this could also help him track down her father and investigate that angle too. "I could swab the seat belt perhaps for epithelial cells. I'd need to visit a drug store first and pick up some supplies."

"I can do better than that if you want her DNA."

Alasdair sprang the lever for the trunk and waved a hand at a purple sports bag.

"She left her gym clothes in the back, and I know for a fact she didn't wash them last time she worked out because she didn't have time. I almost washed them for her but, Mike, my husband, told me that was overstepping."

Thank God for Mike's boundaries. "Can I take this? I promise you I will get everything back to you as soon as possible."

"Anything that helps us find Rowena." Alasdair blinked away tears. "Anything at all."

———

Friday, January 29

Rowena paced the small cabin. According to the little scratched off marks beside the bed, they'd been hostages for two weeks, and she was slowly losing her mind. Their captors had given them playing cards and a cribbage board and a chess board and pieces. It had helped for a little while, but now she thought she might scream from fear, worry, or boredom.

Would a book be too much to ask? Anything would do. The classics, an encyclopedia, Dan Brown.

At least Kurt was with her, and that thought made her feel guilty as hell.

"Wanna work out?"

"No."

"Wanna game of chess?"

"No."

"Want me to teach you close-quarters combat techniques?"

"N—" She whipped around to face him. "Close-quarter what?"

"Self-defense and maybe the odd preemptive strike." The smile at the side of his mouth told her he knew exactly how pissy she was feeling. He probably felt even worse because he was a man of action, and this was his expertise. He was supposed to rescue hostages, not be one. And the fact he was stuck in this damned cabin—she couldn't help feeling it was all her fault.

"There's not a lot of space in here, but we can improvise."

"Let's do it."

He put the chair on top of the bed. "First thing is going over the principles of CQB."

"I like principles."

"The core of it is surprise, speed, and violent action—the latter means using overwhelming force to neutralize threats. In my world, that's a team of highly trained, well-armed individuals coming in hot. For you and me, it's going to mean going in hard and fast and not stopping until the adversary is dead."

She blinked at him.

"I'm not expecting you to kill anyone, Row. Just preparing you for what you might witness. It won't be pretty."

She swallowed. "This is what you did back at the Mozambique border."

He nodded.

"Show me. Show me exactly what you did."

"Row—"

"I want to know." She gritted her teeth. "I won't be able to help with most of this stuff, but I want to know how you saved us and how it might happen again. I don't want to freeze when I should be running or running when I should freeze."

He rubbed his hand over what was now an impressive beard. It gave him a rugged appeal she hadn't expected to find so attractive. "Not sure I can teach all that in the time we have left."

"You don't know how much time we have left." Bitterness leaked through.

His eyes burned a little at that. Mouth firmed. "True. But maybe we should start with some Taekwondo patterns—*poomsae* —to fill the time."

She narrowed her gaze thoughtfully. "I'd like that. How many patterns are there?"

"Twenty-four. They're supposed to represent each hour of the day. First few are easy, and we may not have room for a lot of them in here, but we'll make do. It's a good way to concentrate the mind."

"How good are you at Taekwondo?"

"I attained a sixth dan black belt last year."

"Bloody hell."

He gave her a wry smile. "The longer you do it, the harder it gets."

They faced one another, and he bowed so she copied him. "However, first, we'll start by working on some basic self-defensive moves."

She liked that idea. She was ready to fight her way out of this mess, if necessary.

"The first thing to remember is that if anyone puts you into a position where you need to use any of the things I'm about to show you, don't hold back—unless there are overwhelming numbers. In that case, you're gonna need to find another way to survive."

She knew what he was saying. Mentally. She nodded. She was doing her best not to worry about the threat of rape, but it seemed like a stock in trade to Hurek and his buddies, and she wasn't going to assume she was special in any way. She wasn't special to them. She might be a useful pawn, but she wasn't special.

"After we get through a few basic methods to disable someone, I'll show you how I handled the mercs who were chasing us. Then we'll work on pattern one."

She nodded. She wanted to be a participant in this, not just a girl who needed saving.

"Okay, first thing, you need to go for the vulnerable areas and don't be squeamish about it. Eyes, nose, throat, and groin."

He stripped off his T-shirt, gave her a look. "So I don't get too sweaty."

"Playing dirty, are we?" She raised her brows.

He grinned, and she knew what he was thinking. "Feel free to do the same."

She kept her shirt on, in case the guards decided to see what all the noise was about. This was what she needed. Something positive to maybe help them get out of here. A skill. A power. A distraction. She needed to move, or she was going to go insane.

"I'm going to start with what to do if an attacker comes at you from behind... And try not to emasculate me during training, babe, but feel free to do so to any asshole who comes at you in real life."

She nodded and turned. She was about to learn how to strike back at an attacker, and she wouldn't let all that lovely muscle on display distract her. Not when their lives might depend on it. She needed to learn how to punch back and how to make every strike count. They didn't know when their chance would come, but it would come. She wanted to be ready.

29

Jordan lay spent in the darkness after another energetic bout with Trooper Mires. As good as the sex was physically, it left him feeling dead inside. Even when he'd told himself this wasn't what he wanted, he found himself opening the damned door when she knocked.

It was loneliness and grief crying out for a distraction. Weakness that pissed him off.

He didn't even know where this woman lived or if she had a middle name or how she took her coffee. What was worse, he didn't care. He hated himself for that. He was in no state to be with anyone until he could get his head straight.

It wasn't as if he expected anyone to crack the ice encasing his heart, but he did try to remember his humanity during his few-and-far-between relationships.

This wasn't a relationship. This was emotionless and physical, like a ten-mile run with an orgasm at the end.

But he didn't need a woman for an orgasm, and he should finish this thing before he started to resent her as much as he hated himself. It wasn't her fault. She just wanted sex. A hookup. Any other time, it would have been the perfect scenario, but not right now. Not when he was raw with emotion.

He could hear her quiet breathing as her finger idly doodled on his chest.

She didn't usually hang around afterwards. It was pretty much come and go. Waiting for her to leave, made him feel like the world's biggest prick.

"You didn't call me to escort you home this week." She pouted. The moon shone so bright he could clearly see her expression.

He captured her hand to stop those wandering fingers. "I was away. I didn't call anyone."

Her finely plucked eyebrow rose. "Somewhere nice?"

He couldn't answer questions. Didn't want to talk. "Just work."

She sat up in bed, unabashed about being naked as the silver light outlined her perfect body. Christ if his demonic prick didn't respond.

"What were you doing?"

He found his shirt on the floor beside the bed. Pulled it on. "FBI stuff."

She laughed breathily. "I know that, dummy. I mean what kind of work do you do?"

"It's classified."

"I'm not about to tell anyone."

Why was she suddenly asking questions?

"It's still classified." He tried to soften his tone, which was verging on a growl. "Look, Ellen, I don't think we should do this again."

Her back snapped straight. "Because I asked a couple of questions?"

"No." *Yes.* "I can't talk about my job."

"Because it's *classified*."

He saw the sneer as clearly as he'd seen the smile. "Look, we're not in a relationship. You knock on the door to get laid, and I open it for the same reason."

She smiled slyly in the darkness and licked her lips. "You

don't think that is worth a little conversation?"

He turned on the bedside lamp. Sat up on the side of the bed. He wanted to cradle his head in his hands as a headache worked around the edges of his vision.

"It's not worth my job," he said honestly.

She got off the bed, snatched up her clothes, and stormed into the bathroom. A minute later, she came out looking slick and polished. And pissed. "If you're not interested, don't answer the door."

"If you want anything except to fuck, don't bother knocking."

"Oh, well excuse me. I didn't know the only time I could open my mouth was when I was deep throating you."

Ouch.

"Ellen—"

"Am I wrong?" Those hard blue eyes bored into his.

"Not really." He wanted to drive her away for both their sakes because if she knocked again, he'd probably let her in. Because he was fucking weak and male and struggling to find anything that mattered in his life right now.

She adjusted her hat on the tight bun of her hair, headed to the door. She slammed it behind her with enough force to rattle the glass in the windows.

Fuck.

He went outside and watched her cruiser taillights disappear along his driveway. He glanced up at the security camera and hoped Jon Regan wasn't watching while making acerbic comments that could blister paint to his colleagues. Jordan was doing what the guy suggested, but that wasn't why he'd done it. Having sex was the only time he wasn't thinking about the fact it should have been him on that plane, terrified as it nosedived thousands of feet to bury itself in the earth below. It should have been him in his family home when it burned to the ground taking his grandparents, mother, and sister with it.

He went back inside. Shut the door. Locked it.

Next time, he wouldn't answer the door. The sex was good, but it wasn't worth this self-recrimination.

How was that healthy?

But maybe that was the point.

Feeding the misery, stoking an addiction...punishing himself with mindless sex that made him hate himself even more afterward.

He didn't need a damned escort anyway. He was armed and ready. Let the fuckers come. At least that way, he might figure out who'd tried to kill him and bug him, and why. The FBI would have a lead to follow. Action to take. Rather than nothing but unanswered questions.

After the fire at Rowena Smith's house, Reid Armstrong had been concerned enough that someone was listening into Jordan's calls that the task force had switched over to the same system they ran presidential communications through out of Langley. Jordan had persuaded Ackers to switch HRT communications over too. Until they could figure out what the hell was going on, he wanted to be appropriately paranoid.

He went into the kitchen and dug through one of the cabinets. Pulled out a bottle of single malt. Poured a healthy measure in a cheap glass and then went back to his desk that was set up in the corner of the living room. His body clock hadn't yet adjusted back to Eastern Standard Time after his quick trip across the pond. He'd visited the beautiful historic town of Ironbridge and what little remained of Rowena's burnt-out home, and then he'd driven back to London and gotten the first available flight home, which was early Thursday morning.

While he'd been away, Grady Steel had almost died of a gunshot wound, and some of his teammates had gone head-to-head with some of the deadliest threats on the planet.

The divide between him and his teammates exacerbated the strain he was under. Every mission they did without him drove the wedge between them deeper, pushing them further apart. Ackers had forbidden him to even mention Rowena Smith, let alone Darmawan Hurek, but the guys wanted answers. They weren't stupid. They knew something was off.

Now a new nightmare loomed. Despite the lack of a body, Montana's family had decided to hold a memorial service in a couple of weeks, and Jordan still didn't know how he'd be able to face them.

Survivor's guilt was crippling.

He needed answers. He pulled out his laptop and put on some music. Billie Holiday's emotionally raw vocals resonated with his mood.

He realized he'd missed a call from Reid Armstrong that had come in while he'd been distracted by Ellen. It was early evening, so he called Armstrong back. "Did you get the DNA back off Rowena Smith's gym kit?"

"Good evening to you too."

"Sorry." Jordan rubbed the stiff muscles in his neck. "Fatigue tends to dull my manners, and the triple dose of jet lag doesn't help."

"The lab has the clothes and gym shoes and are confident they'll get her DNA. Analysts managed to figure out that the family tree site she used hasn't mailed her results yet, and that's not surprising as she sent it the day before she left for Africa, and they say about six weeks on the website."

"Can we hurry that along?"

"By the time we do, the results should have come through anyway. My analyst assures me we'll know as soon as the results go live."

"As will anyone who gets pinged as a potential relative."

"If her biological father is involved with her disappearance, it seems unlikely he's the sort to enter his DNA into one of these websites."

"True, but he might have relatives who did. Did you get into her cloud service?"

"We did." There was a long pause. "It was wiped. We have

someone seeing if they can reconstruct anything, but they say it's doubtful."

Jordan swore. "It's as if someone is trying to wipe her existence off the map."

"The most obvious answer is she's doing it herself and is determined to disappear."

"That's what I thought before I spoke to her relatives and co-workers. By all accounts, she was genuinely close to them, and it doesn't explain her house burning down."

"Unless she plans to reappear in a couple of weeks and claim the insurance money."

Jordan grunted. It didn't feel right. "She was financially solvent after the inheritances from her family, and she could have just sold the house. Way easier than getting insurance policies to pay out. Anything on those ghost signals?"

"Our analysts aren't sure. The data looks like it's been corrupted."

Who had the power to do that or was it the byproduct of shitty equipment and an unstable electrical grid?

"Did we get anything from the plane itself?"

"That's why I called. You're sure your place is bug free?"

Jordans' suspicion had spread to his colleagues. "TacOps tells me it is." He hadn't done a sweep since he'd gotten home this evening though. Too busy doing the State Trooper. "Give me five minutes to do a sweep. I'll call you back."

"Feeling paranoid?"

"This whole situation makes me batshit."

"Me too."

Jordan hung up and took out the wand Regan had instructed him on. Started in the bathroom and the bedroom then the living room and kitchen.

Jordan called Armstrong again as Billie Holiday finished singing *Trav'lin' Light*. "All clear."

"Okay. Well, the bomb tech who snuck in the hangar with NTSB said that despite the preliminary findings of the Zimbabwean investigation, she believes it was definitely a bomb that brought that plane down."

What the fuck?

Jordan dropped to his seat as his knees gave out. He took a slug of the fiery whiskey to steady himself.

"She managed to take a couple of photos of pieces of fuselage and swab some of the fragments while her colleagues distracted the officials. She looks like a harmless kid, so they largely ignored her."

"What does our side plan to do about it?"

"First thing is to analyze the swabs and confirm the presence of explosives. She only got back today, and the samples are now at the TEDAC lab in Alabama."

"Any of Kurt or his belongings identified yet?"

"No. If he was targeted, maybe they put it under his seat to make damned sure he didn't survive."

"I think death from an air disaster when you're at ten thousand feet is pretty much a given." At least his friend wouldn't have suffered for long. "Any ideas why the authorities there are lying to us?"

"No. But they're starting to make noises about the West trying to make them look incompetent and as if they are incapable of investigating themselves."

"When in actual fact someone is trying to hide the truth. Why?"

"That's a good question, and I don't have any good answers. Ambassador swears Zim officials are a hundred percent committed to working with us, but that wasn't what the FBI agent said when she was there. They kept them corralled in their hotel and then escorted them to and from the hangar and crash site under armed guard—for their own protection. They were not allowed to talk to anyone."

"Could someone powerful in the Zimbabwean government be responsible for bringing that flight down?" It was a dangerous idea to voice.

"Why?"

"Find the motive, find the 'who,'" Jordan pondered. "How long until the bomb squad finish their tests?"

"Middle of next week. State Department wants this information locked down."

Jordan exhaled tiredly. "I want to know how and why my friend and colleague died." *And who ordered it.*

"You, me, and several hundred other people's family members who are growing more vocal in their discontent. I get the impression the US is going to let the families lead the demands for answers until we have proof one way or another."

"In the meantime, any trail to potential terrorists goes cold. The same way Hurek's trail has gone cold." Hurek was the obvious suspect for this bomb, although he had never used explosives before. Didn't mean he couldn't start.

"I'm trying to get warrants that allow us to start digging into the security footage from Harare."

"I can help with reviewing that."

"I'll let you know when we confirm explosives and the warrant comes through."

"What can I do right now?"

"Take the weekend off."

Jordan took another sip of whiskey and frowned into the glass. "I've got a teammate in the hospital and a memorial coming up and still no answers. It's not exactly conducive to relaxing."

"Task force is taking the weekend. We're in limbo without test results. I'm flying to Seattle for a family wedding on the red eye. I'm at the airport right now."

Jordan had forgotten people had real lives outside work. "Did you discover anything new about the Anders' murder?"

"The case has been closed for lack of evidence."

"Already?"

"Yeah. Anders' company has been sold for a tidy sum, and his wife and kids moved to Cape Town."

"Something tells me Bjorn knew something about either Hurek or the bomb or both."

"Yeah, but how do we prove what a dead man knew?"

"Can we access his phone records or email?"

"Not without a warrant, which I'll request tonight. This is all too big to start cowboying around," Armstrong warned. "It was one thing to follow-up on the Smith girl, but illegally accessing a dead man's phone records during a time when the Zimbabwean authorities are screaming US interference... Can't risk it."

Fuck. This was why people like Hurek escaped without a trace. They didn't have to play by the damned rules.

"I'll just get drunk at home then. Enjoy your wedding."

"I will. My niece. I can't believe she's old enough to get married."

"Must be nice to have a big family."

There was a long awkward pause that said it all. "It is. It really is. I'll call if anything breaks over the weekend, but try to get some rest."

30

FEBRUARY 4

Kurt watched Rowena work through pattern five like a pro. Adding self-defense training and TKD to their daily routine had focused both their minds and bodies and could help them stay alive. He'd already done his workout for the day. Fifty pushups, twenty chin-ups using the tiny lip above the bathroom door to pull himself up on, fifty crunches, planks, squats, and lunges. He'd also perfected the fine art of holding Rowena against the wall and eating her out until she came.

They were making the most of their confinement.

But they'd been held captive for three weeks now, and it was driving him nuts that they hadn't seen land except for a tiny spot on the horizon, once. Had they crossed the Atlantic or were they sailing slowly up the West African coast? From the direction of the sun and orientation of the stars he was certain they were crossing the Atlantic, which was good. Closer to home.

He could be wrong, but he didn't think so.

Was Hurek really planning to go after Quentin and the others? It was sadistic and exactly the sort of thing a man like Hurek would try. The asshole hadn't called him upstairs for a second dinner date yet, which suggested he was biding his time, probably heading to his next hidey-hole before making any sort of contact with the federal government. Or he was bartering with Gilder for some kind of truce. Hurek wasn't in any rush, after all, right now the US thought Kurt was dead. No one was looking for him. As soon as Hurek tried to cut a deal they'd be swarming over every detail of the crash and beyond.

Did Hurek have the results of Rowena's DNA tests yet?

How was Daisy holding up? How was the team doing? Had they caught that motherfucking serial killer who'd murdered Scotty yet?

Rowena finished her pattern and collapsed beside him on the bed.

She stole his can of Dr Pepper and took a long sip. "Bleh."

"Hey, this is a classic."

"It's disgusting. Now tell me something I don't know about you."

"I think I've told you everything there is to know." He huffed out a small laugh. "You know more about me than my family and colleagues combined."

Her eyes brightened. "Tell me about your workmates."

"Fine. You first."

"That'll be easy. I have two people I work with at the library. Betty, who is adorable and has got to be close to eighty. I remember her from when I was a kid going there."

"What," he scoffed, "a whole decade ago?"

She poked him in an area she'd discovered he was particularly sensitive and possibly ticklish, though he'd die before he admitted it. "I thought you'd gotten over the age difference, mister."

"I'll never get over the age difference. I'm the luckiest old fucker in the known universe."

"You better believe it." She tilted her head to face him. "Hey, what did Marianne say to you back at the farm? I know she said something."

Kurt grinned. "She told me how she'd seduced her considerably older husband with a little late-night skinny dipping and that if I was happy to shag you in private, I better make damned sure I was happy to claim you as mine in public too. Otherwise, you'd dump me the way she'd dumped Newt."

"Marianne is a badass. I hope she didn't betray us." A smile played over her lips. "*Are* you claiming me as yours?"

He stared into those pretty green eyes. "Every damned day."

She dipped her chin and wiggled her bare toes. "I hate to break it to you, but I think this still qualifies as the 'shagging in private' part."

He touched her bottom lip with his thumb. "As soon as we get out of here, I'll be happy to tell the whole damned world that you are all mine. Every inch of you."

She made a hum deep in her throat, and he had to stop himself from reaching for her.

"So this Betty woman. Who else?"

"Alasdair. Gorgeous Scottish accent. Quite the hunk. He's a couple of years older than me. Well, actually he's closer to your age." She sniggered and something inside him melted. She still had her sense of humor. It was a goddamn miracle.

"I hate Alasdair."

"He's happily married to a guy called Mike, who is probably the most beautiful creature I've ever met and at least ten years younger than good old Alasdair." She put her hand on her heart and tapped it rapidly.

"Alasdair's okay, but I'm on the fence about Mike."

She laughed, and the sound filled him with a quiet joy. He loved making her laugh.

She sobered. "They're going to be worried sick about what happened to me. What about you? Tell me about the people you work with. Nothing classified, obviously."

"My guys?" Emotion hit Kurt unexpectedly. He'd been trying not to think about his team as individuals and how much they'd each be hurting. "I've been Gold Team leader for the past six years, and it's been the privilege of my life. HRT has three different teams, Gold, Blue, and Red. Gold Team is the best."

"Obviously."

"Each team consists of two seven-person assaulter squads—Charlie and Echo—plus one eight-man sniper team."

"Doesn't seem like enough people considering how much work you have to do."

He nodded. They were often stretched thin, but he, for one, enjoyed being busy. "We have a few operators who are on secondment to various other agencies in the US and around the world, and then there are special missions like this one."

"Maybe you need another team. A Green Team who all have sexy Irish accents."

"What is it with you and accents?"

"Accents are sexy." She eyed him sideways. "Your accent is sexy."

"I don't have an accent."

"Sure you don't." She laughed. "Okay, tell me why you can't have a fourth team—oh, a purple team. That's my favorite color."

"I'll be sure to mention that to the FBI Director when she has to go beg for additional funding to support more operators." He ran his hand over the freckles on her arm. "But it's not just funding, though that's a big part of it. It's tough to get into HRT as we don't take just anyone. We actually base the HRT Selection process on what Delta Force uses to select their recruits, which in turn, is based on that of the British SAS."

She jogged his shoulder. "They do that course not far away from where I live. The Regiment is based in Hereford."

Maybe he could get a secondment with the Brits.

The idea hit him like a sledgehammer. He was willing to change his life for this woman. Assuming they ever got out of here.

He cleared his throat. "Hey, we have our first woman on the teams now."

"How enlightened of you," she said drolly.

He laughed because he'd expected her to be impressed. "I was dubious at first, I admit it." He defended the vulnerable patch on his ribs. "It's the physicality of the whole thing, the grueling nature of the work." He captured her hands. "I've been thinking since I met you how many characteristics of an operator you embody. Grit. Determination. Courage."

"You're just saying that to get into my recently washed pants."

He shook his head. "I'm saying it because it's true. Physicality can be honed, but the mental fortitude? You either have it or you don't, and you have it in spades."

"I'm a wimp. Terrified all the time."

"You're a goddamned warrior."

Emotion traveled over her features. Disbelief, amusement, then a calm kind of acceptance that maybe he meant what he said. "Maybe a wimpy one."

He gave a quiet laugh.

"I wouldn't be dealing with everything half as well without you by my side, but I hate that you're a prisoner too."

He took her hand in his. Played with her fingers. "Same."

That was sobering. And true.

Without the distraction of making sure Rowena was as safe as he could make her, he'd be a wreck. He'd have probably tried to escape already and ended up beaten or drowned at sea with no one to bear witness.

His patience was stretched thin. He needed to get them the hell out of there, but there was still no land on the horizon. Nowhere for them to go.

"Tell me about her. The woman."

"Meghan Donnelly, former Eighty-Second Airborne Division soldier. I don't know her personally, but I watched her go through Selection and crush it. Then she went to New Operator Training School, and I know she made it through because my boss Daniel Ackers called to tell me over the holidays. I requested her for Gold Team."

"Why?" She shot him a curious glance.

He smiled. "Because Gold Team is the best, and she'll be an asset, especially when going undercover."

She snorted. "Tell me about the rest."

The sea was relatively calm, and the sun was going down slowly on the horizon. If the last twenty-one days were anything to go by, they'd have a tray of food delivered in the next thirty minutes. The fact they were keeping them well fed and looked after was presumably in case Hurek decided to try to cut a deal with the US authorities. It wasn't because he was merciful or kind.

"There was some restructuring after I took this mission. An operator named Payne Novak took over from me as team leader. Former Green Beret. He's a big guy, hard ass, hell of an operator. Out of Arkansas. Bomb tech and card-carrying member of Mensa, though he hates anyone to know. Then we have Jordan Krychek who came out here with me. Damned glad he caught that earlier flight out." Jordan would be feeling the worst of the guilt. Kurt hated that for his friend. "He's serious. Dedicated. Hard working. Kind of intense. Loosens up after a couple of whiskeys, but always seems a little haunted. This won't help."

Rowena took his hand and squeezed.

"You sure you want to hear all this? There's a lot of them."

"Yes, because then when they rescue us, I'll know who they are."

That hit him in the chest like a battering ram. The fact she was such a damned optimist.

The letters might have arrived by now—or they could be another six months or lost forever—but Rowena didn't even know about the letters, and she still held out hope. The race between the letters and the DNA results was just another thing he couldn't control, but as soon as they were within sight of land…

"Shane Livingstone, another former Green Beret, from Alabama. Southpaw. He's our breacher or was until he broke his arm."

He grew somber. "The man who replaced him was his best friend, the operator who was killed on New Year's Day. Dave Monteith. 'Scotty.' Left behind a pregnant wife and two kids."

"That's awful."

"Scotty was a great guy." He stared at his hands and wished

he'd had the chance to tell the man how much he'd meant to him. What they all meant to him. He wasn't known for his effusive nature. He regretted not saying the words now. If he ever got the chance again, he'd make sure they all knew.

"Who else?"

"Okay, let me think. Aaron Nash, we call him 'the Professor.' Former biologist. Always thinking things through from all the different angles and coming up with smart solutions. Plays Devil's Advocate like Lucifer himself. Luke Romano, former Army, flies our drones. Seth Hopper, Cas Demarco, and Elliot Zerowski are all former Navy SEALs, but we try not to hold it against them. JJ Hersh, a sniper, one of the few married guys on the team. We have a bunch of former law enforcement officers— Grady Steel, Sebastian Black, Jonah Church, Levi Cruz, Wyatt Voss. Church and Ford Cadell are our main K9 handlers. Cadell is former Marine and a bit of a wildcard, but he's started to settle. Hey, if dogs ever run at you, hold perfectly still. Don't run. Even if they latch on, don't move."

She gulped audibly. "They'd bring dogs to a ship?"

"Sure. Damien Crow, a.k.a. Birdman for obvious reasons, another former Marine, is a tough nut to crack but loyal as a pit bull. Malik Keeme has a good head on his shoulders—always wins at poker. Tobias Hayashi flew fighter jets for the Air Force. Fluent in Japanese, Cantonese, Mandarin, Korean, and Thai. Most of our guys know at least one other language fluently."

"What do you speak?"

"French. German. Dutch. Some Spanish. Enough Portuguese to get myself into trouble."

"I'm impressed."

"Oh yeah?" He smirked at her. "How impressed?"

"I'll show you later." She tangled her long leg with his and stroked his foot with hers. "You have a lot of former special forces people on the team."

He shrugged. "The job lends itself to that. Plus, they get accelerated into the program, and don't have to serve in the FBI for as long as non-military agents before they can apply to HRT. It's a pretty attractive second career for these guys."

"Cool."

"I guess. Who's left? Noam Levitt—former Army medic and should have been a trauma surgeon. The sort of guy girls want to take home to meet their mothers. Guy's brilliant. Keir Turley and Ian Rockwell round out the sniper team—both quiet but solid professionals. Best friends even though Turley comes from a dirt-poor background and Rockwell's parents are the 'house in the Hamptons' variety. Then we have the three FNGs."

"FNGs?"

"Fucking New Guys." He grinned. "Donnelly and two former FBI agents out of Atlanta who helped take down that anthrax terrorist ring last year."

"I heard about that. Scary." Rowena shuddered and he wrapped his arm around her shoulders.

"Will Griffin and Hunt Kincaid. Kincaid was an engineer before he joined the Bureau. Griffin lost his girlfriend—a fellow agent—to those same terrorists. I was worried how he'd cope, but he's figuring it out. That leaves only Ryan Sullivan, a.k.a Cowboy."

"*Cowboy*? Is he bad at his job?"

Kurt laughed. "No. The guy was a literal cowboy. Family has a ranch in Montana, and he can ride like I've never seen and is probably the best goddamned natural shot I ever saw."

"So he's a sniper?"

"Hell, no. He's one of our explosive specialists. Has a different girl on his arm every week." He cocked a brow. "By on his arm I mean—"

She laughed. "I know what you mean."

"If you meet him, don't believe a word that comes out of his mouth, and don't take the bait."

"I suspect you'll be the one taking the bait."

Damn. She was probably right.

"Aside from his sexploits, Ryan's probably the best all-round operator on the teams, but he has a few blind spots. He lost his wife also about eight years ago. Cancer. She was pregnant with their little girl when diagnosed and refused treatment until she gave birth. She died not long after, and from what I gather Ryan went off the rails for a few years."

"He's a single dad?"

"Kid lives back on the ranch with cousins around the same age. I know he misses her, but it's probably the right decision, given we never know when we'll get a call."

"Like you and Daisy?"

"I guess." He pulled a face. "But you'll probably meet him and fall in love, and then I'll have to kill him."

She kissed his cheek. "Probably. Always a sucker for a hot single dad."

Kurt laughed. Jealousy was lowering and not something he'd ever had to worry about before. "He will flirt with you. He can't help himself. Women honestly seem to love him, young and old."

She squeezed his hand. "I think you love him too."

He sent her a look. "I do. I love them all. I just never told them. I'm not the type to say it out loud. Out of practice, I guess." Emotion crowded his throat.

"They know." She sounded so sure.

"I love you."

"I know."

31

The HRT compound was virtually empty. Gold Team had been deployed to Boston on Monday to protect a judge and a former defense attorney from an escaped serial killer.

Jordan was losing his mind waiting for results from the bomb squad to come in. He could probably learn to run the experiments himself in the time it was taking.

His cell rang.

Ackers. "Get in here."

Jordan slipped out of his office, gave Maddie Goodwin a nod as she, in turn, shot him a concerned look. He wasn't sleeping. He'd kept his promise to himself and stopped answering the door when Ellen knocked, and he'd left a phone message apologizing for his behavior but also telling her he didn't want to see her anymore.

And he was holding on to that resolution by the tips of his fingers because sex was a great distraction from all the shit happening right now.

He strode into Ackers' office and closed the door behind him.

"They confirmed traces of Semtex in the swabs the bomb tech took in Zimbabwe."

Jordan sank into the visitor's chair without an invitation.

Since becoming the explosive of choice for various terror organizations in the 1990s, Semtex had been more carefully regulated, and the manufacturer had added a detection taggant to make it more easily detectable.

"What kind of Semtex? Are we looking at old stuff left over from the IRA days or something else?"

"According to the report it's likely Semtex 1A, which is used primarily for mining."

"Which many people have access to in that part of the world." Jordan absorbed the news for a few seconds. "Kurt was murdered. Was he the target?"

Ackers slumped heavily in his chair. "Armstrong had the other passengers run before this and said there were no obvious other targets on board, which doesn't rule out the possibility that there could have been. The warrants to start scouring airport security footage came in. He wants you up there to help."

Jordan nodded.

"I told him no."

Jordan opened his mouth to argue.

"The roads are sheet ice, and with authorities asking people to stay home, I suggested you could do it from here as easily. Maddie can set you up with a couple of extra monitors." Ackers dipped his chin. "I'm worried about you, son."

"No need."

"You look like hell."

An accurate reflection of how he felt.

"Struggling to sleep," he admitted. "Maybe it'll be easier now I know he was murdered." It hadn't been determined by fate so much as human evil. He could fight evil. "When do the FBI intend to release the findings?"

"Not yet."

Jordan didn't understand.

"State wants to dig with some of its sources, figure out who within the government there is pulling the strings regarding this investigation and cover up. That way we hopefully don't alienate the entire country, but rather hand them the means to root out the corruption for themselves."

"And save face."

"Exactly."

Jordan wanted to swear but managed to keep his cool.

"You spoken with the shrink about how you're feeling?"

The shrink?

He'd rather stick needles in his eyes. "Not yet."

"It's time, Jordan. Past time."

Jordan looked away. "I'll make an appointment." For next year.

"Do it this week. And let me know if you or SIOC find any evidence worth pursuing on the security tapes." The man stood and leaned across his desk. "And do not mention a bomb to anyone."

The weight of the deception snapped shut on him like a gin trap. "Not even the guys?"

Ackers' eyes turned fierce. "Especially not the guys. They'll be too angry not to share with someone, and that's how secrets leak. Officially, I shouldn't even know as I'm not on the task force."

Jordan nodded reluctantly and left. His teammates were never going to forgive him for not telling them something this important.

Between him and Maddie, the two of them set up two large monitors on his desk, and he started scouring different feeds from around the airport. It took a couple of hours to map what feed was from where and write that down and figure out where to start. The data had been accessed without Zimbabwean approval, so there wasn't a nice handy map of which camera pointed where. It helped that he'd been to that airport recently. He decided to run through each feed for the twenty-four hours prior to the fated plane's take off, starting with the high-traffic areas.

Analysts at SIOC were running all the available images through facial recognition software looking for any known terrorists or persons of interest. Rowena's uncle, Gamba Moyo, had caught a flight earlier that morning to South Africa. Jordan watched him carefully, but there were no red flags. No bag swaps or anything else that might be suspicious.

Then, several hours later, he found Kurt strolling through the airport without a care in the world.

God.

The loss hit him forcefully in the chest. Pain flashed across his heart.

His eyes blurred, and he blinked to clear them. Rewound the footage.

There was a knock on the door. Before he could answer, Maddie popped her head in. "Heading home before the roads become too treacherous. You should do the same. Daniel left half an hour ago."

He looked at his watch. Five o'clock and dark as a pit outside.

"You're upset?" She came into the room. "What is it?"

He waved her forward to look at the monitor. He pressed play, and she stood behind him with her hand on his shoulder. Her grip tightened as she recognized Kurt, and they both watched him walk through the frame and onto his date with death with a smile on his face.

Maddie let out a long breath. Squeezed his shoulder more gently. "He wouldn't want you to torture yourself. It was a tragedy and not your fault."

He caught her hand. The simple human connection felt better than a thousand rounds of mindless sex. "I know."

"Go home. Take work if you have to, but go home and get some sleep. Take a sleep aid if you must."

"Does whiskey count?"

"Only if you don't get drunk."

"Spoilsport." He turned off the monitors and closed his laptop. "You're right, I can do this at home."

"Will we see you tomorrow, or are you up in DC?"

"I'll stick around here unless Armstrong tells me otherwise. Any news from the guys?"

"Not since the murder yesterday."

"Let's hope they catch Leech soon."

Maddie shuddered. "That poor woman. She's been through so much."

"Yeah." Jordan wasn't the only one suffering, and he needed to get his shit together. The only thing Kurt would ask of him would be to take care of the team, his family, and to identify whoever had brought this plane down so they could face justice.

Maddie left, and he pulled up his email to start a letter to Kurt's daughter, Daisy, but he couldn't get past the first line. Annoyed with himself, he decided to work on it after he'd eaten dinner. Not frozen pizza. For once he would cook from scratch.

He walked outside and got in his car, which had been fixed by the garage and checked over by TacOps. He headed off base behind a solid line of traffic all trying to avoid the worst of the weather that was forecast.

He'd stopped requesting an escort a few days ago. It had been weeks since the incident with the truck, and he didn't like wasting police resources. Plus, he was trying to avoid Ellen. He could look after himself. He kept an eye out for anyone following him, but no one did. He relaxed a little, grateful for his snow tires and four-wheel drive capabilities as he hit the dangerous curves not far from his place.

He didn't see the truck pull out, but high beams suddenly blinded him in the rearview mirror.

"Shit."

The vehicle slammed into him from behind, attempting to force him off the road and down the wooded hillside.

Jordan sped up. Grimaced at the loose traction. He controlled a small skid and sped up again. He also called Armstrong on the hands-free unit.

"Truck's behind me again."

"Dammit. We're calling the local police. Where's your escort?"

Jordan winced. "I didn't call them. Weather conditions are treacherous."

"Can you pull over safely?"

The steep hillside on his right and the sounds of bullets hitting his back window answered for him. "Not right now."

His car lurched forward again as he was rammed.

He skidded and ended up on the wrong side of the road driving alongside the black truck. The driver wore a mask and pointed a pistol at him through the open window.

Jordan slammed on the brakes and controlled the skid—just—his heart hammering as the bullet missed him by inches. He swerved behind the truck, narrowly avoiding an oncoming vehicle who blasted the horn.

"Jordan?"

"Can't talk right now."

He put the brakes on, but his car didn't stop. The truck's brake lights flared to life as it pulled across the road and tried to block him, the driver holding the pistol out the window and aiming at him, firing shots in rapid succession. His car was fast and nimble. He accelerated and nipped through the narrow gap and careened back onto his side of the road, correcting another skid, sweat popping out of his pores. He went around the sharp bend, and his mouth dropped open with horror as a semi came toward him and disappeared around the corner.

The sound of steel crashing against steel and glass shattering had Jordan pulling over to the edge of the road and flicking on his hazards.

He grabbed his cell where Armstrong was talking to someone else but still on the line. "Semi rammed the truck, which was on the wrong side of the road. I pulled over, and I'm on foot heading back to see what the hell is going on."

"Be careful."

Jordan tucked the phone into his jacket pocket with the call still connected. Pulled his weapon and ran up the road. The scene when he got there showed a jackknifed semi with the driver just climbing down from his cab.

"FBI! Stay there!" He pulled his creds and peeked around the engine block. Using it for cover. The road was empty. "Where's the truck?"

"It went through the guardrail." The shaken driver pointed a trembling hand over the edge of the road.

Jordan ran over and looked down. The truck was thirty feet down the steep slope wrapped around a tree. "Call 911. Tell them there's an FBI agent on scene, and they're going to need the fire department. Tell 'em to close this road."

Traffic was already starting to back up, but it wasn't going anywhere anytime soon. The semi was now part of a criminal investigation.

He went back to his car for a flashlight, which he grabbed out of the trunk along with an emergency blanket. He wanted the driver alive. He wanted answers.

He set up a safety triangle blocking the middle of the road, then made his way carefully down the slick snowy bank using trees to brace against and stop his fall.

The driver could be out here somewhere, waiting to take a shot while Jordan tried to help.

He finally reached the truck, which was concertinaed around a large sugar maple. He checked his surroundings, looking for a figure in the darkness. The truck's back window was blown out, and both front doors were mangled. No way would they open without machinery. He could see a figure hunched over the remnants of an airbag.

He tried the back door, but it was locked. Instead, he vaulted into the bed of the truck, crunching through what remained of the safety glass before snaking his way inside via the broken back window. He shone his flashlight at the masked driver.

His head hung at an angle that made Jordan's stomach lurch.

There was a cell phone in the front in one of those dashboard holders, but he wanted this guy's face. He crawled into the front seat, his heart lurching as the truck shifted an inch to the right. *Fuck.*

Carefully he rolled the black knit balaclava up to reveal porcelain skin and a neat blonde bun and broken nose.

He swallowed hard.

Trooper Ellen Mires.

He wasn't even surprised. He wanted to shout with frustration but held it inside. He took a photo of her face and then opened her cell using facial recognition. He went into the settings, changed the passcode so he could get in. and stuffed her cell into his pocket.

Jordan cleared his throat. "Armstrong. You there?"

"Yes. Report."

"Driver of the truck is dead. Went off road and hit a tree. Broken neck." Pretty much what she wanted to do to him. "I know her. She's been my police escort several times and"—He felt like such a damned fool—"we've been intimate sexually." The words felt inaccurate, but it was the best he could come up with right now. "TacOps ran her, said she was clean." He climbed out of the truck the way he'd gotten in and eyed the slope. It was going to be a hard climb back to the road without a rope. "I guess they missed something."

"That's not like them. We'll be there in an hour."

"I'm going to call Regan. He can get to her place and secure the scene."

"Okay. Call Ackers too."

Shit. He was silent.

"Do it, or I will."

Fuck.

———

They met in the briefing room at the HRT compound the following morning. Jordan was exhausted. Daniel Ackers, Jon Regan, Crisco—whose real name turned out to be Special Agent Florence Cisco, hence Regan's truly terrible nicknames—Reid Armstrong and one of the analysts from the task force.

"What do we know?" Ackers asked.

Regan leaned back in his chair. "From what we've found following a deep examination of her communications, she'd been hiring herself out on the dark web for some extracurricular activities in her off-duty time over the past two years."

"As an assassin?" Reid Armstrong demanded.

"Looks like this was her first attempt at the big leagues. Lucky for you, kid, or else she'd have probably slit your throat while you were banging her." But Regan's comment lacked its usual bite. The guy had missed this, but Jordan couldn't blame Regan. He'd known something was off. Women didn't throw themselves at him. He wasn't Ryan fucking Sullivan.

"Why didn't she kill me when she was in my cabin?"

Regan scratched his head. "She was on record as being your escort home that first night. I figure she decided to try to infiltrate your life to either find out information—evidenced by breaking in and bugging your kit bags—or so she could get to you more easily in the future and dispose of you." He stood up and paced. "When we installed those big ol' security cameras everywhere and told VSP they were being monitored, she might have thought twice about killing you during the act."

But she'd still fucked him. She'd been working up to pumping him for more information. No wonder she'd been pissed when he ended it so abruptly.

"The truck?" Jordan hadn't been allowed to be involved in the evidence gathering part of the investigation. He'd been the intended victim. The question was why?

"Provided by the anonymous client." Reid Armstrong scratched beneath his eye. "We tracked it to a dealer in Georgia where it was purchased for cash by someone with a fake ID. We'll try to track it since purchase to the garage where she kept it, but it might take time considering she switched plates."

"You talked to her boss?"

"I did." Ackers stroked his mustache. "He was prickly as a cactus at first—dead officer and all that—but when he realized we caught her in the act of actively trying to kill an FBI agent and had evidence to show she'd taken bribes and used intimidation tactics, he relented. Said she had a good record as a cop but wasn't really a team player. The other troopers found her cold."

Regan opened his mouth and Jordan pointed his finger. "Enough with the snide remarks. The more important question is who hired her and why."

Reid Armstrong yawned. "I have a team following the money. We're also hiring Cramer, Parker and Gray, Security Consultants, because they have a specialty with tracing money through the dark web."

Jordan nodded. They were an excellent firm with solid connections to the FBI.

"Why did someone want me dead?"

Ackers glanced at Crisco. "Can we talk freely, or do you want Agent Cisco to leave the room?"

Reid Armstrong smiled thinly. "If she stays, she's on the task force for the duration, so it's up to her boss."

Regan drew one side of his mouth back. "She can work on the task force but not exclusively. I may need her in other places too."

"Fair enough." Armstrong outlined the overall details of the task force's search for Hurek and the fact a bomb had brought down the airliner probably in order to kill Kurt Montana.

"Somebody thinks the two of you know something," Crisco said.

"Someone with money and means," Regan agreed.

"Which would be great if I actually did know something." Jordan filled them in about Rowena Smith's disappearance and what he'd discovered so far. "The weird thing—"

"It's all fucking weird," Regan interrupted.

"Let him speak," Ackers snapped.

Regan bristled, but Jordan jumped in before the two got distracted by their mutual ire. "The Israelis detected ghost signals from Kurt's cell phone along the Mutare Road and the car

Rowena was driving was found farther along that same road." He showed them on a map.

"You think she stole his phone? Crossed the border illegally? On foot?"

Jordan shrugged. "Can we see if anything happened in that general area around the day of the crash?"

Armstrong frowned. "I'll get a team on it."

"What is a 'ghost' signal?" Crisco's brow was crinkled.

Jordan shook his head. "I don't even know."

"We've dug into this." Armstrong looked tired. "Everything was screwed up because of a nationwide electricity stoppage. My techs think the cell towers were fritzed."

"What if..." Jordan speculated, "knowing what we now know about the crash not being an accident, the power outage wasn't because of some system failure, but instead deliberate?"

Silence descended on the team as that idea sank in.

"None of it makes sense." Armstrong talked it through. "Kurt met up with Anders, told the task force he had a lead to follow that he'd discuss when he got back. Asked them to run a background on Smith. Next day Anders is dead, Smith disappears, and Kurt's flight is blown out of the sky."

"I spoke to him later that night from the airport, but the connection was terrible."

Regan stared at him thoughtfully then sat forward. "Maybe they didn't know that. Maybe they just knew he contacted you but couldn't listen to the content?"

"Perhaps they did bug the uncle rather than your cell, like you suspected," Armstrong added.

"Seems we're dealing with an individual or entity that can tap cell phones and create sophisticated covert monitoring devices and bombs." Jordan couldn't help thinking about the Mossad and how they used these kinds of techniques. But as far as he could tell they had zero motive.

"This sort of sophistication is usually state sponsored, but no way are the Zimbabweans responsible." Armstrong squinted as if he had a headache. Jordan could sympathize.

"Unless they had help." Jordan thought about the Chinese and Russian influence in the region.

"We're spinning our wheels guessing. Let's go find the evidence we need to figure it out." Regan paced impatiently.

He was right. Jordan stood. "I'm planning to dig back into the footage from the airport."

"Crisco can help you with that," Regan offered. "I plan to see what more I might find out about State Trooper Ellen Mires and make sure there aren't any other LEOs hanging out on the dark web. If there are, they are about to have a come-to-Jesus moment."

"Everyone planning on attending the memorial next week?" asked Armstrong.

Everyone nodded miserably.

"Not a word about any of this gets out. *Especially* not to the family," Armstrong stated firmly.

Jordan stared at the ceiling. *Shit.*

The meeting broke up, and he was glad the guys were still away. Lying to them was eating away at his insides. He led Crisco to his office and found her a chair from the briefing room. The compound was quiet as a morgue.

He plugged in his laptop and hooked it all up.

"Wait, you're doing this all by eye? Yourself?"

"I'm looking for things that seem off. Hard to put that into a computer program."

"Well, it seems you're really looking at who and what is loaded onto that flight and any sightings of your buddy, correct?"

Jordan pinched his lips together. He was tired. He'd barely caught an hour of sleep last night. "I guess."

"So, give me five minutes to set up a couple of filters and then we'll start from there."

Fuck. He felt like a dinosaur as her fingers flew over the keys. "Want a coffee?"

"Yeah. Please."

Jordan met Dinah Cohen in the break room.

"Quite the little meeting you had this morning."

He stared at her silently.

"Fine." She rolled her eyes. "I'm not the enemy."

He exhaled. She was right. He didn't have to trust her to work with her either. "You guys find any more signs of you-know-who recently?"

"No, but…"

"What?"

Dinah pulled a face. "We've heard rumors that maybe he has a kid that he cares about. And a wife, but whether he cares about her is up for debate."

A kid? "Any idea where this kid might be?"

She shook her head. "At the moment, it's pure speculation and possibly another red herring, but we're working backwards and trying to see if there's any truth in it. Pity that everyone on that island for any amount of time is dead."

"Except Alice Alexander." The woman had been held with her husband for months on Hurek's Indonesian hideout.

Dinah's eyes widened. She put a finger on her chin as she considered. "Good idea. I'll see if I can get an interview. See if she remembers anything that could tell us either way."

"Go easy on her."

Dinah narrowed her eyes at him. "What exactly do you think I have planned? A cattle prod and a bucket of water?"

Jordan picked up the two coffees. "She went through a lot, and it matters how we treat people like that."

Dinah lifted her hands. "I agree."

He yawned widely. "Sorry."

"You okay?"

He held her gaze. No, he wasn't okay, but he'd handle it.

"Let me know what you find out," he called back.

"Ditto, Krychek. Ditto."

Jordan nudged his office door ajar and placed Crisco's mug on the desk. She was nose to the monitor and had another screen open. She finished whatever black magic she was doing and then sat back, lifting the mug. "Thanks."

A screen appeared in the other monitor then another and another.

"Okay, these are the clips we want to watch first. You see something interesting you click the star icon at the top. Close anything else."

He started watching the arrival of the doomed aircraft from Zambia. The luggage operators loaded the aircraft with bags, and other staff loaded food and drink aboard.

"There's no way I can tell if a bomb is inside any of the baggage they're loading or not. Can we hook into their screening machines?"

"Unfortunately, not." Crisco frowned. "The bomb could have already been on board the plane from Zambia."

Jordan swore and dragged his hand through his hair. "Everything seems to change after he meets Bjorn Anders at that restaurant and he bumps into Rowena Smith. We don't need footage from the airport, we need it on those other two people to see where they go and who they talk to."

A clip caught his eye. He leaned forward. "Hey, what's this?"

He pressed play and a figure that looked hauntingly like Kurt Montana scaled a security fence and left the airport.

Jordan watched it three times and felt his heart roll around his chest like a tumbleweed. He watched it again and then pressed the star button. He frantically searched for other clips of Kurt. Through the airport. Past the boarding desk and down the steps to the tarmac.

"Where's the feed showing passengers getting on that plane?"

Crisco chewed her lips. Typed some instructions. "It's this one here, but the algorithm didn't pick him up. That's *not* surprising as the people are generally facing away from the camera." She let it play from the time Kurt had his boarding card scanned to the time they closed the doors on the aircraft.

Jordan was afraid to believe his own eyes as his pulse

pounded. "Run it again. We'll check off every person from the manifest."

It took an hour, and his hands were shaking by the time they finished.

"He's not there. He follows the woman with the baby and then...he isn't behind her when she climbs onboard." Jordan's throat was sore from suppressing emotion. "He didn't get on that flight." His mouth opened at the implication. "Holy fuck." He lurched to his feet. He wanted to kiss Crisco. He needed to tell Ackers. He needed to tell his teammates, Montana's family.

Kurt Montana never got on that doomed plane.

"Wait," Crisco warned. "Look at this." She found another glimpse of him walking around the outside of the airport terminal before he scaled the fence.

"I have to tell everyone—"

"Krychek. Stop. Think." She grabbed his sleeve. "If the Zimbabwean government suspect it's a bomb, they would have already reviewed this footage. They'd know Montana wasn't on board."

And they hadn't told them.

"Perhaps they didn't bother looking because they assumed he got on board, and maybe they know exactly who planted that bomb so didn't examine the evidence too closely. But," she swallowed, "if they truly don't know it was a bomb and we tell them it was and then they see this footage...he's going to be their prime suspect."

Jordan dropped back down in his seat. "We have to find him first, before news of the bomb leaks, before we tell anyone he's still alive."

Shit, shit, shit. He rubbed his forehead. His throat was as dry as a sandstorm, but joy filled him. His friend was alive, and he was damned well going to find him and bring him home.

32

FEBRUARY 8

Mon., 10:00 p.m. Local Bar, Quantico

Jordan sat in the bar nursing a beer, watching his colleagues who were back after finishing up the op from hell in Boston. Cas Demarco eyed him through the mirror behind the bar with both suspicion and pity as a hockey game played on the TV.

Jordan looked away. The past four days had been torture. To not tell these men the truth about Kurt Montana when they wore their grief tattooed in the sadness of their eyes and the deep grooves around their forced smiles.

They still did their jobs, excelled even, but he knew how Montana's supposed death wore at them, eroded them from the inside out. He'd felt it himself.

But even though he knew Montana hadn't gotten on that flight, he didn't know if the man was still alive. The idea of giving his friends and colleagues hope, only to quash it, didn't sit right either. He did know that Montana had somehow for some reason connected with Rowena Smith and driven on the Mutare Road and then disappeared. The ghost signals weren't anomalies. Someone had tried to erase them from the phone records, and that someone had powerful resources. Lots of resources.

Had Rowena Smith warned Montana about the bomb? No way would Kurt have willingly let that plane take off if that had been the case. Had she known about the explosives? Her phone records had been wiped, as had those cloud files. Her house destroyed. Her uncle had agreed to hand over her laptop to the British Embassy, and they'd started putting pressure on the Zimbabwean police to search for her. Jordan didn't think it would be long before the pressure from her family and friends led to some media releases regarding the missing woman, which might shake something loose.

Interestingly enough, the FBI analysts had tracked Smith across the city to near Bjorn Anders' office the morning of the flight, around the time he'd been murdered.

Had Rowena Smith killed Bjorn and then tricked Kurt into meeting her?

It didn't fit with what the people who knew her had said, but it didn't mean it wasn't possible. Maybe she was a sleeper agent. Deep undercover.

Had Kurt been taken in by a pretty face and a willing body?

He wouldn't be the first, or the last.

Jordan's mood soured. The locals and FBI had suppressed the story of Trooper Mires being a hired killer, and she'd been buried with full honors, having died in a horrific accident. It was solely to try to keep whoever hired her ignorant of the fact the FBI were actively hunting them now.

The fact the Anders' murder case was already closed suggested the authorities didn't want to find whoever had killed Bjorn Anders.

Why?

Rowena's DNA profile had been developed, and the techs were running it through the databases for matches, and also loading it to the other family tree websites. Casting the genetic net as wide as possible. They should have some useable information in the next couple of days. The money used to pay Mires to try to either kill him or fuck him into revealing what he knew had been paid in Bitcoin, and although it was traceable, it was taking a lot longer than anyone had anticipated.

With Montana's memorial looming, he was anxious to resolve this. To find Kurt, who would surely have made contact if he could, which suggested he was either hurt or dead, or being held somewhere against his will.

It was like walking a tightrope, and if he fell off, his friend died.

A pretty blonde with flyaway curls walked inside the bar, and Jordan saw the interest of half the guys stir. She bought a beer then checked her cell. Then she glanced around for a seat. He tried to give out vibes that told her to find somewhere else, but she smiled at him and sat one table over.

"Seems like a busy spot."

He frowned when he realized she was talking to him. He ignored her for a moment then realized maybe whoever hired Mires had decided to try it again with someone more winsome.

He forced a smile. "Yeah."

She held herself tightly together. Knees pressed close. Arms against her sides even when she took a delicate sip of her beer.

Cas Demarco half staggered off his stool and out the door. Was he sick? Jordan exchanged a startled glance with Sebastian Black before the sniper went after the other man.

He hated this situation with every cell in his body.

A few minutes later, Sebastian came back inside. He sent him a sharp nod to say Demarco was okay.

Jordan nodded back.

"You work for the FBI?" The woman looked sweet and guileless. Her eyes were slightly red as if she'd been crying.

He didn't trust her an inch. "If I did, I wouldn't go around admitting the fact to strangers, now, would I?"

A soft smile touched cherry red lips and sent a bolt of desire straight through him. Ellen had worn that exact shade of lipstick.

He hadn't realized how easy he was until these last few weeks. Give him a pretty blonde with crimson lips, and he was toast. They didn't even need to buy him a drink.

She sniffed. "I guess not."

He didn't believe the act for a moment. Did they think he was an idiot? Regan's words came back to him. Keep your friends close, your enemies closer. Perhaps he was playing this all wrong.

"So what do you do?"

"Me?" She looked startled by the question, tapped her painted nails on the table. "I'm a student, actually."

He raised his brows.

"Richmond."

"And what are you doing in Quantico?"

"Family business."

"Is your family in this bar?"

Her tongue slipped out and tracked slowly over her lower lip which she then bit seemingly to hold back emotion. "No. Unfortunately, they're not."

"But you are? Why?"

She squirmed under his gaze which he allowed to travel boldly over her T-shirt that featured a quote from *Hamlet* stretched over pert breasts.

She shrugged, looking miserable. She wasn't very good at this. "Curiosity."

"Curiosity about what?" He let his voice drop and linger suggestively. He used the fact he found himself attracted to this woman to fuel his rage.

"It doesn't matter." She pushed her beer away and picked up her coat before heading outside.

Pissed, he followed her out into the parking lot, stalked her to her car. "What are you curious about?"

"About the Hostage Rescue Team. I know they drink here." Her hands fumbled with her keys. What else did she have in her pockets?

He spun her around and grabbed her wrists so she couldn't pull a gun on his stupid ass. "Who told you that?" He thrust his face close to hers as he transferred both wrists to one hand so he could frisk her for a weapon. "Tell me who the hell put you up to this?"

Tears began pouring down her face. "Leave me alone!" She tried to shove him away from her. "Let me go."

Bitterness welled up inside him, along with hatred.

She stopped struggling and glared at him so fiercely he released her and took a step back. She wasn't carrying anything more dangerous than her face.

"Do me a favor. You might be prettier than the last one, but tell whoever hired you that I don't need any more whores to fuck and kill, so they can save themselves the trouble." Her mouth opened in shock, and her dark blue eyes were massive and terrified. Good. She was playing a game she didn't understand. "And tell them this, I will find them, and I will make them pay for what they've done to my friends."

He held her door open and watched her bolt inside. "And if I ever see you around here again, I'll make you regret it. Understood?"

Those eyes looked at him aghast before she sped away like the hounds of hell were on her tail.

Good.

He watched her go with satisfaction. She wouldn't be knocking on his door, and he wouldn't be letting her in, no matter how pretty a shade of blue those eyes were.

He wouldn't be seeing her ever again, and that suited him perfectly.

———

Thursday, February 11.

Rowena focused on pattern ten. She appreciated the need to be in the moment to make sure she did the movements exactly right. Because sometimes the need to escape scratched at her skin from the inside, desperate to get out like some creature in a horror show.

Kurt sat on the bed and scratched the day off the wall. Twenty-eight. Then he looked at her.

"You haven't had your period."

She was well aware. The idea of being pregnant was daunting in this environment. She'd always wanted a family, but not like this. "I know."

"Pulling out is not exactly a fail-safe contraceptive method." His expression was twisted and full of self-condemnation.

"I know that too."

She gave up on wherever she was in the pattern and started over. "I'd rather be pregnant with your baby than by unknown rapists."

Her stomach lurched because that was what she was probably a product of. Rape. That was why her mother had fled Africa so suddenly. She swallowed. "It's my womb. It should be my choice."

His dark blue eyes looked defeated. This was hard on them both.

"Plus, it could be stress. I remember going into the hospital overnight as a teen. My period was due, but it never arrived. Skipped that whole month in some sort of stress response."

He looked surprised. "That happens?"

"Yes. It happens."

"You'd keep it?" His dark eyes burned. "If you have a choice?"

She held his gaze. She didn't know if he wanted more kids or not. She didn't know what this would mean for *them*. They hadn't discussed a future together. It wasn't safe to be pregnant here, and having a child under these circumstances was dangerous and awful. But she enjoyed the intimacy she shared with Kurt. She wanted that much control over her own body, her own choices. The fact nature might have taken its course was not shocking, although it seemed fundamentally unfair that the consequences varied so much between the sexes.

"I'd keep your baby." She watched his features which currently revealed nothing but intense concentration. She couldn't read him. "If that scares you, you better tell me now because I've always wanted kids. Although I imagined a very different scenario if it ever happened."

He stood in front of her. Tipped up her chin. "In other circumstances, the thought of you having our baby would bring me so much joy. I'd love the chance to be a proper dad this time. But"—he looked around their cramped quarters—"here? It terrifies me. And, just in case you're not already pregnant. No more sex. I'm jerking off in the bathroom from now on."

"There are other alternatives." She sent him a sweet smile. She wasn't agreeing to abstain from making love with him, not when it was one of the things that was keeping her sane.

His lips pinched. "*Row*."

It was about choice and autonomy. And enjoying sex with the man she loved. It was a risk, but a calculated one that she was willing to take. "I have a lot of catching up to do, and I don't think I'm there yet. How often do you think people have sex in a normal relationship?"

"Normal? Depends on the normal. When I was married and home, before Daisy arrived, pretty much every day. After she arrived...probably twice a week if we were lucky."

"So, say the average person, assuming they're in a healthy relationship, has sex twice a week, conservative estimate. So fifty-two weeks multiplied by twice a week is 104 times a year. So over ten years...that's more than a thousand times! We've had sex, what? Twice a day on average since we met? About sixty times. I have a ways to go to catch up, pal."

He closed his eyes and tipped his face up to the ceiling. "You're going to kill me."

She rose up on tiptoe and kissed his bearded cheek. "Can't wait."

He took her face in his hands. "We're getting out of here as soon as we spot land."

She held that intense gaze. "You and me."

He rested his forehead against hers. "You and me."

33

FEBRUARY 12

Friday. Quantico

Jordan sat outside Montana's ranch-style home, wondering if the man were still alive and, if so, where he was and what he was doing. Why hadn't he gotten a message to them? Was he hurt?

On Wednesday, Kurt's memorial had been attacked, and Gold Team were actively hunting the psychopath—another mission he was barred from participating in. Jordan couldn't help feeling some twisted sense of relief about the fact that the ceremony hadn't concluded, though he was grateful no one had been badly injured. He didn't want to memorialize a man who might still be alive. He didn't want to lie to the family or anyone else at the wake Ackers had insisted on hosting for show. Jordan had ducked out of the church as soon as they'd ascertained the bad guy was gone and the danger was over.

He was frustrated by the slow progress of their investigation, but at least people were working on it. Rowena Smith's DNA didn't match with anyone in any of the criminal or military databases, but they couldn't gain access to the Brit's databases. They had an expert trying to whittle down people who might be her biological father. He'd assumed it would be an easy case of this guy or that, but instead there were all these possible connotations. Not only were records spotty and sometimes hard to decipher, but infidelity and incest also confused the issue.

He dragged Kurt's large black bag from the trunk of his new car—the old one had been an insurance write off—and swung it onto his back. It wasn't that heavy without all the weapons and ammo he'd left in Montana's equipment cage, which no one had yet dared to touch and probably never would.

He trudged around the side through the gate to the back door. Used his key to unlock the door and came to an abrupt halt. A light was on in the hallway. Papers lay strewn across the kitchen table. A mug of coffee sat in the middle.

Someone was here?

Ackers had assured him the family had left right after the memorial on Wednesday afternoon.

Jordan lay the bag softly on the floor and eased the door shut. He drew his weapon. Had the person who'd paid Ellen Mires decided to search Kurt's house? Looking for what?

He stepped soundlessly through the kitchen and into the hall-way. The sound of water splashing had him narrowing his gaze. Whoever was here obviously felt comfortable enough to make themselves at home.

Anger, never far from the surface these days, rose inside him, pressed against his forehead, his chest, the knuckle of the finger that wanted to curl around the trigger of his Springfield Custom Professional 1911-A1.

Then he heard singing, and it pushed him over the edge.

He kicked open the door of the bathroom and pointed his weapon at the wet naked figure soaking in the tub.

She screamed and lunged for the towel. He beat her to it and whipped it away, searching for weapons. There was none.

"Shut up. Shut the fuck up." Jordan recognized her from the bar last week.

She drew in a shuddering breath and tried to cover herself with her hands.

"Nothing I haven't seen before, sweetheart. Stop with the hysterics."

Her gaze narrowed into thin blue lasers that would have cut out his heart if he'd had one.

He grabbed the first towel that came to hand and thrust it at her, realizing belatedly it wouldn't cover much. Didn't matter. He had no intention of being distracted. "Get out."

He moved backwards, watching for an accomplice. He motioned her forward then took her arm and held her in front of him while he cleared the ground floor.

She trembled in his grip.

They reached Kurt's bedroom. He swept under the pillows for weapons. Nothing. "Lie down." He pointed at the bed and gave her a light push.

He grabbed a belt from Kurt's closet and caught her on her way to the door. He tied her arms and wrists together and pushed her back onto the bed.

"Leave me alone!"

The kick in the face took him by surprise, but he ignored the pain and the blood and sat on her to capture her legs and ankles and bind them securely together. He wiped his nose, and she started screaming again. He found some socks and a canvas belt and used it to gag her.

This was an FBI matter now. Not a local one. As soon as he cleared the house, he was calling in Armstrong, Ackers, and Regan and they'd figure out what to do with the little hellcat.

The towel had come loose during the struggle, and her eyes were wide with fear. She was beautiful with an almost innocent air. But that innocence was deceptive, and he wasn't foolish enough to fall for the same trap with different bait.

"Stay there while I check the basement for any accomplices. Move and you'll regret it."

The threat was a bluff. He wasn't about to hurt her, but he was happy to scare her into submission so maybe she'd tell them who she was working for.

He headed downstairs, cleared the TV room and the back where the furnace and water heater were. He even shone a flashlight around a small crawlspace. Nothing.

He heard a heavy thump and hurried back up the stairs. He paused mid-step on his rush through the living room. There, on the sideboard, was a large, framed photograph he'd never noticed before, of Kurt with his arm around a blonde woman in a black graduation gown. The same woman who was currently tied up in Kurt's bedroom.

Oh my fucking God.

He realized his mistake with the sense of impending doom like watching an axe about to sever an innocent neck. He strode into the bedroom in time to find the woman pressing the combination of Kurt's small gun safe in the base of his wardrobe with her bound hands. He launched himself on top of her. Rolling them away from any loaded weapons until he had time to explain and apologize.

She tried to head butt him, and he jerked back.

"Wait. *Wait.* Daisy. I'm so sorry. I didn't know it was you. I thought you were an intruder. I am so sorry."

Those deep blue eyes that he now realized were the exact same shade as Kurt's were filled with loathing and hatred.

Fuck. He had screwed this up so badly.

"I'm truly sorry." He became aware he was pressed down on her naked body, and no wonder she looked as if she wanted to kill him. He rolled off of her and quickly scooped her up and placed her on the bed. She tried to kick him again, but he dodged her.

She was a scrappy little thing.

He grabbed a bathrobe off the back of the door and covered her with it. "I'm really sorry. I can explain. Let me—" He reached tentatively for the belt he'd tied around her face and dragged it off.

She spat out the socks. "I'm going to fucking kill you."

Jordan held up his hands in surrender. "You have every right to be angry."

"Every right? Every damned right? How fucking dare you tell me when I have the right to be angry. I'll be angry any time I want to be."

"That's not what I meant. I'm sorry. I—" He swallowed. He couldn't tell her another woman had seduced him in the hopes of uncovering information about her father. "Your father asked me to take care of his place while he was away. I thought you were…"

She was breathing heavily.

Christ. "An intruder. I would never have treated you with so much disrespect if I'd realized it was you."

"On Monday night," she spoke over him, "you said, 'Tell whoever hired you that I don't need any more whores to fuck and kill.' What did you mean by that?"

He blew out a big breath.

"Who did you kill?" Her voice was firm but wobbled a little at the end. She was scared. Who wouldn't be?

He scrubbed his free hand over his forehead. Sat on the bed. "It's a long story and technically I didn't kill anyone. She tried to run me off the road and ended up wrapped around a tree. I thought you were… Look, it doesn't matter what I thought. I'm so sorry for what I said on Monday night."

"You shoved me against my car. I have bruises."

She'd have more from tonight. "Again. I'm sorry. I thought you were a criminal, and that's no excuse. I will do anything to make it up to you." *Except tell you the truth.*

"You scared me." Her voice was small, and he felt like slime. Any lower, and he'd be looking up to people like Ellen Mires, who'd broken her oath for money.

Daisy wriggled under the robe fighting the straps on her wrists. The shoulder slipped lower, and they both froze. She glared at him.

He swallowed with difficulty. "If I undo the restraints, will you promise to hear me out before you call the cops? I am law enforcement. I worked very closely with your dad. I promise from now on, I'll protect you with my life."

She stared at him long and hard. "Prove it."

At first, he didn't understand. Then he realized she wanted to see his ID. He slipped his hand into his back pocket and pulled out his creds. Gold shield on one side. Official ID on the other.

"*You're* Jordan Krychek?" Her features pinched with surprise and what looked a lot like disappointment.

He knew that feeling. "Your father mentioned me?"

She shook her head, obviously lying but he couldn't figure out why.

"The HRT Director told me Kurt's family had left town. I would never have come over if I'd thought you were still here." He slipped his hands under the robe at her feet to undo the belt that tied her ankles together. She lifted her arms from under the robe, and he released her and stood back.

"You may have seen it all before, you sonofabitch," she bit out, "but you don't get to see it again. Turn around."

He did so, and a moment later she swept past him wearing Kurt's oversized blue robe. He followed her through into the kitchen. She opened her mouth to say something when Jordan realized they couldn't have this conversation here.

"Wait." He held up his hand for silence. Whoever had bugged his place could conceivably have bugged this one too. Although, would they bug the home of a supposed dead man?

In case he somehow tried to make contact…

He pulled out the signal jammer Regan had given him and turned it on. Even so, he didn't want to risk saying too much until the place was swept. He wanted Daisy out of this house and under HRT protection, but Gold Team was stretched thin with this hunt for the disgraced Navy SEAL from Louisiana.

She went to speak again, and he put his finger to his lips.

"Want some coffee?" He found a notepad on the table. Wrote, *Careful what you say. Bugs.*

She looked confused and frightened as she hugged herself.

He glanced at the table, saw two photographs and a phone SIM card lying on top of an envelope with familiar handwriting scrawled over it. Then he saw a note saying, "Give this to Jordan Krychek immediately."

He glared at her, and she glared right back, but when she opened her mouth, he pressed his finger to her lips and her eyes flashed with something that wasn't entirely hatred. It punched through his anger like a fist through paper.

Shaken, he moved away.

He wrote. *Don't mention anything important but act natural.* He turned off the blocker because he wanted them to think they were staying here.

"I don't drink coffee with men who assault me."

He felt sick. "I'm going to make some anyway. It's been a long day."

He wrote another message. *Get dressed. Collect all your stuff. We have to leave. Hurry.*

"Take your time. Then we can sit down and talk."

She left in a pissed-off huff, and he searched Kurt's kitchen until he found some large freezer bags. He slipped the envelope in one, the photos and note into separate ones. SIM in another.

He pulled out his cell and snapped images of everything and sent it to Armstrong.

Armstrong called back immediately but Jordan didn't pick up.

He texted instead.

> Unsecured location. Send TacOps around to Montana's home ASAP.

> Take the evidence to the National Laboratory immediately. I'll call them. Highest priority.

> What do I do with Montana's daughter?

> Protective custody. I'll arrange it.

She won't like it.

And Montana would skin us both alive if anything happens to her.

Who's going to do protective duty?

I'll talk to Ackers. Take her to the HRT compound. Don't tell her what's going on.

Jordan grimaced. She already hated him, so what the hell did it matter if she hated him more? He was taking one for the team. Anything to keep her safe.

She came back wearing tight jeans and a black sweater that made her skin look pale and translucent. She'd slipped on Doc Martens, had her coat over one arm and dragged a suitcase that was almost the same size as she was.

"Let's take these drinks into the living room, and I'll explain everything."

"Fine."

He shoved Kurt's bag against the kitchen wall. Picked up Daisy's case and slipped the pieces of evidence into a side pocket. Zipped it shut. She grabbed her laptop case and notebooks. They left the house quickly, and he threw her luggage in his trunk.

"What's going on?"

Jordan shook his head, scanned for a tail while flicking the signal jammer back on.

He floored it. They were close to Marine Corps Base Quantico, and he was relieved when he got there without spotting anyone following him. It would take time for anyone monitoring Montana's house to realize they were in the wind.

"Why—"

"I'll explain everything shortly." He shot her a look. "We need to make sure you and your belongings aren't bugged first."

"Who'd *bug* me?" The skepticism came with a sneer.

He said nothing, got past the guards who'd already been told they were coming. He pulled up near the entrance of the National Laboratory. Got out and removed the photos from the side of her case.

"Hey, those are mine." She followed him out of the vehicle and across the sidewalk, grabbing for the evidence, which he held out of reach.

"It said to give the note to me immediately."

"Which is why I drove back here after school today. To find him and give them to him. I would have gone to the bar and asked around except *some bastard* threatened me last time I went there, and I was too scared." She was getting loud again.

"I'm sorry." He wanted to dig a hole and crawl into it. "Why didn't you call Ackers or someone?"

"I was tired by the time I got to Dad's. I figured I'd have a bath and call Daniel in the morning and arrange a meeting with you at the compound, where I wouldn't bump into the psycho who'd attacked me on Monday night." She narrowed her eyes.

He inhaled a deep breath and prayed for patience. He'd earned her bad opinion with his behavior and rash assumptions, but he couldn't turn back the clock, so they were stuck with the situation.

A Black woman in a lab coat met them at the door, and Jordan handed the things across and signed a chain of evidence log.

"I need copies sent to myself, Daniel Ackers, and Reid Armstrong. This is the number-one priority in the Bureau today," he urged the tech.

"I want copies too. They're mine. I want them back," Daisy said stubbornly as the tech looked at her nervously before heading back into the building. She stood there shivering without her coat on. "When you've analyzed them, I want them back."

"Your father said to give them to me."

Her eyes filled with the glitter of angry tears. "They were the last thing he sent to me. I have a right to them."

Her grief was a dagger to his heart. Especially when he couldn't tell her the truth about her father. Not yet.

"I'll see what I can do. Daniel Ackers wants to meet with you at the HRT compound. We need to go over you and everything for electronic listening devices."

"Fine. Daniel will help me sort this out." They climbed back into the car, and he couldn't meet her gaze. He drove quickly to the compound, relieved to see Jon Regan was already there with Crisco by his side.

"Who are these people?" Daisy chewed on her lip nervously.

"The techs who look for bugs." Although they did a lot more than that. "They are on our side."

She stepped out of the vehicle tentatively.

"I'm sorry for your loss." Regan stepped forward. A better liar than Jordan had ever been. "I would have introduced myself at the memorial, but we were rudely interrupted."

Daisy nodded.

Jordan hadn't noticed her at the memorial. He'd been lost in his own miasma of misery and avoiding the family and his team-mates as much as humanly possible.

"I'm going to need your phone, sweetheart. I have people going to your dad's place to make sure it's secure." Regan held out his hand, and Daisy gave him her cell without a qualm. He handed it to Crisco who hooked it up to something in the back of their van as Regan began running a wand over Daisy's body.

Jordan narrowed his gaze on Regan, but the man was all business. Regan nodded with satisfaction when he'd finished. She hadn't lit up.

Next, he went to the trunk where he went through every single item in minute detail.

"Phone's tapped," Crisco called out. "I've put it in a secure box for now. Maybe we can trace the tap."

Regan nodded. "There's nothing in the case. Anything else?"

Wide-eyed, Daisy pulled her laptop case out of the back seat. "Here."

Regan ran the wand over the laptop case, and his wand lit up. He handed the whole thing across to Crisco who put it in a trunk. "I'll get those items back to you within twenty-four hours."

With that he gave her a nod, and the two agents climbed in their van and took off.

"What the hell is going on?" she demanded.

"It's a classified investigation, I can't—"

She shoved against his chest. "It's about my dad. I know it is." Pissed. "Tell me what's going on. Dammit. Tell me!"

She punched him, and he let her. Then the tears finally started to fall, and she bowed her head. He gathered her against his chest and tried to give her comfort. "I'm sorry. I'm really sorry."

He watched Ackers' car snake along the road, followed by a large black suburban. He recognized the Blue Team leader driving the vehicle and knew she would never forgive him for what was about to happen.

She could add it to his long list of sins.

34

It was Saturday morning, and Jordan hadn't bothered going home last night, too excited by the potential break in the case and disgusted by how he'd treated Montana's daughter. Last night, she'd gone from being glad to see Daniel Ackers to cursing them both out at high volume before Blue Team had physically removed her. And the look of betrayal she'd shot Jordan still bitch-slapped him in the face every time he thought about it.

Christ.

He'd royally fucked up every single interaction with a person he'd wanted more than anything to protect. He should have insisted she stay with him, but she was safer in protective custody.

Dammit.

Kurt would understand, but his daughter would never forgive him, and he'd realized over the past fourteen hours that her forgiveness was something he wanted to earn. He'd slept on a bedroll in his office and showered in the gym. His stomach rumbled. He didn't remember the last time he'd eaten. He was going to have to go across to the cafeteria at the Academy at some point and get some food.

He looked at the copies of the photos that were being run right now. He knew one guy was a much younger Bjorn Anders, and that gave them a timeline to work with for age progression. Another man was Darmawan Hurek of whom they had very few images, period, and another inexplicably looked a lot like tech billionaire Nolan Gilder. If Gilder were involved, it explained a whole hell of a lot about what had been going on over the past month.

Maybe not the why, but certainly the who. It wasn't the Israelis or Russians or Chinese. It was one fucking, out-of-control oligarch who, according to some sources, wanted to live forever.

The photos revealed answers to many mysteries. Hurek and Gilder had both attended university in St. Andrews at around the same time, but there had never been any hint they'd been friends. Had Gilder scrubbed his online history? Definitely. Who were the other men in the photos? Analysts were running them now.

Jordan had called the hotel resort that was on the header of the paper used in the note—the one near where Rowena Smith's uncle's car had been found. They had no record of Kurt or Rowena staying there, nor Kurt's alias, Joe Hanssen. But if someone was willing to bring down a commercial aircraft and attempt to murder an FBI operator on US soil to keep their association a secret, they were more than capable of erasing records of a man and a woman staying at a hotel.

His phone rang.

Armstrong. "Hey, get this."

Jordan heard the excitement in Armstrong's voice.

"We had a break in the case. Took Dulles security about an hour to tag me, but thankfully, the woman refused to give up."

"Woman?"

"A farmer from Mozambique claimed to have information about Montana."

This was it.

"I went over and interviewed her and then brought her to headquarters. She traveled all the way from Mozambique because she recognized Rowena from the Brits' missing person appeal.

And then she saw Kurt's photo in the list of people who were supposed to have died on the flight and guess what? She *saw* them, Jordan. She saw him and Rowena Smith both alive and said they were traveling together as a couple using fake names."

Jordan raised his brows. "When?"

"January thirteenth at her farm."

"They only met two days prior, but they forged enough of a bond to go on the run together?"

"Seems like it. Marianne Van Hoogen said she caught them in her outdoor canteen patching up a nasty wound in Kurt's arm. Spun some story about being lost hikers. But get this, he told her his name was *Joe Hanssen*."

Jordan stood abruptly and walked to the window that looked out over the stark winter landscape. This had to be true. There was no other explanation.

"Why'd she come to Washington? Why not call?"

"She's scared. Says that she gave them a ride to Beira, but after they helped her load fertilizer onto her truck, an armed gang came along and grabbed Kurt. Rowena tried to defend him, and they took her too."

His mouth went dry. A kidnapping? This was a simple kidnapping? Where was the ransom demand? Why had they been traveling on foot across Mozambique in the first place?

"The woman reported it to local police, and they promised to look into it, but she says nothing happened. When she was searching for any kind of mention of it in the news afterwards, that's when she spotted Kurt's photo. After that, she didn't trust the local police not to come looking for her. She's convinced her phones are compromised—we have hers now, examining it in the lab. She's genuinely scared and very, very smart. She decided to book a vacation cruise package to the Caribbean, something that wouldn't arouse too much suspicion. She jumped ship in Jamaica and flew straight here with only her purse and the clothes on her back."

"What day did they get taken in Beira?"

"January fourteenth."

A month ago.

Despair leaked through though he tried to hold it at bay. "We should have had a ransom demand by now."

"Yeah. I'm going to pull in a negotiator as part of the task force, just in case."

Jordan scrubbed his hand through his hair. "Most of them are getting ready for Quentin Savage's wedding tomorrow. Do you think it could be related? Savage's wedding? Hurek? Kurt's disappearance?"

"Maybe. They're on high alert for that."

"You get a load of the people in that one photograph?"

"Yeah. Believe it or not, Gilder is a plus-one to one of the wedding guests."

A bad feeling flitted over his skin. "Could this be some sort of terror plot?"

"I've given Alex Parker the heads up as to a potential situation, and he's hiring additional security to the already massive security efforts they have in place. President Hague is supposed to make an appearance, so no one is taking any chances."

Jordan relaxed a little. If POTUS was there, security would be tight as a duck's ass. "Perhaps we can flip it and use the opportunity to get eyes on him."

"Exactly what I'm thinking too. We have enough agents in play, hopefully we can get something on him."

"It can't be traced back to us unless we have a warrant."

"I already spoke to a judge. It's a sealed warrant. The info is need-to-know—I wasn't even convinced I should tell you."

Jordan bristled, but he understood. This info couldn't leak. "It's dangerous going after this guy." He didn't even want to say his name. "If he has Kurt and he discovers we suspect him, what's to stop him ordering a kill?" *If he hadn't already.*

All this progress in the past few days…it would be unbearable to lose Kurt now.

"I spoke to the FBI Director. I had to. We have massive defense and infrastructure contracts with his company. If he's dirty, they need to know."

"What did she say?"

"Apparently, DoD is already conducting a separate investigation."

"What are the implications of arresting one of the richest people in the world?"

"At least he'll be able to afford a good lawyer."

"Cocksucker will probably be out on bail and on his private island by lunchtime." They were going to have to tread very carefully, the priority for the FBI first being to find Kurt Montana and Rowena Smith. Then they needed to round up all those responsible for bringing down a commercial aircraft and whatever other crimes they were trying to hide that were worth killing so many innocents for. Not to mention putting a contract on Jordan's head.

"What are you doing with the witness who came in?" asked Jordan.

"A protective detail. But she's made a sworn statement under oath, and she's planning to stay in the city for as long as we need her to."

Would it ever be safe for her if she were identified?

"If Gilder is in the city for this wedding, he better not catch sight or scent of her."

"He won't. Right now, he thinks we're ignorant of any involvement on his part. Kurt's letter is the only connection we have. It's circumstantial. It proves nothing, but we're working on it."

"I hate waiting."

"So do I."

"Do you think Kurt's still alive?"

"That's what I'm telling myself until I see proof otherwise. You know Kurt. He's a fighter. I'm going to see who the CIA have in Mozambique. See if we can identify the group that abducted them. Maybe talk to them."

"We need renewed focus on all and any communications out

of Beira at that time. Hey, it's a port, right? We should look at ships on any satellite images around the same period. Track each vessel. See where they are now. Get ahead of the curve."

"Good idea. I'll put a team on it. It's coming together."

Jordan rocked his lower jaw in his hand. "It's taking too damned long. How's Montana's kid holding up?" It was easier to think of her as a kid though he knew she was anything but.

"Last report was she was giving Blue Team hell, and one of them asked if they could sedate or restrain her."

Jordan opened his mouth to object.

"I told them to man up and treat her the way they'd want their sister or mother treated."

Jordan flashed back to her naked body and knew he definitely didn't think of Daisy Montana like a sister or his mother, and if Kurt ever found out, he was a dead man.

As long as Kurt was alive, he'd take that risk.

35

FEBRUARY 15

Monday. Quantico

Monday night, Jordan found himself dragged to the bar where the team was holding an impromptu celebration following the end of another fraught op. Though desperate for answers in an investigation that was moving at a snail's pace, he needed this release.

While everyone in Gold Team sang along badly to Rick Astley's *Never Gonna Give You Up*, a quiet sliver of joy slipped through the cracks of his misery. It was good to see the guys happy for a change. He hoped they could find Montana alive soon and really see them smile.

Abruptly the music stopped, and he craned his neck around JJ Hersh's large form to see what had startled the group. His hand immediately went to his sidearm.

Through the crowd he saw Daisy Montana standing there looking cold and out of breath. He rose to his feet. What the hell? Where was Blue Team? Where was her security?

She caught his gaze through the crowd.

"Ah, hmm." She began to speak, and Jordan started to push through the crowd toward her. "Sorry to interrupt. My name is

Daisy Montana, and I know many of you worked with my dad."

Fuck, fuck, fuck.

"The thing is."

Don't say it. Please God, don't say it.

"I don't think he's dead. I think he's still alive."

Shit.

He reached her and swept her into a fireman's carry and rushed her outside before she could say another word that might jeopardize their investigation and her father's life.

"Let me go!"

He spun around, looking for Blue Team. "How did you get here? Where's your protection detail?"

She kicked at him and raked her nails over his back. "My prison guards, more like. I walked!"

The parking lot was empty of people, but as he headed to his car, he felt the surge of operators following in his wake. He set Daisy on her feet but held onto her arm. Opened the passenger door. "Get in."

Her eyes glowed with molten fire. "No."

"Get in the damned car, Daisy." Anger seeped through. And desperation.

"What is going on?" asked Cas Demarco.

Jordan pressed the magic button on his key fob. "I can't tell you." His voice cracked and he thought he was going to choke on the need to share everything. "You know I can't tell you."

Gold Team were lined up shoulder to shoulder, staring at him like they could see the shadows on his soul.

Shane Livingstone crossed his arms. "But she can. Why do you think your dad's still alive, Daisy?"

She opened her mouth but shut it again when Jordan sent her a glare.

"I know the plane crash wasn't an accident," Aaron Nash stated quietly. "They found Semtex residue on some of the damaged parts."

"Semtex?"

"A bomb brought that plane down?" Angry words permeated the group.

Jordan's gaze flashed to Nash. At least he wasn't the only one keeping secrets.

But they'd already said too much. Enough to get Kurt killed if someone overheard and he wasn't already dead. He looked at each of the men in his team, men he loved like brothers. Made a decision that would probably get him fired and possibly imprisoned, but at least he could live with himself.

"Don't talk about this at *all*. Not one word," he warned. "Meet me at my place. Gold Team only."

With TacOps monitoring his home, it was as secure as anywhere, especially for a group of armed and highly talented professionals.

With a wary look, Daisy finally got in the damned car. He went around and climbed into the driver's seat, pulled out of the parking lot. Cowboy's truck was immediately in his rearview, full of the guys. A hell of a lot better sight than the black one that had tried to ram him off the road the other week.

He called Armstrong and interrupted his panic. "I have her. Tell Blue Team they failed the assignment. Gold Team is taking over. And I'm going to tell her and the guys what we know so far."

"It's too dangerous—"

"I don't have a choice," he snapped. "They suspect something is off. They won't say anything. I'll make sure they understand the stakes. You know it's only a matter of time until we update them anyway. Daisy already told them she thinks her dad is alive."

He flicked a glance in her direction and saw the hurt cross her features. Damn.

"They aren't stupid. One of them already knows about the bomb."

"If any of this leaks..."

"They'll appreciate the stakes better than anyone." He hung up, and he and Daisy stared silently out the front windshield. Finally, he released a breath and with it, most of the anger. He tried to get a grip on what he was feeling. Mostly relief. It certainly wasn't this woman he was angry with. More with himself. "I'm sorry. I should have handled this whole thing a lot better than I have."

She pressed her hands between her knees and looked at him. "Is Dad alive?"

"We don't know if your father is alive, but we do know he didn't get on board the aircraft that crashed."

Her eyes filled with tears, and he reached for her hand and squeezed. She held on tight, sobbing. "I knew it. I knew it." She released him. "Why did you lie to me?"

"I didn't lie to anyone. I've only suspected myself for about a week, and we only had news of a positive sighting Saturday."

"When? When was he sighted?"

"Back on January fourteenth."

Those familiar blue eyes went wide. "That's only two days after the crash, and he's been missing for more than a month now."

"I know, which is just one of the reasons we didn't say anything."

"Because he could still be dead." Her eyes looked haunted in the reflection in the glass as she stared out the window.

"We had a report from an eyewitness that he was taken by an armed gang in Beira, Mozambique. We haven't had a sighting since."

"The photos that he sent me..."

"And the SIM card. Mailed from Zimbabwe prior to that. Contained a lot of information the analysts are still combing through. It's given us suspects—"

"Hurek."

His eyes shot to hers in surprise.

"I keep an eye on the Most Wanted lists, and I recognized him in the photo Dad sent even though he was a lot younger. He's who the two of you were looking for in Africa."

He nodded. "This is classified, so if you leak it, not only will it get me thrown out of the FBI, it might also get your dad killed."

"If he's not already dead."

Jordan jerked his chin. "If he's not already dead."

He reached his driveway and pulled up. He led the way inside in case of any nasty surprises, but there weren't any. He had the feeling whoever had been watching him, trying to kill him, had given up. Perhaps they realized the FBI was onto them or had decided Jordan didn't know enough to be worth the trouble. Or they knew the FBI had the evidence at its labs. He turned on all the lights, revealing the case board he'd been working on that covered almost an entire wall. The drapes were securely closed against prying eyes. He placed the scrambling device on the coffee table in the center of the room to prevent any electronic snooping.

TacOps were monitoring this place constantly, and the perimeter was secure. Regan was probably salivating, wanting to know what the hell was going on right now as most of Gold Team rolled up. Jordan waited until everyone was inside, even the guys who hadn't been in the bar. The phone tree was alive and well in HRT.

The only person missing was Novak. He was in DC.

Daisy sat on the couch, and the guys gave her plenty of space. Instead, they stared at the evidence he'd mapped out on the wall.

Ryan Sullivan turned to face him. "This is why you've been looking like a sleep-deprived, heroin addict the past few weeks? You've been investigating the crash?"

He nodded, flinching at the baldness of the statement and wondering why he even cared.

"You don't think he's dead either, do you?" Ryan narrowed his gaze at him.

"All I know for sure is he didn't die in that air crash." He raised his hand to cut through the uproar as everyone spoke at once. "We don't know if he's alive." He explained about Marianne's sighting of Kurt and Rowena in Mozambique and what had happened next.

Aaron pointed to a printout of the photos Kurt had sent Daisy along with the note and envelope. "That's a young Darmawan Hurek and Nolan Gilder."

"The billionaire?" Livingstone shouldered his way closer.

Jordan nodded.

"Who are the others?"

Jordan had only had confirmation of the identities yesterday. "Leo Spartan, the Zimbabwean UN Ambassador"—which had helped explain who was pulling the strings regarding the plane crash and the Anders' murder investigation— "and a Scottish guy called Dougie Cavanagh, who died in the DRC nearly thirty years ago. They all attended St. Andrews University together and graduated the same year. This photo was probably taken a few years after they graduated. Apparently, they went into business together."

"The implications that a tech billionaire, who owns half the satellites in space and has defense contracts up the wazoo, is best buddies with one of the Most Wanted terrorists in the world is concerning to say the least. Especially when he didn't mention it to anybody." Aaron peered closer at the grainy image of Rowena Smith. Pointed. "Who is she?"

Jordan outlined what they knew so far about Miss Smith.

"You went to England? When?" asked Grady Steel.

"While you were otherwise engaged in Maine."

The man nodded thoughtfully. He still carried a bit of a limp from a recent gunshot wound.

"Let me get this straight." Ryan Sullivan worked through the board. "You and Montana spend six weeks searching for Hurek but find nothing. You leave. The next day Montana has a meeting with this guy, Bjorn Anders, and requests a background check on this woman. Day after that, Anders is found dead, Kurt for some reason miraculously misses getting on that plane and instead sneaks off to meet this same woman." He glanced at another image of Rowena Smith that the Brits had released in their missing person appeal. "I'd probably skip out on a flight if she called me up too, but Kurt probably wasn't hoping to get into her pants."

Meghan Donnelly crossed her arms and rolled her eyes.

Daisy pulled a face. "Ew."

"Your dad has sex, kid. Deal with it. How do you think you got here?" Ryan compressed his lips, mulling over the information. "What about his cell phone data? Or hers?"

Jordan shook his head. "We can't see anything from either of them. Looks like either their messages were blocked, or they were scrubbed after the fact."

"Montana's phone is supposed to be secure. It's supposed to be encrypted," Aaron protested.

"Which is why the FBI has now shifted to communication systems outside of Gilder's Interstellar Company range of influence."

"Only confirmed sighting was in Mozambique?" Aaron studied the board intently.

Jordan nodded. "Farmer caught him cleaning out an infected wound. She gave them shelter for the night and treated him with some pig antibiotics, which she said seemed to help." He walked over to the map. "They were taken by armed gunmen here, Beira, a coastal city."

Aaron shook his head. "He could be anywhere by now."

"No sightings reported in Beira itself. Can't rule out he's being held there, but there's been no ransom demand and no bodies have been found. We've set up a database where analysts at SIOC tracked all the ships that have been within a twenty-nautical-mile radius of the port since the kidnapping. It's a considerable number of vessels, but this way we know where they all are and where they stopped along the way. Analysts are deep-diving the ownership of each vessel."

Ryan shook his head. "If Gilder or Hurek paid some gang to

grab Montana, why not just kill him there and then?"

Jordan shot a look at Daisy who looked shellshocked by the deluge of data. "One of the main reasons I haven't said anything, aside from being ordered not to, was the fact that although we recently figured out he didn't die in that air crash, the chances of him being alive are slim at best."

"Any hope is better than none at all," Cas DeMarco muttered.

"One thing I didn't put on the wall yet." Jordan booted up his laptop. "This morning one of Kurt's neighbors contacted HRT. He's a former Marine. Kurt had mailed him a phone. The phone, and the SIM he'd sent to Daisy, both belonged to Bjorn Anders. Techs are examining them for evidence but check this out." He pulled the image up on his screen of a dead Bjorn Anders tied to a chair. Passed it around. The guys knew better than to show Daisy. "This image was sent to Kurt's cell phone from Anders' cell around the time Kurt is seen taking a phone call before boarding. It was later deleted, but the techs were able to resurrect it."

"Whoever was behind this wiped Kurt's and Rowena Smith's phones, but they didn't realize they had Anders' phone." Aaron nodded thoughtfully.

"Did Smith kill Anders and lure Kurt off the plane for some reason?" Livingstone speculated.

"That was my first thought until I spoke with her family and friends. It doesn't track. What tracks more is she was searching for her father and believed Anders was either the sperm donor or he could tell her who was. She was following Anders, not Kurt, around Zimbabwe. From the witness statement, Kurt and Rowena appeared to be working closely together, and she helped him bathe, and they slept in the same bed."

"Sly dog," Ryan chuckled.

Meghan Donnelly narrowed her eyes at him, laser beams of disapproval.

Jordan continued. "Both Kurt and Rowena Smith's DNA is on Anders' phone and the SIM. Kurt's prints and DNA were found on both envelopes. Also, Anders' call history shows one of his last calls was to Leo Spartan." He pointed to the photograph of the four men again. "And Gilder was staying with him at the time."

"Who's this?" Nash pointed out a picture of Ellen Mires and the crashed truck.

Jordan's mouth went dry. "Virginia State Police trooper who acted as my escort after someone tried to run me off the road as soon as I got back. Only problem was it turned out *she* was probably the one who bugged this place and tried to run me off the road." Jordan needed to be honest but felt like a damned fool. "She initiated a sexual relationship."

"And you didn't turn her down." Meghan Donnelly's expression was unimpressed.

Jordan shook his head and caught Daisy's gaze and felt his cheeks burn. "I did not."

"Another sly dog." Ryan's grin covered his face.

"She died in a second attempt to run me off the road after I told her I didn't want to see her anymore."

Ryan sobered. "What was she after? What did she think you knew?"

"As best as we can figure, they believe Kurt told me something in our final conversation that would lead to the FBI uncovering this group." He pointed to the photo of the four men.

Grady blew out a long breath. "Montana could still be alive."

Jordan stared down at the floorboards that needed staining. Nodded.

"If Gilder's involved, this is big." Aaron looked worried.

"Fucking A."

"That sonofabitch."

Most of the guys had violence in their eyes.

"Can we prove the bomb was aimed at Montana specifically?" asked Aaron.

"We only have circumstantial evidence but…" Jordan pointed to another grainy surveillance image. "Leo Spartan's head of security, Edmund Sabelo, paid a late-night visit to the airport the night before the crash with a piece of luggage that he didn't have with him when he left. It suggests Bjorn Anders told Kurt something that the group didn't want him passing on—at any cost."

They all absorbed that for a moment. They were going to have to reach out to someone in the Zimbabwean government soon and hope Gilder's financial investments in the country didn't hold more sway than the US's political clout when it came to rooting out the possible criminal actions of their UN ambassador.

"What do we do now?" asked Aaron.

"Analysts and TacOps are tracking Gilder's whereabouts and trying to get eyes on him. DOJ is arranging sealed warrants to raid all Interstellar facilities and operations in the US. They'll be passing on any relevant information to Five Eyes and NATO members, but if we move before we know where Kurt is, we risk never finding him. But they can't hold back much longer, not with National Security at stake."

"Where is Gilder now?" Ryan Sullivan asked quietly.

"We were able to get eyes on him at Savage's wedding yesterday, after which he flew to his private island in the Caribbean."

"Can we get any info on it?" Aaron arched a brow. "Perhaps some architectural drawings?"

Jordan knew what Aaron was thinking. Build a mock-up. Start practicing takedowns.

"I'll see what the analysts can dig up without setting off any alarms." He raised his hand. "Here's the thing. The most important take away. You can't talk about this outside this room, not even on base until TacOps checks your phone." He showed them the magic key fob. "This device blocks any electronic eavesdropping attempts, but I don't know if TacOps can give us more of the suckers. We have to continue to act as if we believe Montana is dead. It's business as usual until you are cleared and even then, you have to assume Gilder could have ears anywhere—like your girlfriends' phone or in your apartment."

"I want to rip the motherfucker limb from limb," Ford Cadell growled.

Jordan nodded. "Me too, but we're better than that. We'll get this guy, and we'll put him in a cage to suffer for the rest of his miserable life. But we don't go vigilante. Montana wouldn't approve."

"What about Hurek?" Aaron asked.

"We're digging into all of their history to see if that gives us a clue as to the present."

"Hurek could be sitting on that island sunbathing for all we know."

"Eyes in the sky are taking passes overhead. Gilder's not the only one with satellites. If we take Gilder, I'm betting he'll give us Hurek, but that doesn't mean we find Montana. We'll find Hurek eventually. In the meantime, we get ready and prepare for the op of a lifetime. And we're going to need a protection detail for Miss Daisy here because that's what her father would want." He pressed his lips together. "She got away from Blue Team, but I think she'll find Gold Team a little harder to fox. She can stay here and come into the compound with me during the day."

She sat up, spine like a ramrod. "Don't I get a say in this?"

"Nope."

"I'll volunteer." Demarco stood.

Ryan shook his head and placed his hand on the other man's shoulder. "You get to spend at least one night with De-*lilah* without a maniac on your tail. I'll volunteer as long as I get the couch."

"There's a spare room. TacOps have the perimeter wired, so we'll get plenty of warning, and we're not expecting an attack, not now they know the FBI is on to them."

Jordan swung his hopeful gaze to Donnelly because it was a lot of testosterone they were trying to foist on Daisy. He doubted she'd want him anywhere near her.

Meghan laughed quietly. "I'm in. I'm pretty sure that means Daisy and I are bunking together."

Jordan grimaced. Looked like he was on the couch. Again. But the relief he felt at finally being able to tell his teammates what he knew was immense and worth any price.

Grady sent him an understanding look. Shane Livingstone clapped him on the back. "Good work."

Emotions crowded inside him, all fighting to be free. He pushed them back down as he felt Daisy Montana's eyes, so like her father's, locked onto his face.

Those eyes didn't look as if they'd forgive him any time soon, and he honestly couldn't blame her.

"I've got a question." Aaron held up his hand for quiet. "Who's gonna tell Novak?"

36

FEBRUARY 16

Kurt had started using the light to signal SOSs at night in the hopes someone somewhere reported it to the Coast Guard. So far, no one had come to their rescue, and he knew they needed to save themselves. Tonight, he planned to pop that porthole and find a way to steal one of the lifeboats and get away. They couldn't afford to wait any longer.

The sound of the door being unlocked had all Kurt's senses going on high alert. This was not their normal routine.

Two guards shouldered their way inside, each carrying submachine guns pointed right at them. In a space this small, they couldn't miss if they tried. The game changed in that instant. The world shifted. He'd waited too long.

He stepped in front of Rowena.

A third man came in between the behemoths—the asshole who'd escorted them here that first day. He pointed at Rowena who was peering out from behind him. "Come. Now."

Kurt pushed her back behind him. "Hurek knows the only way I'll cooperate is if she stays with me. Safe."

The man's expression hardened into a sneer. "You overvalue yourself, Mr. FBI. If you don't want to be shot in the next ten seconds, then I suggest you let her go."

Kurt would never let them take her. If he could provoke one of them enough to try to pistol-whip him, he'd snatch the weapon and shoot the shit out of the other guys—or die trying. Then they'd take their chances in the ocean.

The leader took the submachine gun off one of the other guys and slung it over his shoulder. Kurt braced for imminent death even as Rowena's fingers clutched at his waist.

"Take her."

The brute on the left shuffled forward to try to reach around him and grab Rowena's arm. Kurt caught him, twisted him around and held the butter knife he'd spent countless hours sharpening against the goon's exposed throat.

"Let us out of here, or your friend is dead."

The leader's lip curled. He pulled a Glock from his hip holster and shot the man in the chest. Kurt struggled to hold the dead man upright to use him as a shield.

"That was your last chance." The guard gave an evil grin. "I'll be delighted if you make me shoot you too."

Before Kurt could tell him to fuck off or make another move, Rowena darted in front of him, and he watched his entire future disappear.

"No! Please don't hurt him. I'll come willingly. You don't need to hurt him."

She turned to face him as they grabbed her arms and secured them behind her back. Her eyes pleaded with him not to do anything foolish. "I'll be okay. I promise."

She was telling him she knew exactly what might happen to her and that she could face it, as long as he was safe. Love shone bright in her green eyes, and he didn't have an answer for it.

He only knew he wanted to rip off these men's heads with his bare hands.

"She won't be long. General Hurek wants to talk to her." The tone was placating, and Kurt didn't trust the words coming out of that mouth, not even for a second. "If you behave, the men will leave her alone. If you don't… well, you can imagine."

The leader smiled and raised his Glock to Rowena's head, finger on the trigger, as they slowly backed out of the room. They immediately locked the door. Kurt knew right then he'd kill that sonofabitch if he got the opportunity, and he'd smile while doing it.

He stood for a moment, shoulders slumped, head bowed, feeling as if a mountain had been dropped on his head. He'd failed.

Failed himself.

Failed Rowena.

Failed his family and his team.

Failed utterly.

What would they do to her? He couldn't think about it. He couldn't *not* think about it. He shook himself out of his inertia.

He needed to move.

One thing was clear—they weren't coming back. Why leave the dead guy behind unless they were done? Obviously, Hurek had gone with Plan B and bartered Rowena for his own safety.

Would Hurek hold onto Kurt as a wild card? Or would he get rid of him? It was 50/50. Kurt was leverage, and Hurek liked leverage. But if he were rescued, there was nothing to stop Kurt telling the world about Hurek's associates and crimes.

Kurt wasn't waiting around to find out anymore. Now that they'd taken Rowena he had nothing left to lose.

He dropped to his haunches and went through the dead man's pockets. A thin wallet with ID and some US dollars tucked inside. He took it.

A pocketknife.

A *cell phone*.

He unlocked the screen with the fucker's thumb and quickly changed the access code.

He heard a helicopter approach, went to the porthole, and craned his head in time to see an Agustawestland AW109 Grand Versace VIP with fancy black and white paintwork approaching the landing pad. Was that Gilder in the back seat? Kurt was pretty sure it was. Smug son of a bitch.

Gilder must have come for Rowena, which meant he was probably her biological father. Maybe he cared about his daughter. Enough to get her off this ship, which was something. It gave Kurt a slim hope that perhaps she wouldn't be thrown to the crew to be tortured and raped and would be kept safe until he could reach her.

He needed to get the hell out of here and call for help. He took a video of the chopper. Two bars of signal, which was probably connected to the ship's own communication system.

Would Gilder be blocking it? Kurt had no idea, but he had to try to contact help while he had the chance. And perhaps it would go through at some later date even if it failed now.

If he died, he wanted Rowena's rescue to be a priority. He entered Jordan's cell number because it was the first one he could remember.

He stared at the screen in shock as the call went through.

"Who is this?" Jordan sounded annoyed.

Fuck. The sound of his voice hit Kurt like a left hook, but thankfully, training took over and his mouth started working. "It's Kurt. Listen up. I don't have time to explain. I'm on a container ship somewhere possibly in the Caribbean. Not sure of the name or color." *Brilliant observational skills, Kurt.* "Hurek kidnapped me and a Brit named Rowena Smith"—his universe—"on Jan fourteenth. The billionaire Nolan Gilder landed on board in a fancy AW109 one minute ago." He reeled off the tail number. "I believe he's kidnapping Ms. Smith, who we suspect is his biological daughter. And if I were Gilder, I wouldn't be leaving any witnesses behind who could testify against me later. I'm sending you the video right now."

Kurt sent Jordan the short recording and then a selfie with the porthole behind him—proof of life.

The sound of rotors grew louder again, and he pressed his nose to the glass to see if he could spot Rowena, but it was too far away this time. "Chopper now heading approximately northeast based on the position of the sun. Not sure if Row is onboard."

"Is she—"

"She's *everything* to me. Whatever happens, make sure she's —" The signal dropped, and Kurt glanced at the phone in frustration. Then he heard the sound of the helicopter coming back.

Oh hell.

He peered out the window and caught sight of the chopper hovering off the port side. It wasn't the same machine as before, but another Leonardo-made bird, this one a shit-hot military version in plain olive green.

This couldn't be good.

———

Krychek stared at the phone for a moment and then stared at Daisy, who sat working at another desk in his office. "Fuck."

Her eyes were wide. "Who was that?"

He sprinted into Ackers' office as he opened the video on his cell. Daisy ran after him.

Ackers looked up in surprise.

"Just had a call from Kurt. He's alive." He heard Daisy sob. "Get SIOC on the phone. We need them to triangulate the call. Send out the alert for the guys to assemble at Andrews Airforce Base. And get on the phone to DEVGRU. We're gonna need support taking these sons of bitches down, but rescuing Kurt is priority."

Ackers picked up his phone as they all watched the video Kurt had sent and saw the bearded face of their beloved friend and colleague, definitely still alive, but also in imminent danger.

"Let's mobilize everything we have in the area but no details yet." Jordan reeled off instructions, and Ackers started making phone calls. "We're looking for a container vessel."

Daisy grabbed Jordan's wrist and awareness flashed over his skin. She replayed the video, her grip painfully tight.

He paused the video when there was a knock on the open door.

Dinah Cohen stood there, her head cocked to one side. She held up a folder in her hand and took a step forward.

"I thought you might like to know we finally tracked down the truth about Hurek's kid. He's five years old, and he and his mother live in Edinburgh, where he attends a private nursery school. The locals are keeping an eye out in case daddy makes contact."

She placed the folder on the desk.

"We discovered their expenses are paid by a trust. Interestingly enough, the trust owns and operates a container vessel called *MV Mudik,* which happened by some wild coincidence to be not far off the port of Beira in mid-January."

Ackers was already relaying the details of the ship to SIOC.

"You're welcome," Dinah called out to no one in particular.

Jordan rushed back to his computer, pulled up the ship's data from the list, and saw its course plotted on a map onscreen— headed straight for the Caribbean Sea. He found an image on the database.

Daisy stood at his shoulder. Her expression was a mix of grimness and hope. "Is my dad onboard that ship?"

"I think so."

Tears brimmed in her eyes, sparkling like jewels.

Emotion gripped him by the throat, but he had to go. "I need to gear up."

"I want to come with you."

Jordan shook his head. "That's not how this works."

She tilted her head. "I'm not your prisoner, despite what you might believe."

"Your father would want you to be safe."

"My father taught me to take care of myself."

"Not during an op."

"I won't be part of the op. I'm not stupid." She folded her arms. "But I'll be closer if you find him."

Christ. He dragged his hand over his face. Why did he always end up at odds with this woman?

"Talk to Ackers. I don't have time for this." She flinched, and he could kick himself for being so abrupt. He squeezed her arm with what he hoped felt like reassurance. "I'm trying to keep you safe so you're here when your dad gets back. If something happened to you, he'd never forgive me. I'd never forgive myself."

Her lips parted, and he hated himself for noticing the shape of them. The sweet bow of a mouth that was anything but sugar.

"Fine. I'll talk to Daniel. Go. Bring my dad back home safe."

Before he could step away, she grabbed his shirt with both hands and reached up on tiptoe. Kissed him. "For luck. Go."

He froze at the contact and stared into her dark blue eyes for a moment that stretched time. He didn't know why a simple kiss affected him this way.

"Go." She urged again.

He forced himself to leave and not look back.

———

Row was manhandled by the guy with the Napoleon complex and shoved forward forcefully enough that she stumbled several times. She wanted to execute a roundhouse kick to his face, but if she did, she was pretty sure the big man holding the automatic weapon walking a few steps behind would shoot her on the spot. The brief satisfaction wouldn't be worth it. Not when she was fighting for her life.

Kurt would get out. She knew he would. And he'd find her. Assuming she stayed alive that long—so no getting shot. He was probably mad with her for not fighting these men, but this lunatic had looked serious about killing him. The man she loved had survived one bullet this trip. She doubted he'd be lucky enough to survive a second.

And she wouldn't allow that. Not if she had the power to prevent it.

Survival at any cost. The rest could come later.

The prick shoved her again and laughed when she bashed her knee on a metal step and cried out in pain. She couldn't save herself because her hands were zip-tied behind her back. Maybe she should go for it. Smash her foot into this motherfucker's head and hope it knocked him out. Hope the other guy didn't kill her.

"What does Hurek want with me?"

The bastard cuffed her around the head. She was starting to seriously hate this man.

"*General* Hurek will do whatever he wants with you, and you will smile and say thank you, sir."

Fuck you, more like.

He pushed her up another flight of stairs and along the open corridor to the back of the boat.

She stopped at the edge of the deck and watched a black and white helicopter hover above the large "H" before landing.

What was going on?

Was this a rescue?

Why wasn't Kurt here?

She looked away as the wind blew her hair every which way. Once the wheels touched the deck, she was marched forward.

Her mouth went dry, and her heart gave a painful trip. They were taking her away. Without Kurt.

She didn't see Hurek anywhere.

Her feet dragged, and she tried to jerk away from her tormentor. He grabbed her arms and twisted them painfully high. She yelped as he pushed her toward the open door. Inside, Nolan Gilder sat staring at her with avid interest in his eyes—eyes the same unusual color as hers. Something large and ugly crawled up into her throat and made her want to puke.

No.

Beside him sat another man who wore a tailored suit but looked like a gorilla.

"Get in," the gorilla ordered.

The man behind her shoved her into the cabin, and she couldn't stop herself from hitting the floor with her chin. Bright white light flashed through her brain. She rolled onto her side and kicked out with the full force of her leg, smashing her foot into that bastard's face because why not? She didn't have a lot to lose. She smiled grimly when cartilage crunched.

Rage contorted the man's features as he pulled the gun he'd used earlier and pointed it at her. She closed her eyes and braced herself for a bullet ripping through her flesh. The sound of two shots rang out before the door closed, and blessed silence reigned.

She opened her eyes in time to see the gorilla in the black suit put another scary-looking weapon under his jacket. Her mouth went bone dry with a mixture of relief and horror. He'd killed both men who'd escorted her to the helicopter without blinking.

Life meant nothing to these people.

Gilder leaned down and squinted at her with curiosity. "Miss Smith?" He had to yell over the noise of the rotors.

"Yes."

"Are you okay?"

She nodded when she wanted to bark out a laugh of incredulity.

He placed a headset over her ears.

"You look a lot like your mother." Gilder's voice was clear now, but he didn't sound pleased.

Rowena kept every word she wanted to say buried deep inside. She was going to have to be smart if she hoped not only to survive, but to get away from this creep and help rescue Kurt.

She once again leaned on the acting she'd done many years ago at university. Made herself the naive ingénue, which hadn't been that far from the truth back in the day. "You knew my mother?"

Would Hurek have told Gilder he'd admitted to Kurt that they'd gang-raped her mom? She doubted it.

"Help her into her seat, Gerrit." The billionaire was watching her carefully, a hint of impatience in his tone.

Awkwardly, the other man pulled on her arm to get her upright.

"Undo the girl's restraints for God's sake," Gilder said impatiently. "What do you think she's going to do? Attack me while you watch?"

Something shifted in the bodyguard's eyes but was gone in an instant. He didn't like being talked down to but did as he was told. A sleek blade appeared in Gerrit's hand, and suddenly her arms were free again. She rubbed her wrists. "Thank you. Thank you for saving me from that horrible man." She laid it on thick. Let them think she was an idiot. Let them underestimate her.

Gerrit indicated she sit with a flick of his blade.

"Fasten your seat belt. The ride can be bumpy sometimes." Gilder oozed hospitality.

Safety first.

She smothered laughter at the incongruity of her current situation. She clipped the belts clumsily together. They were flying quickly away from the ship. Away from Kurt. Her heart ached. "So, did you know my mother?"

Gilder's amused eyes glittered as they watched her. "Quite well, actually, although we lost touch after she went back to England. I hadn't realized she'd had a child."

She watched him go through the motions of feigning emotion. Acting, just like she was.

"She never told me she was pregnant." He wore her old watch —his old watch, she supposed. He looked at it now. Stroked it with his index finger. "It's nice to know she kept this. She must have thought of me often before she died. That brings me a great deal of comfort."

Rowena smiled as if she were in awe of the billionaire tech guru as opposed to wanting to rip out his throat with her teeth.

He was her biological father. She could see it in the eyes, the nose, in the shape and length of his fingers.

The idea that she shared his DNA made her want to spew all over the white interior of this fancy helicopter, but she was playing a dangerous game with high stakes and didn't think vomit would endear her to anyone. "I never actually knew my mother. She died when I was an infant. I was raised by her brother, Peter. He mentioned that he met you once, years ago." She gave a little disparaging laugh, as if she hadn't loved the man deeply. "I honestly didn't believe him, but he was telling the truth, wasn't he?"

Gilder's rubbery lips pulled down. She was grateful she hadn't inherited those.

"I knew Peter Smith. He didn't approve of your mother and me..."

He was trying to imply they'd been in a relationship, a romance, but she knew that couldn't be true. She didn't believe it. Wouldn't.

Rowena couldn't dance around the issue. This had been her quest, her impetus for following Bjorn Anders around Zimbabwe. If she didn't ask, she'd look like an idiot. "Do you...do you know who my father is?"

He leaned forward and took her hands in his. Looked deep into her eyes, and it was so disconcerting to see the shape and color of hers mirrored in his. He smiled. "Can't you guess?"

"I don't want any more guesses," she spoke more sharply than intended. "I've spent a lifetime guessing and searching for my biological father. I need to know if I've finally found him."

"Yes, my dear. Yes. You've found him, and I couldn't be happier."

God, this was going to kill her. She forced a teary smile and a laugh. "I can't believe it."

"*You* can't believe it?" He laughed like a Bond villain. "I've spent years trying to have a child, not realizing I already had one." His eyes shone. "And, I'm hoping with your help, I might be able to have more."

37

Kurt took a photo of the military helicopter then put the cell in his pocket. The signal could come back at some point. He wondered what the best play would be if he was a billionaire with evil-overlord tendencies.

Had Hurek left with Gilder to cement their friendship while mercs got rid of Kurt and the crew? Not unlikely considering Hurek's track record.

Or was Gilder making sure there were absolutely no witnesses to his latest atrocity? Including Hurek and Kurt. No one to stop him holding Rowena captive for as long as he damned well wanted—except HRT. Jordan would look for her. The boys would find her.

As the side door of the bird slid open and the barrel of an M2 .50 Caliber Machine Gun poked out, Kurt decided he'd figure out the details later.

He dove behind the dead guy and rolled him in front of him as the bullets started flying, ripping through the skin of the ship like fireworks through tinfoil. In terms of protection, the dead man wouldn't help much if there were a direct hit, but it was better than nothing.

The chopper fired for what seemed like hours, seemingly searching for targets before blasting one area after another.

A good thing thermal cameras couldn't see through metal. But what would they do next? Gilder couldn't afford a single survivor if he wanted his secrets kept.

The mercs would go room to room, cabin to cabin, and make sure everyone was dead, and they'd blow the ship so most of the evidence was lost or destroyed by the ocean. He wouldn't put it past Gilder to be able to fake the ship's beacon and place them far away from here when the ship disappeared from radar.

He must pay his soldiers a goddamned fortune to keep their mouths shut, but they wouldn't be able to spend it dead or in prison.

Jordan would be raising the alarm, but it wouldn't come fast enough to help Kurt. He had to save himself, and then he could rescue Rowena from that sonofabitch.

The .50 cal stopped firing. The bird was presumably going to land. A few minutes later, Kurt heard two shots as the mercs began finishing off survivors.

How many were there? That helicopter could hold fifteen troops, but add the .50 cal and you were down to ten to twelve max.

He could see daylight through the side of his porthole now and considered kicking his way out of the cabin. But that would be noisy, and noise would attract attention and make him vulnerable.

Kurt hauled the dead guy up until he was sitting slumped over the desk. Then Kurt stepped into the small closet on the left of the door and settled himself down to wait. Calmed his mind. Settled his breathing. Let his heart rate slow.

He hoped Hurek was still alive. Kurt wanted that guy in a cell for the rest of his miserable life. Gilder too. He wouldn't object to inflicting a little personal retribution, but their long-term incarceration would be enough.

He let his mind quiet. No thoughts of Rowena or the team. Just his wits against those of the enemy. Survival at its most primitive. Predator and prey in the primordial swamp.

A slice of the inner corridor was visible through the holes the bullets had ripped through the interior walls. The light step of purposeful feet went door to door.

A double tap rang out not far away. Another man down.

Kurt didn't know if all the crew were bad guys or simply caught up in an impossible situation. They appeared complicit in Hurek's crimes, but the idea of them being slaughtered, one by one, was sickening.

He kept absolutely still as a pair of legs dressed in black tactical gear walked slowly forward. The merc held matte black SIG Sauer P226 9mms—one of his favorite weapons. One man spoke quietly, and another one laughed in response—two men. They reached his door, and he heard the key turn in the lock. One man came inside. Checked the dead guy who'd become very useful since he'd stopped breathing, then headed back out of the room.

They left the door open.

Kurt turned the butter knife in his hand and stepped soundlessly out of the closet, out of the room and into the nearest merc's shadow. He slit the man's throat before the man could register Kurt was there, and Kurt used his gun to shoot his buddy, first in the leg then in the face.

They both dropped. Kurt dragged them back into his cabin and quickly stripped off the body armor and the least bloodied clothing, including a dark gray neck gaiter that doubled as a face mask and the black knit hat that covered his hair. Nothing in the pockets except a pair of wraparound Oakleys.

He pocketed a knife, both SIGs, and spare ammo. He stuck in an earpiece and listened to South African accented signals.

"Ten minutes to extraction."

He slipped on the glasses and checked himself in the mirror. He could definitely pass for the guy he'd knifed to death.

"Pattern, approaching you on 'C' Deck."

After a slight pause the merc signaled again.

"Roger that," Kurt murmured with a lilt of Afrikaans. He walked out of his cabin and strode confidently down the corridor toward the center of the boat. He turned the corner and came across two more men in black.

"I was beginning to think you got lost. Where's Walters?"

"Dead. One of the crew got a shot off." His accent wasn't half bad, Kurt thought as he shot both men in the face at close range. "So are you." He dragged them into the nearest room and pulled their comms, pocketed more ammo.

"Nine minutes to departure."

Kurt didn't know the layout of the ship but figured there'd be two teams on each level. The more mercs he could take out before he got on that bird, the better for him and Rowena.

"Hurek secure. Found him hiding in the walk-in freezer. If it was up to me, I'd leave him there."

"Boss insisted he is captured alive. Promised a reward."

Kurt slipped down to "D" deck and spotted another pair of assholes dragging a subdued and bleeding Darmawan Hurek between them.

Gunshots were being exchanged on the other side of the ship.

"Here. Take him."

Hurek was thrust toward him as the mercs headed down the corridor to help out their comrades. Kurt put two bullets in their backs. He wasn't proud of it, but this was a goddamned survival situation and not a fair fight. His mission was rescuing Rowena.

"If you want to live," Kurt told Hurek quietly, "stay here and wait for me. Move, and I'll kill you myself."

The terrorist froze, recognizing Kurt's voice, then nodded rapidly. His nose was bloody. His eyes red from crying. The scent of ammonia wafting off him suggested he'd pissed his pants.

There was satisfaction in that, but it wasn't enough. Not after everything he'd done.

Kurt headed down the narrow corridor and poked his head around to see where the gunfire was coming from.

Two men in black had their backs to him firing at what looked like a cook, who was shooting back.

Kurt put bullets in both men. It was like shooting fish in a barrel when they assumed you were on their team.

He'd killed eight. How many more were there?

"Six minutes."

He ran back to Hurek who stood dejectedly where he'd left him. Kurt pulled a neck gaiter off a dead merc and used it as a gag. "Just in case you think the men Gilder sent here to capture you are a better bet than dealing with the FBI. Gilder will kill you, but I suspect he'll do it after he's tortured the locations of all the blackmail material you have on him out of you. Hell, he's slippery enough to say he caught you, collect the reward and make himself look like a goddamned hero." He hurried him along. "We need to get to the helipad ASAP because I'm pretty sure this ship is set to blow."

"Five minutes, guys. Get back here, or else I'm leaving without you."

Hurek's eyes looked as wide and scared as a whipped dog.

Kurt didn't give a shit. "You blow my cover, you say a damned word, or if I even think you're going to say a damned word, I will kill you. To save Rowena. To capture Gilder. In the meanwhile, Darmawan Hurek, consider yourself under arrest. You have the right to remain silent... Use it."

———

Four minutes later, Kurt sat in the back of the helo with his gun pointed at Hurek. The other three remaining mercs high-fived one another and slumped down laughing and grinning about murdering the crew like it was a video game. The crew weren't human. They were marks on a scorecard. The enemy for the right price.

The mercs weren't even particularly bothered by their lost compatriots, although they'd been surprised the crew had put up any opposition.

They turned his stomach, and it made the thought of killing them easier to bear. He held his SIG against Hurek in a threatening manner, acting aggressively because he didn't have the ability to feign joy at their thoughtless slaughter.

His hands were just as bloody, but he'd targeted people who were trying to kill him. He had no regrets.

The pilot pulled up and away from the ship as soon as everyone had piled in. The guy was swearing and genuinely pissed as they hugged the surface of the ocean.

The mercs had cut it fine because these assholes had been having too much fun. How many people were left alive down there? He didn't know, and it sickened him.

Kurt waited for the boom. The distraction he knew was coming.

When the explosion came the three amigos stood up and peered through the windows and whooped like they'd won the lottery. He put two bullets in each of them. Then he stepped over the bodies and knelt on the seat. Put his gun to the pilot's head. "I suggest you listen very carefully."

38

What the actual hell…?

Had Nolan Gilder, her biological father, said he wanted *her* help in having more kids? A fine tremor of fear ran along her nerves.

A boom sounded in the distance, and a plume of smoke grew visible on the horizon.

The ship.

Oh my God. The ship had exploded.

Kurt!

Her eyes went wide, and her fingers gripped the edge of her seat. "What was that?"

"Probably the military operation I instigated trying to arrest that terrible man. Did he hurt you?"

She stared at the black smoke on the horizon. Kurt was on board that ship. Locked in the cabin. Was he dead? Had she just watched him drown—a speck of dust in the distance when the truth was, he was her entire universe?

Devastation crowded her, but she couldn't afford to show even a flicker.

Her insides felt like Jell-O but not from fear. Stress. Anxiousness. Grief that wanted to punch her in the stomach, over and over again, like a pummeling bag. But not fear.

"Of course, he hurt you. Hurek is a pig—"

"No. He didn't touch me." She met his gaze. "The FBI agent who was taken hostage at the same time protected me. He saved me."

"Oh no. Oh dear. I had no idea an FBI agent was also on board." Gilder was a lousy actor. "Hurek tried to blackmail me when he discovered you were Allie's daughter. He knew we were close and suspected I was your father. Sent me a sample of blood to analyze." He frowned out of the window. "I arranged a payment in exchange for your safety and alerted the authorities to Hurek's location. Perhaps they rescued this FBI agent?"

She nodded woodenly. "I hope so. Where are we going? I need to get home and let my friends know I'm okay. My job…"

"All in good time, my dear. I'm taking you somewhere where you can recuperate, and we can get to know one another—my private island."

"Thank you. I appreciate that, but I know my friends will be worried. I need to speak to them." And alert someone about Kurt. Perhaps he was in the water? If anyone could survive, it was him. But locked in a cabin when the ship exploded? Lost at sea? The chances he could survive under those circumstances were minimal.

Tears flooded her eyes. She couldn't help it. Couldn't control the visceral reaction to even the thought of losing the man she loved.

She swiped the tears from her face. She needed to get word to Kurt's family and friends, tell them the truth about what had happened. They deserved to know about his bravery. His courage.

Gilder sent a hooded look at his bodyguard. "We'll try to arrange something once we've had you checked out."

Checked out?

"I can assure you, I'm fine. Healthy as a horse." She smiled determinedly.

A tic formed in his cheek. "You've been through a traumatic experience. Let's let the doctors run their tests, and you can rest before we get to know one another."

That sounded like so much *fun*.

He laughed. "I thought I was all alone in the world, and now I find I have a daughter. We need to celebrate."

Rowena nodded and smiled through what she hoped he'd assume were happy tears. She wasn't stupid. She was just as much a captive as she'd been on the ship, but this time there was no Hostage Rescue Team operator to help her. She was on her own.

———

Kurt relieved the pilot of his sidearm. "Warn your boss or his minions that I'm coming for him, and I'll shoot you."

"And then who'll fly this thing, genius?"

"You won't need to worry about that, sweetheart, because you'll be dead. You just bring us in to land where Gilder usually lands."

He climbed over into the front seat and debated keying into the emergency channel to issue a mayday for the scuttled ship. But that would be a huge red flag to Gilder's people should they be monitoring the emergency frequency. If this were his operation, they would be.

"How many men does Gilder have on his island?"

"Too many for you to handle."

"Let me worry about that. How many?"

"Thirty. Thirty-five highly trained men."

"Including the eleven highly trained men I just *handled*?"

The pilot visibly paled. "Including them."

"Tell me about the setup. Staff."

"He'll kill me if he thinks I talked to you. Hell, he'd kill me for flying you there."

"Sounds like you're pretty much fucked either way. How

about you cooperate with the FBI, and I'll make sure you're cut a deal for your cooperation."

"What makes you think Gilder is going to be held accountable by the FBI? They don't even know you're alive."

The pilot knew who Kurt was. That made him complicit in Gilder's crimes and not just a mindless pawn.

"Think again, sucker." He pulled the cell from his pocket and waved it at him. Unfortunately, there was no cellular signal. "I got a call out before Gilder blocked transmissions. HRT know everything and are going wheels up as we speak."

"The Americans have no jurisdiction here."

"FBI has jurisdiction anywhere US citizens are involved." Kurt pulled on the co-pilot's headgear, grateful they'd used the other front seat for a soldier of fortune rather than a second pilot. He kept the gun aimed at the flyer as he reacquainted himself with the controls. He could fly this bird if he had to, but as he didn't know where Rowena had been taken, he needed the pilot more than he wanted to let on.

"Right now, assuming you survive the next two hours, you're looking at life in a high-security prison."

"I didn't kill anyone."

"Accessory before, during, and after the fact. You ever hear of the getaway driver getting off because he didn't enter the bank?"

The pilot clenched his jaw.

"And once the FBI starts rounding up all the others involved in Gilder's illegal operations, the opportunity to strike deals will go to the people with the most knowledge about his crimes. I doubt that'll include you. I also suspect that Gilder will be eager to eliminate as many witnesses as he can. He'll have nothing left to lose."

Kurt took a breath. Tried not to think about Rowena. Gilder wanted her for some reason. Hopefully, she'd play along until he could get to her. "What's your name?"

"George. George Burnett."

"Well, George. How about it? Want to deal? Or want to rot in prison for the rest of your miserable life?"

"I'll take a deal, but I need witness protection. You have no idea how powerful that guy is."

They were about to find out.

Same way Gilder was gonna find out what the US did to traitors.

"When the US is finished with Gilder, he'll be a penniless has-been. He'll forfeit every defense contract he has, his assets will be frozen, and he'll spend most of his money paying lawyers to keep him off Death Row. The satellites will be appropriated or brought down. Private citizens don't spy on the US without consequences."

He had to believe that. He had to believe the work he and his colleagues did counted for something, and that money didn't change the reality of the law. This was why Lady Justice wore a blindfold. Why they were loyal to the Constitution and not presidents or kings. America was a republic of the people, by the people, for the people.

"Witness protection or no deal." Sweat dripped down the pilot's temple.

"You'll get your WitSec, George, I promise you that. As long as we rescue the woman Gilder kidnapped off that vessel and you testify against him. What does he want her for, anyway?"

"I don't know about any of that." George glanced first at him and then over his shoulder at Hurek. "He knows more."

"He's got a gag in his mouth."

Hurek's eyes were the size of small dinner plates. Whatever the reason Gilder wanted Rowena, it wasn't good.

"Something to do with a doctor he has on the island, the medical research facility. There have been women there. I don't know what he's doing with them, I swear, but...I've never seen them leave."

Kurt's blood chilled.

George glanced at him nervously. Cleared his throat.

"According to the gossip, he's been experimenting with IVF and other stuff."

Kurt frowned. "IVF?"

"The guy is desperate for kids. He can't do it the traditional way, so he's been working with this genetics expert to try to recreate himself and edit out the genes that cause diseases and basically live forever."

Horror filled Kurt. Gilder wanted Rowena for her genetic makeup, not for some long-lost father-daughter reunion. Was he planning genetic experiments or something even more sinister? What would happen if she was already pregnant? Did that put her in greater or lesser danger?

How he wished for her sake she was the product of a doomed romance between her mother and some handsome Scot named Dougie Cavanagh.

"Tell me about the setup. Where is the security focused?"

"Gilder owns the entire island, so the security team is housed on the north side away from where his house is because he hates to see his security staff when he's in residence—the guys think it's because they remind him of the fact most people hate his guts and that's why he needs protection. They also man the perimeter and the roof of his place in Idaho. Plus, they act as a scouting team and protective detail when Gilder travels—kind of like the Secret Service. With everything going on, I suspect they'll ramp up the patrols and bring in more men to replace the ones you killed. Even if you killed every one of them, you still have to deal with his personal bodyguard, Gerrit Vanguard, who's a fucking psycho."

Maybe this was a crazy plan, and yet the element of surprise, combined with overwhelming force of action, might be his and Rowena's best hope. Sitting placidly on that fucking ship sure as hell hadn't saved them in the end, although it hadn't killed them either.

If Rowena died now or was hurt... then he'd failed. He'd

failed. At least he'd contacted HRT. The FBI would figure it out eventually.

"If I can get her, bring her back to the chopper, would you fly us out?"

George was clearly calculating his best odds of survival. "They'll send people after us."

"There's ammo in the fifty cal."

"Not much."

"I don't need much. I'm a better shot than the morons you worked with before." Kurt shifted in his seat. "How far to the nearest island from Gilder's place, and how much fuel would you need?"

"More than I have."

"Can you fill up before we land at Gilder's house?"

"Probably. Yeah. Definitely. It's what I'd normally do. Better get rid of the bodies first though."

His new pal was thinking on his feet. How much he could trust the guy was debatable.

Kurt removed his headphones, but he also removed the pilot's so the guy couldn't contact his base on the sly. Kurt got into the back and retrieved all weapons and ammo. He also took a photo of each face for identification purposes. Then he dragged the bodies to the edge of the doorway.

"Pull any stunts in the next thirty seconds, George," he yelled, "and you're a dead man."

Not trusting his new ally, he held onto the strap with one hand and opened the door with the other. Hauled each dead merc one-handed through the portal and tossed them into the ocean. The pilot watched, but Kurt wasn't about to let go and risk taking a nosedive into the ocean.

He closed the door.

Not a lot he could do about the blood on the floor.

Kurt stayed in the back with Hurek. Grabbed headphones for them both. Lowered the man's gag. "If you give us away, I'll kill you. The US will be happy I escaped and you're no longer at large, so they won't ask too many questions about how you died. You help me. Help me get Rowena Smith to safety, I'll see what I can do with the Department of Justice."

"Immunity?"

"You'll never be given immunity—"

"I can give you Gilder and Spartan on murder. Mass murder."

So that's what they had on each other.

"Your word against theirs isn't going to cut it." He went to raise the gag.

"I have proof! Proof that releases to the press if anything happens to me. That's why I'm still alive!"

Kurt looked at him consideringly. That made sense. "DOJ might cut a deal for that, but if you do anything to betray me or Rowena, I'll—what was that threat you made to your men the day you kidnapped us?—peel your penis with a penknife and throw you to the sharks. And, as you say the evidence will release upon your death, I have nothing to lose, do I?"

"I won't betray you. Nolan would kill me as soon as he tortured the location of the evidence out of me. I'll help the FBI. I'll cooperate. Just save me from that psychopath."

The psychopath who now had the woman Kurt loved in his possession all because of this man's greed.

39

Rowena followed Gilder into a gleaming white, one-story facility with a metal roof that reflected the sun so brightly she'd had to cover her eyes. Inside, a hatchet-faced nurse gave her the once over and walked back into another room.

"Dr. Hendrix is ready. He's through there." Gilder swept an arm to indicate she should keep moving.

Rowena balked. "I really don't need an examination. I'm fine."

Gilder patted her on the back. "You can't be too careful in these situations. As soon as he gives you the all-clear, we'll open a bottle of bubbly and celebrate by the pool."

Because that's what a kidnap victim wanted most.

Gerrit stood by the door, making it clear there was no way out.

Her trepidation increased, and she had to pack it all inside so she didn't freak the hell out and run away screaming. She went into the other room and found the nurse standing beside a middle-aged white guy, tanned, thin blond hair, hunched over, with small beady blue eyes. He looked like every Nazi asshole she'd ever seen photos of.

Classical music played in the background.

The doctor patted the bed, which also had restraints and metal foot stirrups, the kind used during a smear test. Her heart fluttered, and for a moment she thought she might pass out.

What if she was pregnant? What if the baby she maybe carried was all she'd have left of the man she loved? How would that play with Gilder's desire for her to somehow help him have more children?

"Come sit." The doctor ordered. "We'll do a quick exam and take some blood to test."

Blood?

"For what?"

The doctor looked startled by her question.

"The usual. Iron levels. Deficiencies. STDs."

STDs?

"I wasn't raped," she insisted.

The doctor's expression was condescending while trying for sincere. "There's no shame in what happened to you."

"I'm thoroughly aware there is no shame for someone who has been raped. The shame should always be reserved for the rapist. But I wasn't touched. Kurt Montana wouldn't allow it."

She didn't look at Gilder. She knew her mother would never have willingly slept with this piece of shit. The idea of being the product of rape was painful, but thanks to Kurt's warning, she was prepared and knew she was strong enough to deal with it.

What was that old saying—"be careful what you wish for"?

Gilder rolled his eyes. "Let them take your blood pressure and run their tests. No reason to be difficult."

Difficult?

Wasn't that always what women who knew their own minds were branded? *Difficult.* Because having a brain, having thoughts of their own might contradict the fantasy of the all-knowing, all-seeing man-god and that was in-*fucking*-convenient.

"Okay." Her voice was like sugar. "I'll submit to having a medical exam, but I'd prefer to have it without an audience."

She stared at Gerrit, although everyone in the room was a

goddamned stranger. As far as she knew, he was the only one with a gun.

Gilder blinked in surprise and stared at the scowling bodyguard. "Oh, of course. Wait outside."

Great.

Gilder caught her hands together in his. "I can't tell you how excited I am. To know that I'm not alone in the world."

"Yes." Rowena forced some real emotion. "I finally have a family. I finally have someone to love." She knew she was laying it on thick, but the man lapped it up.

"Dear Rowena. You, my darling girl, are going to be the answer to all my prayers."

She kept her expression one of idiotic happiness and watched Gerrit head outside.

The doctor patted the bed again. "You must be very excited to know that you are the daughter of a billionaire."

She scowled at him, then realized he was serious. "I hadn't thought about it. I was too busy worrying about survival after being kidnapped."

The doctor and nurse exchanged sly smiles. "Of course you haven't."

They thought she was lying. Who'd care about money in this kind of situation? "I was held captive by a notorious terrorist for *weeks*. All I cared about was getting out of there alive." *With Kurt.* "And going home." *With Kurt.*

The doctor and Gilder exchanged a glance she had no trouble interpreting. She wasn't going home.

She pushed thoughts of Kurt out of her mind. She needed to honor him by escaping. She couldn't fly a helicopter, but she could surely drive a boat. How hard could it be?

She let them take her height, weight, blood pressure, temperature. She sat on the side of the bed as the doctor used a stethoscope to listen to her chest and heart.

"You are in remarkably good condition. Of course, a low-calorie diet is optimum for longevity."

Longevity?

"We'll devise a regimen for optimal nutritional health with minimal calories."

She raised her brows. Yippee. "Exactly what type of doctor are you?"

The doctor and nurse exchanged a glance.

Were they married? *Did it matter?*

The doc ignored the question and pulled out a syringe along with several vials. Damn, did they want to bleed her dry?

She let him draw blood and label the tubes with F1.

F-fucking-*1?*

Was she a fruit fly?

He pulled out his clipboard. "When was the date of your last period?"

She sat up. "I beg your pardon?"

He glared at her. "When did you last menstruate?"

"What the hell does that have to do with you?"

"Don't be embarrassed. I'm a doctor."

But he wasn't her doctor. He was Gilder's doctor.

"I'm not embarrassed. I'm trying to figure out why you're asking such an invasive personal question."

"Medical." Gilder licked his lips. "The female reproductive cycle is part of your overall health, wouldn't you agree?"

Rowena did agree, but she didn't think that was why they were asking. She didn't want them to know she might be pregnant. They'd find a way to terminate it. How she went forward with that choice was her decision. Not theirs. "If you must know, I started my period the day before yesterday." She hoped it would keep the questions and the chance of a physical exam at bay.

The doctor's eyes lit up and went to Gilder's. "That is perfect. We'll start with the injections immediately. If the blood results suggest disease of any kind, we can wait a month."

Wait a month for what?

"Injections of what?"

"Nothing to worry about." The doctor patted her arm in what

was supposed to be reassurance and felt like a threat. "Nurse Leslie. Bring the syringes. Let's put her out first so she's not uncomfortable. We'll do a quick pelvic ultrasound to check your ovaries first."

"My *ovaries*?" And then she got it. They wanted her eggs. Gilder's desire to live forever flashed into her mind. He wanted to use her to help him beat basic human mortality. She hoped he got run over by a damned bus.

Nurse Leslie carried over a metal tray with two syringes in it.

"You want to help me, don't you?" Gilder leaned down to stare at her with his creepily similar shade of eyes and obsequious turn of his lips.

"Of course, I want to help you, Daddy dear." She was so grateful for all the times Kurt had shown her how to fight.

She grabbed the syringe in one hand, the metal tray in the other. She sank the needle deep into Gilder's side and depressed the plunger. His surprise and horror were comical even as he slumped immediately to the floor, unconscious.

She smashed the tray as hard as she could into the temple of the doctor who was trying to grab her. He toppled like an oak. Nurse Leslie began to run for the front door, and Row grabbed her arm and thrust her against the wall, shoving her arm high behind her back. She pushed her into a supply closet and closed the door, locking her inside.

Row prayed Gerrit didn't hear the commotion. Wagner's Valkyries were taking flight on the speakers, and that helped muffle the sound.

The doctor was coming around, so she hit him over the head again. She'd turned into a feral animal. She didn't care.

She didn't know how long the doctor would be out and knew she had to run, now. This was her one shot. She headed through the back of the building and thankfully, there was a back exit. Yay for fire codes!

Once Gilder caught her, there would be no more pretend Mister Nice Guy. She'd be strapped down and prodded and raped by medical practitioners who believed they had the right to access her body with or without her consent.

Outside, she looked around, relieved not to see anyone. She ran away from the house and the gorilla, along a wide, white path lined with palm trees and incredible flowers. She heard shouts behind her and increased her speed. She headed for the ocean in the hopes she miraculously found a boat.

There would be no real rush for Gilder and his men. This was a private island, and they presumably knew every inch and potential hiding place.

Her breath sawed in her chest, and she wished she'd drunk some water before she'd legged it. She didn't know where she was going, but she ran flat out as far and as fast as possible. She came to the end of the manicured grounds where the tiled path turned to sand. She heard the sound of approaching rotors. Dammit. A helicopter. She ducked as it went overhead, and then she veered right. Up ahead was a small cove with a sandy beach but no boats and nowhere to go. Left was a headland.

Sounds of pursuit were getting louder.

She headed toward the beach. She wasn't giving up. She wasn't letting them take her without a fight.

———

The helicopter pilot refueled without meeting another merc at the pumps.

Their luck was holding. So far. They weren't far behind the insane billionaire. Half an hour at most.

A lot could happen in half an hour, but Kurt forced himself not to worry about it. He'd find Rowena, and they'd get out of here. And maybe the odds were stacked against them, and perhaps he wasn't doing what he should do—wait for the troops and plan for a prolonged hostage rescue effort—but the things that man could do to Rowena during that time...

An unexpected blitz attack from within could work. He knew it could.

A call came through the headset.

"Echo Tango Foxtrot. Be on the alert for an escaped female on the island. White. Long dark hair. Do not shoot. Repeat, do not shoot. Must be recaptured unharmed. She isn't going anywhere, so search and report back." This last was spoken with jaded amusement. "Last seen heading toward the north cove."

Kurt peered out the window. Pointed. "Over there." He held George's gaze. "Time to choose which side you're really on, buddy."

The pilot pressed his lips together. "Fuck it. I'm sick of this gig. These assholes have never been friends of mine, and Gilder is a creep. Let's get the girl before they do."

They swooped low and headed toward a small cove with a beach made of sugary sand.

Rowena looked up in fear then glanced behind her. There was nowhere for her to run. No escape. She glared toward the helicopter, blinded by the sun. Then she began wading into the water.

And that was part of the reason he had fallen in love with her. Her grit. Her determination. She was easily outnumbered. As far as she knew, the bad guys held every ace, but she kept on fighting

"Hover in front of her. I'll try to get her on board." He opened the side door and leaned out. The downdraft blew water directly into Rowena's eyes, and Kurt doubted she could see with the spray, but she kept swimming purposely around the chopper.

Some of Gilder's men appeared on the top of the hill.

Kurt turned to the pilot. "I'll arrange for you to collect that reward on Hurek if you don't betray me, George."

The man nodded. "You've got my word."

Kurt nodded and then, with no choice but to trust the guy, he dived into the water and arrowed straight to Rowena with a powerful front crawl.

She fought him. Not recognizing him. Not seeing who he was.

With the noise and disruption of the helicopter, it was impossible for her to see.

He caught her elbow before it took out his nose.

"Row. Row. It's me. Kurt."

Her head caught his chin, and he saw stars before she finally realized who he was.

"Kurt!"

He could barely hear her over the bird, but he read her lips and saw the joy that filled her face. He urged her to get in the machine. Gilder's men were on the beach now. Shouting instructions he pretended not to hear. It wasn't deep. He boosted her into the cabin, then followed up behind.

"Strap in," he told her. He circled his finger over his head. "Let's see if we can take out the fuel depot and other bird before we get the fuck out of here."

"Roger that."

Rowena looked between them with wide eyes. Kurt handed her a pair of headphones and grabbed a set for himself. Hurek tried to make himself invisible in the other corner.

They flew a short distance out, and when Kurt had the fuel pumps in sight, he opened the sliding door and pumped a short burst of bullets into the gas pumps. For a moment, he didn't think they'd ignite, and then suddenly, there was a great whoosh and a burst of flames that licked at the helicopter as the pilot expertly navigated the blast wave.

"Does he have boats?"

"Sure." The pilot grinned. "Super yacht and some RIBs."

"Let's put a few holes in them too so these bastards can't go anywhere."

"Hell, yeah." The pilot circled around the island.

Kurt spotted Gilder's fancy six-million-dollar helicopter and pointed. "That first."

The pilot nodded.

Kurt opened the door and fired two-seconds' worth of bullets into the engine of the beautiful-if-gaudy-for-his-tastes machine.

Some of the mercs fired back, but the helicopter was out of range of handguns, and a quick hail of bullets at their feet from the big gun made them scatter.

George circled to the marina. Sure enough, a massive white boat was docked along with four inflatables and a couple of dinghies. Kurt took great delight in firing that gun, hot spent cases flying, bullets hitting just below the waterline on the super yacht and then ripping through the RIBS like a psycho through a shower curtain.

"We're done. Let's go, George." He slammed the door closed and safetied the weapon, turned to Rowena who sat dripping wet, teeth chattering in the sudden quiet.

"I thought you were dead." Her eyes filled with tears as he sank to his knees in front of her.

He pushed her hair back from her face. "I've got you, babe. I've got you." He kissed the salty tears from her cheeks. "I have to go talk to the pilot. You're safe now. You're safe. We're getting out of here, and Gilder is stuck in his little paradise. Unlike you, he isn't brave enough to swim out."

He slipped quickly into the co-pilot's seat. "You got a map of this area?"

The pilot handed him a tablet, and Kurt took it, zooming in on a small island in the Caribbean.

Kurt pointed to it and gave him the coordinates. "Take us there."

"What's there?"

"Refuge."

Kurt used the radio to call the Coast Guard and make a full report of the latest happenings, including the sunken container ship and the fact that Nolan Gilder, yes, *that* Nolan Gilder, had kidnapped a British national and held her against her will on his private island after attempting to murder a member of the FBI.

The actual charges were going to be long and complex. Then he had them patch him through to Daniel Ackers.

"Kurt? I am so glad to hear your voice, son."

"Glad to be talking to you, sir." He looked back at Rowena's dark eyes watching from the back seat. She seemed frozen in place.

She was in shock.

"This is an unsecured channel, but I wanted to touch base and let you know I'm alive. I completed my mission. And," even better, "I have with me a British national who went missing at the same time I did. We have a friendly helicopter pilot who helped us make our escape. We couldn't have done it without him."

George looked at him gratefully.

"Hang on—" Ackers was cut off.

"Dad? You're okay?"

Kurt's heart squeezed as his daughter's voice came unexpectedly over the line. "Yes, honey. Sorry to worry you like that."

"I love you, Dad." He could hear the tears she was crying.

"I love you too, baby. I'll be home soon. Promise."

Ackers sounded gruff over the airwaves. "It's going to be good to have you back, Kurt. I'm too old for this shit." They both laughed. "Everything is in motion. You concentrate on getting to safety now. Leave the rest to us."

40

Rowena sat in the back of the helicopter as the pilot landed on the end of a slender ribbon of tropical beach. Her teeth wouldn't stop chattering.

A group of men approached cautiously down the beach, weapons drawn. She didn't know who these people were or where they'd landed.

They removed their headsets as the rotors wound down.

"I'm gonna need to search you when we get out and officially detain you before I can talk to the AG. Standard operating procedure. Plus, these guys won't allow you to wander around the island, not with their loved ones here, so accept the restrained hospitality, and I *promise* I will talk to the justice department ASAP and get that plea deal sent through. Once it's signed and they've run some background checks, we'll get the WitSec thing started." He held out his hand to shake the pilot's. "Trust me to come through for you. We wouldn't have gotten out of there without you, and I won't forget that."

She loved that about him. He kept his word.

The pilot nodded, looking apprehensive but understanding.

"George, I'm gonna need you to step out of the machine and lie on the ground. Arms wide over your head. You'll be safe here.

I give you my solemn oath that no one here will hurt you—unless you do something stupid." Kurt watched the man get out, then he turned and met her gaze. His eyes softened. "Ready to meet some of my friends?"

She nodded rapidly. "Friends?"

"I didn't know they'd all be here, but am I glad to see them."

"We're safe?"

"Safer than you've ever been in your life, babe."

A shiver fluttered over her skin, emotions catching up to reality in slow motion. It was hard to believe their ordeal was over. Impossible really. She wanted to know how Kurt had escaped from the ship. She wanted to know everything—like who these people were—but other things needed to be taken care of first, and they had time now.

They had time.

She fumbled with her seatbelt. Kurt climbed over the middle console and took her hands, led her as if she was some delicate creature and opened the door. He climbed down, and she saw the shocked surprise on the faces of two approaching men and one woman.

He ignored them and lifted her down. She held onto his waist. Looked into his deep navy eyes. "Kurt, he's definitely my father. Gilder." She swallowed hard. "I share that mad man's DNA."

Would he turn away from her? Be repelled?

His eyes were steady as he stroked his hand over her hair. "Thankfully, you favor your mother."

Her throat closed.

How could she not love this man? She hugged him, and then he kissed her, on the mouth in front of all his friends. She wrapped her arms around his neck and kissed him back.

A voice called out. "What was it he said to me and Haley that time?" the taller, dark-haired man asked. "'Never had a declaration of love at a takedown before.'" He gave a good imitation of Kurt's gruff, no-nonsense tone.

Kurt pulled away. "This isn't a takedown. You guys *missed* the takedown." He held her hand and drew her forward. "Guys, meet Miss Rowena Smith. She prefers to be called Row, but in my head, I always call her Rowena. This is Unit Chief Quentin Savage, SSA Eban Winters and Special Agent Mallory Rooney. And boy, do I have a present for you guys."

Kurt walked around to the other side of the military chopper still holding her hand. He let go, and she stepped back. Another man was zip-tying the pilot as he lay in the sand. Then he helped George sit up and stepped over to greet them.

Kurt held out his hand to the man. "Hey, Parker. Row meet Alex Parker, another friend of mine and Agent Rooney's husband."

She smiled at him and wished she didn't feel like everything was going to fall around their ears. "Are you *sure* we're safe?"

Kurt framed her face. "The only place more secure is the HRT compound in Quantico."

"Debatable." Alex Parker cocked his head. "I could get inside the compound without raising any alarms, and you'd struggle to penetrate the house after all the modifications we made this past year."

"I think we should put that to the test sometime, but for now, good," Kurt responded.

"Are we expecting trouble?" Parker's silver gaze scanned the horizon.

Kurt shook his head. "It's not impossible, but with George's help"—He pointed to the pilot—"we disabled the ability of our enemies to pursue us. As far as I'm aware, Interstellar doesn't have fighter jets under its command, so we should be safe enough. Navy and Coast Guard are on the way, and DOJ has been informed of the threat, so I hope to hell they're taking it seriously."

Savage shook his head. "This sounds like a hell of a story. You're supposed to be dead. What happened?"

"It's a very long story that I will tell you in full soon. But what's going to be of most interest to you guys is the fact I completed my mission." Kurt opened the door and pulled Hurek out of the helicopter and into the sand.

Eban Winters' and Quentin Savage's expressions changed from amused curiosity to pure hatred. Eban punched Hurek hard enough on the chin to make him roll back in the sand.

Rowena startled, and Alex Parker drew her back to stand beside him.

Kurt hauled Hurek back to his feet. "You want a go?" He addressed Savage. "This is your one and only chance, and he's earned it. After today, Darmawan Hurek will be handed over to the DOJ, and he'll be out of reach."

Savage's black eyes glittered with rage. "He's getting a deal."

Kurt gave a slight nod. Savage looked furious.

"You want a pop? This is the time."

"I'd rather watch him get a lethal injection," Savage gritted out.

"I'm game for another pop *and* giving him a lethal injection," Eban agreed.

Hurek cowered like the coward he was.

Kurt took a step forward. "I get it." He pointed to his bearded face and then to her. "After what we've been through, I really get it. But can you trust me to do what's right?"

Both men paused, drew in long breaths, and then nodded.

"Okay." Kurt nodded in turn. "We need to start interviewing him as to where he hid evidence of mass murder committed by Nolan Gilder and Leo Spartan. I offered him immunity from the charges of kidnapping me and protection against Nolan Gilder's long reach."

Both men exchanged a calculating glance and then looked back to Kurt. Nodded again.

"I need to debrief him and get the immunity deal for my pal, the pilot, rolling. You guys have a place we can use? I'll need internet and a printer. We need to secure this information ASAP before Gilder is able to intercept it."

"We built a new office building. We can lock Hurek in one of the new bunk houses we have, which are secure and have bathroom facilities. Your pilot friend can stay in the other one." Parker pointed off to the right.

Kurt turned to Row, took her hand, and kissed the tips of her fingers.

The fact he wasn't hiding their relationship, that he was being open despite the fact she knew he still worried people might judge him harshly for being older than she was, filled her with happiness. "Will you be okay with these guys? Someone's going to have to take your statement about everything that happened."

She looked at his friends who all gave her concerned looks. She hugged herself. "I'll be fine."

Mallory stepped forward. "Come with me. You look like you could do with a drink and a change of clothes." She eyed her up and down. "I bet Haley will have something you can wear. We can take your statement in the kitchen while these guys set up everything we need."

She led the way, and Rowena followed, looking over her shoulder at the man who was now her center. Her heart.

He watched her with a pirate's grin.

Suddenly, her heart felt lighter. He wouldn't be letting her leave if he didn't think she was completely safe. He had work to do.

They were free.

She followed Mallory up the steep path to a house built into a cliffside. Mallory was talking, but Row wasn't really listening. She felt lightheaded suddenly. Weak.

She arrived at the door and was met by a tall, stunning blonde wearing skimpy shorts and a bikini top. Beside her stood a redhead in a beach coverup, a mass of curly red hair tumbling from a ponytail as she jiggled a baby in her arms who was holding a strand of her hair in an attempt to eat it. The redhead looked vaguely familiar.

Mallory walked forward and lifted the rosy-cheeked baby into her arms, gently disentangling the woman's hair from the baby's powerfully clenched fist. "This is Haley Cramer, Darby O'Roarke, and this little cherub," she kissed the round cheek of the bright-eyed baby, "is my daughter, Georgina." She slid her onto her hip, and they all looked at Row curiously.

Row seemed to have forgotten how to talk. She stared at these women, wondering where to begin.

"I have some shockingly good news." Mallory jiggled the baby. "Kurt Montana is alive and on the beach with the guys."

"He's alive?" Haley's mouth dropped open. "How is that possible?"

"I don't know yet. There's more." She stared at the redhead. "He has Darmawan Hurek in custody. Here, on the island."

Darby O'Roarke sagged against the wall, her pale face draining of all color.

Haley went over to her and hugged her.

"He's in custody. He can't hurt you anymore, Darby," Mallory assured her. "Eban hit him, but he was so pathetic Quentin didn't even bother."

"I'd like a shot at him," Haley muttered angrily. "I want to beat him until you can't recognize him."

Then Rowena realized why the women were so familiar. They'd both been kidnapped by Hurek last year, then rescued by the FBI. She'd seen their faces on the BBC news.

"Kurt's working to get some information out of him to help nail Nolan Gilder for some pretty serious crimes. He's convinced Hurek he'll be getting some sort of immunity deal."

The other women stared with matching expressions of outrage and horror.

"What he didn't mention was a whole host of other crimes Hurek can be charged with." She glanced at Rowena. "Not to mention what the Brits can throw at him. He's not getting away with anything. He's not going free."

Darby drew in a shuddering breath then released it. "Okay. Between you two, Eban, Quentin, Alex, and Montana, I have to believe I'm not in danger. But I'd like to face him. Here on this island. I want to face him when he's tied up and helpless and I'm the one with the power."

Mallory nodded. "We can arrange that."

"Can I take a kitchen knife?" Haley sounded only half-joking.

"It's your island. Anyway," Mallory brought attention to Row as she stood awkwardly in the hallway, "this is Rowena Smith, Kurt Montana's..." She tilted her head. "What do you prefer? Girlfriend? Lover? Partner? Squeeze?"

"Let's go with partner."

"Montana is really alive?" Darby whispered.

"Yes."

"And apparently doing *very* well for himself." The blonde's eyes gleamed. "I'm so glad. I also cannot wait to tease the hell out of him." She touched Row's shoulder. "Ignore me when I call him a cradle snatcher. It's not personal, but I owe him a few *comments*."

Rowena gave a soft snort. "Oh God. Please don't. It took me ages to wear down his resistance."

Haley gave a loud laugh. "Ha. I can see him trying to fight you off—for five whole minutes. Come on in. I'm going to help you clean up while you feed me enough fodder to have him squirming for weeks if not *years*." Haley wrapped an arm around her shoulders. "Let's have a drink and some food."

Row stopped short. There was no subtle way to ask this. "That sounds great, and I could really use a drink, but I don't suppose you happen to have a pregnancy test here? I don't want to drink alcohol if I'm pregnant, although I could murder a glass of water too."

Haley stopped and gave her a look of concern. Darby's expression turned stricken.

"No. Not that. I was very lucky. I wasn't raped. Kurt protected me, and then Hurek decided I was worth bartering for. Otherwise, I would have been. I realize that," she admitted to the other women. "But we didn't have any contraceptives except for the obvious, and we were stuck in a cabin together for more than a month with little else to do except learn some self-defense moves and…" She swallowed. "You know."

Haley stared at her for a long moment, then she began laughing so hard she bent over at the waist. "I'm so sorry. I don't know why that seems so funny to me. Probably the stress of seeing that helicopter coming this way. Brought back some bad memories."

Mallory kissed the baby and handed her off to Darby. "I have some. We're not trying for another baby yet, but we had a scare a couple of months ago which seems to be how we roll. I bought a couple of tests and got my period on the way home from the drugstore. They're still in my bag."

Row followed the women into the open-plan lounge with the most fantastic view of the sun as it began to set. She felt like she'd once again been thrown into an alternative reality.

Mallory disappeared into a room and came out with a box that she handed over.

"Come with me, Row." Haley took her into the master bedroom and opened the drawers. "Sun dress or workout gear?"

"Workout gear would be great. Thanks."

Haley scooped up some items and pointed to a bathroom that looked like a spa. "Take as much time as you need. We'll be in the kitchen when you're ready."

41

Kurt sat at a table opposite Darmawan Hurek in the bright new office space. The view of the ocean was incredible, but he'd rather be looking at Rowena. Parker had set up cameras to record proceedings that were being beamed via secure satellites along classified channels—not owned or operated by Interstellar —straight to SIOC where the FBI director and AG were watching as the US drew a net around Gilder's tropical paradise.

The documents from the AG had come through. Hurek sat reading them, then took the pen off the table to sign it.

"You agree to waive your right to legal counsel?" Montana asked.

"As long as you stick to the agreement." Hurek crossed his arms and raised his nose as if he were superior. Hard to do when you wore the pants you'd pissed yourself in.

They didn't have time to wait for a lawyer, which might come up at a later date, but by that time Hurek would hopefully be in a high-security facility or extradited to the United Kingdom or Indonesia for crimes committed.

Kurt had agreed to not press charges for kidnapping him, etc., etc. What Hurek failed to understand was that the DOJ could independently press charges for the attack on a federal agent, and the Brits could prosecute him for what had been done to Rowena. Then there was what he'd done to Darby O'Roarke. Quentin. Haley. The Alexanders. Not to mention the coup he'd tried to initiate in Indonesia.

And maybe Kurt was letting him off easy. Maybe he should have shot him and dumped him overboard while he'd had the chance. But he wanted Gilder and Spartan and whoever else had murdered hundreds of innocents just to try to shut Kurt up.

He wanted them exposed for the diseased minds they really were.

"Talk me through what happened."

Mallory brought Hurek a cup of coffee and placed it in front of him. He took it without thanks. Just another woman serving his needs.

Kurt and Mal exchanged a silent glance as she sat beside him. Alex stood near the door. Off camera but very much guarding his wife from any potential threat.

"After I left Indonesia last August, I made my way to the DRC, where I had some friends. Last October, I was made aware that certain intelligence services might have spotted me in the town, and I decided to head to my next refuge."

So Hurek had left the DRC before they'd even arrived. At least the intel had been good at the time.

"Who warned you?"

Hurek glanced at the camera. Swallowed. "Leo Spartan."

"Zimbabwe's UN ambassador?"

"Yes." He sipped his coffee.

"Where did you go next?"

"The container ship called *Mudik*. I'd bought it several years prior via a shell company in my grandfather's name. The crew were men faithful to me after I left the Indonesian Army."

"Deserters."

Hurek's lips thinned. "I was their General. They stayed loyal to me."

And loyalty was everything to dictators.

"Did your friends Nolan Gilder and Leo Spartan know where you were?"

"Not at that time. Leo told me to go to one of his houses in Namibia, but our friendship had been strained since the FBI attacked my island. Leo and Nolan thought I was becoming a liability."

Kurt didn't call him out on his bullshit even though the FBI hadn't attacked a damned thing. He was giving the guy enough rope to hang himself.

"I didn't trust Nolan and Leo not to dispose of me the same way they disposed of another friend of ours years ago when they had a lot less to lose."

"We'll get to that. How did you contact them?"

"We communicate via Tor."

The Onion Routing network enabled anonymous communications and internet use—a place where the dark web thrived.

Alex brought a laptop over. "Sign in."

Hurek hesitated. "What if Gilder tracks us?"

"He won't," Alex stated baldly. "Firstly, he and his people simply aren't that good. Secondly, all his companies and operations have been shut down. Thirdly, he probably knows Haley Cramer owns this island, and if he has any way of organizing or directing hired guns—which he doesn't, but if he did—the best way to make sure it's not worth his while is to expose all of his secrets as quickly as possible. Sign in."

Hurek did, and Alex got to work.

Kurt took a quick look. All the messages were there. The pissed-off note from Leo after Bjorn Anders had given Kurt Dougie Cavanagh's name that night back in January that felt like a thousand years ago now. The decision to blow up his plane and arrangements to get rid of Jordan Krychek in case Kurt had been able to relay any information during their brief phone call.

The fact Bjorn had lied and betrayed him made him feel sad.

"Print it all out. Let's get a hard copy."

"So Leo ordered the bombing of the aircraft. How long after it took off did you realize I wasn't on board?"

"I had nothing to do with it, but within a few hours they noticed your cell signal was moving in the opposite direction. He sent mercenaries after you." He tapped his short grimy nails on the tabletop as if the people who'd died in the crash were of no consequence. "I put the word out that I'd pay more for you alive than anyone else would pay for you dead. I *saved* you."

"Marty Sinclair?"

"One of Leo's."

Sonofabitch. He glanced at the monitor and saw the FBI Director writing a note, presumably arranging for Sinclair's arrest.

"Leo knew I had more contacts in Mozambique than he did, and I could operate more freely there than he could. When you called Mr. Sinclair to arrange for an extraction, he called Leo, and Leo contacted me on our server—as you can see. They expected me to kill you on sight."

"Why didn't you?"

Hurek smiled. "I find people often have their uses. The FBI had already proven they'd go to a lot of effort to get their people back, and I thought I could possibly use you as a bargaining chip or as a shield. Then I saw Rowena Smith wearing that watch, and I realized immediately who she was."

"Gilder's daughter."

Shock rippled around the room.

"Talk me through that."

Hurek looked uncomfortable for a moment. "I told you already."

Kurt ignored his discomfort. "On the record."

Hurek went through the disgusting attack on Allie Smith again, Kurt pulling out details that mattered.

"And when Dougie Cavanagh began to suspect what had happened to the woman he had feelings for—what his friends might have done to her..."

"He thought he was in love." Hurek dismissed the notion with a swipe of his hand. "The fool was writing to her. It was only a matter of time until he went to see her, and she'd have told him what happened." He bit his fingernail. "Then..."

"What?"

"Something happened at the mine."

"What mine?"

Mallory handed him a bottle of water, and Kurt cracked it open. He felt rock solid. He had this sonofabitch exactly where he wanted him now. Sweating. Scared.

Hurek looked away. "The mine the four of us owned together under another shell company."

"Tell me about what happened at the mine."

"It was a very profitable endeavor, and we all became very rich from it very quickly."

"Was it legal?"

"Strictly speaking, although, of course, Nolan had bribed certain people to buy the rights for a song."

"Why such a big secret if you weren't running blood diamonds?"

"Blood diamonds." Hurek spat his derision. "Most diamonds are blood diamonds."

"What happened at the mine?"

"The workers. They kept demanding better pay and working conditions. That's what Dougie was dealing with the night Nolan...persuaded Allie Smith into his bed."

It was rape, but Hurek had already confessed to that on the record. And perhaps it wasn't prosecutable at this stage, but it set the stage as to exactly what these men were.

Evil.

"Allie left the next morning. And the mine foreman was killed by one of the miners. Nolan went crazy. He took some of our security people and a machine gun, and he went to confront the workers." Hurek looked sober. "He opened fire and killed every one of them. Every last one. Even the children." Hurek looked off to the side. "That was the first time I understood who my friend really was."

"But you stayed in business together. You stayed friends."

"What was the alternative?"

"Go to the authorities."

Hurek shrugged. "They'd have killed me if they found out."

"So you doubled down," Kurt guessed.

"They killed everyone at the mining camp. Women and children. Dragged the bodies to the mine and then flooded the whole system. Nolan put the blame on a local warlord. Bribed some of the officials, and no one ever asked any questions. They're still there, the bodies. I have the original deeds in a Swiss bank box along with some photographs I took without Leo or Nolan knowing at the time."

"What happened next?"

"I headed back to Indonesia. I was independently wealthy now and saw what might happen if Nolan ever decided to turn against me. He knew I had some documents, and I told him even back then that they were secure but if anything should happen to me, I couldn't guarantee they wouldn't make their way to various news outlets."

"How did Dougie Cavanagh react to everything that happened?"

"He was away the day of the massacre. He'd taken himself off to a town twenty miles away and drunk himself into a stupor. By the time he came back, Nolan had fabricated this whole story about the warlords that he seemed even to believe himself."

Despots had a habit of drinking their own Kool-Aid.

"We went our separate ways for a short time, and then we all met up again in South Africa after Nolan's parents died a few months later. He got drunk and was pissed about that watch. Blamed Allie Smith for taking it. I mean, she had stolen it, but Dougie defended her, and they got into a huge fight. It came out that Dougie had been writing to her, and after he went to bed, Nolan said they both had to go. Allie had been taking photographs all over the camp and at the mine. They were both loose ends that threatened us. After she died, Nolan had someone go through her belongings while her family was at the funeral. They removed all the photos they found in her room that might be compromising."

But Kurt suspected he hadn't taken the negatives. Rowena's friend John had those.

"After Dougie died—"

"How did he die?" Kurt asked with light curiosity as if murder were only vaguely important.

"Leo arranged for someone to kill him. A bar fight in the middle of nowhere. Looked like an accident. Then he had your friend Anders pack up his belongings and send anything except papers or photos back to his parents in Scotland along with a hefty check."

Bjorn had kept one photograph secret all these years. Had he used it as a form of blackmail the same way Hurek had? Kurt doubted he'd ever know.

"Once Dougie was gone, we drifted apart, although we kept in contact via secure means." Hurek gripped his fingers. "If it wasn't for the FBI arriving on my island last year, we'd have likely carried on like that forever."

"Then perhaps you shouldn't have attacked that conference and kidnapped a federal agent." Kurt scratched his beard.

Hurek shrugged again. "I saved them."

"Why d'you kidnap Darby O'Roarke? Same reason you took Rowena to start with, right? A body to keep your men happy."

Hurek kept his mouth closed. Perhaps he was smarter than he looked. He wasn't admitting to more than he had to.

"We need the information for the Swiss lock box." Kurt pushed a piece of paper across the desk. "Write it down. If whatever is inside corroborates your story, we'll talk about next steps."

Alex and Mallory put Hurek back in cuffs and escorted him to his overnight accommodations.

Kurt turned to the AG and FBI Director on the monitor. "Do

we have enough evidence to prove Spartan and Gilder conspired to blow up the commercial airplane?"

They'd discussed his suspicions earlier, and Kurt had discovered the FBI had already figured out the crash hadn't been an accident.

"We have video footage that potentially ties Spartan's security team to the bomb. Gilder was staying with him at the time. We believe they conspired to murder Bjorn Anders and to prevent you from contacting your colleagues and getting back to the US using any means possible. Combined with Hurek's testimony and those messages on the dark web, it should be enough to convince the Zimbabwean authorities that Spartan is acting against the best interests of their country."

"Is it enough for a warrant to approach Gilder's island and apprehend him?"

"As he's been actively trying to harm federal agents and use his satellites to eavesdrop on classified information, we have more than enough for a warrant. Good work, SSA Montana. Great to have you back."

He nodded impatiently. Time for them to take that sonofabitch down. Time for him to find Rowena.

42

Row wasn't pregnant. Relief and sadness played tug of war on her face in the mirror. She wasn't sure if part of the reason she'd wished for it was that age-old desire to bind a man. That was no reason to bring a child into the world. That was selfish and short-sighted. Rowena didn't need a man and didn't want to force a future with Kurt. He was exactly the sort of man to stand by her for that reason alone. She wanted a future with Kurt because they loved one another. Only that.

They'd both been through a traumatic experience, and both needed time to recover and reassess.

Except, she already knew exactly what she wanted.

She pulled on the clothes Haley Cramer had given her and dried her hair. The luxury of conditioner and a hairdryer was wonderful, but she could live without them if she had to. She wasn't sure she could live without Kurt.

She sat for a moment on the bed and realized she felt more comfortable in this room alone than going out to meet strangers. But these were Kurt's friends, and she knew they'd want answers.

She hung the towel and cleaned up the bathroom. The view from the room was magnificent, but she was still worried Gilder might have some trick up his sleeve where he escaped and came after her like some maniacal villain.

Her father.

The monster.

She shuddered.

She made herself walk through the door. In the living room, which had its own amazing view, she found Haley and Darby sitting around with glasses of what looked like champagne. The tall, dark-haired man from the beach sat on the couch. His dark eyes watched her with compassion in their depths.

The baby kicked at her toys as she lay on a play mat. Rowena felt a wave of longing for something that had been far out of reach in the past. But now...

Haley jumped to her feet. "We're celebrating Kurt coming back from the dead and your rescue. Would you like a glass?"

The room seemed to hold its breath until she nodded.

Empathy filled Haley's expression. "Probably a relief at this moment."

"I have to admit I'm a little disappointed but relieved too." Rowena hugged herself.

Haley headed to the open-plan kitchen brushing a gentle hand down Rowena's arm as she passed. "Emotions are complicated at the best of times. They're allowed to be. We understand what you're going through better than most, but it doesn't mean we know how you're feeling."

"What happens to you doesn't define you," Darby added quietly.

"Damned straight." Quentin Savage—that was his name—spoke up.

The baby, Georgina, started to fuss. Quentin got down on his knees and began entertaining her by batting the various toys dangling above her.

Haley handed Rowena a flute of sparkling champagne and raised her glass. "Here's to safe returns and new friends."

Rowena drank and thought back to the last time she'd had

champagne. Back in the hotel in Zimbabwe before she'd thrown herself at a relative stranger. It was hard to imagine he hadn't always been part of her life. "I can't believe the danger's over."

"We're as safe as we can be here, and reinforcements are on the way," Savage assured her. "You're lucky we're here to be honest."

Darby suppressed a grin. "What they're not telling you is Haley and Quentin got married on Sunday. They foolishly invited us all here afterwards. As if we'd be silly enough to say no."

"Congratulations."

Haley smiled. "Thank you. Something good came out of our abduction even though it was absolutely terrifying at the time." She sat beside Darby and took her hand. "More than one thing."

"I should probably take your statement, so we're done by the time Kurt and the others are finished." Quentin stood and Darby got down to play with the baby.

Rowena's hands began to shake as she thought about what she'd done in Bjorn Anders' office. She bit her lip. "I don't know whether or not I need a lawyer."

Quentin's intense gaze softened. "I realize you don't know us, but we know Kurt Montana. If he thought you had anything to worry about, he wouldn't have told you to make a statement. He would not have done that. We won't record it. I'll let you know if I think there are things you should get legal advice about, but I doubt it. If what I think is about to occur happens, the US will owe you a great debt."

"He's my father…"

"He's a sperm donor at best." Haley's voice was scathing. "And if you need a good lawyer, I'll pay for the best."

"Thank you. I don't know what to say or how to repay your kindness. I do have some money…"

"You don't have to repay anything. You helped Kurt capture a man we've been after for months. A man responsible for…" Savage's throat worked as he trailed off.

"Unspeakable things." Darby looked up from where the baby kicked at her toys.

"A man I'd happily pay to see dead." Haley arched her brows at Quentin as the side of her mouth twitched. "Were such things allowed."

Savage shot her a smile.

"I thought he was getting a deal? I thought you were mad about that?"

Savage shook his head. "He'll have a deal for some of it which does piss me off, but the US isn't the only country that wants him —it's probably not even the one with the most right to prosecute him. The gravity of his crimes means he's never getting out of prison alive—he just hasn't figured that out yet."

Relief filled her, and then she thought of something else. Rowena looked around for a clock. "What time is it? I need to call my family and co-workers. They'll be worried sick."

Quentin checked the clock on the stove. "Six thirty. UK is four hours ahead of here, I think."

Haley nodded confirmation.

"But," Quentin chewed his lip, "I think you should hold off until the arrests have been made. I hate to say that, but I suspect by the time they wake up in the morning, you'll be able to speak to them without jeopardizing any current operations. Come on. We'll use the kitchen counter so these two can eavesdrop, if that's okay. Otherwise, I'll spend the next week being asked question after question I can't answer—and you can walk me through the basics of what happened as much as you can without feeling uncomfortable."

Rowena pulled up a stool and started talking.

———

Kurt might have been tired by the time he finished with Hurek, but he sprinted up the steep path, eager to get to Rowena. He walked into the main house and paused at the scene in front of him.

Rowena sat at the breakfast bar with Quentin. Rather than the scruffy shirt and jeans she'd been wearing for the past month, she was now barefoot in skintight Lycra shorts and a running top, covered by a baggy, sky-blue T-shirt. Her hair was shiny and clean, brushed and tied back in a neat ponytail. His sexy librarian.

She looked beautiful and perfect and, oh, so young.

She looked up as the door shut behind him. Stood and took a hesitant step forward. "Is it done?"

He shook his head. "Hurek's been interviewed. It's over for him. Agents are waking up bankers in Zürich to retrieve the evidence he has stashed away there. Teams are gearing up to arrest Gilder on the island."

He was worried for his men, but he could do nothing about that except trust in their training and abilities.

"Hurek's under guard?" Haley queried lightly, but there was nothing casual about her expression.

Kurt nodded. "He's secured, and the guys are gonna take it in turns overnight. Until the Feds turn up to take him into custody."

"Rats. I was hoping I might get to beat him with a stick."

He understood. And despite the fighting words, he knew she was worried. There was no way any of them were letting Darmawan Hurek escape this time.

Rowena bit her lip, looking suddenly unsure.

Remembering Marianne's words from what felt like an eternity ago, he walked over to her and opened his arms, grateful when she walked straight into them and held on tight. He spotted the champagne glass on the counter, surprised by the force of the disappointment that hit him. She wasn't pregnant.

Didn't matter. But he was oddly disappointed.

Foolish man.

After a moment, he stepped away, aware he was still wearing the clothes he'd stolen from a man he'd killed earlier that day and that his beard itched like he had fleas. "I need to clean up."

Haley Cramer stood and pointed to a door on the right. "I've set the two of you up in that room. It's not as big as some of the others but has a jet tub."

"It's probably bigger than we're used to."

"So I heard—a small cabin with not much to do." Haley's smile was all innocence that he didn't believe for a second. "Darby gathered some clothes that should fit you both and a razor if you want it. Although, I must say, the beard does add a dash of roguishness to that handsome face... I may have a whole new appreciation for beards." She wiggled her eyebrows suggestively.

Savage grinned.

"And you a recently married woman. Congrats, by the way. Sorry to gatecrash your honeymoon." Kurt walked over to her and accepted the kiss she gave him.

"If you need food there's plenty in the fridge." That smile again. "You'll need to eat to keep your strength up."

He accepted the fact he was gonna get ragged on. He'd earned it. And this was only the start. Dealing with his hangup might be the hardest challenge he'd ever faced, but he was game if Rowena was. He headed toward the bedroom door, grateful when she came too.

Once inside, he closed the door so they could finally be alone together. He cupped the back of her head. "Are you okay?"

Her lips parted. Her eyes were uncertain.

Was this what she wanted? Or did he need to give her some space? "I thought I'd lost you earlier. I'm sorry I let them take you."

"I didn't give you any choice—"

"And we are going to talk about that."

"I would never let you sacrifice yourself for me." She sucked in her lips. "It's not fair to ask."

It wasn't, but her sacrificing herself for him wasn't fair to ask either. That discussion could be tabled until another time. A time when her green eyes didn't shine with tears as she gripped his shirt. "I thought I'd lost you. When the ship exploded. I thought you were dead. That I'd left you to die." She pressed her hand to his chest, and his heartbeat sped up. "It was the single worst moment of my life."

She threw her arms around his neck, and he wrapped his around her, closed his eyes and finally let himself believe she wanted to be here. With him. Together.

After a minute of simply hanging on, he managed to squeeze out the words, "You're sure he didn't hurt you?"

She pulled back. Wiped her eyes. "I played along with him. Pretended to be all 'oh, my long-lost father, thank goodness you rescued me.'" She batted her eyelashes then grimaced. "While he eyed me like an egg bank."

Kurt clenched his jaw.

"Then I stuck him with a hypodermic full of anesthetic the doctor had planned to use on me to conduct a quick pelvic exam —as you do to people recently rescued from kidnap situations."

Anger reared up inside him. His fists clenched.

"Then I used my new ninja moves to beat up the doctor and nurse."

He was impressed despite himself. It was one thing to practice, another thing entirely to execute, but in survival situations instincts kicked in.

"Stuffed the nurse in a storage room. Then ran out the back door." She looked away. "When I got to the sea I just didn't care anymore. I refused to be turned into a lab rat, and I thought you were dead."

One last tear escaped, and he wiped it away with his thumb. "You fought with everything you had, and you won. You saved yourself."

A grin wobbled on her lips. "You certainly helped. I would have drowned otherwise. What happened on the ship?"

He rolled his shoulders as the ache of battle returned. "Gilder sent his mercs to kill everybody on board. I took care of them. Grabbed Hurek and convinced the pilot to work for the FBI."

Her eyes scanned his face, fully understanding his meaning. "Impressive."

"Not really. A lot of people died."

"Not your fault."

"Some of them were definitely my fault."

She cupped his cheek. "You did what you had to do to survive."

He nodded. He'd deal with it in his own time. He checked out the clothes on the bed. They should fit.

"I'm going to take a quick shower."

Rowena nodded and followed him into the bathroom. He didn't know if it was a habit left over from their time in captivity. Perhaps she didn't feel safe alone.

He didn't mind the company, but he worried about whether she was really okay.

He stripped off, climbed in the shower. Then stepped back in surprise when Rowena joined him.

She pressed her naked body against his, and he was hard in a heartbeat.

"We never did get to the shower sex part of our relationship, now, did we?"

"I guess we didn't." Kurt leaned back against the wall and smiled down at her.

"You want to lock the door?" she asked.

"Nobody's coming inside."

Her mouth tilted to one side as she murmured, "Except, perhaps, you."

His fingers tightened on her hips. His mouth went dry. "Are you sure?"

She nodded. Swept her hands through his wet hair and brought his mouth down to hers, stopping an inch away. "And I want you to put that beard to good use, one last time."

"Yes, ma'am."

She grinned.

He'd created a monster. A wonderful, confident, amazing monster who knew what she wanted and wasn't afraid to tell him. She was perfect. The love of his life. His equal in all ways except years lived. The woman he wanted to spend the next fifty years worshipping like a goddess if she'd let him.

43

Jordan Krychek straddled the metal bench on the outside of one of HRT's MD530 Little Bird helicopters as the pilot buzzed so close to the ocean he swore the skids brushed the top of the waves. Ford Cadell and his K9, Hugo, sat behind him, the dog's muzzle resting on Jordan's shoulder. The rest of Echo squad filled the chopper to capacity.

They weren't going far.

Adrenaline burst through his system. The mood of Gold Team and HRT in general had flipped since news of Kurt's escape and survival had spread. But they couldn't afford to get cocky.

DEVGRU were taking the security barracks on the north side of the island. HRT had the medical center, guest cottages, and Gilder's house where the billionaire was holed up. Before they'd cut him off, he'd been broadcasting a tale of being attacked by American forces.

The pilot put them down on the outskirts of the main building. Thermal cameras hadn't revealed any hidden heat sources. The guys quickly disembarked and ran for cover, spreading out and taking positions.

No one fired at them.

Jordan followed Shane Livingstone and Will Griffin as they led the way toward the medical center. Live feeds of their night vision and thermal cameras were being broadcast directly back to SIOC.

Shane set a small explosive charge on the door. This way if the place had been rigged to blow, they wouldn't get caught in the blast wave. They hunkered down behind a low stone wall as Shane counted down to zero and pressed the button on the detonator.

The doors popped off their hinges and fell askew. The guys charged in with practiced precision, all of them noting the two bodies on the floor. Middle aged. One male, one female, wearing white lab coats. Gun shot wounds to the head.

Eliminating witnesses?

Jordan took up the rear, covering their six.

"Hey," Aaron Nash shouted. "You're gonna wanna see this."

Jordan came forward and poked his head through a door into a room which contained several liquid nitrogen freezers.

Aaron put on big gloves to remove the lid and pulled up a weird ladle-like tube. "Looks like we have biological samples." Aaron peered at the labels. "Labeled with first names." Aaron frowned as he placed the samples back in storage and replaced the lid. He walked back into the main room. The other operators had cleared the rooms and stood watch, front and back.

"We found three women in separate rooms that were probably kept locked," Livingstone stated. "All shot dead. Two were visibly pregnant."

A cold shiver of alarm ran down Jordan's spine.

Aaron stared at the equipment. A fancy microscope with large monitors attached. Centrifuges. Machines Jordan didn't recognize.

Aaron tapped one white box. "This is a CRISPR machine used for gene editing." This was why they called Aaron "the Professor." As a former biologist, he knew stuff none of the others had a clue about.

Jordan's mouth went dry. "Was this son of a bitch trying to make clones?"

"Sure as hell looks that way."

And the dead women were the incubators.

Livingstone gave the signal, and they started moving to join up with Charlie squad and the snipers outside.

The authorities were expecting a long siege. HRT was fine with that. They'd wait forever and a day for this motherfucker.

But the doors to the house were wide open, as if inviting them in with welcoming arms.

Luke Romano sent in a drone that could see through doors using Doppler radar. Hugo went next, searching for anyone they hadn't spotted lurking in the shadows.

Crouched behind another low wall, Jordan had to wonder what drove people like this. Nolan Gilder had everything money could buy, but it still wasn't enough.

"He's held up in the panic room," Aaron muttered.

"How long do you think he can last in there?"

"Months. Until we find the air supply and pump something else in there instead."

"Yeehaw." Cowboy slid down beside them.

"Worse places to be stuck, I suppose, but we might have company before then." Aaron shrugged a shoulder. "According to Novak, before they cut off his communications, Gilder was in touch with his lawyers and is expecting them to arrive any moment to save his ass."

"Will they?"

"They'll try."

Jordan thought for a moment. "I have an idea."

———

An hour later, the remaining security team had surrendered to DEVGRU after they realized they were outnumbered and there was no escape. None of the mercenaries wanted to fight it out with SEAL Team Six. According to more than one of the mercs, Gilder had gone crazy after Rowena Smith had escaped, shooting many of his own people. His personal bodyguard, Gerrit

Vanguard, had finally taken his gun away and hauled him into the panic room.

Now Gilder was waiting on those lawyers to arrive and save the day.

HRT would do everything they could to prevent that.

Negotiator SSA Jennifer McCreedy was talking at Gilder and his bodyguard via a throw-in speaker they could presumably see and hear as Tactical Command had left them with eyes and ears for now. Gilder had cameras all over the island, so he had to know he was completely surrounded. McCreedy was explaining the situation and offering Gilder safe transit to Washington, where they could discuss everything that had happened and clear up any misunderstandings.

Jordan's lip curled.

It wasn't that he didn't respect negotiators. He did. They saved lives. Probably more lives than HRT did, despite the fact it was their motto. However, pretending Gilder wasn't some sadistic freak curdled his stomach.

He was so full of anger about what this guy had done, it made it hard to be impartial. Made it hard to want to treat him with the respect he was due as another member of the human race. Gilder hadn't treated the women he'd lured here with respect or decency. According to some of the surviving staff, the women Gilder brought here rarely left.

Tactical Command had taken control of everything within the panic room. They controlled the temperature. The lights which now blazed around the compound. The information they had access to. If their plan didn't work, they'd manipulate the airflow.

HRT wanted Gilder and his last remaining bodyguard to see they were surrounded and outnumbered and not going anywhere that didn't involve handcuffs and leg irons.

The noise of a helicopter stirred the air beneath the bright half-moon. A deep red Bell 505 helicopter landed close to the Little Birds.

Jordan and the rest of the team took up defensive positions as they watched a leggy brunette, wearing an expensive charcoal gray suit with pale pinstripes, a crimson blouse with a fancy tie at the throat, and matching skyscraper heels step out of the chopper along with her sleek black leather briefcase.

Jordan stepped into her path as the pilot geared the engines down and other members of HRT checked the machine for weapons. He raised his hand to stop the woman's progress. "I'm afraid this is a restricted area."

"I'm from Peterson, Winchester, and Gladwell. I'm here to see my client." Her crimson lips matched the shoes, and she tilted her head while giving him a crocodile smile. "Nolan Gilder. If you could point me in the direction and inform him that I'm here."

Jordan lifted his chin. "Mr. Gilder is not currently receiving visitors."

She handed him a stiff white business card. "He'll see me. I'm making sure my client has his rights respected and documenting the damage you have done to his reputation." She cast her gaze around the scene that looked like a military zone. "And to his property."

She swept past him, and he tried to grab her arm, but she slipped by him with a look of outrage on her pretty features. "Touch me again and I'll see you in court."

He held his hands wide. "I'm not letting you go inside and risk this becoming a hostage situation, lady."

She threw back her head and laughed. "You're the ones causing the situation. My client has done nothing wrong."

"A few dead people would tell you otherwise, but they can't. Because they're dead."

She reared back a little. "Let me pass. This is my choice, and I'd like to put an end to this siege before my client gets hurt. He must be terrified." She glanced around again and shook her head. "If you could show me the way?"

Jordan rolled his eyes. "Fine. Your funeral."

He led the way through the front door to the back of the

house, nodded his head toward the steel vault door behind which Gilder and his bodyguard hid.

"You'll have to withdraw." She tapped her foot impatiently and insisted. "No way would my client open the door when there are so many guns pointed at him."

Shit.

He reluctantly lowered his carbine. "He's not walking free of this."

"Is that a threat, Mr... Sorry, I didn't catch your name."

"Not a threat. You bring him out, and we'll arrange transportation back to the States. You can join him every step of the way." His expression narrowed as he watched the door locks turn, then slowly open.

The woman stepped inside, and the door began to close. Tension stretched across every neuron of his body, across the airwaves. Sweat trickled down his back. Ryan Sullivan stood beside him wearing an expression that would have scared any other man.

Thirty seconds passed, and the doors opened again.

Meghan Donnelly stepped out with Nolan Gilder's arm wrenched high behind his back. Her hair was a little mussed, the knot on the bow of her blouse undone and trailing. Apart from that she looked fine.

Thank God.

Ryan Sullivan grabbed Gilder and thrust him none too gently against the wall.

Jordan rushed forward and pointed his weapon inside the vault. "Where's Vanguard?"

"Unconscious." Meghan put her hands on her hips.

Jordan stepped past her and cuffed the prone figure. Then he dragged him out into the hall by his feet and frisked him for weapons. The guy had a backup pistol at his ankle and another at his back.

He grinned at his fellow operator. "*That* was fucking amazing."

Donnelly smiled back. "Hardest thing was wearing these damned ankle breakers."

"Where did you get the outfit?"

"Haley Cramer and the captain of the frigate helped fudge it together."

"That was fucking hot," Grady Steel high-fived his Charlie team partner.

Romano eyed Donnelly like he'd never seen her before.

Nolan Gilder sneered. "I'll make you pay for this. All of you. Don't you know who I am?"

"You mean the rapist guy, or the guy who murdered his best friend guy?" Ryan Sullivan hauled Gilder in front of him.

Gilder sputtered. "You have no proof."

"Or the guy who was trying to clone himself using unwilling women?"

"They all signed an NDA. I'll sue those bitches into the ground if they say one word."

"They won't have to say a word." Ryan shoved the guy so he started walking. "The Medical Examiner will be able to figure out the whole story from their corpses."

"That was him." Gilder gesticulated wildly with his head as he indicated Gerrit Vanguard, who was now fully conscious. "He went crazy shooting everyone."

Gerrit's eyes glittered, but he stayed silent.

"I guess we'll be able to piece that together from ballistics and DNA we collect from each of the weapons we find, won't we?"

Gilder's expression became sullen. "I don't know what you're talking about. I want my lawyer. My real lawyer. This was entrapment!"

"You'll get one. As soon as they finish with you at Gitmo." Ryan started marching him out.

Gilder's expression twisted again, this time with horror. "You can't take me to *Gitmo*."

"Sure we can. You're being held on terrorism charges, motherfucker. It's called the Patriot Act. Considering you're probably of Dutch origin, I think you'll like the uniforms."

With that he was gone.

Gerrit Vanguard was slowly being brought to his feet by Romano and Steel.

Jordan blocked his way. "How could you work for somebody like that?"

Vanguard gave a nonchalant shrug. "It paid well."

"Enjoy spending it in prison, asshole."

44

I t was after midnight, and they should've been sleeping in their soft beds. Instead, they sat on the beach beside a large bonfire, drinking beer, watching the flames grow taller and taller —everyone, that is, except for Alex Parker, who was on guard duty for the next hour, and Mallory, who was watching the baby and probably enjoying some much-needed sleep.

What would that be like? Dealing with a baby again? The idea grabbed hold of something in Kurt's chest and squeezed hard.

Rowena lay on a blanket in the sand with her head on his thigh as he stroked her hair. She'd fallen asleep, and the light from the fire coated her cheek in gold. He didn't know what he'd done to deserve her, but he planned to earn her love every day, over and over again, until his last breath.

The soft breeze brushed the bare skin of his arms. He rubbed his clean-shaven jaw, feeling more like himself again and definitely looking more like the guy he remembered in the mirror.

The sound of helicopter rotors in the distance caught their attention. Kurt watched the men's hands drift lazily to their weapons. Parker had found him a spare holster for his purloined SIG. Haley stood and threw on another couple of pieces of firewood, her gaze going east to track possible dangers in the night sky. Darby's eyes grew larger, haunted by flames. Eban put his arm around her shoulders and held tight. The smile on her lips when she looked at the negotiator both broke Kurt's heart and filled him with pride.

She'd survived.

She'd endured more than all of them put together and had the best revenge by living a good life and being happy.

They'd taken her to see Hurek earlier. A pathetic man. Condemned. Doomed. Too stupid to realize it. Hurek had cowered before this slight young woman with flames for hair. Begged her for forgiveness.

She hadn't given it, and Kurt couldn't blame her.

The chopper was getting closer. He tried to ease away without disturbing Rowena, but she woke.

"What is it?"

He didn't want to scare her but didn't want to lie either. "Helicopter coming this way."

She stiffened and sat up. "Gilder? Or someone planning to rescue Hurek?"

"Neither." A voice came out of the darkness, and Alex Parker slipped into view. "Just received a call. Gilder's in custody. No casualties on our side."

Kurt released a deep breath as he stood.

"Who's in the chopper?" asked Eban.

"A few friends who needed a place to bunk down for the night. I offered. I'll grab some blankets and some more beer. Hurek is secure. He's not going anywhere." Alex dropped a case of Samuel Adams in the sand.

Kurt pulled Rowena to her feet and felt his heart start to pound as he stared at the silhouette of not one but two Sikorsky UH-60 Black Hawks.

He knew who was on board those machines.

The birds came in to land one at a time, either side of the Leonardo. The guys piled out before the pilots started shutting them down. They raced across the sand, and Kurt murmured to Rowena, "brace yourself."

He had to fight back tears as he found himself embraced and swept up and carried around on people's shoulders like he was in a parade. They swept Rowena up too, whose laughter reached him over the noise of celebration.

"Put me the fuck down!" He was laughing too hard to put any force into the order.

Finally, they lowered him to the ground, and he found himself engulfed in a rugby scrum of Kevlar and testosterone. When they stepped back, he stood face-to-face with Jordan Krychek.

"You're late," the other man told him in a gruff voice.

Kurt nodded. "Had a few delays."

Jordan's gaze shifted to Rowena. "Nice to meet you, Miss Smith. Your colleagues back in Madeley library were worried about you. I was able to inform them, discreetly, that you were okay."

"You spoke to Betty and Alasdair?"

"I even met them." He held out his hand to shake. "Jordan Krychek."

Rowena shook his hand. "Nice to meet you. Kurt was worried about you."

"Was he now? I was worried about him too. Glad he had you to keep him company." Kurt didn't miss the smile trying to twist Jordan's lips. All the guys had a gleam of amusement in their eyes along with relief. "By the way, Marianne says hi."

"Marianne?" Kurt and Rowena exchanged a look.

"Came all the way to DC in order to help."

"Oh my God. I'm so glad she's okay."

He wrapped his arm around Rowena's shoulders and pulled her close. It was a relief to know Marianne hadn't betrayed them.

"You arrest Marty Sinclair for treason yet?"

Jordan nodded. "He was *extracted* earlier."

The guys all took turns introducing themselves to Rowena before helping themselves to a beer and settling down on the sand around the fire. Haley, Darby, and Quentin had run up to the house for some food, which appeared in the form of giant hot dogs that they cooked in a large pot over the fire.

Meghan Donnelly held out her hand to him. "Pleased to meet you, sir. Miss Smith."

"Congratulations on making it onto the teams, Operator Donnelly."

"Thank you, sir."

"Call me Kurt."

"Call me Row." Rowena shook her hand enthusiastically. "I've heard a lot about you."

Donnelly's eyes widened. "How is that even possible?"

"FNGs." Rowena grinned as everyone within hearing distance laughed.

"Donnelly just saved us weeks of sitting on our asses." Ryan Sullivan stood behind the female operator, his eyes full of mischief, wearing that smile that always had the ladies salivating stretched across his too handsome face.

"Did she now?"

Ryan nodded. "Pretended to be Gilder's high-priced attorney, waltzed straight into the safe room, and then took them down."

"Single-handedly?"

"You betcha."

"What about his bodyguard, Gerrit-the-gorilla?" Rowena covered her mouth in a sign of distress.

"Him too." Ryan sounded like a proud papa showing off at a parent-teacher conference.

Rowena stared at Donnelly with a look of fierce admiration. "I want to be like you when I grow up."

"Me too," said Ryan.

Donnelly flicked a look up and down him. "No danger of that happening any time soon." With that she headed toward the beer.

"Ouch." Kurt winced.

"Not sure what I did to upset her this time." Ryan stepped forward. Held out his hand first to Kurt, then to Rowena.

He clasped her hand in both of his. Kurt gritted his teeth.

"So this is why you took a month off to go on an all-expenses-paid cruise around the world. I can't say I blame you."

Kurt put his arm around Rowena again, and she beamed at Ryan. "You must be Cowboy."

The other man blinked. Tilted his head to one side in inquiry. "Exactly how did you know that when I'm not even wearing my leather chaps?"

"I could tell you." She grinned at Kurt, and he knew he was about to pay a price for his insecurity. "But then Kurt would have to kill you." Taking Kurt by surprise she pulled him in for a kiss, not letting him draw breath for a full thirty seconds. He didn't exactly try to get away.

Rowena was staking a very public claim, and she was doing it because of his fragile ego. Finally, she let him go, holding his gaze for a few moments before they both realized the whole gathering had gone quiet. Only the gentle tumble of waves broke the silence.

Ryan stood there stock-still, as if scared to move. Then he started clapping, and so did everyone else. Whistling, hollering, making Kurt glad it wasn't light enough to see his reddened cheeks.

"I'll have what she's having," Ryan called out and headed off to greet the others by the fire.

Kurt drew Rowena in close and murmured in her ear, "No, he damned well won't."

"Don't forget to tell them you love them."

He rolled his eyes, then swallowed. "They know."

"I love you."

He smiled. Kissed her again. "I know."

45

It was only a week or so since Gilder had been arrested, and Kurt found himself standing beside a pretty arched bridge painted a rusty red color that spanned a wide, deep, muddy-looking river. They'd spent the day before yesterday in DC with Marianne. He'd shown her and Rowena some of the sights and promised to catch up with the orange grower when they returned. The US had agreed to let Marianne stay in the country on a three-month tourist visa, and she'd decided to rent a car and tour the National Parks before returning home to Mozambique.

"The really cool thing about this bridge, aside from it being the first major bridge in the world to be made of cast iron, is that it was made mainly using woodworking principles rather than industrial techniques."

Kurt wrapped his arm around Rowena's shoulders, glad they both wore warm coats. He knew she was acting as tour guide in an effort to avoid the emotions that would surely surface soon. "It's pretty."

She beamed at him. "It is."

The town was quaint and old-fashioned, and considering it was the heart of the industrial revolution, remarkably green and wooded.

"Okay." She straightened her back. "I'm ready now."

She gripped his hand and tugged him along.

She'd forgiven him for not telling her that he'd taken and mailed the photographs back to the States. She understood his reasons. Earlier that day he'd copied all her mother's photographs that her friend John had developed and sent them to SIOC. They'd contained images of the four friends and photos of the local miners, plus enough geographical data to tie them to the site of the mine. That mine was being drained before the macabre process of trying to identify the bodies could begin.

The amount of evidence of Gilder's wrongdoing was piling up so high he wasn't ever getting out of prison. Leo Spartan had raised hell, but the Zimbabwean government had been persuaded by the evidence the US presented to them regarding the mine, the plane crash, and the mercs who'd been sent after Kurt. He'd been placed under house arrest with no contact to the outside world.

Not enough in Kurt's eyes, not yet. But considering the anger from the local population when the accusations became public, they'd have to deal with him properly then.

Hurek was being held in what he thought was protective custody. As soon as they had all the goods on Gilder, the Feds had decided to let the Brits and Indonesians vie for extradition.

Kurt's bet was on Indonesia winning first because if Hurek went to the UK they wouldn't extradite to a country that had the death penalty, and Indonesia sure as hell did. He was really hoping the guy got exactly what was coming to him and that Kurt could keep his promise to Darby, Haley, Savage, and Winters that justice would be done.

They slowly crossed the bridge and headed right. Down a dirt track for about a quarter of a mile.

He'd introduced Rowena to Daisy, who'd been so happy that he was home safe she hadn't cared he was in a relationship with someone almost her age. He'd been shocked by what Krychek had told him about being bugged and almost killed by a state police officer. Gilder had tentacles throughout law enforcement, politics, and industry. Weeding them out was causing a whole lot of damage control and back-pedaling from people who should have known better. The Interstellar Company was filing for bankruptcy protection after precipitating a stock market crash that had rocked the Nasdaq elite to their cores.

Row had lost almost everything too.

Birds sang in the woods behind the lane. The smell of smoke hung in the damp afternoon air. The faint acrid scent of destruction. They reached a small wooden gate painted a green close to the shade of Rowena's eyes. He pushed it open, and they walked down an uneven path through an overgrown garden that was probably incredible in the summertime, but right now looked decrepit and decaying. The walls of the house stood proud, scorched red brick unprotected from the elements by the lack of a roof. The inside was completely gutted.

Rowena gathered herself and walked around the back. A small greenhouse had lost some panes of glass, probably due to the intense heat of the fire. Rowena's eyes grew glassy as she stared at what little remained.

"I feel as if I've been erased from this place. Like my whole family has been erased."

He held her hand, his heart breaking for her. "I'm sorry you've lost so much. I know you have insurance. You could rebuild it. I could help."

"It wouldn't be the same." She shook her head. "I loved this house. I hate seeing it destroyed—but being here, seeing that there is nothing left. Honestly, it's kind of freeing." She sniffed. "I spent way too much of my life thinking that if I simply knew who my father was, I'd finally figure out the missing pieces of myself." She moved away when he tried to comfort her. "But being Gilder's daughter doesn't define me. What defines me are the people who raised me and loved me. What defines me is knowing you and I survived terrible things and that I can rise from these ashes and build the future I want. The future I deserve."

He was so damned proud of her.

"Row," he swallowed. Christ, he hadn't felt this nervous since he'd been a teen asking a girl on a first date. And maybe this was a bad time but... "I was wondering if you'd like to build that future with me, either in the US or here."

She blinked. "You'd move here for me?"

"Babe, I'd move mountains for you."

Through her tears, she smiled that quirky smile of hers. "I can't see you settling down in a town like this."

It was tiny. And very English. "I'll move wherever you want me to." He'd spent his whole life putting his work before his personal life, before his family—as if he alone could save the world. But the guys had more than proven they could manage without him. "I can also talk to the guys at Hereford about working there for a couple of years. Or," he took her hands in his, "you could come live with me in Quantico. I'm planning on taking that promotion. I'll be home a lot more. We can find a house you like." He stared over her shoulder. "It won't be as old as this one, but we still have some historic sites to visit, if you remember."

Her eyes shone. "I remember."

He sank down to one knee, ignoring the way the damp earth saturated his jeans. He could still contribute while making a new life, a better life with Rowena. He produced the ring he'd bought in the Tiffany store at Heathrow Airport when she'd been in the restroom. The diamond was simple and elegant—hopefully conflict-free—its setting a vibrant yellow gold.

"Row. Will you marry me?"

She stared at him in shock for a few seconds before nodding and pulling him to his feet and slipping the ring on her finger. "Yes. Yes, I'll marry you. I love you."

He took her face in his shaking hands and kissed her.

Joy washed away some of the pain from her features, and he knew he'd picked the right moment after all.

"Let's go tell Betty and Alasdair the good and the bad news."

He pulled her to a stop. "What bad news?"

"That I'm moving to America, assuming they'll have me. They'll need a new librarian."

Stress fell away from his shoulders. "The US better have you, otherwise they're going to need a new HRT Director."

Saying it out loud made him realize how proud he'd be to lead such an incredible group of people, but only if Row was by his side.

"Why don't we get married here? At the registry office." She circled around him barely able to contain her obvious excitement. "We have a week before you have to get back, and hopefully, we can start the immigration process more easily if we're official. I can plan a party for my friends here. Daisy might be able to make it?"

"Don't you want a big white wedding? The dress? The flowers?"

"We can always do a fancy ceremony later if we want to." She clutched his hand in her right and admired the ring on her left. "Unless I'm rushing you."

"You are not rushing me. I cannot wait to start our lives together." He shook his head and tugged her away from the ruins of her old life, into the future with him.

———

Turn the page for an exclusive bonus scene, featuring Ryan Sullivan and Meghan Donnelly!

BONUS SCENE

R yan Sullivan watched Meghan Donnelly walk down the
sand, kick off her combat boots and pants, then slip into
the warm waters off the private Caribbean island. Gold Team
were camped out on the beach after a successful operation that
had concluded in the arrest of an internationally wanted terrorist
and one fucked-up billionaire. Most importantly, they'd found
their beloved team leader, Kurt Montana, back from the dead.

Ryan glanced around.

Most of the guys were asleep on blankets. The fire had died
down but was still giving off significant heat. It was a little after
two a.m.

He frowned.

Didn't she know it wasn't safe to go off swimming alone in the
ocean at night. Hadn't she watched *Jaws*?

Aaron Nash opened one eye and flicked a tired look at him
that suggested one of them should go after her and that it wasn't
going to be him.

Dammit.

Not like he'd be able to sleep until she came back anyway.

Ryan eased slowly to his feet and headed toward the water's
edge. Perhaps he could keep an eye on her from the shore. He

scanned the flat surface, but it was too dark to see clearly when the moon kept disappearing behind slow-moving clouds. He couldn't see her.

He growled.

He stripped off his shirt and his tactical pants, left them in a pile in the sand near Donnelly's clothes.

Fuck it.

He stripped off his underpants too, no point getting them wet when nobody would see anything anyway. He slipped soundlessly into the water, enjoying the coolness against his hot skin. He waded out past the gentle breakers, wondering where the hell she was. The black water looked unbroken as far as he could see.

He swam out while doing a quick 360.

Members of the Hostage Rescue Team were combat swimmers who had been drown-proofed both in the pool and in the sea—which didn't mean they couldn't drown—more that, they did it slower and with more grace than regular people. Most of HRT operators were also advanced scuba divers.

All that to say, Meghan Donnelly should be fine in the water alone, so he should head back to the beach and mind his own damned business.

But where the hell was she?

He heard something break the surface close by, a rush of relief washed over him at the sight of her slick black head rising out of the water.

She startled and then released deep breath. "Jesus. What are you doing here?"

Ryan rolled his eyes. "Thought I'd take a quick dip before trying to get some sleep. What do you think I'm doing out here?"

"Were you worried about me?" Her voice rose incredulously—as if he were the crazy one.

"I'm a big believer in the buddy system."

Her snort told her exactly what she thought of that. "You know I'm a grown-ass adult, right?"

He kept quiet.

"I'm a former soldier, an FBI agent, a highly trained operator."

"I'm not doubting your skills, Megs."

"Just my judgment, apparently."

It wasn't that. "Didn't you ever watch *Jaws*?"

"Didn't you ever watch *The Meg*?" she countered.

He exhaled heavily, knowing he was being overprotective. "I was worried."

"If you'd done this a few weeks ago, I'd've thought you were trying to get into my pants."

Ryan showed his teeth in a feral grin.

"Now I know you're all talk."

What?

"All talk?"

"I've been watching you."

The idea sent fear skating along his nerves. Fear and something else, something equally unpalatable.

"You're attentive, and you flatter the ladies—*all* the ladies, young and old—laying on the charm, flirting the same way you breathe. Yet for all your reputation, I haven't seen you actually go in for the kill."

"The *kill*?"

"Yeah, you know. The wolfish smile, the hand on the small of the back as you escort your latest conquest out of the bar to find any available surface to…you know." Water lapped against her T-shirt-clad chest as she shrugged.

He gave her a wolfish smile now, though he doubted she could see it. "Yeah, well, you weren't in that private jet a couple weeks ago, now, were you?"

He wasn't sure why he needed to keep reminding her of his base nature. Except he knew why.

"Just before I tried to seduce you. Yeah, I remember." Her words were murmured vibrations off the heavy expanse of water. Neither of them wanted anyone else to know what had happened that day.

"Yeah, when you were crying over the fact you lost your dad. What am I, a complete asshole?"

The memory of her body pressed against his, her lips on his skin was enough to make his body burn. He was glad it was nighttime, and he was neck deep in the ocean.

"So if I hadn't been grieving, you'd have taken me up on my offer?"

"Hell, no."

She turned away. "Ah. Of course."

"Of course, what?"

"I don't even know why I didn't think of that."

"What?" He'd missed something.

"You don't find me attractive."

He dragged his hand through his hair. "I told you that night. I don't sleep with colleagues."

"I am literally the only female on the teams, and I know you aren't bi. That rule seems highly convenient as it only applies to me."

Did she really think he'd created that rule so he could reject her without hurting her feelings?

"Darlin', if you weren't my teammate, that night would've taken a whole different turn, and we would've been making use of *every* available surface in your house."

Even the thought terrified him. Once he started with her, he was terrified he wouldn't be able to stop.

She cocked her head to one side as if deciding whether or not he was telling the truth. "But you wouldn't have stayed, would you? Because the staying over, not the fucking, would've been too much like cheating on your late wife."

He swallowed hard and looked away. He wished he hadn't told her those private things about himself and Becky. He didn't even know why he had, except he'd recognized the depth of her grief after losing her father, understood the magnitude of her pain. He swam a little ways away from her.

"Running away?" Her voice was disembodied in the darkness.

He guffawed. "From what?"

"Everything."

He hated to acknowledge that she might be right. "Do you wish I'd taken you up on your offer? Is that what this is?"

It was her turn to swim a little further away.

"Maybe."

Maybe?

"I mean, it's obviously just physical for you. That's all I want. Good clean sex. At least then I'd get rid of the itch plaguing me without worrying about all the other bullshit."

His heart rate ramped up right along with his blood pressure. He was familiar with the itch.

"I guess I'll have to use your method. Go pick up a strange guy next time I have a night off. Find a motel. Screw his brains out."

He tightened his jaw against the image of Donnelly with someone. Anyone. It was none of his damned business what she did with whom. He was in no position to preach.

"You could always get yourself a good vibrator."

She threw back her head and laughed loudly, probably attracting attention from those on the beach. "Trust me, I don't need any advice on vibrators from a guy. Not even the God of sex."

God of sex?

It stung like a whiplash.

Before Becky there had been no one.

After Becky…

"Then what do you need a guy for?" He sounded pissed, even to his own ears.

"The kissing. The physicality. The unpredictability of the act. The weight of a man against me. The illusion I'm not alone for a few hours."

He closed his eyes because he understood the need for that kind of connection.

"You have a favorite bar when you go to pick up women?" she asked.

What the fuck? "Looking for tips?"

"Sure. Why not? I haven't had a boyfriend, or sex for that matter, since I applied to HRT."

She floated on her back and his eyes followed her whether he wanted them to or not. Her long legs were bare. The black T-shirt clung to the top of her thighs and made his fingers clench.

"I'm out of practice flirting. If it doesn't involve gun oil or gun powder, I'm not sure I remember how to do it anymore."

Thoughts of Donnelly and sex were not good for his sanity.

"You want me to teach you how to flirt?"

"Why not? I know you're good at it. That's what all the guys say. Though I haven't witnessed it personally." She mumbled the last.

"You shouldn't pick up strange guys in bars, Megs, it's not safe."

"Every time a woman goes somewhere alone with a guy, it's potentially not safe. At least I know how to fight."

The thought of anyone attacking a woman drove him crazy.

"Can't you try a dating app or something?"

Donnelly snorted. "That last serial killer put me off."

She treaded water and moved a little closer.

She gazed up at the stars. He gazed at her.

"What do you want out of life?" He had no idea where that question sprang from or why he was foolish enough to voice it.

"I've been focused on this for so long. I don't even know anymore." Her arms swayed slowly through the water.

"You want to get married? Have kids?"

A flash of moonlight revealed a frown. "I spent most of my life trying to make my dad proud. Now he's dead, none of that seems to matter anymore."

"No way you only got into HRT because you were trying to please your dad."

She swam even closer. "Why do you say that?"

"Because."

"Because what?"

She wanted a real answer.

He sighed. "Because you were born for this, Megs. Look at today. You walked into that vault on those high heels and took out an armed bodyguard and a deranged billionaire single-handedly. You didn't do that because it would make your dad proud. You did it because you could. Because you're a damned good warrior."

He was close enough to see that vulnerability move across the features. The vulnerability she tried so hard to hide.

"I wouldn't mind getting married but it's not as important as finding the right person to share my life with. I don't think I want kids." She hunched her shoulders. "It's not that I don't like them. I just don't think I'm built for the stay-at-home-and-look-after-them business."

"Not everybody is." He stared up at the moon's silver light catching the edge of a cloud. "I certainly wasn't." Being a shitty father to an amazing daughter was probably his biggest regret. Not that he'd win any awards for any of his other relationships.

He'd been a good husband, once. Turned out he was a terrible widower.

"It's easier for men."

He smiled softly. He wished that wasn't true. "Yeah, it is."

"What do *you* want out of life?"

Ryan inhaled. What did he want? He wanted to not remember that he was missing a part of himself. He wanted to not remember that he'd once had everything and lost it all. Except, recently, he had started to forget his grief for whole chunks of a day without the aid of sex or whiskey. The memory of Becky's long, dark hair and pretty face were fading now. Maybe it was simply time dulling the edges of his memory like sandpaper against the edge of a blade. Or maybe it was something else. "You'll find someone."

"Ha. Well, it's a pity you said no. You'd have saved me a lot of time and effort if you hadn't. We could have had a no-strings hookup, and no one would have ever known. Neither one of us would have to risk dating a serial killer. What do they call it? Oh, yeah. *Friends with benefits.*"

The breath ripped from his body, and his heart threatened to beat itself to death against his rib cage. She was joking. She *had* to be joking.

Didn't she?

He was about to strike out for the shore when he spotted something behind Donnelly.

Triangular fin about eight inches tall, slowly sliced through the water behind her. His mouth went completely dry. He watched her flinch away as the shark brushed past her.

Donnelly swore.

"Don't panic. It's probably curious rather than hungry, but you and I are gonna swim back to shore so that we don't become this fish's next meal."

He heard her swallow and saw her nod. They set off at a calm, leisurely pace, no thrashing in the water like a wounded beast. Strong, sure strokes.

Ryan skimmed his gaze over the water, looking for the telltale torpedo. The *Jaws* theme music ran through his mind in tune with the beat of his heart.

They ate up the distance through the water into the shallows, and he thought they'd left the wild creature behind until he felt a telltale brush of abrasive leather against his bare skin.

It swam beneath him, and fear engulfed him as it headed toward Donnelly. He grabbed the animal by its pectoral fins and thrust it up into the air. It was shallow enough to stand. And he found himself yelling at Donnelly to run while he staggered through the water, carrying the six-foot-long bull shark thrashed its tail and gnashed those deadly teeth in a frantic bid to escape.

Donnelly reached the shore, and the water was only at his

knees now. He turned around and flung the animal as far as he could before staggering onto the beach.

He and Donnelly stood side-by-side breathing heavily as they stared out to sea.

"Oh my God. Oh my fucking God!" Donnelly's teeth were chattering as she grabbed her towel from where she'd left it.

His lungs were bellowing. "*That's* why you always swim with a buddy."

After a moment, she started laughing and bent over at the waist, filled with mirth.

"Ryan." Aaron Nash came up beside them. "Did you hurt that poor shark?"

"Tried not to." Ryan shook his head. "The damned thing scared about a decade off my life. I think we're even."

Meghan was still laughing. Some sort of delayed shock response?

He sent her a worried look. "Are you okay?"

She nodded and started laughing again.

"What the heck is wrong with you?"

"I'm never going to get the image of a naked Ryan Sullivan wrestling a shark out of my brain."

"Me neither," Aaron agreed.

Ryan had forgotten he wasn't wearing any underwear. "Shit." He looked around for his clothes and went over and pulled them on.

"Are you sure he didn't take a bite, Ry?"

Ryan could hear the laughter in Aaron's voice. "Still more than enough left over."

"Which I can vouch for." Donnelly chuckled as Aaron sent Ryan a startled look.

"Dude. I never touched her."

"You better not have."

"I swear." Jesus, he saved her from a shark attack and was now getting *that* look from his friend and colleague. "The only blood in the water is my reputation being savaged."

Meghan started to shiver.

"You have dry clothes to wear?"

"I'm not a child."

He was well aware.

"You don't have to mother me."

The last thing he felt was parental, but at least making her mad was familiar and safer territory.

"You'll catch your death."

He heard her grind her teeth as she snatched her things and stalked up the beach. He grinned.

"Playing with fire, Ry?"

He looked at his buddy. "Watching out for my fellow operators."

Friends with benefits?

She was the one playing with fire. He didn't intend to get burned.

———

Thank you for reading *Cold Truth*. I hope you enjoyed Kurt's and Row's story. Are you ready for the next exciting installment of the Cold Justice® - Most Wanted series?

Order *Cold Heat*...the next Romantic Thriller from *New York Times and USA Today* bestselling author Toni Anderson.

If you enjoyed this book please consider leaving a review at your favorite vendor or on your socials. Reviews help readers find books that might be right for them. Thanks so much!

USEFUL ACRONYM DEFINITIONS FOR TONI'S BOOKS

ADA: Assistant District Attorney
AG: Attorney General
ASAC: Assistant Special-Agent-in-Charge
ASC: Assistant Section Chief
ATF: Alcohol, Tobacco, and Firearms
BAU: Behavioral Analysis Unit
BOLO: Be on the Lookout
BORTAC: US Border Patrol Tactical Unit
BUCAR: Bureau Car
CBP: US Customs and Border Patrol
CBT: Cognitive Behavioral Therapy
CD: Counterintelligence Division
CIRG: Critical Incident Response Group
CMU: Crisis Management Unit
CN: Crisis Negotiator
CNU: Crisis Negotiation Unit
CO: Commanding Officer
CODIS: Combined DNA Index System
CONUS: Contiguous United States

CP: Command Post
CQB: Close-Quarters Battle
CRISPR: Clustered Regularly Interspaced Short Palindromic Repeats
DA: District Attorney
DEA: Drug Enforcement Administration
DEVGRU: Naval Special Warfare Development Group
DIA: Defense Intelligence Agency
DHS: Department of Homeland Security
DOB: Date of Birth
DOD: Department of Defense
DOJ: Department of Justice
DS: Diplomatic Security
DSS: US Diplomatic Security Service
DVI: Disaster Victim Identification
EMDR: Eye Movement Desensitization & Reprocessing
EMT: Emergency Medical Technician
ERT: Evidence Response Team
EV: Electric Vehicle
FOA: First-Office Assignment
FBI: Federal Bureau of Investigation
FNG: Fucking New Guy
FO: Field Office
FWO: Federal Wildlife Officer
IB: Intelligence Branch
IC: Incident Commander
IC: Intelligence Community
ICE: US Immigration and Customs Enforcement
HAHO: High Altitude High Opening (parachute jump)
HK: Heckler & Koch (a German firearms manufacturer)
HRT: Hostage Rescue Team
HT: Hostage-Taker
JEH: J. Edgar Hoover Building (FBI Headquarters)
JTTF: Joint Terrorism Task Force
K&R: Kidnap and Ransom

LAPD: Los Angeles Police Department
LEO: Law Enforcement Officer
LZ: Landing Zone
ME: Medical Examiner
MO: Modus Operandi
MVP: Most Valuable Player
NAT: New Agent Trainee
NATO: North Atlantic Treaty Organization
NCAVC: National Center for Analysis of Violent Crime
NCIC: National Crime Information Center
NCIS: Naval Criminal Investigative Service
NFT: Non-Fungible Token
NOTS: New Operator Training School
NPS: National Park Service
NTSB: National Transportation Safety Board
NYFO: New York Field Office
OC: Organized Crime
OCONUS: Outside of the Contiguous United States
OCU: Organized Crime Unit
OPR: Office of Professional Responsibility
POTUS: President of the United States
PT: Physiology Technician
PTSD: Post-Traumatic Stress Disorder
RA: Resident Agency
RCMP: Royal Canadian Mounted Police
RIB: Rigid Inflatable Boat
RPG: Rocket-Propelled Grenade
RSO: Senior Regional Security Officer from the US Diplomatic Service
SA: Special Agent
SAC: Special Agent-in-Charge
SANE: Sexual Assault Nurse Examiners
SAS: Special Air Squadron (British Special Forces unit)
SERE: Survival, Evasion, Resistance, and Escape
SCIF: Sensitive Compartmented Information Facility

SD: Secure Digital
SIOC: Strategic Information & Operations
SF: Special Forces
SSA: Supervisory Special Agent
SWAT: Special Weapons and Tactics
TC: Tactical Commander
TDY: Temporary Duty Yonder
TEDAC: Terrorist Explosive Device Analytical Center
TOD: Time of Death
UAF: University of Alaska, Fairbanks
UBC: Undocumented Border Crosser
UNSUB: Unknown Subject
USSS: United States Secret Service
ViCAP: Violent Criminal Apprehension Program
VIN: Vehicle Identification Number
VSP: Virginia State Police
WFO: Washington Field Office
WMD: Weapons of Mass Destruction